KESSLER PARK

a novel
by Clifford Morris

ISBN: 978-0-615-38975-2

Library of Congress Control Number: 2010933833

FOR INFORMATION CONTACT;
Clifford Morris
2716 Wentworth Drive
Grand Prairie, TX 75052
682-367-9082

Printed in USA by
Morris Publishing®
3212 E. Hwy. 30 · Kearney, NE 68847
800-650-7888 · www.morrispublishing.com

This book is dedicated to

my parents, Bradford and Dorothy Morris

Acknowledgements

A special thanks to so many people who read, encouraged, and provided useful input into the completion of this story. It wouldn't have been possible without the many hours contributed by Kati Thompson, Linda Hull, Lois Raymond, Glenda Strange, John Morris, Carmen Goldthwaite, Bill Woodrow, Fred Hedgecoke, Tony Skur, George Goldthwaite, and all the accomplished, aspiring, and energetic writers of The DFW Writer's Workshop.

CHAPTER ONE

THE FALSEHOODS THAT CUT THE DEEPEST are those accepted as truth; for what can exceed the heartache of learning you've lived a lie?

Judge Desmond J. Nolan stared briefly at the courtroom over his hawkish nose and settled into his seat behind the bench. The proceeding would be brief, but the implications profound. The defendant, Jonathan Evans, would serve the time, but his family would suffer, too.

"Would the defendant and counsel please stand."

The judge read each chapter and verse of applicable statutes where the defendant, Jonathan Evans, had been found guilty. Brandon sat behind his father, between his mother and older sister, and his face flushed hot. His ears burned as he listened to the judge's condemning lecture.

"Over a two-year period, you embezzled and misappropriated nearly one million dollars from your firm," the judge recited. "These were withdrawals and transfers not authorized by senior management or part of your prescribed duties. This was not money you needed because of a life threatening illness. You weren't being extorted by another party. You devised a bogus paper trail designed to enrich your bank account and to cover up your own bungling of business matters. And you pulled others into the slime with you to hide your incompetence.

"Mr. Evans, you are hereby remanded to the Texas State Department of Corrections for a period of not less than five or more than fifteen years. Further, you are ordered to pay restitution in the full amount embezzled from the firm and pay a fine of twenty thousand dollars."

For seven months, Jonathan Evans had vociferously protested his innocence. When the trial began, Brandon sat in the courtroom for three straight weeks while testimony was given, tedious evidence presented, and witnesses examined.

His father despised people who talked a good game, but then fell short when results were measured. In spite of his demanding ways, his driven personality inspired Brandon. His father's professed innocence was all Brandon needed to hear.

When the testimony ended, the jury deliberated all of an hour and a half. The verdict was guilty on all counts. Until that moment, Brandon had cloaked the damning evidence in a cocoon of excuses. During the trial, he hadn't listened to a single witness with an open mind. The judge's sharp announcement shook him, and he felt strangely sad for a man who hardly gave him the time of day.

Today, from three rows back, Brandon caught the side view of his father as he stood behind the defendant's table. His suit appeared worn and limp. His body slack, his shoulders drooped as he listened to the judge. His father's body language expressed a defeat he hadn't seen before, and the sight turned Brandon's emotions. His heart filled with disgust. The man was a fake. A cowardly bully who lied about his innocence, and when it came time to pay the piper, hung his head like a scolded schoolboy. There stood a man he knew would quickly browbeat others to tow the line to his warped perception of hard work, but when things got tough took the easy way out. The last thing he saw was the sad spectacle of his handcuffed father being led away by a squad of uniformed officers.

Brandon touched his mother's hand as it rested in her lap. He wanted to say something, but wasn't sure she wanted, nor needed, any words of support. She knew the kind of man she'd married. She hid her face behind huge sunglasses. Her stoic expression indicated she just wanted the courtroom spectacle to end. She appeared strangely relaxed, her face a countenance of serenity. She may well be thankful to be rid of his father for awhile. He wasn't an easy man to live with, not for any of them. Seated on his other side, Brandon glanced at his older sister, Christine. She had her eyes closed, holding a tissue on the bridge of her nose. He doubted if she had shed a single tear, but if that was the effect she was going for, the pose was fitting.

One of their father's attorneys came over, expressed self-serving condolences and mumbled canned lines about appeals.

As the courtroom thinned out, the three of them left in silence. Brandon drove the women to the family home, then headed off to his apartment. His middle sister, Ella, had remained home near Denver. She hadn't seen the need to attend a boring white-collar trial and wasn't concerned about being kept abreast of events. She wasn't particularly surprised about the hole 'good ole dad' had dug for himself. She figured after all his speeches about self-reliance, he could damn well dig himself out of his own predicament without her help.

Brandon sat alone in his apartment. Confusion rattled his thinking. He wanted to help his father if there was something practical that could be done. Equally compelling was the notion to distance himself from a man whose ego knew no bounds. He had learned from his father, though it was more by watching than being taught. The man had hardly been there for him. And now, he had to advance his own business career without the convenient contacts his father once enjoyed.

The next morning, Brandon doodled at his office desk. He had hardly slept. His thoughts were still with his dad. What goes though one's mind when he knows he'll wake up to bars on the door for years to come?

Brandon knew the situation of his current employment was now untenable. No longer could he follow the long road to corporate success. Now he had to make some really big money. By an act of sheer will, he would force an idea from the pencil he held and embark upon a decisive plan of action.

His confined cubicle dwelt in the midst of eighty others, cast in glares and shadows of harsh florescent lights. The constant hum of indecipherable voices reverberated around him. The air wafted of churned dust, stale coffee, and half-eaten lunches. Everybody stuffed into one huge floor, squared and partitioned. Brandon had his own four by four square feet, his tiny assigned space. Only the crack of sunlight atop the covered wall-high windows confirmed another world outside.

A recent business degree from Texas State had garnered him a cubicle at Hoyt, Fitzgerald, and Greer, a starched-collar, by-the-book investment firm. There, he hawked retirement plans by phone to small businesses via a canned pitch guaranteed to mentally euthanize even the most receptive business owner. He worked on commission. Until now, the meager pay in his weekly envelope had been sufficient to support his single lifestyle. But his current income was peanuts compared to the score he wanted and racked his mind to conceive a plan. His brainstorming session drew a blank, and the pencil snapped in his hands.

Brandon stood and peered over the partition at another cellmate in the next cubicle. "Hey, Mark, how about Julio's after the grind?"

"You don't have to twist my arm, but . . ." The guy shook his head. "I have take Karen to her mother's. Maybe tomorrow."

Brandon slipped back into his chair and pulled himself up to the desk. He looked at the sheet of paper in front of him and tried to focus on the endless columns of black type. The sea of phone-book size letters and numbers seemed to pulsate under his gaze. A hazy mirage of light appeared to hang over the page. Only the movement of his ruler down the list provided any clarity, and he dialed a new number.

"Good afternoon, is Mr. Douglas in?"

"I believe he's still here. Whom may I say is calling?" The receptionist sounded tired.

"I'm Brandon Evans, ma'am, with Hoyt, Fitzgerald and Greer. How are you today?"

"Ready to go home. Is he expecting your call?"

"Yes, I believe he is."

"I'm asking if you've spoken with Mr. Douglas before. He's quite busy."

"I understand completely. I intend to be brief."

"Mr.," she interrupted.

"Evans, ma'am."

"Mr. Evans, have you spoken with Mr. Douglas before?"

"No, I haven't. My call is simply to introduce myself. You would allow me that, wouldn't you, especially if what we do would be of service to Mr. Douglas?"

"I'd be happy to take a message. He'll call you back if he's interested."

"I wish you were *my* executive secretary," Brandon said. "I can see how much Mr. Douglas relies on your efficiency. And I appreciate what you're asking. Couldn't I speak with him for just a minute? I promise that's all it'll be."

Brandon heard a sigh at the other end of the line.

"Just a minute," she said. "Please be as brief as you can."

After thirty seconds of cowboy radio that served as music-on-hold, another voice came on the line. "This is George."

"Good afternoon, Mr. Douglas. My name is Brandon Evans with Hoyt, Fitzgerald, and Greer. I just wanted to call and introduce myself."

"Hoyt and who?"

"Hoyt, Fitzgerald, and Greer, Mr. Douglas. We're one of the largest administrators of employee contribution plans in Texas. Currently, our funds average a nine point two percent rate-of-return."

"You talking about retirement?"

"Yes, sir." Brandon prepared to shift his speech into second gear. "We have conservative to aggressive offerings to meet your employees' risk tolerance and a solid track record of outstanding performance."

"Young man, I'll never get to retire around here. They'll be carting my lifeless carcass out of here in a wheelbarrow."

"I understand perfectly, sir." Brandon smiled into the phone, knowing full well his agreeable attitude came through in his voice. "Our real service is keeping valuable employees at your company. When important employees have a solid benefits package, even when they're making most or all of the contributions, they don't look for greener pastures elsewhere."

"Employees?" Douglas laughed. "There's just me and my secretary. Didn't she tell you that?"

Dead silence stuck in the line for several beats. "I hadn't asked," Brandon said. The steam in his delivery escaped faster than the air in a busted balloon.

"We both fund our individual retirement accounts. Beyond that, we wouldn't have enough money to pop a zit on your boss's butt." Douglas's raucous laughter continued. "Thanks for calling, but no thanks."

The line went dead. Gloom descended over Brandon's thoughts with mind-numbing sluggishness. He wanted to sleep and drift away. He stared at the clock, and his eyes glazed. Why did it always take longer for four p.m. to roll around once three-thirty arrived than it did at three?

When the clock finally struck four, Brandon tossed his paperwork in his desk and rose from his open cell, feeling the warm sweat around his collar. He walked into Julio's Bar & Grill six minutes later. His mental fog lifted, his sour thoughts transformed. He headed straightway to a table of business rookies from other firms he'd met in recent months.

"What's on tap?" Brandon beamed.

"Old Tree Bark for me," replied a tall fellow with a narrow face and sharp nose, "black as licorice and thick as eggnog."

"I'll bet. I think I'll have something lighter."

"It must be European or at least imported. No beer allowed at this table today if you can pronounce the name at first reading."

The group chuckled and raised their bottles in mock salute as the waitress walked by.

"I'll have one of those," Brandon said to the waitress. "Anyone else?"

The rest of the group was ready for another, and he bought a round. When the waitress returned, Brandon made a production of his five-dollar tip and rolled it tightly, length-wise, and wrapped it around a large button on her blouse. She pulled back, slightly annoyed, but broke into a genuine smile when he said, "Only one thing more pliable than this bill, beautiful, is my heart in your hands."

A cheer of raised bottles went up. "*Salud.*"

Brandon soaked up the accolade, winked easily to his friends, rubbed the cold bottle between his hands, and took a long draw on the contents. He swept back a lock of black hair that continually fell into his eyes and surveyed the bar, taking special notice of the female scenery. The workday was over, and he inhaled a refreshing breath of relief. He finished his beer and, for a moment, studied the empty bottle, put it on the table, and announced to the group. "Son of a bitch, it's Monday and I'm already beat."

Wide eyes stared back at him, and an uneasy flicker of silence invaded the group. It wasn't the profanity that instilled the quiet, but rather the fact this was a table of corporate greenies, soon to be properly designated wannabes. His blatant remark tended to let the genie of self-doubt from the bottle. Any reference to their low positions on their company's totem pole, and how much they worked for how little they were paid, brought up thoughts they were loathe to consider, and his drinking buddies weren't inclined to heap praise on anyone who did.

Brandon noticed the reaction and laughed. "Oh, hell, I was just pulling your chain. I need another beer."

Another cheer rose from the table along with a bottle salute. Brandon looked around at the packed happy hour bar, then back to his drinking comrades. He knew the tall guy's name was Charles, and he was a banker. He already looked like a banker and talked like one. He seemed competent, industrious, and destined to run a trust department someday or become vice president of internal paper shuffling at a major financial institution. But Charles was a banker, little doubt about it, and Brandon knew he didn't want to be one.

The stocky guy's name was Lance, and he'd mentioned 'computer programmer' when describing his vocation. Brandon couldn't rightly remember anyone, including himself, ever asking him again about his work. He understood how computers presented a challenge in the sense technology was always on the move, but how could a career be fulfilling if all you did was develop software or write code? Where was the human interaction? A person would have to come out from behind the servers just to get some sunlight.

He wanted to be his own boss and make his own way. That's what his father had done. Jonathan Evans had been born and raised in Ohio, the son of a man who made millions designing automobile engine performance devices. The two men had a

14

falling out thirty years ago, and his father took his new bride and an inheritance of sorts and moved to Texas. Brandon's grandparents were dead now. He could remember visiting his grandparents only a couple of times in all the years of his childhood. Once in Texas, his father built his own career. First, he worked as a salesman of oil field service equipment, then as a partner in an energy exploration venture. Wealthy beyond most men's wildest dreams, he found the temptation too great to keep his sticky fingers out of the company till.

Brandon knew the road to a big payday depended on continually dealing directly with people, working in sales. He was selling now, but it was small stuff. To score big, he needed to handle a significant transaction. He stopped the waitress as she passed and ordered another round.

Vic was one young man in their happy-hour group he wanted to know better. Vic bought his share of drinks and seemed well liked by everyone. From previous table banter, Brandon knew Vic worked for a commercial real estate developer. Personally, Brandon believed the way to real wealth was accomplished in the stock market, though he had only a business education as the foundation for such beliefs. As he now knew, until he had some real money to invest, wealth in the market was just an elusive dream.

The idea of commercial real estate development intrigued him. Since he didn't yet know where he would find his passport to the top, he was more than willing to learn. For now, Vic was going to become his new best friend.

Corporate scandals and plane crashes were acceptable happy-hour topics of conversation. Yet, a detailed discussion of what each of them actually did at work seemed all but taboo. Brandon knew he would rather chew broken glass than answer truthfully about what he did from eight to four. Everyone was defined by who he worked for or by an innocuous title that provided a label, and everyone pretty much left it at that.

As much as Brandon wanted to talk about Vic's line of work, he needed another point of reference in which to broach the topic. It wasn't a problem. He had a conversation starter that seldom failed. As acquaintances came and went, Brandon cornered Vic's attention across a couple beers.

"You live up on the north side of the city?"

"More east I'd say," replied Vic.

"Well, that's closer anyway . . . to the lake, I mean."

"Johnson Lake?"

"That's it. Smoothest, cleanest body of water for a hundred miles. You ever been on it?" Brandon asked.

"No, been up around the place, though. It's pretty."

"Oh, it's more than pretty. You should see it from the water."

"Never had the chance."

"I've got a boat. Use it almost every weekend. My girlfriend and I ski some, but mostly we just drift on the water."

"Sounds like fun."

"You want to join us this weekend? You and a friend?"

"That sounds great, but I have to work Saturday."

"We'll be there Sunday," Brandon said without missing a beat. "Just meet us at the Dawson Marina at ten."

CHAPTER TWO

BRANDON AND CINDY ARRIVED AT THE MARINA shortly after nine-thirty loaded with ice chests. A rising sun slowly burned away the morning mist. The lake shimmered silvery blue. Water lapped the piers mixed with the subdued gurgle of propellers pushing boats away from the dock. Sunlight stabbed the water at harsh angles, and the two of them dropped their sunglasses in place as they prepared the boat, and waited for Vic to arrive.

Cindy's adventurous disposition placed her atop the list for spur of the moment excursions. For years she had been a readily available date. At five-feet-four, she was compact with full breasts, toned legs, with a gift for conversation and a daring attitude. She also possessed an anchored sense of the acceptable, useful around Brandon's unpredictable antics. She wore a lime-green two-piece with yellow trim that accentuated her copper skin and had her shoulder-length, black hair swept behind her ears with the aid of a barrette.

She had known Brandon since high school. They had dated briefly in junior college and had reconnected when Brandon returned from Texas State. She had been on the boat many times, and knew her way around the lake. She was always available to answer the call as Brandon's girl Friday, especially if it meant spending a day on the water.

Vic arrived at the appointed hour, fully dressed in nylon sweat pants and a billowing white, long-sleeved shirt turned up at the collar. His nose was painted with zinc oxide and a wide-brimmed hat pulled snuggly on his head. He escorted a slender brunette he introduced as Gail, and full introductions were made all around as they pushed away from the dock.

Brandon's father owned the boat. It had been purchased three years earlier as a restoration project, but it quickly found its way onto a list of worthwhile, yet unfulfilled intentions. The boat was both quaint and disconcerting, certainly out of place amid the sleek fiberglass speedboats and elegant sailboats at the marina. She arrived with the name *Betty Sue* burnt into her stern and for the time being the name remained. She was thirty-four feet long with a covered pilot house, high gunwales, and sleeping accommodations for six. She had a spacious rear deck with two, six cylinder in-board engines. Those who wished to ski could easily do so with only one caveat—stay in *Betty Sue's* draft.

Attempts to traverse her massive wake guaranteed an incredible wipe out.

They headed to the center of the lake, northeast toward the dam. Brandon turned the wheel over to Cindy. The men went to lawn chairs and an ice chest on the rear deck and settled back, each with a cold longneck.

Vic looked portside across the lake. "Very nice. It's a beautiful lake—and a great boat."

"It works for me," Brandon said. "Nothing better than spending time on the water."

"Guess I never thought how peaceful it could be out here."

"It sure takes the edge off after a busy week," Brandon said, warming to the sound of his own voice. "I come out here, relax and recharge, all without the expense of leaving town."

Vic nodded in agreement. "What do you do, if you don't mind my asking?"

"Investments mainly and company retirement plans. It's not real glamorous, I guess, but it pays the bills. How about you?"

"Me?" Vic smiled under his broad hat as if the question about him amounted to less than nothing or was humorous at the very least. "I'm what you call a land man."

"That sounds interesting."

"Hardly. It's fairly routine." Vic popped the top on another beer and took a swig. "I buy corners."

Brandon smiled. "Now what does that mean?"

"Well, the company sends me out to scout for commercial land in front of population growth. We buy for national retail and restaurant chains, so we know what sizes and locations they're looking for."

"Sounds like a blast."

Vic shrugged. "Oh, it might be if I got a commission for buying a parcel of land below list price, but I don't. It's all rather straightforward. Once I find a suitable property, the home office handles the negotiations. I get paid a salary, so it doesn't matter how many deals I work on."

"Yeah," Brandon commiserated, "that does sound lame—money wise, I mean." Brandon's brow pinched and a distant gaze clouded his eyes. "But I thought there were big bucks to be made in real estate, especially commercial real estate."

Vic seemed to study him for a moment. "The way to make the big bucks in real estate is to find some valuable land before anyone else wants it, before anyone else realizes its value."

"Yeah," Brandon said. The casual statement, laden with common sense, washed over him like a heavenly message. His mind immediately contemplated untold riches. It required simply that he unearth value trapped in a tract of dirt. The wealth he sought might lie around any corner. He could no longer disguise his rapt interest and sat before Vic mesmerized, awaiting knowledge.

Vic continued. "If you're looking for something like that, I'd suggest you look in the heart of the city rather than on the outskirts. There are a lot of older neighborhoods and business districts where the land isn't being put to its best use."

Brandon interrupted. "Best use?"

"Sure, say you find a run-down, half-abandoned strip retail center. It isn't producing any real rent for anyone. The buildings are an eyesore. You buy up the property on the cheap, take the headache off the poor sap who owns the place, and tear down the buildings. Then you'll have a piece of land that can be put to better economical use. In the process you make a sweet profit."

Brandon listened intently. He soaked up every word even as his mind raced ahead, visualizing a map of the city, contemplating how he might start. It made perfect sense. Buildings and houses, neighborhoods and shopping centers, even schools and churches were born and grew, lived and died, just like people. Areas of town got redeveloped all the time.

"One more thing," Vic said, "actually the most important thing. Before you get all carried away with what I just told you---make sure you have a buyer for the property you're working on. Make sure someone wants the property. It's the only way to guarantee that someone will pay your price. Negotiate all you want with your sellers, but don't invest a dime until you find a ready and willing buyer."

"So, how do you do that?"

"Work both sides of the street simultaneously," Vic said with a sly smile as he stood. "Mind if your girlfriend shows me how she operates this ship?"

"No, no, go ahead, enjoy yourself." Brandon was instantly lost in thought. One idea made its way to the forefront of his mind and stuck. With land, one or two deals could make a person absolutely rich. No more penny-ante, po-dunk business transactions where you had to talk to a thousand people to sell a hundred and hope that half of those stayed on the books. With land, a person could afford to put in the time and effort to complete the big score. He would compensate for his lack of experience with sheer determination. He would learn what he needed to know along the way. He finished his beer and walked into the pilot house.

"How you doing? Enjoying the lake?" Brandon didn't wait for a response as he took the wheel. "I'm going to head over to the Point Marina so we can get some sandwiches and gas. Then I've got to head back. Sorry, but I just remembered, there's something I have to get done back in town."

CHAPTER THREE

RICK STANTON CLOSED THE BAKER'S
BACK GATE and headed up the alley to his next
stop. His massive hands played with the trove of
objects that found home in the deep pockets of his
overalls, a roll of electrician's tape, little clamps
attached to shiny swivels, a lucky half-dollar he
never spent, crayon stubs of delightful colors, a lost
or discarded woman's engagement ring, a cracked
marble, and an assortment of smooth pebbles and
tarnished keys. Each was a treasure in its own right.
Each had a special significance or held a personal
delight. He fingered through his pocket, brought
one out and looked it over as he moved along,
examining it for the hundredth time as though it
were new, then put it back, and reached in his other
pocket for something else.

Several blocks away Sherman Porter snoozed
fitfully in his front porch swing. The vibrant buzz of
a tenacious gnat kept his daydream on the edge of
consciousness, but bothersome only when it landed

on his ear. An absent swat of his hand, a pinky finger to rub away the tickle, and Sherman was in dreamland once more, fully attending to his nap.

Sherman and his wife, Grace, had raised three boys in the house at 408 Lancer, from the day each came home from the hospital to the day each had gone on to lives and wives and homes of their own. An oak's gigantic sprawl of branches dominated the front yard and stood impressively over the lawn and street. A cozy veranda stretched either side of the stone steps where Sherman rested. The porch spanned the front of the house around to an east-side door that offered a second entry into the parlor. Now nestled in the shade, the porch had been a popular meeting place over the years because of its location and inviting openness, a gathering point for celebrations by many, a place of neighborly evening conversations among three or four, a private sanctuary for family discussions between Sherman and Grace alone.

Rick stopped at the thigh-high, wrought-iron gate, fumbled with the latch, and walked on up. "Afternoon, Mr. Porter," he said, as yet unaware that the object of his greeting was asleep. He waited and received no reply. "Mr. Porter, Mr. Porter." His cry grew louder as alarm spiked his words.

Still Sherman napped. Rick ran up the porch steps to the front of the porch swing, grabbed the old man by the shoulders, and shook him. "Wake up, Mr. Porter, please wake up."

Sherman's eyes flew open, but he couldn't see. His lungs gulped for air, but he couldn't breathe. His brain still listened to the faint, rhythmic beat of insect wings, but the gnat had become a giant mantis. He pulled in his arms to defend himself, but the attack ended as quickly as it began.

"Mr. Porter, I thought you was . . . was . . ."

"Good lord, Rick, you trying to kill me?" Sherman worked himself out of the swing.

Rick was relieved he hadn't come upon a dead man.

"Don't ever do that again, you hear?" Sherman pointed at the swing. "If someone is dead, they're not going to be sitting up in a swing. Do you understand?"

"Yes, I know, it was just that you didn't---"

"I was sleeping. You know the difference between dead and sleeping, right?"

"Yes."

"Well, don't ever do that to me again. Don't do it to anyone. If you want to talk to someone and they're sitting up, just keep calling their name. They'll answer you sooner or later." Sherman grabbed a straight-back chair from beside the front door and plopped into it as he caught his breath.

"I'm sorry, Mr. Porter."

Sherman dropped the subject. He had to. A response to Rick's apology would only perpetuate the topic, and they would be going back and forth all afternoon.

"Why you here today?" Sherman asked.

Rick thought for a moment. "Oh, I'm going to start on the paint job on the back of the house."

"You want to start that now?"

"Yes, sir. The sun shines best this time of day so I can see my work better."

Sherman nodded. "Okay. All the supplies you'll need are on the back porch."

"I'll do you a really good job, Mr. Porter."

"I know you will," Sherman said as he leaned his chair against the house and folded his hands behind his head.

Sherman's house was in serious need of maintenance, as were many houses nearby. The sad state of the Victorian homes that comprised the neighborhood summed up Rick's reason for moving to this part of town. Restoring old houses was his passion. Fixing the neglected and broken fulfilled an inner purpose. Most of the resident owners were elderly. If something didn't have to be fixed immediately, it fell down their list of priorities. If it were up to him, Rick would replace warped window casements and attend to broken porch and balcony railings—restore the architectural masterpieces to their bygone years of glory. But decades of minimum attention kept him busy in basic duty, replacing rusted plumbing and old wiring. For many of his customers, it was all Rick could do to keep their old houses in a decent coat of paint.

Hours later, the descending veil of darkness prompted Rick to suspend his painting on Sherman's house. No longer able to easily see his work, he glanced over his shoulder, caught the final beams of a disappearing sun, and climbed down his ladder.

He had finished another day's work, and he knew all was in order. But his mind struggled, just for a moment, to recall his next task. He knew what it was, and he knew it would come to mind. Yet, something in his brain mocked him. His head didn't play fair; this he instinctively knew. He walked to the front of the house. If the thought didn't come to him soon, he would knock at the front door and talk to Mr. Porter. But then he knew. The increasing darkness gave him the clue he sought, and he realized it was time to go home.

Rick lifted his head and watched as the stars revealed themselves against the growing blackness of the sky. He accepted each moment for what it was, content and appreciative of the present. The brain that fought him at every turn when he tried to coalesce and clarify an elusive thought was the same mind that defended him against the negativity that inevitably came his way. His reasoning ability and memory were more than adequate. He could hear and retell a story. He could learn a task and repeat it again and again. His memory served him as well as it could. Though it sometimes left him confused for a moment, his tyrannical brain tossed in a special blessing when failures, disappointments, and disparaging remarks came his way. It simply filed such experiences in the wastebasket of the inconsequential and irrelevant.

Often he came across to others as such a simple individual where nothing was expected of him beyond the availability of his strong back. At other times, Rick came up with unexpected insights that garnered him a second glance and generated a curious admiration from those who heard him.

Last week, at the home of Cecil Nance, Rick expressed a confident observation about the task at hand. A monstrous armoire occupied a second floor bedroom. The room was now an office. The wardrobe closet took up needed space. Because of its size, Cecil thought it would need to be sawn in two to get it down the staircase. To him it was just a large wooden box that had outlived its utility.

"Actually, Mr. Nance, we can carry it right out."

Cecil and his adult son gave Rick a deprecatory glance and headed up the stairs with a power saw.

Rick followed on their heels. "If you turn it on its side, it'll go right out," he said. "That's the way it came in."

Cecil stopped and offered an unconvinced shake of his head. "You haven't lifted it, Rick. It weighs a ton. It had to come in here in pieces."

"No, sir," Rick said, his smooth, non-judgmental tone so easy to bear even when he was in disagreement. "It came in one piece and it'll go down those steps a lot easier than it came up them."

Cecil glanced at his son, then at the armoire, then back at Rick. "Why do you care?"

"Well---I guess, I can just tell it'll go out the way it is, and I don't want you to have to go to a bunch of trouble if you don't have to. Besides, maybe it's worth something. Don't people buy old stuff like that?"

That was Monday. By mid-week Cecil had sold the armoire to an antique dealer for a handsome sum.

Rick stood at the door of his one-bedroom apartment and reached into his breast pocket for the only important key he carried. He didn't have a TV, but listened to the radio constantly while at home. His coffee table was piled high with fishing and wildlife magazines. A single volume on Texas wildflowers was the only hardcover book he owned.

Ten months previous, his parents moved him to this older, established part of the city accessible to important services and stores without the need of a vehicle. Considered safe in spite of inner-city decadence that plied its money-grubbing version of capitalism in the pool halls, liquor stores, and payday loan outlets that littered its nearby streets, it proved a struggle for his mother to let him go. She still made the ten-mile trip across the city twice a week to check on him and bring him extra household supplies. But it had been the right move. He had to learn to live on his own, make everyday decisions for himself, and experience life away from his boyhood home.

His dad had shaken his hand, clasping it between the two of his, and hugged him. He knew his parents loved him deeply, but figured if they ever pulled themselves together and left, he'd take a walk around the block and check out the neighborhood for himself. Now, almost a year later, he felt as though he'd lived at the apartment for years.

He was about to turn the key in the lock when he heard approaching footsteps.

"Hey, mister, I was hoping to ask you something."

Rick turned and listened, attentive yet expressionless.

"You been living here long?"

"Ten months," Rick replied.

"Me and my wife've only been here a month. By the way, my name's Todd." The lanky fellow extended his hand.

"Well, hi, I'm Rick." They shook hands.

Todd was lean, a tinge of red in his hair. His words were easy-going and his mannerisms friendly, but his eyes emitted a darting energy that hinted of a mind working harder than necessary. Todd's easy banter halted imperceptibly as he looked closely at Rick, and within a heartbeat his entire approach and vocal inflection turned, and he got to the point.

"Hey, let me ask you, I need to get some milk for my daughter. Could I borrow a ten? I can pay you back at the end of the week."

"A ten?" Rick wasn't sure.

"Yeah, ten dollars."

"Oh, some money."

"Yeah, just ten dollars. Till the end of the week."

Rick reached for his wallet and opened it. He knew what dollars were, and that some were worth more, and you could buy more things with the dollars with the bigger numbers. What purchases he did make were usually with a credit card his parents oversaw. He didn't need cash, though he always had a few bills on hand.

Rick reached for a bill. "This is ten dollars, isn't it?"

Todd nodded. "Now that I'm thinking about it, could I borrow this one?" Todd reached into the wallet and pulled out a twenty. "It would sure tide me over till the weekend and I'll pay you back then."

Puzzlement overtook Rick's expression as he thought. He watched as Todd folded the bill and stuck it into his shirt pocket. "You'll pay me back?"

"Sure thing, man. Thanks a lot, you're a big help."

CHAPTER FOUR

ETHEL BARNES busied herself crocheting another scarf. She donated her voluminous production to the church's perpetual clothing relief drive. There could never be too many scarves and shawls to warm and clothe the cold and naked.

She camped in front of the television for Dr. Phil, her favorite program. She never missed the program unless the ladies at the church needed her assistance. But Ethel didn't care for all the talk of personal addictions or the seamy details of life's tribulations, so she watched with the volume off as she tended to her needlework. She was sure Dr. Phil was dispensing sound advice to his guests, and that's what mattered most.

For Ethel, life was pleasant, though routine, and comfortable because she was in familiar surroundings, her home of fifty years. She had a housekeeper who came by once a week and Meals-on-Wheels every weekday at noon. When she wasn't knitting, she scooted from room to room on the first floor of her Victorian home where she sorted through boxes and moved things around, but never threw anything out.

She lived in the glow of table lamps that were always on, covered with parched paper shades strung with cloth tassels. Her living room was an emporium of porcelain figurines of animals and clowns, babies and birds, all peering forlornly from behind curved-glass cabinets. The walls were hung with a hodgepodge of picture frame clusters, the floor a maze of kilim rugs. In one corner stood an upright piano, now closed and silent, having long ago played its final note.

Ethel sighed as she looked up from her handiwork and rested her hands in her lap. She had everything she could possibly ask for. Marvin had provided everything before he passed. He had been a good man, an attentive father, a gentle husband. He'd been an especially good provider, thirty-seven years as a senior partner at one of Atherton's largest law firms. Ethel knew she would never want for anything material. Even though it had been fifteen years since Marvin worked there, the firm helped her free of charge with the occasional legal matter. She'd been peeved when they removed 'Barnes' from the name of the firm, but she tried to understand. After all, Marvin had sold his partnership interest when he retired. They were good people at Dustin, Cushman and Childs.

She got up and moseyed over to the doll case. Was that dust on those dresses? That cabinet was supposed to be airtight. She peered into the glass case and was sure she saw dust on the garments. If the dolls needed cleaning she would have to do it herself. She didn't want the housekeeper handling her precious dolls. Most of the collection had been purchased over her lifetime on spur-of-the-moment impulses. She was so enamored by their facial expressions and the cut of their delicate clothes. She perused them all and whispered their names. Ethel realized she had a doll collection of considerable size. The dolls were the tip of the iceberg of all her souvenirs, knick-knacks, antiques, and heirlooms collected over the years and crowded into every cranny of her house.

A knock came, and Ethel shuffled to the front door. Meals-on-Wheels had already come and gone, but maybe she had forgotten about an unscheduled arrival. At any rate, she didn't want to miss a visitor. Unhurried and unperturbed, she cracked the door and greeted a young man in a wrinkled green shirt carrying a shabby leather satchel.

"Good afternoon, ma'am. It sure is nice to find you home. I hope you're having a wonderful day."

"Thank you, I do believe I am."

"My name is Todd Simms, a student at Adams High, and I'm introducing folks to new magazines to earn enough money to go on a field trip next month."

If the young man was still in his teens, he was the oldest-looking kid who ever set foot in a public school, an observation that struck Ethel immediately, and she wasn't a big reader these days, a fact she did express to Todd.

Todd peered into the house past Ethel's shoulder. "Ma'am, I know I have at least one periodical that you'd like, and I'm allowed to give away one subscription free if you'll just let me show you the list."

"Well." His voice sounded so hopeful, and he did seem like a nice person.

"Could I just come in and sit for awhile? You don't have to buy anything. I've almost sold all I need to anyway."

"I guess that would be all right." She stepped back from the door.

Todd stepped past the decoratively carved oak door into a mahogany foyer with a built-in desk beside a coat closet. A wide staircase with curved balustrade led up from the right. An archway announced entry into the living room and its twelve-foot ceiling, richly engrained hardwood floors, and its floor-to-ceiling pea green anaglyptic wallpaper, the raised relief brushed with copper highlights.

"This is a nice place you have," Todd said. His eyes surveyed the bric-a-brac that littered the hutches, lamp stands, and tables. "I see you have an exquisite collection."

Such words were more than enough to strum the emotional strings of a lonely woman in a house full of inanimate stuff. The comment contained the very flattery that reduced Ethel to a self-indulgent gossip. Though this fellow was a complete stranger, she almost blushed. Todd was obviously an intelligent young man, a connoisseur of fine things. "Well, thank you," she said. "I've accumulated a lot—more than fifty years worth—too much, I know."

"It's all quite beautiful."

"Would you like to see my favorite doll?"

Todd ignored the question. "May I sit here, ma'am?" He took a seat on a footstool beside her wing chair and waited until Ethel situated herself. "May I ask your name?"

"Oh certainly, it's Barnes."

"Mrs. Barnes, do you have any pets?"

"Just my finches over there. They're being quiet now," she said as though she were able to control the behavior of the birds.

"Take a look at this, Mrs. Barnes. It's one of the most amazing magazines I've ever seen."

Todd spread the magazine under the glow of a lamp and flipped through a bird magazine with detailed color pictures. He showed her another magazine on antiques that included a small article on porcelain dolls.

"One of these, whatever one you choose, I can let you have for free," he said as he got out his order pad. When it came time to get a check, he told her, "it's only $89.95 for six months and your first magazine will arrive in two weeks."

She wrote the check. It wasn't worth fussing about anyway. He seemed like such a nice boy, and besides, it was nice to have someone stop by today. Todd took the check and told Ethel again how nice it was to meet her, and what a lovely house she had.

As he left, he slipped a rectangular silver tray from her foyer desk into his sample case. It was the only thing that looked valuable amid all the junk she had around the place. And he didn't bother to mention that her subscriptions were all part of a package. If she didn't care for *Field & Stream* or *Sports Illustrated*, she could always throw them away.

CHAPTER FIVE

BY THE TIME BRANDON GOT CINDY
back to her apartment it was mid-afternoon. He
hurried home, changed clothes, and called the
downtown library. On Sundays it closed at six.

For Brandon Evans, visits to the public
depository of knowledge and enlightenment were
few and far between. He didn't have a library card
and was far more inclined to pick up a video than a
good book. But he knew of the extensive map
collection at the city's downtown branch, and he
sped down the relatively empty streets to get there
as fast as he could. He hoped the detail in the
collection of city maps might give him a clue as to
where to begin a property search.

Vic's information struck him as brilliant;
amazingly simple, yet brilliant. Why hadn't he
figured it out on his own? If he could find an area of
urban blight and decay, a tract of land pleading for a
new beginning, then he could revitalize a parcel of
unproductive dirt. Soon he'd be counting his money

in five figures per deal instead of three figures per week.

He found the aerial view of the downtown business district in a neatly alphabetized rack of hanging maps and moved to spread it out on a nearby table. A weather-beaten drifter snoozed at the table, dressed in a winter coat and hunting cap in spite of the outside heat, while a book slipped from his hand. He jumped when the maps hit the table, dropped his book, and scowled as he jerked awake.

"Don't be making faces at me, old timer. You aren't supposed to be sleeping in here. Go outside and sleep."

In a labored slow motion, as though his body had been molded into the chair, the shaggy fellow pried himself from the seat and moved away, a fierce backward glance left in his wake.

Brandon immediately dismissed the exchange and concentrated on the map. He'd grown up in Atherton. He knew the city's downtown streets as well as anyone, and yet, the aerial view cast the downtown geography in an entirely new perspective. The use of color made it possible to see every street and building at once. It was all quite fascinating; it also didn't help. He realized he must drive every street to find any empty and boarded buildings, those pleading for tenants, the others crying for maintenance. He would start at Main and Broadway and work his way out. Hours later he ended his search only because the falling shadow of dusk cloaked the streets and he needed to find a filling station.

The next morning he called in sick. In two days, he could collect his paycheck for the previous week and leave Hoyt, Fitzgerald, and Greer forever, without notice. He'd tap Cindy for some living expenses. He'd gather investors, one way or another. Once freed from the straightjacket of a written script, he would smooth-talk the most reluctant investor to get on-board for a bona fide real estate opportunity. He would make his telephone not just a tool, but a weapon, an instrument to seductively exploit the festering piranha of greed that dwelt in every soul. He would raise the money needed to tie up a prime piece of investment property.

During his drive the previous day in and around the inner city, an area around the downtown hospital, just south of the freeway, appeared to warrant further investigation. There he found a number of one-story office buildings, clinics really, each with impressive titles, an oncology institute, geriatric resources, hyperbaric wound care, and women's center. Yet, directly across the street nothing existed but empty, trash-littered lots.

A pharmacy called home a building with a façade of crumbling stucco. Numerous storefronts stared vacantly at the curb, grimy plate glass a vestige of more robust times. Doctor's offices occupied art deco buildings of the 1940's next to a modern four-story, glass cube---home of the local office of the American Cancer Society. Everywhere was a mishmash of undisciplined property use.

An apartment building, yellow stucco trimmed in white, stood near the entrance to a parking garage. Half a block away, workers loitered on the sidewalk around a temporary labor storefront, smoked and gossiped while they waited for work, and sat on the curb content to let the passing traffic serve as entertainment.

Brandon parked his Trans Am and got out. A block from his car he saw a young woman, pert and petite, arms full of books, head up the steps to the apartment building. He reached her before she fully entered her security code.

"Excuse me," he said. Unalarmed, her gaze met his. "You live here I imagine?"

"Yes." She evaluated him with interest.

"I was just wondering, are these units available for anyone?"

An easy smile came to her mouth. "They are if you want to be a nurse."

"Oh, a dormitory?

She nodded.

"Is this the only one?"

"No, there's three more on the other side of campus and another is going to be built right over there." She pointed to an empty lot a half block up the street.

"I see. Are all the nurses in training as pretty as you?" A mendacious tone ran through his words, but still she smiled.

"Have a nice day," she said as she opened the outer door and dismissed him with a turn of her head.

Brandon frowned at her quick dismissal. He was just trying to be charming. A feeble attempt, he quickly admitted. He wasn't up to full speed before noon.

A high canopy of lush greenery a few blocks away pulled his eyes from the stark commercial street of mismatched shops and squat office buildings. He headed for the shade of the trees before he resumed his drive of the area. Within several hundred paces he walked into a secluded residential neighborhood of rich foliage and ancient architecture named Kessler Park. He felt as though he had stepped back in time. The picket fences and narrow streets spoke of a bygone gentility. The view was both astounding and depressing all in one glance. What had once been could be fully imagined. What currently existed could be plainly seen.

The streets were lined by ancient Victorian homes made almost entirely of wood with expansive porches and impressive balconies. Once inside the entry columns that marked the neighborhood, a new ambiance enveloped the street. The trees held in a sweet shade and the insect buzzing and chirps of birds were magnified. But the houses had seen better days. Time had marched through the neighborhood and left its erosive scars.

Before Brandon could fully contemplate everything around him, a man approached along the sidewalk, and Brandon called out. "Excuse me. Could you help me?"

The man halted and eyed him skeptically. "What?"

"Just wondered if you live around here?"

"Not far." The young man continued to survey him with suspicion.

"So you know this neighborhood?" Brandon asked.

Brandon waited as the fellow seemed to ponder the question for hidden meaning. The guy was about his age, tall and lean with sandy hair, wearing painfully out-of-date polyester pants stitched with thick white thread at the pockets. His lime colored shirt appeared to have been retrieved from the hamper. He carried a worn leather satchel. After a few seconds, without giving the man's reluctance any special thought, Brandon continued.

"The reason I ask is that I'm thinking about buying property around here. I just wanted to know more about the neighborhood."

"Like what?"

"Oh, like what do the houses go for? Who might be looking to sell, general info like that."

"Uh-huh." The fellow's tone said he didn't believe it. "Ever heard of a realtor?"

Brandon did his tried-and-true open arms affectation. "Why use a middle man if you don't have to?" His brain generated a flurry of reasons why he'd be looking for property by walking the streets, but then, their eyes fully met, and in one instant they each took measure of the other, and Brandon knew it was best just to lay out his cards. Maybe this guy could help him, maybe not, but if he expected to get anything useful, he'd have to tell it straight. For in that moment, Brandon knew, when it came to the instinct to go for the fast buck, their DNA was the same. "Let me put it this way,"

Brandon said without missing a beat. "Maybe you'd like to make some real money."

"Sure would." The other guy nodded.

"Let's go down to that diner and get some coffee."

The corner diner was an Atherton landmark. Norma's was a neighborhood meeting place for businessmen, doctors, and winos alike, with big-boned waitresses and old-timers whose wives kicked them out of the house every morning. Coffee was sold by the refill. It was either that or rent out certain tables by the hour.

The atmosphere was a din of scraping chairs and tinkling silverware mixed with the steady drone of four dozen animated conversations. The menu was irrelevant. Order the special and the food would be on your table in less than a minute. The walls were a disjointed spread of autographed pictures of long dead, and longer forgotten, local celebrities collected by the restaurant's original owner, now himself among the dearly departed. Everyone was friendly and chatty, likewise aloof and indifferent.

The two young men sat down and ordered coffee. The waitress popped her order pad with a pencil, glanced at the clock on the wall, and said two words, "Lunch hour." Brandon got the hint and ordered two specials.

"My name's Brandon. Brandon Evans, what's yours?"

"Todd," the other man said. "So you think there's money to be made in all those old hulks of dried kindling?"

Brandon searched Todd's face. "Maybe—I'm not sure yet."

"Well, let me tell you straight up," Todd said as he poured a stream of sugar into his coffee. "There are a few absentee investors already playing landlord down there. Tenants are there, but they can't pay a decent rent. I know, I've heard. The tenants willing to live there don't have the income to allow rents to be raised. So if you're thinking of buying an old mansion or two and playing landlord."

Brandon shook his head. "Not what I had in mind at all, but you know a lot more about the area than I do. Tell me, who lives in those houses?"

"Real simple," Todd said. "For the most part just old people waiting to die. They're the homeowners, the people who have been around for years. Like I said, there are a number of rentals, too, with a bunch of foreign families in them and kids all over the place. I'd bet the people who own them would love to get them off their hands."

"You have any idea how much they're worth?"

"Not really. I don't think I've ever seen a *For Sale* sign in the neighborhood. Maybe it's because nobody wants to sell, but I bet it's because nobody wants to buy."

Their lunch specials came, and Brandon picked at his mixed vegetables as he listened to Todd analyze the area.

"You know," Todd continued, "you look at those houses and you can see they were really impressive a long time ago, but now, and I've been in a bunch of them, they're junk. None of them had plumbing to start with, and if they did, it was that galvanized crap, all rusted through by now. Few of them have air conditioning, window units maybe, but all that open space ain't worth shit if you don't have some cool air around here come summertime, if you know what I mean. I don't see how anyone can make any money on those houses unless you got a boat load to fix them up."

"Well---" Brandon searched for a few choice words. He knew he'd found the land he sought and the glow of discovery warmed his core. Todd's oration made it obvious. Now he would fill in the blanks and develop the strategy. There it was, land near the center of the city, currently being used no more productively than as a hospice for crumbling homes. But it was this very detail, that it was a residential neighborhood, historical in fact, that had sheltered it from scrutiny.

Truth was, he didn't have a plan. Brandon struggled for an idea. If he could just put flesh on an approach where he first gained control of the properties, he would then have time to pitch development ideas to potential investors.

"You're missing an important detail." Brandon leaned across the table and spoke in a whisper. "I'm a developer, not a landlord," he said. "The value there is in the land, not in those houses. Those houses have to go. Once that land is cleared, it'll be more valuable because it'll be ready to be redeveloped. The sooner all those old houses are torn down, the sooner the real money will be made."

"So how'ya gonna do that?" Todd now leaned across the table himself.

"Get those folks to sell their houses." Brandon concocted an idea on the fly. "Not for cash now, but for when they have to move out, or for funds payable to their heirs. Make it an amount that's larger than anything they think the house is worth. Tell them they can live in the place until they're ready for their heavenly reward, a transaction presented as prudent estate planning."

Todd nodded all the while. His smile of gray, square teeth grew larger and larger. And then Todd whispered the words that caused Brandon's heart to flip with joy. "You know, you don't have to give those people anything of value. They'll sign anything, anyway."

Brandon could hardly contain his excitement. "What do you mean?"

"You're talking about making them an offer on their house, explaining a real estate contract, talking about money." Todd shook his head. "Big waste of time. Half of those people wouldn't know what you were talking about. The other half wouldn't be interested."

"How do you know this?"

Todd's lips parted again in a gray smile, and he spoke in an unctuous tone that gave Brandon a sudden chill. "I've been around here for awhile, my friend. I've sold these people everything from pots and pans to magazine subscriptions. They're my clientele. Most of them are so absent-minded that when I come by with one thing today, and two weeks later show up with something else, they don't even remember that I've been there before."

"So, you'd suggest what?"

"Simple, my friend. You get us some real estate paperwork and we start making house calls. Let's see, I've got a few boxes of greeting cards we can use as samples. I haven't done that one in awhile. We tell them that we're selling cards for every occasion of the year. Those old folks love that sort of crap. I doubt if they ever write anyone, but they think they will. Anyway, my friend, we have them sign your paperwork. You mail them a box of cards in a week or so, and those poor saps won't know the difference."

Brandon's guts buzzed with pure energy even as his conscience fought with the knowledge that he sat across a table from a petty crook, and a badly dressed one at that. But hadn't he been searching for just such a ploy? Hadn't he known he would gladly defraud someone, especially where there was no threat of violence? Greed quickly settled the issue in favor of Todd's idea. Brandon was on board. He would do his part, though it scraped a nerve every time Todd used the irritating words, my friend.

"All right," Brandon said, "so how many homeowners do you figure are in the neighborhood?"

"Except for the rental houses, they're all owner occupied, my friend. They've been there for ages. Let's see, in that original development there's probably a hundred-twenty houses, maybe a few more. How many properties do we need to sign up?"

"As many as we can. I'll make it well worth your while now, and with a piece of the action down the road." Determination now set Brandon's expression. All friendliness left his eyes, all charm absent from his words. If this guy was willing to cheat old ladies, then he'd tell him whatever he thought he wanted to hear. He would work with this street punk, but only because he had to, and in the meantime try to forget he was actually following his lead. "I'll be here Wednesday at nine sharp."

"Hey, friend, how 'bout maybe forty dollars till then?" Todd asked.

Brandon picked up the check and got up from the table. "No—you'll have to wait. I'll be here Wednesday."

CHAPTER SIX

BRANDON WENT BY AN office supply store and rummaged through every aisle searching for pens and paper, white-out and generic business documents. Then, he headed to an afternoon appointment he needed to keep. Why he had felt the need to volunteer? He wasn't quite sure. At age twenty-four, he had plenty of activities available to occupy his time. He hardly needed to pin himself down with uncompensated obligations. If his past held an unpaid debt he was duty bound to repay the reason wasn't readily in his thoughts. Now, with the exciting possibility of redeveloping an undervalued parcel of land, he wished his hadn't made the commitment.

A memo posted on the company bulletin board had asked for volunteers. A benevolent responsibility would provide a badge of civic involvement. At the time, he didn't think it would be so difficult. After today's discovery of the old neighborhood, he intended to separate himself from any association with Hoyt, Fitzgerald, and Greer as soon as possible. If he had to, he could always drop the volunteer bit, as well, express his heartfelt regret, and move on with whatever excuse came to mind.

But now he had known the kid for a month, and already Brandon felt similarities between the two of them. He also wondered if he hadn't gotten in over his head. Today was his first visit to the boy's home. All three previous meetings had been at the agency headquarters. Brandon knocked and waited for someone to answer the door.

The boy's name was Jake. At least that was the name his mom snapped when she wanted his attention. During Brandon's only meeting with the woman at the initial Big Brother interview at the agency office, she quickly conveyed her eager desire to have another adult involved in the boy's life. A man would be good; actually any adult would do. The woman was hyper to a comedic extreme, constantly digging for items in her purse, eyes darting about the room. She made Jake stand up, introduce himself, and shake hands.

Jake had just turned thirteen. He had a broad nose of dull freckles and oily chin of fresh zits. He had managed to get his mother's approval for his thick brown hair to be shaved high and close on the sides. His hair looked like a hanging shock of dead corn silk, and about as cool as boxer shorts sprouting from an open fly.

But Jake's brown eyes expressed an inner pain. His wide-eyes watched adults cautiously, hopefully. Brandon saw walls of emotional detachment being erected. He recognized the look and demeanor in himself at that age. He figured there was still time to reach out and possibly turn the tide of emotional isolation brought on in large part from Jake's fatherless environment. Brandon wasn't overly enthusiastic, but decided to give the Big Brother thing an honest effort.

A girl, about eight, in a dingy cotton dress answered the door. She inspected Brandon as though he wore or held a clue to his identification, and she was supposed to guess the purpose of his presence.

"I'm here to see Jake."

"Jake," she turned and shrilled. "There's a strange man here to see you."

The floor was wall to wall scuffed hardwoods. Cereal bowls littered the coffee table. Across from a cratered gray couch the TV flickered with the volume down and no one watching. Jake appeared from a back room, trudged toward the door in a mass of baggy pants, and untied tennis shoes.

"I'm ready," he said, two words that pretty much covered a greeting, introductions, and a summary of his day to that point. Jake walked out the door and led the way to Brandon's Trans Am.

"So, what would you like to do?" Brandon asked as he turned the ignition.

"I don't care. You decide."

"I've got a ball and several mitts. How 'bout we stop at the park and throw it around?"

Jake glared from his limp position. His body seemed to expand inside his baggy clothes as he sat up straight, and a smirk grew at the corners of his mouth. "You're kidding, right?"

"No, I wasn't. What's wrong with that?"

"Play catch—oooooooohhhhhhhh. I love it."
Jake laughed. "My big brother's going to play catch
with me."

Brandon felt embarrassed, though he didn't
know why. He wasn't an athlete, tennis the extent
of his sport activities, but he could certainly throw a
ball around. At least the kid had opened up. "Was it
really all that funny?"

"Funny enough. I was thinking more like
checking out the arcade at the mall."

"We can go by there," Brandon said, "but not
first thing. I figure you have your face stuck in a
computer screen enough of the time."

"What's that supposed to mean?"

"It means we're going to do something physical
first . . . like bowling or roller skating or shooting
hoops in the park."

"Bowling whoopee," Jake said, his eyes fixed
on the windshield in front of him. "If you want
some competition, how about you take me on at
virtual NASCAR, ten laps, best time wins."

"Yeah, real competitive," Brandon said, "see
who has the fastest thumbs."

"No, it's real. It's like driving a real car."

"You ever roller skate?" Brandon asked.

"What?" Jake couldn't have made the word
sound more disgusting if he'd spit something from
his mouth.

"Okay, then bowling, that's competitive. Best
two out of three games."

"And after I beat you, we'll go to the arcade?"

The kid was more assertive than initial impressions had conveyed, and cocky, too. Maybe pressures around his home kept his personality under wraps. Maybe Jake was taking a liking to him, though he didn't expect to hear comments of appreciation anytime soon. Brandon smiled to himself even as he raised his eyebrows. "You outscore me, we go to the arcade."

Two hours later, they headed to the mall. Jake marked in almost every frame. Jake won every game. Brandon had a nagging feeling he'd just been hustled.

"You roll a pretty mean ball," Brandon said as he tried to inject some levity into the statement.

"Yeah well, it's nothing. I've been playing in summer leagues the past few years."

"You're good. Why didn't you tell me?"

"You didn't ask."

The arcade was in the mall basement and took up half the lower floor. Once inside, the place pulsated with the lights of the Vegas strip. Several hundred machines blinked and flickered, chimed and buzzed.

Jake led the way to a virtual car race and fed several dollars into the machine before Brandon could offer to pay. "Watch me," Jake said. His face beamed with delight.

Jake drove a perfect ten laps in four minutes, thirty-five seconds. Brandon sat behind the wheel and gave it a try. After wrecking five times, he finally brought his car around the prescribed course just shy of ten minutes.

"Not too good. I'd say you've got a lot of work to do." A playful sarcasm coated Jake's words.

"I'll just watch. You go ahead and run another circuit."

"No, no. Got to have competition." Jake fed more dollars into the machine.

"Hey, Jake. You don't need to pay for this. It's supposed to be my treat."

"No sweat. I got plenty," Jake replied.

"What do you mean, plenty? How much you got?"

Jake ignored the question and began a new race circuit. When his turn came, Brandon ran the course again. His spread against Jake's time was worse than the first go around.

"I've got to make a phone call," Brandon insisted when Jake was ready to play again. "I'll be right back." Brandon made a brief tour of the arcade, then returned and watched Jake for half an hour as he ran the track, oblivious to anyone else around.

When Jake finally finished, Brandon observed his broad grin as Jake headed his direction.

"Second best time on record." Jake exclaimed.

Brandon led the way out the door. "Want something to eat?"

"Yeah, maybe some ice cream."

They stopped for treats, found a booth, and Brandon studied the boy's demeanor. "You dumped around forty dollars into that machine."

Jake's bright expression quickly fell downcast and moody.

"That's a lot of money to spend on a game."

"So?"

"Couldn't you spend that money more usefully?"

Jake scrunched his face. "It's my money."

"Uh-huh," Brandon said as he watched the boy over a spoonful of strawberry sundae. "The reason I ask is it's kind of important to spend money wisely." Jake didn't respond, and immediately the silence between them thickened. "Is that the best way you could come up with to spend forty dollars?"

"It's my money," Jake shouted, his eyes fierce with indignation.

"Okay, and where did you come by that much money?"

"What?" Jake just stared. "I don't go asking you where you get your money."

"Does your mom know about all that cash?"

"Who are you?" Jake pushed his way out of the booth and glared at Brandon from the side of the table. "Nobody asked you to butt into my life. Why don't you mind your own business? I didn't ask for you. I don't need you." Jake turned and sprinted for the mall escalator.

"Jake, come back here." But the boy was gone. Brandon looked for him throughout the mall, but finally gave up the search. He called the counselor at the agency office and reported the incident, but didn't call Jake's mom. He realized he'd pressed too hard on the point. They were still getting to know each other. All he'd wanted to do was to emphasize the value of a buck, but it was more than two months before he laid eyes on Jake again. It was getting dark as he headed to the one place where he could always find a helping hand.

Cindy answered the knock at her door with a paperback in one hand, a cigarette in the other. She was neither enthusiastic nor perturbed that Brandon had arrived, once again, unannounced.

"Hi, babe, glad to find you home." He gave her a phantom peck on the cheek.

"Pretty good chance," she said mockingly, "like I'd be running around with work tomorrow."

Brandon unloaded five plastic bags filled with office supplies across the sofa.

Cindy smiled to herself. Her evening had changed for the better. Brandon would have a story, not too plausible perhaps, but a story nonetheless. The fact he looked at the bags as though they held the key to Solomon's temple was proof of that. She was about to hear another tale. The episodes were entertaining, if little else. She would try to nod in all the right places.

Even though his adventures usually ended poorly, costing her sleepless nights and needed cash to extricate both of them from his escapades of grandeur, she never tried to stop him nor seriously stand in his way. Though she knew better, she would go along for the thrill of the ride. She wanted him and whatever kept him close. Besides, whatever was coming would beat the bland predictability of the book in her hand, so she took a seat at the table, put out her cigarette, and set the paperback aside.

Brandon bounced about with the enthusiasm of a child. His chest swelled with such animated bluster Cindy prayed he'd speak quickly before he burst.

"I tell you, babe, I hit the mother lode."

"I can tell, and it was all right there at Office Depot."

"I hope your printer works. I bought extra paper. I need you to help me put a few things together."

Cindy picked up a box of greeting cards. "You setting up a booth at the arts and crafts fair?"

Brandon scanned the real estate contract. "Okay, go ahead and laugh. I got the inside track, babe. This gig is going to make me rich."

He gave her a quick summary of his plan to alter a purchase agreement for greeting cards and combine it with the bottom half of a real estate contract. He explained how he intended to cut and paste and transfer the signatures to actual Texas real estate contracts later. Then, he rambled at length about the targeted neighborhood and the residents who lived there. Still, his whole plan woefully lacked details. "I'm getting into the real estate development business," he stated with the air of an implied heavenly blessing.

"Sounds like a definite plan," Cindy said as she crossed her legs and lit another cigarette. "So how much you figure it's all worth?"

"Well, don't know exactly—just yet. Don't know how many lots there are. But, well jeez, let's see. If there are a hundred and twenty houses, give or take, and with the size of those lots there's no more than three to the acre, that's at least forty acres down there, maybe more."

The concept of forty acres caused Brandon's expression to explode in awe, for even as he remained soaked in ignorance, forty acres was a huge number, especially in the center of a city where land was valued per running foot. Developed commercially in some way, that patch of land had to be worth tens of millions.

Cindy noticed how the realization flushed his face, how he became even more animated with pent-up energy than when he had walked in the door. "Will it make me rich, too?" she cooed behind a plume of smoke.

"It'll make you rich, too, babe. It'll make you rich indeed."

He approached her and his fingers toyed with the hair along her temple. She leaned back in the chair and closed her eyes as his fingers ran gently behind her ears. Brandon moved behind her, placed his athletic hands on her shoulders, and with firm, yet tender pressure, kneaded until her muscles loosened, and the tension in her body melted away through his fingertips.

"This is our chance, babe, one-way ticket to uptown."

The words, spoken slowly like a lullaby, rolled over her mind. She wanted desperately to believe. She could listen to him talk like this forever, his words so mellow yet invigorating, as soothing to her hopes as his fingers were to her body. When he talked like this, the allure was intoxicating, but she knew from experience his schemes consisted of more wishful thinking than substance.

Even so, she would help him any way she could. It was at times like these, when he talked in glowing terms of business deals and infinite possibilities while he touched her that anything seemed attainable. Delicious shivers ran over her skin as her mind nestled in the warm conviction of his voice. She knew Brandon as a persuader, a motivator, a driven individual. It mattered little that he was short on details, follow up, and actual business acumen. He made life exciting. When he had a big idea on his mind, he belonged to only her.

CHAPTER SEVEN

IN AN ENVIRONMENT of high-stakes
cronyism and back-stabbing duplicity, Darrin Riley
plied his craft in the Atherton mayor's office.
Officially, he was the legislative liaison. It was vital
for him to keep abreast of important issues,
including smoldering pockets of public sentiment
that might ignite into political flash fires in the
corridors of city hall. Any thorn stuck in the
mayor's backside on any particular day also found
its way onto his list of priorities.

Riley didn't handle public relations, so he
neither spoke officially for the mayor nor wasted his
time providing inane copy to mindless reporters. He
wasn't responsible for the mayor's daily appearance
schedule either. Insuring the mayor's appearance at
the opening of another food bank or women's
shelter was left to others. Yet each and every day,
Darrin Riley left his firm and guiding hand indelibly
imprinted upon the business of the Atherton city
government.

On this cloudy morning Riley sat at his desk in his corner office on the third floor and indulged his thoughts about the history of his dynamic city.

Such a curious mix of circumstance and destiny gives birth to a town. Beginning as a few campfires and tents, the spread of makeshift shelters pushed outward, spurred by countless individual decisions. Haphazardly it devoured land beyond its initial encampment. Often, natural landmarks denote the initial location of settlements that flourish into immense cities. Rivers provide a source of transportation as well as water to a nascent community. Towering cliffs near a mountain offers shelter in the foothills. Other towns find beginning in the caressing arms of a fertile valley or at the edge of a game-rich forest.

For Atherton, TX, Mother Nature's contribution to the town's establishment was endless acres of prairie sod. The bounty of the land was measured in prairie dog mounds. Brutally cold in winter, blistering hot in summer, days on end filled with the constant companionship of a maddening wind. Trees of any height were a rarity, the panorama from horizon to horizon viewable from a single spot.

But covered wagons did stop as America moved west after the Civil War. People drank and washed from the flow of water that sprang from nearby rocks and meager streams that ran with strength only after spring rains. People unloaded their wagons of possessions and supplies, and set to work. For the landmark of the new town was known, but not yet seen. It was to be the growing ribbon of steel that would connect a nation, the inevitable western push of the railroad.

The town got its name from Colonel Chester R. Atherton, former adjutant to General Meade of the Union Army, now superintendent of the railroad in North Texas. This designation pleased the colonel in no small measure as it fit nicely with Ohio and Missouri towns already named after him. Lumber was hauled in and four-square shacks erected overnight, some as homes, others as businesses, streets quickly drawn and named, and the town began to grow. As a prospering center of commerce, with the cash from cattle and cotton, the city pushed across the land and made its mark upon the map.

It was early in 1874, soon after Atherton's initial spurt, a carpetbagger from Illinois named George Kessler platted a rectangle of sixteen crossing streets on the southern edge of the downtown. Construction materials had advanced beyond square posts and rough-cut boards to machine-sawn beams imported from the east. Elegant scroll-sawn braces adorned the eaves, carved cornices and railings, double-hung windows that actually opened and closed. Precision cut stones of terra cotta, limestone yellows, and slate grays added color to foundations and steps. Second story balconies and wide staircases completed the grand details and left an unmistakable air of sophistication about the new homes.

At the turn of the twentieth century, the neighborhood of Kessler Park was the must-have address for the business and professional elite of the city. The well-heeled of Atherton mingled on their cool, recessed porches, in their fashionably appointed parlors, and around luxurious well-tended lawns and gardens.

In time, home styles changed and newer neighborhoods were built. When the stock market crash of '29 hit, the glory days of Kessler Park had come and gone. Atherton's upper crust had moved west nearer the museum district and botanical gardens. Still, the homes of Kessler Park were known to be well built, prized for their craftsmanship, and enviably located near the heart of the city.

But then, an odd combination of economics and geography came along and changed Kessler Park forever. In an effort to build more roads, a decision was made to expand an existing east-west street into a major four-lane highway through the city. Immediately citizens were divided on the issue. Many neighborhoods would be affected, not just Kessler Park.

But in the area around Kessler Park, the project hit its most troublesome snag. The highway was designed to parallel the six-line railroad as closely as possible. But a critical rail line ran into the warehouse district on the eastern side of downtown. An overpass needed to be built to let the rail spur pass under, which would cut Kessler Park in half. Thirty stick-style and twenty Queen Anne homes were demolished to make room for bridge spans and supports, and the original splendor of the area was diminished, irreparably severed and scarred.

Within a few years the two separated neighborhoods assumed new identities. The area on the north side of the freeway and closest to downtown was renamed Richardson Terrace in honor of the mayor at the time. The smaller neighborhood, now south of the four-lane highway and separated from the prestige and vitality of the city's heart, languished like a neglected orphan. But the neighborhood didn't relinquish its historic and honored title. The area continued to be known as Kessler Park.

As the twenty-first century opened its arms, Atherton, TX, claimed the designation as the fifth largest city in the state. Atherton had economic muscle and with it, the political clout that accompanies a robust city. Those in possession of authority and influence jealously guarded their hold on power. In a city of nearly a million citizens, there were nine council seats, eight districts, and one at-large seat elected as mayor. Currently, all seats were held by businessmen who had been active in party politics for years. Term limits were non-existent. Two seats had been passed almost by edict from father to son.

Riley refocused his attention to his computer screen, his cool green eyes scanning e-mails. Before him was follow-up correspondence from the Britton Cattle Equipment Company's attorney to an official request that had crossed his desk last week. The company planned to expand their cattle equipment manufacturing operation by adding twenty-five acres of manufacturing and storage capacity beside their current operation. The land was already properly zoned. What the company wanted was property tax abatement for ten years to help finance its expansion. Riley had seen it all before. The addition neither warranted nor qualified for such exemption. They would hire a handful of additional employees at best. The company would quickly recoup its expenses through increased sales. The e-mail was hogwash, the request completely outside the established guidelines for tax abatement consideration.

And yet, that didn't mean the request wouldn't be approved. The Britton Cattle Company already had Don Martin, councilman from the Sixth District in their hip pocket. Riley could count on councilmen Fitzpatrick and Brunner's support because Martin had signed on to support their pet project, the renovation of Duck Creek Park.

The mayor could be persuaded to vote for anything that made campaign contributors happy. More important, Councilman Joe Thompson of District Four already owed Riley favors for previous political skirmishes waged and won, all in the name of efficient, effective government. Riley could collect a favor from Thompson on the proposal and get the cattle company's request approved.

Since Britton Cattle would now be in Don Martin's debt, the councilman needed to be informed of the lengthy efforts the mayor's office had gone to secure a favorable outcome for one of Martin's most important constituents.

Immediately, Riley knew that the Britton Cattle Company could get its ten-year tax abatement. The cattle company's request was resolved in Riley's mind. The fact that it would be weeks before the documents were ready, months before the appropriate city departments gave their blessings, and even longer before the city council finally voted on the matter didn't concern Riley in the least. The passage of a reasonable length of time was just part of the necessary and orderly process of city government.

As he dialed the phone, Riley contemplated on what new matter he could best use Councilman Martin's new found vote.

CHAPTER EIGHT

AT EIGHT SHARP WEDNESDAY
MORNING Brandon jumped though the row of
newspaper racks that lined the curb in front of
Norma's Diner, pushed through a bustle of patrons
paying their checks at the register, and searched the
tables for Todd.

The restaurant was packed, an A.M.
menagerie of urban humanity. Young men in greasy
ball caps sat at the counter shoveling their mouths
full of eggs while they flirted with waitresses as
they picked up their orders. Groups of retired men
relaxed in clouds of smoke and waved for more
coffee. Businessmen in pressed suits sat in booths
of cracked vinyl and carried on as if they were in
the plush surrounds of swanky hotels. Couples with
tyrannical toddlers made good use of available
high-chairs and extra napkins, and the obese of the
neighborhood waddled in for their morning fix of a
couple thousand calories of sausages, pancakes, and
cream.

The air wafted with an aroma of bacon and cigars, warm maple syrup, and fried potatoes, aromatically delicious, yet overpowering. The vocal din was undulating and indecipherable.

Brandon found Todd seated in a booth sipping a Coke. Todd's attire and appearance was more repugnant than Brandon remembered. He had to be getting his clothes at Goodwill. Todd wore a tan shirt with a narrow red tie, a painful contrast to Brandon's crisp blue dress shirt.

Todd's gaze darted about as Brandon took a seat. Todd's shoulders were nervous even when they were still, and his mouth worked overtime on the ice cubes in his Coke as he sucked on them and spit them back in the glass.

"I knew you'd show up," Todd said.

"Been here long?"

"Just got here."

Brandon noticed three crushed butts in the ashtray with another burning. He felt on edge and decided to make their stay in the diner brief with just coffee and a donut, then get to work. But when a bright-eyed waitress and her little pink apron stepped to the table, he changed his mind. She leaned on her hip as though it were a stool and cast a provocative glance his way.

She was a big girl, one of millions who could tote five plates on one arm and never drop a slice of toast. She wore combed-out blonde curls that framed eyes full of mischief; a face generous with the eyeliner and an obvious affinity for rouge. Still, she had a youthful cuteness, and a sparkle in her eyes testified that she hadn't been at the work so long that she detested the very people she served, and it was the twinkle that caught Brandon's attention.

Apparently she liked her job, or at least liked people, enough to flirt harmlessly with a good-looking guy or laugh at an old geezer's silly joke. She flipped through her order pad, popped her pencil on a blank form, and said, "Wad'll it be, guys?" She used the plural, but kept her attention on Brandon.

"Got a special?"

"Link sausage and a short stack for three ninety-nine."

"I want more than that," Brandon said as he skimmed the menu.

"How much more?"

"What?" Brandon lowered the menu, caught the glint in her eyes, and laughed. "How about breakfast in bed?"

"It can be arranged," she replied.

"Could I get some more Coke?" Todd said.

"What's your name?" Brandon asked.

"Unless I'm wearing the wrong name tag, it's Rita." She bent over, and he could read the narrow badge with lettering the height of a typewriter ribbon above her large breasts. "And you are?"

"The guy who's going to be leaving a nice tip." Brandon beamed his magnetic smile.

"Well, I'm glad to meet you, Mr. Tipper." She said the last two words with an exaggerated enunciation and gave him a wink.

"I'll take two eggs over medium, hash browns, and bacon." Brandon smiled again as he handed her the menu.

"Could I get some more Coke?" Todd repeated, rattling the ice in his glass.

The waitress gave Todd a haughty glance that said volumes in a micro-second, then flashed a quick, puckered smile toward Brandon. "Be right back."

Brandon leaned back in the booth and gave Todd the once over, neither enthused nor disheartened by what he saw. He would make the plan work with or without Todd. "I have everything we need in my car." He went through a complete rundown of what he had prepared, including how he had doctored real estate signature pages to make them appear like an ordinary order form.

Todd's ears were on point. His eyes opened wide as though his brain needed extra light to function. Brandon almost chuckled at the intense expression that gripped Todd's face as he analyzed his every word.

"I went online and ran off the tax rolls for all the streets we'll be working. We'll know exactly who the homeowner is at each address and whose signatures we need," Brandon concluded.

Todd nodded, but his expression indicated his mind toiled to keep up with the presentation. Finally, he asked one question that seemed to be squirming at the forefront of his thoughts. "So exactly how do I fit into all of this?"

Brandon studied Todd's silly expression. "The money? What do you think would be fair?"

Todd's cheek twitched. "Listen, I know you're going to make a killing if this all goes through, so I figure to get my share."

"When all this goes through," Brandon interjected, "I'm just talking about today, or the next few days—as long as it takes to get these names signed up."

Todd leaned across the table, and his voice became a hushed growl. "What do you think I am, stupid? You think you're going to play me for some kind of chump? I know good-n-well you won't need much of me once we get those signatures. I want my money now. Up front. When I deliver, I expect to get paid."

"Hey, hey, ease up." Brandon felt his shoulders pressing the back of the booth. "I'm going to pay you. I expected to pay you—today, all right? You need to relax."

"Yeah, I'll relax." Todd's lips enunciated every word as his pink face erupted into a scarlet blush. "I want twenty dollars for every signature I get, plus a hundred bucks for the day."

Brandon noticed looks from other tables glance their way. Tiny trails of sweat ran down his sides. He knew he had a couple hundred bucks in his wallet, maybe, and a maxed-out Visa. Unless he hit up Cindy, there was no way he could meet Todd's demands. At the same time, as he watched Todd uncoil back in his seat, he was elated. He expected Todd to try to squeeze him for a grand or more. What a smuck, two-bit hustler. He'd sell the rights to a gold mine for a carton of smokes and a six-pack.

"Okay, a hundred dollars plus twenty for each one, but I'll have to give you a check."

"No checks, mister big-shot developer. You do realize what we're gonna do, right? I know you don't really want to be paying me with a traceable check." Todd dropped all pretense of being a collaborative partner. "Just maybe, mister hot-shot, you're all talk and wishful thinking. You need me in the worst way and you know it."

The waitress returned and Brandon picked at his breakfast while Todd slurped his Coke and sucked on the ice.

Brandon despised himself and so loathed Todd at that instant he was unable to fully perceive the depth of his revulsion. But he had to go on. He knew he would wade through whatever cesspools of deceit lay in his path to see where the road might lead. "I'll pay you cash at the end of the day," Brandon said.

"Now you're talking, college boy, and I need a hundred to get me through the day," Todd said.

"A hundred? Maybe twenty for a pack of smokes and lunch." Brandon pulled out two tens and tossed them across the table, downed the last of his coffee, and left two bucks under his cup. "Let's get going."

"I thought you were going to leave her a big tip," Todd said with a smirk.

CHAPTER NINE

BRANDON AND TODD drove to the
neighborhood and parked at the corner of
Cummings and Garrison. "Go with me to a few
houses and I'll show you how this works," Todd
boasted. "These people will open the door to
anyone wearing a smile and in most cases invite
you in."

The first house on the block sat on a narrow lot
with a small front yard close to the sidewalk, a
Queen Anne cottage with terra cotta stone steps.
The second-story balcony hung over the lower
porch where matched railings highlighted the
breezeways. A decorative tower with mansard roof
stood above a bay window. The house was painted
brown with dark red trim, and a recent paint job at
that.

Todd knocked, and they waited. Finally the
front door moved. A generously proportioned old
gentleman with huge reading glasses and a week's
worth of whiskers answered. Skin hung in pleats
under his jaw, small black moles dotted the bridge

of his nose under rheumy eyes. He held a crossword puzzle book in his hand as he opened the screen door.

"Mr. Warren, good morning. I'm Todd Simms. I'm sure you remember me. I wanted to get by as quick as I could today to tell you the wonderful news." Todd let the end of his sentence hang on the air for one long beat, then he beamed his dingy smile and continued. "I found out I owe you a partial refund. This is my associate, Brandon. May we come in for a minute?"

"A refund for what?"

"Your magazine subscription with the six bonus puzzle books."

"Oh, yes, when are those going to arrive?"

"I have all that information in my book." Todd tapped his booklet. "May we come in?"

Mr. Warren shuffled in house slippers across hardwood floors and led them to the dining room where they all took a seat. Todd sifted through some papers and announced, "Mr. Warren, your first magazines should be arriving any day now. What I came by to tell you is our marketing campaign did so well, the entire package you ordered is forty percent cheaper. Isn't that great?"

Mr. Warren seemed to give the entire notion considerable thought, then agreed it was indeed a wonderful turn of events.

"I just need you to approve the refund here, and you'll be getting a check in the mail."

The gentleman looked at the paper as Todd handed him a pen. "How much did you say that refund would be?" he asked.

"Well, let's see." Todd played with some papers, then announced, "You're gonna get back $31.20." Todd shut up and remained silent. Any attempt to make the amount seem like a big deal would only focus unwanted attention.

Mr. Warren studied the paper. Todd and Brandon waited. Breathless anticipation hung over the signature line. The old man appeared to start reading, but then, sign it he did. Todd collected the document and trumped up the whole event. "I'm so glad to have saved you some money, Mr. Warren. That check should arrive in a week to ten days. We'll let ourselves out. Have a nice day, Mr. Warren." Todd shook his hand, and the young men left.

Todd beamed a cheesy grin all the way to the sidewalk. "Piece of cake, like I told you. Talk about whatever they're interested in, sell them whatever they want. I just thought of the refund angle as I walked to the door. If they like the greeting card idea, sell them greeting cards, but first you got to grease the front door. That's what I call it. You got to get them to like you or show them something they'd like to have. Want me to do another?"

"No, I get the picture," Brandon said. He found Todd's act less than enthralling, more akin to a shell game than a sales presentation. "Let's each work a side of the street and meet down at the end. How far is it?"

"Eight blocks."

Brandon walked across the street and looked up at the huge two-story, wood-frame house adorned with steep interlocking pitched gables, two

76

ribbed chimneys, and a weathervane-topped turret. It was a magnificent testament to architectural genius and detailed craftsmanship of years gone by. It was also a relic, a steeple of rotten kindling. He would sweet talk and cajole whoever lived here until he got what he came for. Now determined to have more signatures than Todd when they met at the end of the block, Brandon opened the gate and headed up the walk with a focused mind.

The porch was deep and expansive. An exquisite sunburst window, no more than six inches high, adorned the top of the entrance, but the door itself was dry and splintered at the bottom as though it couldn't tolerate another sweep across the porch. Brandon looked at it all and, to him, it made no sense. The houses required too much maintenance to be economical. They had too many decorations and not enough functionality, enormous dining rooms, but dinky closets. Brandon saw the deflected roof lines, dry, curled shingles, warped and splintered clapboards. It was as though the components of every house just wanted to reach the ground and rest. For now they stood, structural members welded into one over time, ornate architecture and quaint details held together by petrified spider webs.

A short woman answered the door. She looked up at him with a white smile of false teeth and a new perm of blue hair.

"Good morning, ma'am. My name is Brandon Evans, and I have a new selection of greeting cards right off the press for every occasion you could imagine." He beamed his smile and opened the box.

"I'd sure like to show them to you. I know you'd find a few you'd like."

"I thought kids peddled those," she said without the slightest change in her cherubic expression. "Come in, I'll take a look."

Brandon followed her into a cavernous home with twelve-foot ceilings. She took a seat in a chair surrounded by TV trays and end tables covered with reading material and embroidery, and motioned him to her davenport.

"Now let me see," she said.

"These three are samples of our new birthday cards." He passed her the cards, one in a cartoon motif, the second sentimental in tone, the third with religious verse. "No matter whose birthday it is or what mood you're in, we have a card for every birthday."

She seemed enamored. He had no idea why. Maybe it was the artwork. Maybe she had someone in mind who should receive a card. Brandon waited patiently until she looked up.

"They're very nice," she said.

"With our special promotion you'll receive six cards every month, plus one card specific to that month, such as a patriotic card in July in tribute to Independence Day. I don't need any money today. You'll receive a coupon book and pay only after you receive your cards."

"How much are they?"

"Five dollars a box, and that includes shipping." Brandon paused and hoped the off-the-cuff presentation would be enough to get her to sign. "I just need your approval here."

"Can I have these?"

"Well, those are samples, ma'am. You'll get yours in less than a week." He watched her pull the cards to her breast and begin to sway like a school girl with a private letter. For a second he thought she was putting him on. Then he wondered if she wasn't just a senile old coot who whiled away her days waiting for someone to knock on the door. "If I can have your order I guess I can let you have those."

She signed. Brandon took the order form and read the name. "Mrs. Nance, is it?" She nodded. "Clara. What a lovely name. Is there a Mr. Nance?"

"Oh sure. My Cecil is somewhere in the back."

"Could we holler at him? I need his John Henry, too."

She pushed a button attached to her end table. "He spends all of his time in the garage," she said as she admired the greeting cards as though at long last she had found something she had been searching for all her life.

Brandon waited in silence, both perplexed and tickled at her display. Soon a skinny gent appeared. He wore blue jeans and a long-sleeved shirt buttoned to the throat. He had brushed off his shirt and arms, but an abundance of sawdust still powdered his whiskers. He appeared neither perturbed nor appreciative that he had been interrupted. He seemed accustomed to seeing his wife perusing a salesman's wares.

"Honey, this man has some holiday cards I want to buy. He needs you to sign his paper."

"Mr. Nance. My name's Brandon." He extended his hand. "I trust you're having a great day." The old fellow glanced at him not in an unfriendly way, more as though he were a distasteful son-in-law whose presence made him contemplate the shenanigans being committed with his daughter. Mr. Nance took the clipboard and signed the form. Without a word he returned to his woodshop.

A curiosity bubbled in Brandon's mind as to what Mr. Nance was working on, but he knew better than to ask. To do so was to invite a lengthy conversation. He had to keep his inquisitiveness in check. He sensed the old timers would talk your ears off if they got wound up, and all the while think they were sharing insights of universal interest.

"Thank you very much, Mrs. Nance. Your first box of cards will arrive shortly. I can see myself out."

"I can hardly wait to see my first box of cards."

He stepped off the porch, headed to the gate, and enjoyed the warm glow of satisfaction. He had gotten the signatures he sought, both of them, husband and wife, with no problem. By the time he reached the gate, the glow was gone. She seemed like a nice lady, and he had just promised her greeting cards every month. Why exactly? He had to get original signatures on his paperwork. He walked to the next house. But how was he going to deal with the un-kept promises?

CHAPTER TEN

IT WAS ALMOST TWO WHEN BRANDON reached the end of the block. He counted the signatures he'd gathered— seven. He'd knocked on at least thirty doors and talked to someone at almost every stop, but between the hard-of-hearing and the mentally infirm, he felt as though he'd spent a good part of the time talking to himself. One woman was more than willing to chit-chat all day long, but only from her second story window.

He studied the last house on the block, a weed-infested eyesore surrounded by a broken down chain-link fence, a mangy brown mutt asleep on the porch. A mildewed couch and rusty stove sat along the fence and propped up drooping branches. Splintered beveled struts grudgingly held up the front porch roof. The fascia, cornices, clapboards, and posts pleaded for paint. The sight of the place made him weary. He crossed a side street, basically a paved alley at the edge of the neighborhood, walked thirty yards across a littered field to the back of a retail strip. When he came around the building, he found himself at Noble's Pawn Shop front door within sight of the hospital's main building, a twenty-story tower several blocks away.

Traffic rolled along Sixth Street with a steady, uncongested hum. A few people waited at the corner for the next metro bus. He was now out from under the cooling shade of the giant trees. The afternoon heat cooked the air, the street and parking lots radiating sweltering thermals. He walked in search of a place to buy a soda, and headed in the direction of an outdoor event marked by colored balloons and a gathering of people on the other side of the street.

He found a convenience store a block away. The place was grimy and claustrophobic, with the lingering scent of spilled milk left to permeate the cracks on the floor and curdle in seclusion. He could venture down the aisles if he turned his shoulders and wondered if the place carried a single product that hadn't exceeded its expiration. The counter was a maze of low-hung cigarette and lottery ticket dispensers. Brandon bought a 7-Up. A bum hanging around the pay phone hit him up for spare change as soon as he got out the door, and Brandon told him no.

At the corner, he waited for the light to change, crossed the street, and approached a gathering of fifty to sixty people. Red and white balloons were tied to stakes around the perimeter of a vacant lot. A makeshift dais with a lectern stood before the audience seated in rows of folding chairs. It appeared that the proceeding had just begun. A slim woman in a stylish blue suit and white silk blouse with ruffles at her throat took her place behind the lectern. Her hair was auburn-orange, pinned up in back, and appeared iridescent in the sunlight. Her skin had a caramel coloring. Her eyes were dark, yet expressive, with a radiance of their own. Even her shapely legs, accentuated by her cobalt-blue heels, were graced by the caress of the afternoon sun.

Intrigued, Brandon eased himself into a vacant chair, his eyes fixed on the alluring speaker.

"Good afternoon. Let me thank you all for coming," she began. "My name is Katherine Cramer, vice president with the hospital. Today, Saint Anthony's Regional Medical Center breaks ground on our sixth student dormitory for the school of nursing. We are well on our way to meeting our goals for the twenty-first century, and it's all due to the hard work of people like you and the thousands of families we serve."

A polite applause moved through the audience.

"St. Anthony's is a leader in providing healthcare throughout the region. Our medical campus handled 38,000 admissions last year, delivered 4,500 babies, responded to 60,000 emergency room visits. We have 1,100 licensed beds, and 1,400 physicians work within these facilities. This campus offers specialized care in neuroscience, transplants, orthopedics, digestive diseases, and trauma.

"With today's ground breaking, we'll add dormitory rooms for sixty more on-campus nursing students. St. Anthony's is committed to training qualified nurses to meet the ever-growing, ever-changing healthcare needs of our community."

Brandon became mesmerized by the lyrical quality of her voice and the way her words drifted into the pleasing notes of song. A round of applause awoke him from his daydream. A rotund gentleman took the podium and said a few words, then everyone seated on the front row picked up gold-plated shovels, and in unison turned a spade of dirt. Everyone clapped again.

As the ceremony concluded, Brandon watched the woman mingle with dignitaries and honored guests. She moved about with the skill of a politician and the grace of a socialite. He worked his way in her direction without any sense as to what he would do. He just knew he had to meet her now. With his quick wit and assertive manner his only resource, Brandon knew he could only fail by not trying. Whether she was the person he needed to speak with or not, she could likely point him in the right direction and pave his entrance into the upper echelons of the hospital's hierarchy. As she turned, he stepped in her path.

"Mrs. Cramer, I know this is a proud day for you and the hospital. Please let me introduce myself." He gained eye contact and held it, his expression relaxed, his eyes friendly but without the virile adolescent charm that likely would be unwelcome or at best premature. "I'm Brandon Evans. I work for the Heritage Group, and I have a piece of property that I know would benefit the hospital. May I call your office for an appointment?"

Her gaze took a snapshot of his face. His easy manner bought him an extra second, his youthful good looks a dozen more. He thought he saw a turn at the corners of her mouth. Brandon waited silently for her to respond, positive anticipation etched on his face, eye contact maintained at all cost.

She had the beginnings of tiny lines around her eyes and a petite nose. Her upper lip had a little flip to it like the crest of a tiny wave, and up close, her dark eyes seemed even more appealing and mysterious. "Mr. Evans did you say?"

"Yes, Brandon—Brandon Evans."

"Fine then, Mr. Evans. I'll let my secretary know you'll be calling." The mystery in her eyes receded behind a veil of professionalism. "She'll schedule you for ten minutes." With that, she moved on and greeted another person.

Brandon continued to watch as the gathering dispersed. Though he didn't know if he'd accomplished anything, he was ecstatic over what had just occurred. His mind replayed the tape of their conversation. He knew he'd said the words *property, benefit hospital,* and *appointment*, and she'd said yes.

Certainly something good would come from that. It most certainly would. It had to.

As he reached the edge of the vacant lot, he realized that Todd would be waiting for him at the end of Cummings Street. He broke into an easy run back to the neighborhood. He couldn't help himself. The afternoon heat blistered the air, but he increased his pace. Once again behind the pawn shop, he jogged through the lot that separated the neighborhood from the retail strip. He jumped, cheered, and punched his fist in the air. He had a contact in the hospital's administration. The scorching heat had him feeling totally alive.

He found Todd in the shade, leaning against a tree, smoking a cigarette. "What happened to you?" Todd asked.

"I was looking for a bank to get you some cash, but there's none over there. How many did you get?"

"Twelve."

"Very good. This is going to work out. It'll just take some time. Let's start up the next block," Brandon said, his tone dripping with optimism.

"After I get some lunch. How many did you get?"

"Seven. I admit I'm not as good as you, but then this is your territory. I expected that you'd do better than me."

"Bet your sweet ass. I can get in the door and close the deal once I'm in," Todd said, his attitude instantly bolstered by the compliment.

"While you're eating, I'm going to the bank. You work the east side on the next street, and I'll work the west. We'll meet again at the far end."

Brandon headed back to his car knowing full well he was finished knocking on doors for the day. Let Todd do the grunt work for twenty bucks a pop. He saw the same woman who clung to her second-story window and refused to come down to talk to him, now out on her lawn giving directions to a house painter. He stopped and watched as the old woman squinted at the house, pointed with her cane, and spoke words he couldn't hear, scooted ahead two steps, craned her neck, and pointed some more. Within a minute she waved her hand menacingly at the sun and waddled back inside the house.

Brandon couldn't resist the urge to open the gate and approach the handyman. Maybe he could learn something about the old lady. He looked at his list of property owners and ran his finger along the address—Mrs. Hunter. Brandon stopped in an apex of shade afforded by the high angle of the roof and looked at the work being done. The man was scraping loose paint from exposed roof struts and decorative rafter tails. Brandon let his eye follow the thick beam that set the edge for the second floor and travel down the massive support at the corner of the house. There wasn't the slightest deflection or bow. There was no doubt, the roof ridge hadn't moved an inch since the day it had been set.

The man on the ladder was a big fellow, dressed in denim overalls and a long-sleeved print shirt. Brandon's footsteps clicked on the stone walk as he approached the house, but if the worker heard his approach, he didn't turn to look.

"Good afternoon."

"Hi." The man on the ladder kept scraping.

"You painting the entire house?"

"No, just working on these under hanging supports. They don't get the attention they need. If they aren't properly painted, they'll dry out and split. That can hurt the whole roof."

Good grief, he's going to give me a carpentry lesson. "Listen, I was wondering—do you know of any houses for sale in the neighborhood?"

The question caused the worker to stop scraping. "I don't watch that sort of thing, but—no, I don't think so. Mr. and Mrs. Thomas on Poplar might have to move 'cause Mrs. Thomas is doing poorly, but I don't think they want to sell."

"Why wouldn't they want to sell if they have to move?"

"Don't know. Guess you'd have to ask them."

Brandon paused. "You do a lot of work around here?"

"Yep, I sure do. Restoring houses is what I do."

"Well, but, haven't a good many of them outlived their usefulness?"

The worker hesitated, stuck his scraper in his tool belt, and descended the ladder. On the ground standing beside Brandon he appeared as a bear of a man. He was thick across the chest with big hands and a wide stance. But his demeanor was as relaxed as a convert at prayer meeting. His bright blue eyes appeared as though back lit by stars, and something about his expression indicated a sincere intention to be helpful.

"You sounded full of questions so I figured I could take a break for a couple minutes and try to help you out," the house painter said.

Brandon was taken aback, not sure if he should be appreciative or insulted by the straightforward response. The man's statement sounded like sarcasm, but his body language didn't confirm it.

Brandon's upbringing had taught him the wisdom of cynicism. He'd endured his mother's pretense of caring. All she ever did for him was nothing more than a litany of charades designed to boost her ego, impress her friends, and indulge rather than love him. He had listened for months to his father's adamant denials of business wrongdoing only to see him convicted in a court of law. For years, since he could remember, Brandon filtered what he heard through three distinct and separate screens—what does the other person have to gain, what are they trying to hide, and why are they telling me this? No one told the truth; this he already knew. If this guy suddenly wanted to be so helpful, he must have an agenda of his own.

"So what would you like to know?" the house painter asked.

"I just keep wondering why with these houses being so old and all, why there aren't more vacancies?"

"Oh, they have so much room, and it's so close to downtown."

"Yeah, but it must cost a fortune to maintain them. Why not buy something newer?" Brandon's tone grew more puzzled with every question.

The house painter smiled as though only someone as familiar as he could ever fully understand the attachment these homes held. "Many of these houses have been in the same families for years. Many of these folks are elderly. They probably could move, but they want to live out their years in a place they call home."

Still, the explanations didn't satisfy Brandon. It all seemed so impractical, even silly, to stay in a house where many owners didn't even have the extra money to fix the front gate. He repeated a question he'd asked before. "But, really, haven't these old houses outlived their usefulness?"

The house painter's face remained relaxed, his demeanor calm, but the cheerful glow from his blue eyes faded and a look of sadness settled on his features. "How old do you think you'll be when you've outlived *your* usefulness?"

Brandon studied his face and saw that the fellow was dead serious. "That's not a fair comparison."

"Why not? Why should you be the judge of someone's house anymore than someone should be the judge of you? Maybe usefulness has more to do with something being wanted than how it looks."

Brandon was at a total loss for a reply. He didn't agree, but didn't know what to say. The house painter preempted any response, when, after the silence between them hung for too long, he said, "I see I've answered all your questions. Have a good day. I need to get back to work."

CHAPTER ELEVEN

LATE AFTERNOON SHADOWS CREPT
over Kessler Park. Todd waited alone at the corner
of Linden and Poplar. He hadn't seen Brandon
entering or leaving a house on the other side of the
street since he began working Linden Avenue. The
blue Trans Am wasn't parked anywhere along the
curb. Todd stood under a misshapen elm, half its
limbs dead or broken, lit a cigarette and surveyed
the street. He would wait. Todd knew the signatures
he held were worth money in the bank.

The greeting card ploy worked like a charm.
He had twenty-three signatures. The squatty woman
with the pale gray eyes who wanted to serve him
iced tea took more time than it needed to. He should
have let her pour him a glass when she first offered.
One couple wanted to ramble all afternoon about
their great-grandchildren. He smiled and nodded
and they never let up. He finally excused himself as
politely as he could and walked out.

He had twenty-three signatures after one day's
work—$460 cash up front for the names plus $100

just for making an appearance. He relished the thought of watching Brandon's face when he forked over the cash. For paydays like this he would knock doors every minute the sun was up until everyone who owned a house in Kessler Park had signed on the dotted line.

He flipped his cigarette butt into the street and checked his watch. It was almost five. He could get to the pawnshop before closing, but figured he'd wait until tomorrow. Todd knelt and rummaged through the leather satchel that held his paperwork. He turned a little clock over in his hands. He thought it was real gold when he took it from the hunchback's bureau, the stooped fellow who couldn't look straight ahead. Now he wasn't sure. The clock was six inches across with an intricate face and hands. He could probably get five bucks for it. The proprietor at the pawn shop over on Fannin Street, paid maybe ten cents on the dollar for the stuff he brought in, but he didn't ask questions.

Todd looked over a serving tray. It looked like silver. It was worth something at any rate. He liked trays. They fit easily in his satchel. He reached for the porcelain doll deep at the bottom of the bag. He pulled her out and studied her in the sunlight. She was a beautiful little thing. Her face was hand-painted with delicate red lips and a blue velvet dress with white buttons and lace at the sleeves and hem. She even wore tiny blue shoes.

Todd admired the figure. She was truly a gorgeous piece of work. He congratulated himself on such an exceptional score. Most of the old folks had so much clutter in their homes it was hard to identify the good stuff before it was time to go.

For an instant he didn't want to pawn the exquisite little doll. It might bring a dollar. The doll would sit on a shelf and collect dust or be thrown in a box and forgotten. Todd handled it gently now and turned it, admiring the facial details and the fine garments, and wished he'd never laid eyes on the thing. He also knew he had to sell it for whatever it would bring. He needed every dime he could get.

His three-month-old daughter's hunger was insatiable. It was unbelievable what eight pounds of squirming fat cost to maintain. His wife didn't work and would use the baby as a continuing excuse not to. Mona was a chubby girl of nineteen, raised in a welfare home by a single mother and an endless string of uncles. As long as she had cigarettes and cable TV, she kept her complaints to a minimum, but Todd's limited options to earn a decent income generated constant pressure between them.

He didn't have a car or decent clothes. Wherever he applied for work, they would shake his hand, go through the motions, and thank him for coming in. That was always the end of it. He was just a little too shifty, wore a second-hand jacket that didn't match his shiny pants. His fingernails were too dark. Too much of the street seeped from his pores.

When he and the missus rented their one-bedroom flat for $360 a month, the only job he could get was selling magazine subscriptions. He could work his butt off at a car wash up the block for minimum wage and pathetic tips, but the door-to-door selling at least gave him a way to increase his income if he buckled down and hustled. Lifting items from his customers came later. He wasn't proud of it, but after awhile the thievery didn't cross his mind.

When Brandon Evans came along, it was the lucky break he'd been praying for. He wasn't about to let the college kid think he was especially appreciative. He kept things square, asserted himself in the business relationship, but deep inside Todd was thankful and relieved. He'd help Brandon every way he could and even take the con to another neighborhood if Brandon wanted. He'd get the old folks to sign, one way or the other, as long as it kept cash flowing into his pockets.

By the time he threw his fifth cigarette butt into the street, he was more than impatient. It was a quarter past five, and Brandon hadn't shown. He began walking toward his apartment. He would go past the diner, see if Brandon's car was around. Brandon had said he was going to the bank and would be back. It pissed him off to be stood up, but it didn't matter. He would find him sooner or later. Mr. Brandon Evans better have the money. Todd was pretty sure he would. The guy was too hyped up about getting something for next to nothing to just change his mind.

CHAPTER TWELVE

FIVE DAYS AFTER THE GROUND-
BREAKING CEREMONY, Brandon headed to the
hospital and his appointment with Katherine
Cramer. He rode the elevator to the eighth floor of
the Saint Anthony's Medical Tower, mentally
rehashing every important point he wanted to make.
He checked the knot of his tie, patted down his
jacket, and pulled at his sleeves.

He'd spent forty dollars on a maroon and green
striped silk tie, and one-fifty for a pair of patent
leather shoes. He got a manicure and his hair
trimmed. He knew he looked sharp whatever he
wore. The expenditures were window dressing. His
most powerful feature to impress, reassure, and
persuade cost him nothing. It was his constant
companion. He could always count on a favorable
response to his easy smile.

He found suite eight-ten guarded by ceiling-
high, inch-thick glass doors, and stepped into a
luxuriously appointed reception area lined with

gaudy paintings of blurry swans on shimmering lakes. After a lengthy wait an escort directed him down a glass-lined corridor where Katherine Cramer met him at the door of her corner office.

"Good morning," she said. "Please have a seat." She moved behind a polished mahogany desk.

Under the indoor lighting her hair looked darker than the orange-tan hue Brandon remembered. With a stunning blend of brown and fire, her tresses looked like her mahogany desk, a rich mixture of chocolate and flame. Brandon figured she was in her early forties. Her light gray skirt hugged her thighs. A simple gold necklace complimented her modest loop earrings. Her movements were precise. Even the angle of her head and the speed of her turn lent a professional bearing to her presence whether it was conscious or not. Her caramel skin looked delicious, her dark glistening eyes captivating. Brandon felt the need to swallow, and he lowered his head so she wouldn't see his nervous reflex.

"So—you have a piece of property you'd like to tell me about?" Her tone invited openness, but her demeanor indicated the existence of an invisible moat.

"Yes, I do." He quickly regained eye contact. "The Heritage Group specializes in commercial property. For the past year we've focused on downtown properties that might benefit from value-added development or redevelopment. As you are well aware, there are many underutilized strips of property around the hospital, but most are small and scattered."

He wanted to ask if she agreed with that observation, but decided against it and continued.

"We've been assembling a tract that consists of forty contiguous acres nearby. My research leads me to believe it could best be used for St. Anthony's expansion."

She moved forward in her seat.

"The hospital is going to continue expanding to keep up with Atherton's population growth, correct?"

She nodded. "Yes, the hospital administration is committed to the growth of our facilities and services."

"And please correct me if I'm wrong, but many of the physicians have their clinics in old, cramped buildings. Couldn't a new physician's clinic and office complex, managed by the hospital, generate a significant additional income for St. Anthony's?"

Her gaze dropped. Her hands appeared. She placed them on the edge of the desk and brought them together slowly until they were one on top of the other. Without answering his question she said, "You're putting together a parcel of forty acres?"

"Yes, ma'am, the land between here and the freeway."

Her eyes went up and to the left, and her lips tightened as she worked to locate the parcel in her mind's eye. He had hit a nerve. When her gaze came back to him, it no longer contained any friendly receptivity. Her blood pressure had jacked up a point or two, that he could tell, and she was about to grill him for information or possibly challenge him on some point. To get even a qualified commitment from her would achieve his objective on this first visit.

But before she said a word, she did the one thing he hadn't expected. She smiled at him in a way that indicated she didn't take him seriously. "Are you speaking of that old neighborhood with nineteenth-century houses?"

"Does that surprise you?" He had to stay ahead of her.

"Well, I'm sure that neighborhood has an historical designation."

"No, ma'am, none whatsoever." He paused a beat to let his tone permeate the statement. "Wouldn't that be an excellent parcel of real estate for the hospital to utilize in the years to come?"

She hesitated again. She seemed in no hurry to reveal the scope of her contemplations. Within seconds Brandon caught the dead air and continued. "At this point The Heritage Group is looking for an end user who would contract our professional services to acquire the entire tract. At the present time we have more than sixty percent of the lots under contract."

Katherine Cramer pursed her lips, and her eyes brightened with interest. "And how, may I ask, are you going about this acquisition?"

"I'm sorry, ma'am, I'm not at liberty to discuss our professional strategies, but I do want to work for you if you see merit in this tract."

Again she became absorbed in thought. Brandon noticed how the tightening and rolling of her sensuous lips was a reflexive manifestation of her thought process. "I would say that, until now, we haven't considered expanding the hospital in that direction."

"With all those mature trees, it is a beautiful area, wouldn't you agree?" Brandon let the first glimpse of his boyish smile flicker through.

"Large, mature trees are an asset, no doubt about that," she admitted.

"What we have to offer, Mrs. Cramer, is one united tract just across Sixth Avenue. It can be obtained for a reasonable price because the homeowners are ready to sell. In addition, this land can be acquired in a relatively short time so that the hospital could move ahead with expansion plans that may just be on the drawing board." Brandon paused a moment, then added, "I can have the papers drawn up to allow the hospital the first right of refusal when the property acquisition is complete. May I get that started for you?"

She studied his face intently. A respectful air between equals attached to her expression. He knew before she said a word, she was going to agree to his proposal. Now he had a solid contact at the hospital, a connection inside the most obvious end user for the land.

"I think that would be helpful, Mr. Evans. I'll discuss your proposal with my colleagues as well."

"Thank you for your time." He shook her hand. "I'll call early next week." He couldn't help but beam his friendliest smile. He caught himself just before adding a charming wink.

Brandon was ecstatic. He was equally apprehensive. Katherine Cramer paid attention to his presentation. He readily observed her interest in the spontaneous twitch of her eyelids and the contemplative expressions that crossed her face. Yet she held closely the full nature of her interest. Her responses indicated she'd never seriously considered the old neighborhood as a target for hospital expansion. If that were truly the case, he may have captured her imagination entirely.

She didn't ask many questions. She gave him the go ahead, said she'd check into it further. It all sounded encouraging. He figured she'd make a phone call or two. The dozens of individual owners in Kessler Park provided his sense of security. Who in his right mind would go in and negotiate with each resident? If she believed even half of what he said, he'd be her point man on the project. She could find out a few things about him if she dug deep enough, but she could never know for certain that he didn't have a substantial part of Kessler Park already under contract. A warm euphoria glowed within him as he left the hospital grounds. He was on his way up, one of many mega deals, and his very first one would put him near the top.

Paying Todd every day was putting a serious crimp in his available resources. Todd wanted to knock doors every hour of every day, whenever it was even conceivable the old folks would be up and willing to answer their doors.

Brandon wondered what had he actually been paying for. He had acquired original signatures under false pretenses. The residents of Kessler Park hadn't sold anything. Their intent had been to buy greeting cards or magazines. There were no sales figures as to what the properties were worth or what the owners would accept as payment. No dates had been set for them to move out. Todd had gotten the best end of their ruse with no obligation to see the plan to completion, and limited exposure if they got caught.

The only value in the signatures was as a tool, a calling card, a marker to assert his claim to the properties to prospective buyers along the line of hogwash he fed Katherine Cramer. Only if a potential buyer thought he had already done the leg work would they be inclined to work with him. Vic's admonition to secure a buyer before he made final deals with the sellers sat at the forefront of his mind. But now, a sense of misgiving filled his gut. He hadn't secured anything. He'd only deluded himself. What if he found someone ready to make a purchase offer today? What did he have to deliver? Nothing.

He'd already paid Todd more than twelve hundred dollars. It was too much for the little he'd received. Why was it that he could never see the next step in a business plan until he had poured sweat and dough into the scheme? Why did he always jump at ideas without thinking them through? Was it his natural unbridled optimism, or was it just a case of ingrained stupidity? Whatever the shortcomings that led him into so many boxed canyons of financial gloom, he wasn't a person to quit. He'd fight his way through the inadequacies of his approach and triumph in the end.

Few of the elderly homeowners could be realistically thinking of passing on their houses. One look at the surrounding area, the problems inherent in the old structures, and any young family would turn tail and run for the suburbs. Wouldn't it be better to plan ahead and save their loved ones the burden of selling? He'd been in a few of them. No matter how much care and upkeep continued to be invested, it was obvious the houses were near the end. Eventually the neighborhood was going to change. New houses weren't going to be built there. What existed around it was too commercial, too urban. When the change came, it would be drastic and complete. Brandon knew he had to keep at it, stick with his original instinct, and be part of the conversion.

He decided he'd shut Todd down for the time being. Todd could go back to what he'd been doing. He didn't want too many people hollering for their greeting cards before he had secured a definite buyer.

As he drove down the freeway, Brandon strained to consider his next step. Spontaneity was his strong suit, not planning. But now that events were falling into place, he was forced to look ahead. He found himself headed toward Cindy's apartment. For several weeks now, she'd listened to his plan, encouraged him when she could, remained silent when even he knew he was talking only to convince himself. She had lent him a thousand dollars of the money he paid Todd and let him use her credit card to buy his new clothes and fill his tank.

He pictured her for a moment and wondered why she hadn't moved on. She was certainly attractive enough, sociable, informed, and witty. Yet she'd completed two years of junior college, then settled into a nine-to-five job behind a department store jewelry counter.

She listened to him. There was a subtle quality about her that could soothe anyone's frazzled emotions. But for an anxious individual like himself, Cindy's ability to bear his stories and stroke his fragile pride instilled rebirth. Sometimes she seemed so enamored by his tales, as if his Pied Piper oratory would carry her to the summit of secret desires. In many ways he took advantage of her. He took up her time whenever he needed a sounding board for his grandiose ideas. He was just glad she was there, though he gave back so little in return.

She smoked too much. She could afford to lose a few pounds. Though they had been intimate, the relationship was not. Occasionally, Brandon would pull her to the bedroom, his day a cascade of pent-up pressures, his male hormones demanding release. They would strew her bed covers, sweat in each other's arms, and exchange bodily fluids, but hardly a word. Brandon wasn't sure why he didn't tell her how much he enjoyed being with her in bed. He felt safe and happy during those few moments while they were staring at the ceiling, catching their breaths. Maybe she'd be critical of his performance. When their sexual romps ended, he felt awkward. For all of his talkative nature, he avoided any discussion of that subject.

He hardly spoke any words of appreciation in her direction, though he always went back and looked her up, especially when he needed support. He needed her patient listening. He needed her un-maxed-out credit card.

Even now he wanted to see her and tell her about his meeting at the hospital. His father wasn't around to encourage him, and he would have to show substantial progress on the venture before he'd get much of that anyway. His mother was consistently aloof, more interested in her social calendar than what her children were doing.

So he sought Cindy's advice, though she knew even less than he did about commercial real estate. As he pulled into a parking space, he realized that specific information about real estate wasn't what he wanted or needed to hear. He wanted Cindy to tell him he was on the right track as long as he kept plugging along. He wanted her to tell him that he was going about it the right way and doing the right thing. He wanted her to soothe his anxious soul and push the gnawing demon of doubt from his mind.

CHAPTER THIRTEEN

BRANDON'S SALES PITCH stirred Katherine Cramer's curiosity. The information demanded her attention. The proposal intrigued her. Even if it proved unrealistic, after all the land in question was currently an established residential neighborhood, the young man's presentation was compelling. He seemed knowledgeable, his demeanor self-assured. With eleven years in the hospital's property management department, five of those in her current position as vice president, she knew immediately, if the land was available, the hospital was interested. More than interested, if that plot of ground became available, the hospital would move heaven and earth to buy it. She had to know more.

She called two staff managers and asked if they had heard anything about the Victorian neighborhood to the north. They hadn't. She called the county Register of Deeds, but they couldn't help unless she had lot and block numbers. She immediately enlarged a city map on her computer, printed a copy of Kessler Park that included street names, and dispatched a secretary to the county courthouse with specific questions to get answered. Then she called another number, an infrequently called number, but a number she kept in her Rolodex for days just like this.

"Riley."

"Good afternoon, this is Katherine Cramer."

"Well, good afternoon. To what do I owe the pleasure of your call?"

"You sound like you know why I'm calling."

"No, I guess I'm just glad to hear a different voice. Never a dull moment at city hall some may say, but in many ways it's the same old routine."

"Boring, don't say boring. I won't believe you," Katherine tried to sound professionally sympathetic. "Getting council members to work together is a challenge, I'm sure, but there's got to be a reward in that."

"It would be easier to get toddlers to share their crayons. How can I help?"

They had known each other for ten years, though neither could recall when they first met. They crossed paths at benefits for autistic children and the Independent Living Foundation, an agency dedicated to assisting mentally challenged individuals. They were seated at the same table at one of the city's year-end galas to recognize Atherton's exemplary citizens. Riley worked in the mayor's office. When Franklin Patterson became the city's highest elected official, Riley readily accepted the offer to join his staff. Within six months he was the mayor's right hand man.

Networking within the business community was just another component of being a true professional. It wasn't long before each knew the other's line of work. In the upper echelons of both hospital administration and city politics the quality of personal contacts embodied the life blood of continued success.

"You know we just broke ground on a new student-nurse dormitory?" Katherine said.

"Yes, I read about it. That'll be a nice addition, I'm sure."

"None too soon either. There's a tremendous demand for nurses. I mention the dormitory because the pressure on the hospital to expand will continue for years."

"I follow you. What's come up?"

Darrin Riley knew he didn't get phone calls from Katherine, nor other high ranking executives, unless they wanted something. It would take up his time and expertise without being reflected by even one additional dollar in his pay envelope. But money wasn't what got him up each day. Being kept in the loop was a reward in and of itself. The benefits of skillfully-placed favors returned home like well-trained pigeons. Being the puppet master of Atherton's political muscle was worth much more than money.

"The hospital is always looking to acquire good parcels of land for future development," Katherine said, "especially large contiguous tracts that can be master planned. We've purchased several retail strips in the past few years including the quarter block at 9th and Wentworth where the Lora-Locke Apartments used to be. But all of those tracts were small. Today I was presented with an interesting proposal---a proposal that approximately forty acres near the hospital soon would become available."

There was a gap of silence on the line. "My, that's interesting." Riley knew a parcel of that size near the hospital would indeed be worth looking into. "You say soon?"

"Yes, this company is working to unite all the lots in a residential subdivision, get the zoning changed to commercial, and sell the parcel to the highest bidder."

"That is ambitious," Riley said. "There's usually a holdout or two, especially once the word gets around."

"That's what I thought, but this agent tells me they have 60% of the lots already under contract. If they have that much work done, they must think they can put it all together."

"Where is this land?"

There was another gap of silence on the line. "Please understand I'm calling because I respect your expertise. I know you know how to get things done. St. Anthony's would be interested in this property. I'd appreciate your complete confidence in this matter."

"Of course."

"It's that enclave of Victorian homes between the hospital and the freeway."

"Oh, yes." As Riley pictured the hidden neighborhood in his mind's eye, an inspired grin came to his lips. He leaned back in his plush office chair and put his feet on his desk. Far from being another tedious inquiry, this phone call made his afternoon. His political instincts began to stir. The phone receiver nestled against his ear like the warm brush of a lover's cheek.

"Have you heard anything about that neighborhood selling out or requesting a zoning change?" Katherine asked.

"No," he assured her, "but I can check into it."

"My concern—the reason I called, is if the acreage is coming on the market, I want the hospital to be first in line to acquire it. I'm certain the hospital board would approve the acquisition. If the land is being shopped to me, then I imagine it's being shopped to others."

"The best way to avoid that," Riley said in a reassuring voice, "since the hospital is an institution serving the community, is to move the acquisition from a private transaction to a governmental process."

"Could that be done? It's not like the hospital has any immediate expansion plans for a parcel like that."

"It can be done. Besides, when you're dealing with residential property, it's about the only way to unite all of those individual lots. It's clean, relatively quick, gets things done faster than waiting on a real estate outfit to put it all together. Everyone gets a decent price for their property, you're happy, the public is happy. The proceeding may generate news for awhile, a few people complain to the newspaper editor, but after a few months everything is back to normal. Life goes on."

"So you're talking about . . ."

"Maybe we should have lunch," Riley interrupted. His mind shuffled though the political markers he could call in to support such a measure and the favors he would acquire from the hospital in return. "We could talk specifics then. Do you have some time tomorrow?"

"Tomorrow would be fine."

"Let's make it a late lunch, say 12:45 at McLinty's, on Main across from the federal building. They have nice tables in the back."

"Tomorrow then," Katherine said, "12:45."

CHAPTER FOURTEEN

SIX WEEKS LATER

As morning sunlight lit a shaft of dust beside the window blinds, Myron knew it was at least seven. And if it was past seven, he had to get up.

He had yet to move and remained on his back, stared at the ceiling, and resisted the urge to even try. Finally, he eased his legs over the side of the bed and pulled himself up by the headboard into a sitting position. He scratched his head, confounded by his forgetfulness. Immediately, he realized, once again, he had misplaced the ruby star. He was certain he'd laid it on the nightstand. It wasn't there. Where had he left it this time? A helpless confusion gripped him as he looked about in vain.

It was just a simple charm, but it meant a great deal to Delores. She took it off each night before bed, but insisted it be placed around her neck each new day. She cherished the brooch, now a necklace, as a lover remembers a caressing touch. With her good left hand she could reach it, touch and turn it, and find comfort. Myron perpetuated the daily routine because it bolstered her spirit. Her will to fight the daily struggle of existence was rejuvenated by the sentimental keepsake, a talisman to thwart her pain, an amulet of cheer. It seemed like such an easy task, though Myron had been misplacing many things of late.

He rubbed his fingers on his thighs until feeling radiated in his hands, then grabbed the headboard and, with a rocking bounce, stood on unsteady legs beside his bed while his six foot, two-inch body unfolded as much as stiff joints and atrophied muscles would allow. He shuffled in a tight circle and retrieved his robe from a hook beside the door.

The ruby pendant was nowhere to be seen. To him it was little more than a trinket, pretty but hardly valuable, a garish thing with a red rock center with tiny diamond studs at the end of onyx radii. The pendant Delores called her ruby star was slightly larger than a silver dollar. Forty years ago he'd bought it for an occasion he had now forgotten, if there had been any occasion at all. Back then Delores hardly wore it. Now it was her favorite piece of jewelry. Myron didn't know why the ruby star made her happy; he just knew it did.

Delores slept in the next room, on a hospital bed where she spent most of her days. A thin cushion of hard rubber served as support as she couldn't tolerate a soft mattress of any kind. She suffered constant discomfort, the result of a car accident fourteen years earlier. Delores and Myron hadn't slept in the same bed since.

Myron looked for the ruby star everywhere as he made his way to the kitchen. He passed Delores in silence. To touch her now was to start their day, a regimented routine of pills and pillows, and changing from night clothes, one labor intensive garment at a time.

He took a store-bought oatmeal cookie from a tray and poured himself some milk. Another hot and humid day lay ahead. During these free minutes, Myron simply listened to the coffee pot gurgle, watched the birds flitter from tree to tree, and the squirrels jump and skitter along the fence. He still had Delores and he was able to help. She still laughed at his jokes and told him her never-ending stories from her days as principal at Eisenhower Elementary. For quite some time now, life was a series of simple days, and as each one came it was enough.

"Myron, you there? Help me."

"I'm here. I'm coming." Myron ran a glass of water and scooted to her side. He lifted her and held the glass so she could drink from a straw.

"Do you want to turn?" he asked.

Delores groaned and imprinted her nails in his wrist. She pushed her face into the pillow and tried to rise on an elbow while she protested in raspy breaths she not be moved in the least. Myron gently turned her frail body, put a pillow between her legs, and propped more pillows behind her so she could rest on her side.

"I need my pills, four of them."

"You're not to have more than two in the morning."

"I need more." She raised a bluish, tight-skinned hand, in supplication for her plea.

A familiar knot of pity swelled in Myron's throat as he watched her breathe with precise, rhythmic breaths.

"I'll be right back."

He hated the ruse he now must play, a strategy he devised years ago. It was the only option he had, his only choice to keep her with him, lucid and able to converse. Myron took two allergy tablets from the cabinet, the same size and shape as her narcotic, and returned to her side along with her regular dose. He hated himself. His actions forced her to endure additional pain, but he couldn't overmedicate her either. He prayed she experienced some placebo relief. He did, after all, give her the number of pills she asked for. Her lips barely opened as she took the pills and sipped from the straw. She inhaled quickly. Her face relaxed. Their eyes met, their gazes lingered, and silently she thanked him again for his never-ending love and care.

"I want to get in my chair," she said.

"Are you sure?"

"I want to eat sitting up." Her face scrunched as she spoke. "I want to see the morning. I won't be in anymore pain sitting up." Determination laced her voice with an inflection that proclaimed her statement as self-evident. "I have to move. It's Thursday, right? Rick will be out back. You can get him to help."

"Maybe I should call the hospital. We can ask the doctor to give you another injection."

"No! No more hospital. I'd rather die than ride in that ambulance again, the way they drive." Through a crust of dry tears she gazed at him. "No more hospital. They don't help me there. It's all pokes and prods. I want to stay right here, in my house, with you. You take care of me better than any of them."

Myron tried to smile. "Feeling better?"

"I'll feel better when I get moved. I just want to be up, at least for awhile."

Myron dressed her in slacks and pullover blouse, then repositioned pillows around her hips and shoulders. "I'll see if Rick's here."

Out the back door, onto the enclosed porch, Myron opened the screen door, and the sun warmed his cheek. He saw Rick in the alley, approaching the back gate, his tool belt around his waist, an old canvas bag full of supplies slung over his shoulder.

Rick was a huge bulk of a young man, dressed in faded overalls and a colorful, long-sleeve print shirt of pinks and yellow. He wore a scruffy green ball cap logoed with a bass out of water fighting against a hook. He surveyed the backyard garden as he approached the house and jerked his gaze in surprise toward the back door when Myron called his name.

"Good morning, Mr. Holmes," he replied. His blue eyes beamed with instant energy as he looked up, shading his gaze from the sun. Sweat ran from his sideburns down a strong, symmetrical jaw. It was an attractive face that returned Myron's greeting, a face one might call handsome except the right eyelid that didn't open as fully as the left.

Rick had suffered a head injury as a boy. But to look at him, a person was unlikely to notice anything amiss. Rick made no mention of his morning or the growing heat, but waited patiently for Myron to make his wishes known.

"Would you help me put Mrs. Holmes in her wheelchair?"

"Oh sure, sure thing, Mr. Holmes."

Myron led the way into the house and maneuvered Delores' wheelchair beside her bed.

"Good morning, Mrs. Holmes. Your flowers are looking pretty today."

"I'm sure they are, Rick."

"I'll give them extra water. It's going to be hot today, but the sun makes them stand up tall and beautiful, too. Do you want to see them?"

"Certainly, I'd love to."

Rick easily picked up Delores by himself and placed her in the wheelchair. Myron watched and remembered when he easily tended to all of Delores' needs. He could still do most of it, but it became harder every day. An ache of ineptitude filled him, though the feeling was hardly justified. It just hurt knowing he couldn't fully care for his wife of sixty-three years.

Delores moaned and bit on her lower lip, but didn't complain as Rick set her in the chair.

"I'll roll you to the back porch," Rick said, a sparkle in his voice as though he were about to let her in on a secret known only to him.

He wheeled her through the kitchen and easily out the back, down a ramp into the garden where they stopped under a cove of shade beside a hackberry tree. Neither said a word. The scenic array of colorful blossoms consumed their attention.

Rick's diligent work throughout the summer nurtured a garden that covered the entire back yard. A narrow footpath led to the withered detached garage, and a wider path of crushed stones meandered through the flowers. The wash of color contained an earthly rainbow. The yard was full of orange Trumpet Creepers, white dogwood, Indian Paint Brush, and wild azaleas. Bluebonnets waved in the breeze along with other flowers in colors of peach, pink, lavender, and reds. Delores scanned the yard with delight. "You're a wonderful gardener, Rick. Please take me over there."

Soon, with the warm sun climbing overhead, Rick returned Delores to the house where Myron fed her in the kitchen. Rick accepted an offered glass of lemonade, drank it, returned to the backyard, and began his gardening.

A knock came at the front door.

"Morning, Roger," Myron said as he answered.

"You need to sign for this one." The postal carrier leaned against the door jamb, his powder-blue shirt drenched in sweat. A ceiling fan blew a tepid breeze across his crimson face as he removed his cap and wiped his forehead with a wet handkerchief. "Every house in the neighborhood is getting one of these, and I have to get a signature for every one. I won't get through today till dark."

"Something certified," Myron said as he signed the card. "Well, Roger, I guess that means it's important." Myron returned the card and pen and took the rest of his mail. "Try to stay cool."

Except for the envelope he signed for, Myron threw the mail on an entryway table. With two hands on the arms, he eased himself into his favorite chair. The return address was printed in raised lettering, the envelope made of high quality paper with a textured finish. It was from the city. Myron's curiosity grew as he turned the envelope over in his hands. His property taxes were paid. Why had he received a certified letter from the city?

Myron usually opened letters by knocking the contents to one side of the envelope and ripping off the end. But something told him he may want to keep this correspondence, so he retrieved a penknife from his pocket and sliced along the flap. Inside he found a single sheet, fancy paper with a watermark, embossed with the city of Atherton's official seal.

He leaned back and read slowly until the meaning of the correspondence took shape in his mind. At first, an imperceptible hollowness invaded in his chest. Warming blood drained from his extremities, a clammy coolness settled on his skin. "No, they can't do that," he muttered under his breath. The letter fell from his fingers. He leaned his head back, his eyes stared, unfocused at a high spot on the wall, and his body receded into the armchair as though he were shrinking.

From across the room, Delores watched Myron's collapse. Her coffee cup slipped from her and fell to the floor. She hollered at the top of her voice.

"Rick, help me. Rick, come in here. Please come quick."

Only silence answered her cry.

"Rick, help. Rick, come here."

Lumbering steps pounded across the back porch. A violent slam threw open the kitchen door. Rick's large frame soon filled the archway between the dining room and parlor. His eyes flashed between Delores' frantic pointing and Myron slouched deep in his chair, his slack arms draping the armrests.

"What is it?"

"Check him, please. Something's happened."

Rick dashed to Myron's chair and knelt beside him. Rick touched his arm. Myron sucked up a huge breath and fought his way up and out of the chair. His lower lip quivered.

"They want to take everything I have," Myron said. The letter lay on the rug like a ruinous stain. A slight, but unmistakable tremor overtook his body as he tried to stand.

"Sit down, sir. Who wants to take what?"

"My house, my house," Myron mumbled.

"Why would anyone take your house? You live here."

"They want my land. They want all the land around here." Myron raised his gaze and searched Rick's face with a pleading that Rick tell him what he'd read was a mistake, but the young man's bewildered expression confirmed he was still processing what he'd just been told. Myron brought his thoughts inward, his fingers plied his face, and audible sighs rolled up the walls.

"Rick, get that paper there and bring it here," Delores said. "I want to read it."

Rick wiped his hands on his overalls, pinched the letter at the corner, and took it to Delores.

She read it, and a gasp escaped her throat.

City of Atherton, Texas
Planning and Zoning Commission
CAUSE N0. 515167-9002
Dear Property Owner,

You are hereby notified that on August 10th, the Atherton Zoning Board will conduct a public hearing to consider the petition of St. Anthony's Regional Medical Center to initiate CONDEMNATION PROCEEDINGS for the purpose of proceeding in EMINENT DOMAIN all properties from 800 through and including 1500 South Atoka, Ashford, Linden, and Cummings Streets, and 300 through and including 700 West Bensen, Lancer, Garrison, and Poplar Streets, and to change city zoning designation from Residential R-1 to Commercial C-4.

Atherton City Charter Sec. 18, 21 sub. D-F

"I can't move. Where would we go?" Myron talked to himself, his gaze remained high upon the wall. "It would cost more than they would ever pay me. I don't want to go nowhere."

Rick went back to the old man's side and put his hand on his arm. "Now don't get all upset. Whatever it is, there's got to be something that can be done. You're making yourself sick and there's no good reason for that."

Myron sat up. He studied the young man's worried expression. Myron swallowed and forced himself to gather his thoughts. "Rick, you're absolutely right. I'm okay now. Why don't you go back to work? I have things I need to get started on myself."

Rick's blue eyes lit at Myron's declaration. "Okay then, I'm going back to work, Mr. Holmes." Rick took a few steps and turned. "You'll be okay?"

"Yes, Rick. I'll be fine."

Myron swiveled his chair toward Delores, and for several minutes he stared across the room without actually looking at her. Finally, he shuffled across the expansive parlor and took a seat beside her wheelchair. "Rick doesn't understand, and wouldn't even if I'd tried to explain. I saw no reason to keep him in here worrying about us."

"Are you okay, dear?" Delores asked.

"Yes, over the shock of it, I guess."

Myron saw her grimace. The blunt realization of the official letter rolled a wave of doubt against her breast, and he saw that Delores needed reassurance. "What are we going to do?" she said.

Myron took her hand and patted it as he spoke. "I don't know yet. I just don't know. But please don't worry. You've said yourself many times, worrying doesn't help a bit." Even as he spoke, a debilitating uncertainty took residence in his guts. Myron found no comfort in idle optimism.

"I'm scared. Where would we go?" Delores asked.

"I want to go outside for awhile," Myron said without answering. He pushed her wheelchair out the front onto the wide porch beside a row of high bushes that blocked the morning sun. Myron left her there as he shuffled along the veranda to the far side of the house, now lost in thoughts of his own. He made his way down side steps off the dining room, through overgrown hedges, out on the lawn. Myron walked to the front gate, turned, and gazed up at his home. It was a tired, worn relic from another era, similar to all the houses in the neighborhood built just after the Civil War. Most were erected on spacious lots with fences of white pickets or ornamental iron, built primarily of wood. The only stone in their construction was used for foundations, steps, and chimneys.

His Victorian home nestled under a canopy of giant oaks that covered the house in a broad shade. Sagging branches licked the rusty crests of its cast-iron ridge and scraped the mildewed wooden shingles. Dead vines encased the outer walls in a brown cocoon, and living vines searched unceasingly for crevices between the clapboards and anchors across the eaves.

The old structure seemed to sigh as the day grew warmer. Its antiquated geometric protrusions and steep roofs, stylishly grotesque in comparison to the straight lines of modern architecture appeared to struggle to remain erect. Grime covered the stained glass of the bay windows. The balcony off the upstairs bedroom sagged. Insects buzzed in the rising heat, and tired birds rested away the late morning in nests tucked under the eaves. The motionless air accentuated the drabness of the house, and the splintered, picket fence posted sentry on little more than history.

Never before had Myron seen his house as such an ancient structure in so much need of maintenance and repair. Rick mowed their lawn and made minor repairs around the house, but he was in too much demand to spend all his time with them. The backyard garden had been the compromise, the one beautiful, well-maintained aspect of their home. It brought the greatest joy to Delores. The garden hinted at the bygone splendor of the old residence.

Why did the city suddenly want his property? According to the notice, the city intended to take all the homes in Kessler Park. Myron couldn't reconcile the thought. The city had actually started the process to take his home. The idea was unimaginable. A cascade of touching memories involving his home swelled within him. An ache of loss filled his heart though nothing had yet happened. He was eighty-seven years old. He thought he might cry. It was a struggle to walk to the porch. He sat beside Delores and absently patted her hand.

"Maybe the city means to buy folks out one at a time. . . when we're ready to move of our own choosing." His words tapered for the lack of conviction, and he forced down a lump in his throat. He knew he was concocting a plausible lie for his wife's benefit, and her expression clearly indicated she wasn't buying it. Still, he wanted to reassure her. But every ounce of resolve in his heart melted away faster than he could muster more to shore his confidence. He gazed at Delores, completely unable to project a grain of confidence or kernel of hope. What if he had to put her in a nursing home? His chin quivered again. "If they make us move, I don't know what we'll do."

"Dear," Delores said after a long silence passed between them. "Would you get the ruby star for me? I'd like to put on my necklace now."

CHAPTER FIFTEEN

THE NEXT DAY, WHEN RICK GOT UP, he immediately made his bed. Then, in order, he shaved, washed his face, got dressed, fixed two slices of toast with cinnamon sugar and butter along with a bowl of Cheerios, and finally brushed his teeth. It was a routine he adhered to without contemplation and with such physical precision as to appear choreographed.

When all was complete, he checked his calendar. His daily schedule listed where he was to be each hour, everything from doctor appointments, to when his mother would be stopping by. His remodeling and maintenance jobs included the address, name of the homeowner, and the time he was expected. Rick perused the entry beside the X that he had crossed through yesterday. Today he was to meet the Klines and Stewarts at the neighborhood park to erect a wooden wall on the west side of the picnic area.

The neighborhood park occupied a corner at the intersection of Linden and Poplar on a previously weed-infested lot that dwelt in the midst of Kessler Park. Once the location of an elegant Victorian Queen Anne, the structure was abandoned after a fire gutted it in the 1940's. The owners at the time had no insurance to restore her to her original charm, so the passage of time brought down the house with the help of derelicts who squatted there and burned her stick by stick to keep warm in winter. All that had remained were the broken remnants of a stone foundation.

With the lot too small to be of commercial value, the eyesore grew with the weeds. Some of the houses nearby were now multi-family rentals, void of loving care, sectioned off by chain-link fences protecting plastic tricycles and yapping dogs, with rusty appliances as lawn ornaments on grassless yards. Their former grandeur was now disguised in peeling paint and hidden by un-pruned branches.

Transportation around the Kessler Park neighborhood was available at the bus stops and with personal shoe leather. The primary income for the working idle was found at the corner blood bank. The rest of the odd lot of haggard humanity that milled the rundown streets along the perimeter of Kessler Park were content to receive whatever food stamps and their day-labor checks would provide. The neighborhood milieu was more disgusting than dangerous, and the conscientious homeowners who lived in Kessler Park were left to dispose of the litter that blew into their yards and pick up the wine bottles that lay at the curb.

It was with this reality, as the urban elements around them putrefied, the homeowners of the nineteenth century subdivision decided to create their own small park. It began just as talk, then someone hauled away the junk, and someone mowed the lot. Others poured 3 x 4 foot concrete slabs and bolted down metal benches. Everyone knew the park belonged to all, an integral member of the neighborhood. Now, without assignments, schedules, or much discussion, most able-bodied residents spent time each month maintaining their island of shrubs and blossoms.

Before the park was built, most homeowners were caught in a state of depression about the economic forces that conspired to reduce their property values. Many had lived in their houses for decades. The reverse gentrification that swallowed their neighborhood was hard to accept. They weren't wealthy people. They came from hard-working families who had bought in the area because of the charm of the houses and proximity to downtown. Now they were stuck in a declining part of the city with little they could do but be on about their lives. The park became a source of inspiration and accomplishment. Once again a measure of pride came to the little area of Atherton, TX, named after the man who built the subdivision back in the 1870's.

Rick was the first to arrive and quickly busied himself pulling weeds. Because of the considerable expanse of the lot, much was sown with native wildflowers. A thick blanket of Cloth-of-Gold yellow flowers shared the sunlight with orange clusters of Standing Cypress, red Pheasant's Eyes, and Wild Blue Indigo. Throughout the garden Indian Paintbrush and Texas Bluebonnets stood tall and proud.

He worked carefully around the plants, kneeling between them when he could, bending to the ground when limited space required. Butterflies skipped among the blossoms as the day warmed. A platoon of hungry bees filled the air with a pleasing hum as they sampled the botanical cuisine. Rick was about to weed a stand of bluebonnets when a group of kids called to him from the street.

"Hey, mister, whatcha doing?"

Rick turned in the direction of the sound as four youngsters ran up the original stone steps built into the earth. He stretched his back and wondered where his co-workers were. He gave the youngsters his full attention, with a vacant yet receptive countenance as though the juveniles may have something for him or be in need of his assistance.

The kids were all in their early teens dressed in faded blue jeans and rock band T-shirts. The lone female was a chubby girl with bobbed hair who appeared simultaneously thankful and reluctant to be there, and endured the possessive draping of one boy's arm as though she were a post.

The largest boy had a head of shaggy, brown hair, a heavy brow, and a substantial head start on a case of adolescent acne. Another boy was long and gangly, with a head too big for his shoulders. His body moved in jerks of energy as he looked about and surveyed the vast assortment of floral color.

"Pretty cool. Why didn't you tell me about this, Dan?"

"I didn't know it was here."

"You could get your mom something pretty, Jake. She might cut you some slack."

"Why don't you mind your own business? I thought we were going to the mall?"

"Hey, mister, so what is this, a flower farm?" asked the third boy who kept talking as he surveyed the garden and leaned on the girl.

"A flower farm?" Rick wasn't sure what the question implied.

The boy's blue eyes caught the morning light. An engaging smile appeared as a jocular lilt coated his words. His leadership in the clique with unchallenged dibs on the girl not only allowed, but required he ply his cleverness and expose anything that may prove of interest on an otherwise boring summer day. "Yeah, do you grow these and sell them to flower shops?"

"Oh, no," Rick said.

The four teenagers all waited. Finally, the shaggy headed boy said, "Oh no, what?"

"Well, no, this is a park for people to come and sit and walk and enjoy," Rick replied, pleased with his complete and accurate answer.

The leader of the group paused before responding and studied Rick. A subtle smirk curled at the corners of his mouth. "So the flowers are for us, too?"

"Sure, the flowers are for everyone."

"And you take care of them, right?"

"Yep." Rick smiled. "I like to take care of the flowers."

The boy stepped away from the girl and made close eye contact with Rick. "A big guy like you---you like to take care of flowers because you're a bumpkin, right?"

The lanky kid let out a hoot, but Rick took no offense. He didn't catch the implication of the boy's tone or know what the word meant.

The boy gazed about the garden. "You like flowers don't you, Ashley?" The girl mumbled a feeble affirmative, and the boy continued, "These blue ones are pretty." He stepped between the rows. In a heartbeat he grabbed a stand of bluebonnets and yanked the flowers, roots and all.

"No," Rick cried.

"Can it, Farmer Brown. No one is going to miss a flower or two."

Maybe the boy had been bossing around his friends too long. Maybe his arrogance knew no bounds. But in a split second he became acutely aware of his grave miscalculation. Rick snagged the boy by the skin and muscle of his collar with his massive, calloused hand. The kid groaned and dropped the flowers. His friends sprang for the street. Rick hauled the boy to the edge of the park and dropped him in the dirt. With the clarity of a bullhorn and the authority of a drill sergeant, Rick said, "If you want to come back, don't do that again."

The boy struggled to his feet, his face contorted in agony. He hobbled half a block to

where his friends waited. Then he turned and yelled
up the street, "You're gonna pay for that, you
retard. You're gonna pay."

CHAPTER SIXTEEN

RICK RETURNED TO THE SITE of the carnage. He surveyed the mangled flowers, uprooted and broken. There was nothing he could do to save them. He knew people often put cut flowers in fancy bottles and took them indoors to admire. Yet, it was beyond his comprehension why someone would violently rip beautiful, growing flowers from the ground. He sat in the dirt and rolled the wounded plants in his hands.

As Rick tried to make sense of what had happened, Beatrice Morgan arrived at the park. She was an active woman in her early sixties with a fleshy face, her long snow white hair pulled tightly over her head and tied in back. Rick told her of the incident, but she seemed unconcerned.

"Don't let it bother you, Rick. Folks around here may not be using this park much longer."

He couldn't believe what he'd just heard. Why would she say such a thing?

"I could use your help at my house, Rick. Would you come and help me?"

"I'm supposed to be here until one o'clock. We're going to build a fence."

"Not today. Plans have changed. No one else is coming."

"Is anything wrong?" Apprehension at the change of schedule crinkled worry into his forehead.

"It's okay, Rick. I'll explain it to you at my house. You can make some money this morning, and you'll be doing me a big favor."

Beatrice turned in the direction of her house and Rick silently followed. As they walked she told him of her needs. "I've got two rooms of furniture I've been meaning to move for ages. Today I'm going to get it done. A moving company is bringing over a truck. I'm going to put it all in storage."

Rick listened, and although he didn't care one way or the other, her explanation didn't make much sense. Why would someone pay good money to store furniture when she had room in her own house? "Are you buying new furniture?"

"No, no," her voice seemed to drift.

They arrived and went inside where she offered him a seat in the parlor. "Would you like something to drink?"

"Yes, ma'am, maybe a glass of water."

His gaze drifted about the room. Rich oak wainscot covered the walls behind antique credenzas and glass enclosed china cabinets. Delicate lace valances bordered the high double-hung windows silhouetting a perfect balance of view and sunlight. A modest amber chandelier hung from the ten-foot ceiling. It was one of the smaller houses in the neighborhood, but cozy, and well kept.

Beatrice returned with a glass of water. "Let me show you what we need to move."

In the bedroom Beatrice swung her arm around the room. "All of this needs to go." She set her hands on her hips while Rick took it all in. A queen-size bed was piled high with boxes and plastic bags stuffed with bedspreads and quilts. Stacks of hardback books saddled a weathered vanity. Mismatched drapes hung over a cheval mirror. Three side-by-side dressers were covered with columns of framed pictures nestled back to back. More stacked boxes filled every corner in the room.

"Are you moving out?" Rick asked innocently.

"We're all going to be moving soon, I do believe."

"Where? Who?"

"Everyone in the neighborhood, Rick. The hospital is going to buy it all and build new buildings here."

"What do you mean, everyone? Mr. and Mrs. Holmes don't want to move nowhere. The Porters neither. I can think of a lot of folks who don't want to move."

"I don't want to move either, really, but I will if they pay me enough."

"Who?"

"The hospital, Rick. They want to buy the land. They want to buy up the whole neighborhood."

"But people live here," he said as though the sheer truth of the statement would be sufficient to make the entire proposition go away.

"Yes, they do," she agreed.

"Well then, the hospital can't have it, right?"

Beatrice stopped her sorting. His simple logic had her gazing at him more closely. "Sometimes..." she said, and she stopped and swallowed. The dejected expression that sprang to his face the instant she began to speak brought moistness to her eyes. She took a deep breath and began again. "Sometimes, Rick, neighborhoods change." His body language forced her to stop again.

His hands were at his sides. His innocent blue eyes appeared as though he had just lost his favorite pet. She made room for herself on the bed and sat. Then, she took his big, calloused hand and held it between her own as she gazed into his questioning eyes. "The people in charge, Rick, give a place like the hospital special privileges. The hospital helps everyone and the hospital is for everyone. So when the hospital needs to get bigger, the people in charge give the hospital special consideration. If they need more land, the people in charge will help them get it. Do you understand?"

Rick's eyes were wet now, and he gently pulled his hand away from hers. He thought about the people he worked for. Many were old and feeble, and he knew they didn't want to move. He thought about the grand houses, and how, when he first moved to his apartment, he sought work among them because they were so inspiring. He wanted to work the craft he had learned. He wanted to repair and restore the century-old structures to the way they used to be.

Now he knew why Mr. Holmes had been so distraught yesterday and had almost collapsed on his living room floor. Rick's face changed, a firm determination set his jaw.

"No! People live here. Not the hospital or nothing else is going to get this land." He looked at Beatrice and frowned. "I'm sorry! I'm not helping you move nothing." With that he stormed through the house and out the front door.

Beatrice's mouth fell open as she witnessed his change. Never before had she seen such intense and decisive behavior from him. The incident served as a personal wake-up call. If Rick was incensed, maybe she should reconsider her options before hastily moving out. She went straight to the phone and called the moving company. "I've changed my mind about moving anything today. If I need to move any of this stuff, I'll worry about it later."

CHAPTER SEVENTEEN

NOT A HALF BLOCK FROM Beatrice Morgan's home, Rick stopped in his tracks. His breath came in labored gasps. An ache crept up the back of his neck, a slow spread that settled at his temples. Destruction of the flowers, Beatrice's explanation of the city's official letter, and now the glaring sunlight all conspired to initiate the pain. He wasn't to get all worked up. It was bad for his head. The resulting headaches might last for days and leave him tormented, sick, and temporarily blind.

The notion people he knew and cared about would be forced to leave their homes without consent required a line of reasoning he was unable to comprehend. And who was he supposed to be angry with? It was beyond his understanding to be upset with the hospital. In his mind, the hospital was good. But Mrs. Morgan said the hospital was going to take the property of others just because they wanted it.

He sat on the curb beside a stop sign at a shaded corner and pressed and rubbed behind his ears. He had to force himself to breathe slowly, to concentrate, to take deep breaths. If not, the tentacles of pressure would continue their relentless march past his temples and grow with throbbing intensity until they met between his eyes.

Rick had no idea how long he sat and rubbed, but his efforts were ineffective. The afternoon sun glared off the cars and concrete. He shielded his eyes as he walked. He needed to get back to his apartment and lay in the darkness of his bedroom. He tried to check the time on his wristwatch, but his eyes wouldn't focus. The sun's glare seemed to boil his eyeballs. He walked as a blind man, one eye barely open. With a pinky finger on one temple and a thumb on the other, he squeezed his forehead as though he was holding together his skull. He shuffled along as quickly as he could, a seven-block journey ahead of him before he had any hope of relief. Rick tripped on a slab of broken concrete, buckled by a massive tree root, and fell to his knees.

Across the street, three boys snickered, then ran ahead. The leader huddled his cohorts, and they hatched a plan in the middle of the street.

The boys ran ahead, putting every obstacle they could find in Rick's path. They moved a large downed tree branch across the sidewalk. Rick's toe nicked the top of the log, and he stumbled. The boys bit their fists to keep from laughing. By the time Rick reached the next block they had crates, garbage cans, and open gates in his way. The agony in his head was now all-consuming. He had no awareness of his tormentors.

Ahead, the lower branches of a tall pine extended past a fence line. The boys jumped the fence, put all their weight and muscle against one branch, and forced it back as far as it would go. Within seconds Rick hobbled by, and they let the branch fly. It swooshed forward. Thick pine needles and sappy bark smacked Rick in the face and knocked him on his back. The boys, egged on by their vengeful leader, roared with laughter. Rick didn't hear them. He'd been knocked cold. Even before the sucker punch by the tree, the debilitating pain had him near paralysis. Now he lay in the open, directly exposed to the heat of the afternoon sun. The boys scampered over the fence and ran away.

For hours Rick lay where he fell. He was hidden from the street by parked cars. He lay in front of Wallace and Lydia Baker's home, friendly octogenarians, who employed him off and on but they seldom ventured out. He was found by the one person who never had him far from her thoughts.

Ann Stanton had gone by Rick's apartment. When he hadn't arrived home by six she went in search for her son. She made phone calls to the people on his daily calendar. Beatrice informed her he'd been at her house earlier. Ann set out on foot to scour every block between his apartment and the Morgan residence. She found him sitting in the grass holding his head, still confused, but his breathing was steady, and he recognized her.

"Mom," he said.

She helped him up in her strong, yet gentle hands. She examined him quickly, saw two unsightly scratches on his face weren't bleeding, brushed leaves from his hair, and took his hand. The top of her head barely came to his shoulders. Her demeanor remained calm, her face a granite bust of determination. Though bewildered as to why he was sitting on a street corner at that hour, she didn't display her anxieties to him. It was enough to deal with the reality of the moment. Since that other Saturday long ago, she lived her life one day at a time. Since that devastating morning, just having him had been enough.

During his public school days, Rick arose at dawn on weekends. Saturdays were not to be wasted. A day of boundless possibilities and unbridled energy in the life of a twelve-year-old would expand time as he and his friends spent endless hours at play. The bonds of home had begun to loosen while the ropes of responsibility were still stored away. At such an age, life is lived simply because it's there. It needs neither explanation nor analysis. It's a time replete with curiosity because it's short on experience; a vast sea of days filled with wonder because it is wonderful.

Rick jumped into the same pair of blue jeans he'd been wearing for a week and stumbled down the hallway past the bedroom his sisters shared, pulling on a T-shirt while on the move. He found his mother in the kitchen, hot breakfast sizzling, and he spied a stack of cinnamon rolls on the counter. He poured himself a glass of orange juice which he proceeded to down between bites of pastry.

"Bye, Mom."

"You know, I was fixing this bacon for the girls, but then I remembered how late they like to sleep. Your dad's already gone. I guess I'll have to give it all to Skippy."

Rick reached for a paper towel to use as a napkin. He blinked his gleaming blue eyes in thought. "I know what you're doing, Mom," he said with an inflection of uncomplicated honesty that makes a parent smile.

"I'm sure I don't know what you mean," Ann Stanton said. Rick refilled his glass while she turned the bacon.

"It's called reverse psychology."

"My, that's a big word."

"It's two words."

"Well, I hope it was okay to do that, whatever it was."

Rick took a drink and pulled a chair up to the table. "It's okay, Mom. You do it all the time anyway, 'specially when you think I'm going to run out the door."

"Hmmm," she said with a proud gaze upon her son, "so maybe you have time to have some bacon, or should I give it to the dog?"

Rick put down his glass and looked directly at his mother. "I've got time, Mom. That sure smells good… and some eggs."

By the time he left the house he had on a clean T-shirt and jeans to go along with a hearty breakfast. The crisp morning air met the warming rays of a rising sun as Rick broke into an easy trot for the two-block trek to the Masters' back yard. He called to Danny Trotman who had emerged from his house. Rick and his friends had little use for clocks, but everyone arrived right on time. Six boys and Adam Masters' older sister, Donna, called the Saturday morning meeting to order as they surrounded the well-used trampoline.

Benny and Paul climbed aboard first as they always did. They were slightly bigger and could jump fractionally higher than their classmates. They spent all of thirty seconds warming up before they propelled each other high above the roof line with their staggered jumps. They flew spread eagle high into the air, descended with heads down, landed with split-second suicides of tucked heads, then giggled with carefree abandon as they strove once again to achieve altitude.

Donna took her turn and bounced through a series of demure seat landings and lazy back flips.

Adam and Rick took their first rotation. They rocked back and forth across each other with alternating front and back landings. Then, they tried to propel each other to new heights with well-timed counter jumps. The maximum ascension for all of them was about a half-body length above the roof's eaves. The vertical power in their ninety-pound bodies had upper limits.

"We need to extend a stick from the chimney over the tramp," declared Benny.

"I don't have nothing long enough for that," Adam quickly determined.

"That won't make you jump any higher," Rick said.

"It'll give us something to shoot for," Benny retorted.

"What for? We can't get near that high."

"I know what we can do," Paul said. "Let's set up that ladder and jump down from the roof."

"And do what?" Rick was incredulous. "Go fly off in the grass?"

"Whadda ya mean?" Benny and Paul asked in unison.

Rick thought his statement self-evident, but he proceeded to explain. "Well, if we jump from the roof, we'll hit the tramp at an angle. That means you won't go up. You'll fly off that way." He pointed to the back fence.

"That sounds like fun," said another voice in the group.

"No, no," Benny shouted. "We should run off the roof, you know, up and out, and come down straight on the tramp." He beamed. "We'll fly to the top of the chimney for sure."

Everyone surrounded Adam except Rick. "Let's set up the ladder, okay?"

"I don't know." Adam hesitated.

"Yeah, one time for everyone, just to check it out."

"Don't do it," Donna admonished as the boys surrounded the heavy wooden ladder from where it lay in the grass and began to raise it like the

143

flagpole at Iwo Jima. "Mom," she cried out, but Mr. and Mrs. Masters had left on errands.

Benny's shoes touched the asphalt shingles first, and he stared at the tramp from his new perch. All eyes were on him now. Everyone was more than willing to let him have the honor of going first. Even his best friend Paul, watched his every move in eager silence from the best vantage point of all at the top of the ladder.

Benny swallowed, took two steps up the roof, focused all of his attention on the center of the tramp, and took off. His speed and distance calculations were perfect. His body flew out over the tramp and hung for an instant in mid-air. His feet impacted the tramp just short of dead center. His forward momentum carried his body toward the edge. Another few inches adrift and he would have landed in the yard. But when he came down, his heels hit the last square inch of the landing surface, his toes dangled across the springs, he recoiled back toward the center of the tramp, and bounced around in a circle like there was nothing to it.

A cheer rose from the lungs of his friends, a round of adulation filled with absolute astonishment. In that instant, Benny achieved the pinnacle of neighborhood stardom. The event catapulted his prestige, a rather lucky outcome that nevertheless amped his reputation for the rest of his public school days, a feather in his cap that would never fade. Benny caught his breath and soaked it all in.

Other boys scampered up the ladder already arguing who would go next. Paul won the slot and made a three-step takeoff. His trajectory decidedly overshot the target. He hit the far edge of the tramp, flailed the air as he flew ten feet into the yard, did a belly flop in the grass, skinned his hands, and came up with an agonized grin that crinkled his face, ready to go again.

Next, Adam stood at the roof's edge staring at the concrete patio below that separated him from the tramp. He backed up the roof, ran, and jumped with all his strength, and repeated Paul's performance. He trudged back to the tramp wiping both hands on his jeans, a dejected look of pain and humiliation etched on his face.

Rick took the position. He wasn't afraid of the jump, and had every intention of landing on the tramp and remaining. He could see that he didn't have to jump high. He was high enough already. The key was to jump forward only as far as was needed to reach the center of the tramp. It was one, two steps then jump, same as a basketball lay-up. He made his short run as everyone watched in horrified disbelief.

Rick's takeoff step was an inch too long. His toes hit just beyond the roof line. The gutter at the eave obscured the fine demarcation of the actual roof and gave way when his weight hit, offering no support. His forward thrust lacked any power as he sprang. His body fell away, crashing onto the concrete deck below. It was a ten-foot drop that might as well have been fifty. Rick landed on his head and shoulder. An ugly splat reverberated across the yard as though someone had whacked a body of water with a large, flat paddle. Rick didn't move. Donna screamed. The other boys stood about, wide-eyed, immobile with shock.

Donna gathered herself and rushed to his side. "Call 911," she commanded. True terror strained her voice when she saw the blood.

Adam ran for the back door. The others circled the grotesque form, a lump of little boy, his arms thrust backward, fingers of his right hand stuck straight into the air. He hadn't even a split second to break his fall.

"Let's turn him over," Benny said.

"Don't touch him," Donna demanded.

"He's bleeding. You can't just let him bleed."

Donna yelled, "Get me some towels—NOW." A second passed. None of the boys moved. She sprang for the house herself. "Don't touch him."

By the time the ambulance arrived Rick's bleeding had stopped. Donna had managed to work a towel under his head, but no one thought it mattered. He hadn't moved. He hadn't moaned or coughed or done anything.

EMS personnel worked on Rick for ten minutes before they lifted him up on a gurney and slid him into the back of the ambulance. Adults were now at the house. The backyard gate was opened. The ambulance pulled away quickly in a strobe of pulsating lights. Everyone stood in silence looking down the street for several minutes well after the ambulance had sped away.

The phone rang incessantly at the Stanton home. A parade of neighbors banged on the door. Ann rushed to the hospital in a carpool of concerned friends. Michael Stanton was contacted by cell phone, a putter in his hand on the eighth green of the municipal golf course. An emergency had arisen. He needed to go to the hospital. He floored his golf cart across active fairways and tee boxes in a beeline to the clubhouse and arrived at the hospital shortly after his wife.

An excruciating forty-five minute wait followed. When the doctor finally appeared he told them more about their son's prognosis by his demeanor than mere words could ever convey. The worry in his eyes was unmistakable, his despondent step revealing. He ushered the Stantons into a private corner and sat with them. The doctor kept his eyes up, catching their terrified expressions even as he gazed past them.

"He has a concussion. He's on support to make it easier for his body to deal with this period." The doctor took a deep breath and readjusted his gaze. "He has some deep facial lacerations. The critical period is the next two to three days."

"I want to see him," Ann said.

"You can look in on him, but only for a moment. He's in the best of hands and getting the best of care. We just have to give injuries like these some time."

"Time for what?" Ann insisted.

The doctor stood, pursed his lips, and swallowed. "Time to determine the full extent of his injuries."

Now the doctor had said what he came to say. He turned the next critical hours over to the divine hands of God. The Almighty would place a healing hand on their comatose child or bear him gently back to heaven. He left the grief-stricken parents without another word.

A few minutes later, a nurse led the Stantons to Rick's ICU bed. The sight was difficult even for Michael to take. Flashing monitors lined the head of the bed. Tubes ran from everywhere across his prostrate body. His head was wrapped. Cotton pads covered his eyes. Only the familiar nose and mouth were visible.

Grief and fear consumed Ann as she squeezed her husband's arm with one hand and the bedrail with the other. "What's happened to my beautiful little boy?"

The blast of a car horn jolted her back to the task at hand. Arm in arm, Ann walked with her darling boy as she helped him to his apartment. She remained at Rick's side throughout the weekend. Rick tossed through hours of fitful sleep that alternated with intense interludes of commode-hugging vomiting. She was there through it all to pat his hand and hold his head. Rick's reaction to Beatrice Morgan's revelation brought on a spike in blood pressure and his headache began. The slap in the face by the pine branch exacerbated the migraine, and by time he was well enough to eat and go back to work, it was Monday.

CHAPTER EIGHTEEN

AGAIN, ANN STANTON WAS AT RICK'S SIDE, and with him she would remain until he was back on his feet. Before Rick's boyhood injury, she'd been a successful real estate agent. She was elegant and efficient, a top producer who served on numerous Realtor committees. Two weeks after Rick came home from the hospital, and it became clear he was going to need untold hours of care she quit her real estate career and came home for her son.

With unyielding determination, she got Rick back into the public schools to learn with children his own age, even though he progressed at a slower pace. She taught him how to read again. They labored endless hours that he might speak distinctly. They worked on words used in everyday conversation and practiced for months how to pronounce common words correctly.

As time passed and his mind adapted, she encouraged him to explore the new and different found within the pages of books. Rick learned from books even though he couldn't understand every word. Whenever frustrations surfaced, she backed off only to revisit the task at a later date, when she encouraged him to tackle the subject again.

Ann Stanton was the youngest of six children, doted on by four older brothers, a prom queen and cheerleader. She met Michael, her future husband, at the University of Oklahoma. She was twenty-four when she gave birth to Rick, her eldest child, happy and healthy, another blessing among many bestowed upon her and her family, the good fortune of an assiduous work ethic and genetic providence. Within a few years two daughters joined the family. Ann fulfilled her role as wife and mother with a steady devotion to family and involvement in the community.

Ann was thirty-six when Rick fell from the neighbor's roof. On that day she lost the joy that filled her soul. Though the shock and grieving over the accident soon ended, the sadness never did. Within days, her life turned upside-down. She rearranged her schedule forever. Her days working outside the home were over; her days of community activities resigned to the past. Though the future would hold days of praise and applause, even satisfaction, the laughter in her life had been stolen. She faced endless hours of toil to rehabilitate a previously perfect child who, at the very least she prayed, would be able to cope and manage in the world. She faced an all-consuming challenge, and a grim reality set in, a reality that told her that her work would never end, not until she took her final breath.

"Mom," Rick said over a bowl of Cheerios, "I sure am glad you're here."

"So am I," she replied as she buttered them each a slice of toast.

"I was really sick, huh?"

Ann nodded. "Yes, you were." She never elaborated on his difficulties with him or anyone except his doctors.

"I'm feeling better now."

"I'm glad to hear that, dear."

"Mom, did you know that the hospital is trying to take everyone's house?"

"No, whose house?"

"The people I work for who live in the big, old houses. The hospital wants them all to move. That don't seem right to me 'cause I haven't heard nobody say they want to move."

"I hadn't heard about that."

"Well, it's true, Mom. Mr. Holmes got a piece of paper in the mail, and he almost fell off his feet when he read it. And Mrs. Morgan wanted me to help her move a bunch of stuff she didn't want to move in the first place, 'cause she's for sure that she's got to move."

"You want me to find out what it's all about?"

"Sure thing. I don't like it. I don't like it at all." Rick thought for a moment, then added, "I'm going to stop it one way or the other."

"What do you plan to do?" Ann asked, knowing full well he would need her help to formulate a plan.

"Well, I think I should go see everyone and see if they got the piece of paper . . . and see if they don't like it either."

Ann's eyes lit up, and she smiled to herself. "That's exactly what I would do, too. You can take around a form for them to sign if they don't want to move. It's another piece of paper called a petition."

"Can I start now?"

"Why don't you finish what you're eating and go take a shower. I'll get your petition ready."

"Sure thing."

Once alone in the room, Ann went to the phone. She had little contact nowadays with people she had worked with at her real estate office. The manager there had retired several years earlier. The elected officers she'd served with on the Board of Realtors had been replaced long ago. But she knew a woman named Beth Dinkle from the city's business task force. She might still be at city hall and know something about this particular condemnation proceeding. Ann made the call and asked around.

After several transfers, Beth Dinkle came on the line, and Ann reintroduced herself.

"Are you familiar with the condemnation application initiated by St. Anthony's on the neighborhood just south of downtown? It's an area known as Kessler Park?"

"No, I'm not," Beth said.

"That's quite an historic area. It has eighty to ninety foot trees. The neighborhood is well over a hundred years old. I can't imagine any group would be granted the right to demolish an area like that,"

Ann said, the incredulousness in her voice pressing for information.

"I know the area you're talking about," Beth replied, fully in agreement. "The hospital wouldn't be allowed to redevelop the neighborhood if it's been designated as an historic area, but it would require such a designation to prevent it. So, if, as you say, a condemnation proceeding is already in the works, I'd say the hospital has already done their homework on that point."

"You mean the city would entertain the destruction of a neighborhood like that?"

"It's possible."

Ann was startled by the acquiescent tone that came through the phone. "How is that remotely possible? Some families have lived there for generations. Others have spent small fortunes restoring those houses."

"Well, the bottom line is that the city council is not going to buck the big employers in the city. That's been my experience anyway." A hint of apology laced Beth's words. "Whenever the university or the airport wants more land, they get it."

"But the hospital---how could they possibly justify a claim for more land? There's vacant land around them now and plenty of run-down retail strips they could buy up before they needed to kick elderly people out of their homes," Ann said, her voice rising.

"I'm just telling you what I've seen happen before. In all likelihood the hospital doesn't need the land now. They might not even have a use in mind. It could be that they want to start the process now so they can get the land at cheaper prices than they would have to pay in the future."

Ann squeezed the phone receiver and wished she had the strength to break it in two just to release a sudden surge of pent-up anger. She forced herself to count to ten while a long, uncomfortable silence settled in the line.

"Are you still there?" Beth finally said.

"Yes, I'm here. I just have a hard time believing this sort of playing with people's lives takes place when there's no pressing community need."

"Sorry I couldn't give you better news. I'd be happy to check into it and get back to you about the application."

"I'd appreciate that, Beth." And with that, Ann hung up.

A few minutes later Rick emerged from his bedroom in a new pair of stiff blue jeans, an olive and blue plaid shirt, and his same hiking-style work boots. "I thought I'd better dress up to go knocking doors."

"You did the right thing. I think you look wonderful."

"Thanks, Mom."

She handed him a clipboard with several sheets of lined paper, each headed with the words

SAVE KESSLER PARK PETITION.

"So I should get everyone to sign these papers?"

"Yes, as many as you can. Each person should write their name one time, one on each line. Here are some extra pens in case one quits working."

"I'll keep those nice people from having to move when they don't want to," Rick said in a determined tone and headed for the door. But then, with his hand on the door knob, he paused, turned to face his mother, and with an inflection of doubt asked for the reassurance he sometimes sought. "Mom, can I really help my friends?"

"Yes dear, you can. You most certainly can."

CHAPTER NINETEEN

RICK STEPPED FROM HIS DOOR, clipboard in hand. He took a deep breath of fresh morning air, his mind alert, filled with purpose. The seriousness of his weekend ordeal never entered his thinking. He had a personal assignment to save a special neighborhood, and the crisp, sweet smell of morning invigorated his mission.

He strode with plodding steps from his apartment door to the moss-encrusted, cement columns that stood either side of Ashford Street, crumbling monuments that hailed a faded welcome to the west entrance of the neighborhood. Etched in tarnished bronze on each column, eight feet high in all capital letters, were the words KESSLER PARK. Extending out, down the street from each column, were the remains of a red brick fence now crumbling and obscure in a tangle of overgrown vines and fallen limbs.

Rick stopped at the first address on the block and looked closely at the house. He couldn't recall if he knew the occupants, all the more reason to knock on the door and make their acquaintance. He walked up the undulant sidewalk, across a splintered porch, and let the brass knocker set in the door fall twice with metallic clanks against the plate. The door moved back, and a woman in a house dress of faded prints appeared in the opening. Her face was a morass of winkles, but clear, friendly eyes peered back at him behind fleshy eyelids.

"Good morning, ma'am, my name is Rick Stanton, and I live just up the street. I bet you got one of those con-dem-naton notices from the city, and, well, I have a paper here for folks to sign that says you don't want to sell---and you shouldn't have to."

At first, the woman watched Rick and his nervous manner with a polite forbearance borne of countless propositions from cookie-selling Girl Scouts. But when she realized he was circulating a petition, she grabbed her chin, and all she said was "My, oh my."

"Would you like to read my paper, ma'am?"

She turned back into the house. "Louis, come here."

A minute later a short fellow, bald and toothless, appeared in the doorway. He wore blue/green striped suspenders over a white T-shirt that didn't cover his belly, and cocked his head, looked up at Rick, and squinted into the sun's morning glare.

Rick swallowed and picked up in the middle of his speech. "Good morning, sir, I bet you got one of those con-dem-naton notices from the city---"

"Sure we'll sign that, young man," the old boy interrupted as he pushed back the door and stepped onto the porch. He took the clipboard from Rick without another word, and beamed a broad smile of pink gums when he saw the blank paper. "We're going to be the first, mother." He swirled the pen in an exaggerated scrawl that took up three lines. "Anyone ought to be able to read that." He handed the pen and board over to his wife. "You're doing a fine thing, young man, a fine thing. Nobody should be forced to move from their house."

Rick could only stare. He didn't know anyone would be so appreciative, but felt a warm glow of satisfaction from the man's compliment.

"That's a fine thing," the fellow said again. "Come back and see me when you get signatures on all of those pages."

"Sure, mister." Rick studied the writing and tried to pronounce the names.

The old fellow jumped in again. "Hilker— we're Louis and Judith Hilker."

After the first stop, Rick lost all perception of time. Only a pang in his stomach prompted him to check his watch. At half past two he headed for a burger shack. He placed an order and waited on a concrete seat under a metal umbrella. He had three pages of signatures. He counted them carefully, one by one. After he ate, he went straight to the Holmes' residence, put the sprinklers in the flower garden, and set them to run for thirty minutes. He got

Myron and Delores' signatures while he was there. He visited with Delores as she sat in her wheelchair, an open book spread across the blanket across her lap. He assured them he'd return the next day to tend other chores around their house.

He headed back to his apartment, eager to call his mother and tell her of his success in collecting signatures. The elation that lifted each step dissolved into inert horror as he passed the community garden at Linden and Poplar. An entire patch of bluebonnets had been torn from the ground, broken and cast about the lot. He shook his head and looked again. The destruction was undeniable. He was struck sick with disbelief.

Twenty feet of flowers had been uprooted and strewn about. Other flowers had been trampled in the destruction, but the bluebonnets had been the target of the crime. He was unable to fathom why anyone would do such a thing. Sadness quickly overcame his initial shock and he fell on his knees in the dirt. Gently, he handled the broken stalks around him.

He too had been broken, this fact he knew, and had known for years. After the accident, when he was again able to form thoughts and communicate, again aware of his surroundings, Rick understood he'd been put back together. For that reason, he dedicated himself to repair and nurture things no matter how old or outdated they were. The destroyed bluebonnets made his powerful body ache because, because no matter what he might do, he knew they could never be fixed.

That should never happen again. The old city lot, now a neighborhood park, was so vulnerable. He wanted to stand guard and protect the park day and night, but knew that was impossible. And yet, anyone could come along and damage the elm saplings or undeveloped hedges or the flowers. The beautiful array of flowers was most at the mercy of cruel and idle hands.

It may well have been an act by the people who were trying to steal the homes of his elderly friends, an attempt to scare neighborhood residents. Now he had another duty. He must protect the garden even as he mounted a coordinated resistance to the city's official notice.

Five blocks later, Rick walked into Redmond's hardware store. He could buy whatever he needed with his credit card, but knew a fence wasn't the way to go. A fence would keep people out. The park and garden was for everyone to use and enjoy. He needed an idea to protect the garden without restricting people's ability to come and go. Rick wandered aimlessly through the aisles looking for anything to spark an idea.

"May I help you?"

Rick pulled his attention from the jumble of thoughts swirling in his mind and focused on a young woman in a green vest who waited for him to speak. After a long pause, he said in a tone of bewilderment, "I don't know what I'm looking for."

Her brown eyes brightened with a calming assurance. "That's why I'm here. What kind of project are you working on?"

Rick explained his dilemma, speaking rapidly with the passion of injury. "I know it was people who did it, but I don't know how to protect the park."

Throughout his story, she focused on his face, and listened to it all. He felt better when he finished just by the way she listened. Her eyes were most striking, insightful, soothing. He observed her patient attention as though he was the only customer in the store, and he noticed her round, dimpled cheeks. Rick could tell from her attention she would do her best to help him. Her attentive patience exceeded a clerk's usual assistance regarding a purchase. Her entire demeanor put him at ease. "You got anything that would help?" he said in an exasperated finish to his tale.

She pulled her gaze from his face and looked each way up the aisles. "Well, we have electric fences to keep pets in their yards, but that wouldn't deter a person." She glanced back at Rick, her sincere words complete evidence she had adopted his problem as her own. "We have outdoor lights, but that wouldn't stop anybody either. Let's see." She led the way to the back of the store, obviously deep in thought.

"I've got an idea." Her eyes sparkled. "Follow me." She led him to a far corner and began thumbing through catalog pages that hung from a shelf. "These are the poles we carry. We have plastic and aluminum of various lengths." She turned and gazed into his eyes. "I was just thinking. There's nothing a person who's up to no good hates more than a camera. Now we don't carry cameras, but who says they have to be real." But her suggestion had lost him. Without missing a beat, she slowed her delivery and explained.

"You could mount fake cameras that move back and forth on the poles. Let me show you." She pushed a portable ladder against a shelf and brought down some little motors. "These are called actuators. They can automatically move fake cameras back and forth at the top of a pole. Everyone would think they were being watched, but only a dishonest person would worry about that."

On the ladder she was now at his eye level and their gazes lingered. She handed him an actuator and he took it without looking. He saw her lips move, but forgot what she was saying. He perceived the weight of a silence even as he enjoyed the length of the moment. He was enamored by her presence, alarmed by a twinge of delightful terror, aware in some way his interest came from more than the softness of her features and her helpful attention. He soaked it all in, unconcerned as to the reason for its occurrence, unable to utter a sound even if he had wanted.

She swallowed and lowered her eyes as though she had to see each step in her descent. He reached for her arm and helped her down the ladder. "Oh, thank you," she said.

"You're welcome." Rick took a deep breath. "I like that idea. I think four poles would be enough. So I'll need four of these things, right?"

"Yes, four."

"I'll have to get someone to help me. I'll come back tomorrow and pick them up."

"I can have everything in the back ready for you. What name should I put on them?"

"My name? I'm Rick. . . Rick Stanton."

"I'm Lena."

"Oh," was all he could say.

She paused, her brown eyes widened, waiting it seemed, should he have another question.

But any words he might have spoken were caught in his throat.

"I'll have your ticket at the register. I have to get back to the front now." She headed down the aisle, hesitated for an instant, and turned back. "Nice to meet you, Rick," she said, then she was gone.

CHAPTER TWENTY

THE CURIOUS ENCOUNTER with the sales lady remained fixed in his mind, as was the carnage at the neighborhood garden. Still, Rick remained anxious to tell his mother of his success collecting signatures. In the few hours he knocked doors, he had created a tsunamic reaction among the elderly residents. No excuse now seemed sufficient to remain passive and accept the outrageous intrusion by the hospital without mounting a vigorous opposition. If a friendly lad with nothing to gain was willing to mount a protest on their behalf, then it dawned on folks they should unite in a common defense.

Rick hurried home and called his mom. His thoughts were a tangle of strange feelings, something more than the satisfaction of a job well done. He couldn't get the vision of the young woman at the hardware store from his mind. His stomach felt queasy. Why her? He didn't even know her. Other people had helped him in the past and talked to him nicely, and he hadn't had this sort of inner glow, this disturbing queasiness.

When he touched her arm as she descended the ladder, it gave him the strangest sensation. He wanted to say something right then, but nothing came from his lips. He wanted to hold her arm, even let her hand sit in the curl of his fingers, but she had stepped aside. Though they had talked for just a few minutes, he felt deserted when she walked away. He couldn't remember her name. Did she think he was someone else? He couldn't understand what she did, and yet, she had cast a spell over him that drenched him in a tingle of pure delight.

He reached his mother on the phone. She listened patiently as he gushed through the events of his day. He talked about getting people to sign his petition with the enthusiasm of a boy finally getting a kite in the air, and his voice sank, laced with despair as he spoke about the vandalism in the community garden.

Ann listened without comment. She knew he went through swells of emotion on nearly every topic. His view of the world was an untarnished testimony of simple yes and no, and her eyes grew moist as she listened. He was articulate and insightful. It mattered not to her that her twenty-eight-year-old son told his stories with the breathless exuberance of a seven-year-old.

"Yes, your dad can bring the truck over," she said as Rick concluded in a rush of words.

"When?"

"I'm not sure. He's not here now. But I have something to tell you. Myron Holmes called. Everyone is excited about your petition drive, so they're having a community meeting tomorrow night at the Holmes' house. They want you to be there."

"Me?"

"Yes, you. Mr. Holmes said everyone he talked to definitely mentioned your name."

"Why me? I don't know anything about meetings."

"I don't know, dear, but I think it has to do with the fact you helped them see they have to join together if they want to save their neighborhood. I think you helped them realize they don't have to just sit and wait and let their houses be taken."

"I told you, Mom. Those folks like where they're at, and they shouldn't have to move if they don't want to."

"I know you did. So you should call Mr. Holmes now and let him know if you're going to be there."

"I'll be there if they want me. I'll call him now."

The neighborhood meeting was scheduled to begin at 7:15, but people began arriving at six. Myron gathered some men, and they moved Delores' special bed and support board from the dining room out to the back porch and brought in stacks of dusty plastic chairs once used when they held Bible studies on the lawn. Delores sat in her wheelchair greeting all arrivals with a beaming

166

smile, the best pain tonic she'd had in months. The kitchen bustled around pitchers of iced tea and Ritz crackers. Lydia Baker brought a tray of her famous, folded-bread triangles filled with a concoction of cheese and ham and, after instant consumption and enthusiastic praise, wished she had brought more.

A steady influx of neighbors filled the dining room, poured into the parlor, and spilled into the vestibule where people took seats on the staircase. Someone brought out folding chairs that quickly lined the veranda where pipes and cigars were lit and old acquaintances picked-up on long-overdue conversations. Crickets sang harmony with the voices as the sun descended below the canopy of giant oaks, and as dusk settled across the lawn, fireflies sprinkled the bushes out beyond the porch lights.

At the scheduled hour Myron stood in front of his fireplace and the massive mirror that dwarfed the mantel and called the meeting to order. The first floor lights were all turned on. The windows opened so everyone outside could hear. Rick stood by the side door into the dining room as Myron called for everyone's attention.

"Good evening, everyone. I see so many familiar faces. Many of you I haven't seen in awhile. Anyway, we have some serious business to discuss. But before we get started, we have a young fellow to thank for getting us to this point, and I want to be sure you all have met him. Rick, step in here where everyone can see you."

Polite clapping accompanied the turn of heads toward the doorway, but Rick instantly froze where he stood. The very sound of his name called in front of the large group pumped anxiety up from his toes like a geyser, a blush rose out of his collar. Rick stared down at his feet. He had attended because he'd been asked. Maybe, in the back of his mind, he understood his name would be mentioned, but he didn't know he'd be introduced. Being the center of attention, especially in front of so many people, scared him beyond reason, but nevertheless it did.

"He's the best carpenter around. Rick, step in here so everybody can see who you are."

Cecil Nance opened the screen door and motioned to Rick. "Just for a sec, Rick," Cecil said. "Some folks have never met you."

Rick took two short steps, enough to get him through the door. His shoulders were stiff, his body language strangely fearful. The applause sputtered as friendly smiles morphed into expressions of bewilderment and pity.

Myron quickly interceded. "I think Rick's just a bit overwhelmed by the attention, but we appreciate the petition drive you undertook on your own, Rick. We all appreciate you very much." As everyone settled back into their seats, Myron cleared his throat and looked about at the throng of humanity squeezed into his house. "Now the reason for our meeting. It seems like some big shots downtown want to tell everyone in this neighborhood what to do. The city, at the behest of the hospital, wants to demolish Kessler Park."

A rumble of protests flared through the house. The friendly neighborhood gathering quickly changed into a hoard of angry citizens with a single target of their ire---St. Anthony's Regional Medical Center. A chorus of blurted opinions filled the air.

"We ought to sue 'um."

"The hospital has to prove they need this land."

"Someone should write the attorney general."

The pressure valve of civility popped on the gathering's pent-up outrage. The sudden and heartfelt outburst provided a needed catharsis for everyone's suppressed doubts and fears. Myron raised his hand to bring calm even as he watched Ethel Barnes shake her tiny fist.

"Maybe we should hire an attorney to represent everyone in Kessler Park," Myron said when the voices died down. "We would each chip in to retain legal counsel."

A brief silence settled over the house, then someone asked, "How much would that cost?"

"I don't know yet, but we need professional help. Going it as a group would be a lot cheaper than going it alone."

"Mr. Holmes, may I make a comment?" Dan Beckerman stepped forward. He was a stocky man, easily the youngest person in the house other than Rick, no older than mid-fifties. He lived in the neighborhood and owned three majestic, two-stories with bevel-crowned chimneys and had turned them into multi-unit, walk-up rentals. He moved from where he stood along the dining room wall to stand beside Myron at the fireplace.

"I believe many of you know me. I'm Dan Beckerman, and I've lived at 918 Linden for nearly ten years. I agree with all of you that the notice from the city was shocking and insulting, but it's important to understand, the city is just beginning the process. We have plenty of time to get all the facts. I say we should. Who knows what the hospital is going to offer for our properties. It may be twice what the properties are worth on the open market."

"Wait a minute." Sherman Porter pushed his way through the front door and stood in the center of the parlor. "I don't care what they're offering." He glared at Beckerman. "I don't want to move."

"Well, okay, but listen," Beckerman said, "haven't any of you thought about being closer to grand children or great-grand children?" He turned and faced the other side of the room. "What about more money for medical bills? How about a house where it's easier to get around? Until you get all the facts how do you know this isn't the answer to some prayer?"

"An answer to your prayer maybe." Beatrice Morgan rose from the couch, her white hair shining like a halo beneath the chandelier, and pointed at Beckerman. "Nobody is going to pay us anything close to what we paid for our properties because the overall neighborhood is so old. My property taxes keep going down. That doesn't happen when values are increasing. It's people like you who cause so many eyesores on some of these streets that it ruins the neighborhood for the rest of us. Why don't you take care of those magnificent houses you bought? Wait—don't even answer that. I don't want to hear your excuses. But you're the last person around here to be telling the rest of us what to do with our property."

An eruption of applause filled the house, but Beckerman held his ground.

"Do you all really want to fight the hospital and the city?" he said. "Rather than trying to pick a fight, we should be making the most of this eventuality."

"There're the ones who picked the fight," came a voice from the top of the stairs.

Beckerman shook his head, sniffed hard, and tried to find room to maneuver. "I'm telling you, a legal firm is just going to take your money. If the hospital wants the land, the city council is going to go along with it. If we're going to organize, we need to do so to get the best possible deal we can, not to fight the inevitable." Beckerman looked about as daggers of loathing came at him from every face in the room. Otherwise the house fell silent, for all of five seconds, when Sherman dismissed Beckerman with a swat of his hand and launched a counter attack.

"I for one didn't come here to talk about how to make it easier for the city to steal my house. Did you?"

The chorus of no's was deafening.

"If you ask me, the hospital has their eye on Kessler Park because they think a neighborhood of old folks will just roll over and let them have it for a song." Sherman's voice built toward a crescendo. His face grew fierce as he led everyone through a line of thinking they found perfectly plausible and a balm to their wounded sensibilities.

"They don't need this land. No! Good heavens, there's plenty of open space further south. They want our beautiful trees and to be closer to the freeway. That's it, I'm telling you. They don't have any need right now. They just want it."

Indignant cries mixed with some choice profanity. Those in attendance bared their perceived ill-treatment as though it was the worst offense they had ever experienced in their protracted lives. Sherman wound them tight as a coiled spring and fanned their indignation. They shared a common bond. Each was being marginalized and exploited. They must stand together or perish alone.

No longer the center of attention, Rick watched the emotional brush fire with pride and growing bewilderment. He had never seen his elderly friends so animated. He understood that each and every one of them had been under a lot of stress, and this meeting was their first opportunity to air grievances. He was supportive of them and always would be. He hoped they could come up with a solid plan to save Kessler Park.

Ideas swirled in the air. A bee hive of conversations dissected every proposal that floated on the wind, and after a while a consensus seemed to emerge. As emotional flames cooled and the vocal volume diminished, Myron took the reins of the meeting once again.

"Okay, first of all we're going on a letter writing campaign to the city commissioners. Who wants to participate in that?" Almost everyone raised their hand. "Louis, would you make a list? We need to write letters to every councilman every day, and rotate the list so that every one of them hears from every one of us before this is over. Agreed?" The proposal carried unanimously.

"Second, we need to hire a high profile law firm to represent us. Agreed?" Everyone cried 'aye' and raised their hand. "I'll look into that and report back."

"Third, we need to picket the hospital. We can hire some younger folks to help us, but if you can walk, you need to be on the lines. We'll get the newspaper and the TV stations covering us, too. If the hospital plans to kick a bunch of seniors out of their homes, I think everyone in town should know." Myron couldn't help but grin as he concluded. "Agreed?" The affirmative shout was overwhelming. "Opposed?" The house fell silent, then erupted in a healing peal of laughter.

Kessler Park hadn't died; it had been reborn. A sleepy, stagnating urban neighborhood found a new life that only human love and resolve could provide. The battle had just begun, but the white flags were now locked away. If Kessler Park was to pass, it would do so in struggle, not acquiescence. If Kessler Park was to die, the conquerors would have to battle for their victory.

CHAPTER TWENTY-ONE

AS BUSY AS HE WAS, Brandon never forgot Jake. On several occasions, he called the house and made appointments, only to be stood up when he arrived. He knew he didn't need the ongoing hassle. The kid was easily a delinquent in the making without much hope of changing course. And yet, he couldn't shake the kid. The new school year had begun and he was curious what the Jake was up to. Maybe it was just in his genes to be a sucker for lost causes.

On a hunch, he stopped by the mall arcade. Jake was there. He'd graduated to a contraption the size of a small car, decked out to look like a fighter jet with all the dashboard avionics, switches, and sounds of the real thing. Brandon stepped beside him as Jake exited the game room.

"Well, imagine running into you," Brandon said.

Jake stopped, glared, and tensed like he'd been cornered.

"You can relax, you know. I'm not the principal."

Jake grunted even as a glint of amusement flickered in his eyes.

"You got a minute? I wanted to apologize for the other day."

"Yeah," Jake said.

Brandon figured he'd gotten to first base. A two-word response from Jake might mean he'd reached second.

They headed to the ice cream stand, then found a booth.

"It wasn't my intention to butt into how you get money. My dad was pretty strict with me about treating a dollar like it's worth something, because it is. If you have money in your pocket, I don't want to see you broke when you need something really important."

Jake remained quiet, but looked him in the eye. It appeared he was listening. "So, what's been going on at school?" Brandon asked.

"Same boring stuff that don't make no difference."

"I'm sure there's a lot going on at your school. There's probably something you like, even be good at, if you just look for it."

"Yeah, whatever."

"I'm serious. I bet you take shop. You like that, don't you?"

Jake rolled his eyes. "Making magazine racks ain't real challenging. They don't let us build anything really cool."

"Like what?"

"Well, like an entertainment center. That would be fun, and something a person could use."

"But that's something you'd like to do, right?" Brandon asked.

"I guess."

"I bet there are a lot of things around school you'd find interesting. That is, if you'd spend as much time looking for something worth your talent as you do dismissing it." Brandon made little circles in the air with his spoon as though the implication of his speech held a universal truth. "It pays to do the best you can. When you give things an honest effort, things can get quite interesting."

Jake remained silent.

"Listen, they hold drag races south of town on Saturday nights. Would you like to go to that?"

"Sure," Jake said.

"Tell your mom, and I'll pick you up at six. You need a ride now?"

"Yeah, that would be good. I should already be home by now.

- -

In the weeks that followed his meeting with Katherine Cramer, Brandon worked feverishly to sign up the properties of Kessler Park. With Cindy's help, he scanned original homeowner signatures into the computer, pasted them on the correct line of the Texas real estate contract with appropriate legal descriptions and purchase prices. For the time being, he left the date line blank.

He asked around what commercial properties were selling for along Sixth Avenue and what residential property values were nearby. He thought of completing deeds, filing fifty or so properties with the Hall of Records. He knew it wasn't the time for property tax bills to go out, but worried such filings might trigger a return notice back to the residents who hadn't actually sold anything. More than that, he realized he didn't want to pay the filing fees.

The sight of the bogus documents infused him with a sense of accomplishment, a self-induced illusion that he was actually in the real estate game though the documents were as worthless as Confederate currency. It was just a start, Brandon assured himself. His initial contact with homeowners would eventually lead to authentic transactions. Cindy was less than enthusiastic. She helped him only because he asked. More than once, she winced when she read over the reproductions, and she remained silent when he played for encouragement.

He procured a so-called 'investor list' and spent endless hours pitching by phone his 'sure-fire downtown Atherton development.' After hours of effort, he had a measly $21,400 on deposit in his property acquisition account and a truck load of let-me-think-it-overs and half-hearted maybes. The bulk of the funds he collected came from parents of college chums who knew him personally, liked his outgoing drive, and thought it a rather quaint notion to speculate on a real estate venture.

Brandon sent Katherine Cramer a letter thanking her for her time and called her once and they spoke briefly. She said she had submitted the proposal to her superiors. The matter would be taken up in the near future by the hospital board.

He began walking through the neighborhood in the evenings, introducing himself to homeowners he'd meet, getting acquainted on a more personal level. He liked talking to the burly, simple fellow he found working every day at a different house. It seemed he was the designated neighborhood handyman. One day he'd be replacing the broken planks on a porch, the next day painting the side of a house. Brandon would get his attention with a general comment about the quality of his work, then ply him for information about the residents. Always polite and generally informative, the big guy only spoke in generalities when it came to discussing his customer's future plans. The ole boy seemed content just being outdoors practicing his trade.

Brandon's cell phone rang.

"Hey, partner," Todd said. Brandon caught the cocksure tone.

"What's up?" Brandon wished he hadn't answered.

"I was knocking a few doors, trying to nail down more signatures, and I ran into something might be of interest."

"Yeah and."

"Some old dried-up bag-of-dust tells me there's a guy in the neighborhood passing around a petition. Well, I don't pay her no mind, but later I hear it again. This fella I'm talking to is all excited. He don't want to hear nothing I have to say, so I ask what all the fuss is all about. He shows me an official notice he got from the city."

"Notice?"

"Partner, if my guess is right, someone has made an end run on you or is trying to beat you to the punch."

"What are you talking about?" Brandon listened intently now.

"The old fella showed me a condemnation notice," Todd said. "The city is in the process of taking this land for itself."

"What?"

"Yep—I saw it, official as hell. They already got a hearing scheduled early next month."

"That can't be."

"Yeah, it can," Todd said. "That's why I'm calling. I thought you'd want to know."

"Damn!" A debilitating hollowness invaded his guts. "The city? I don't get it. Why would the city need that land?"

"I don't think they do. The city just issued the notice. I read the whole thing. Another party is involved."

"Who?" An interminable wait followed.

"The hospital . . . the hospital's in on this, too."

Brandon snapped his cell phone shut and fell into a chair. A wave of disbelief rolled over him like a smothering blanket. Heat radiated from his face. For a minute, struck immobile by the sucker punch of treachery, he just sat and tried to breathe.

But it wasn't in his genes to take a reversal lying down no matter if it was a misunderstanding or outright deceit. He saw Katherine Cramer's face in his mind's eye as he pulled off his sports shirt and rummaged through his closet. She had to be at the bottom of whatever the city was doing. He grabbed a white shirt from a hanger and the first tie within reach. Katherine may have thought he would just slide away as an inconvenient memory, but he didn't play that way. She would tell him. She would answer one way or the other. She would explain why she had gone behind his back.

Brandon drove straight to the hospital. No time better than the present to make a traitor account for her duplicity. He fought to keep his cool as he stepped into the reception area. Handle it just like another appointment. Maybe Katherine had an explanation for this turn of events. Maybe he was included in this change in strategy. But again, despite his innate inclination toward the positive, he knew this reasoning was folly, and he detested himself.

He walked past the receptionist.

"May I help you?"

"I'm expected."

"Wait. You can't---"

Her office door was open, and she was there. He walked right in with a set jaw, but his hands were down, his palms open. He tried to move casually, approach her desk with a professional bearing, but his heaving chest betrayed his agitation, and he felt like a school boy late to class.

Katherine Cramer's eyes widened when he strode in, but the rest of her calm exterior remained fixed. She rose, moved around her desk, and sat on the front of it, her hands on either side of her body lightly gripping the edge. She never broke eye contact. Her gaze became increasingly pointed down the bridge of her nose.

"What do you want?"

For a second Brandon could only glare. He actually didn't know where to start. The fact he brought her the deal now hardly seemed worth mentioning. That her guard was up was proof enough that she knew exactly why he was there. She had probably rehearsed exactly what she was going to say to get rid of him and didn't even perceive his unannounced presence blatant enough to call security.

"I thought we had a deal?"

She let his words hang in the air. Much better to remain quiet and let any power in his question die of stagnation than to actually reply. Finally she spoke, but not to answer him.

"Mr. Evans, I work for the hospital. We have procedures around here we're required to follow."

"Meaning?"

"It's my job to explore every possibility for the hospital."

"You didn't even have the courtesy to call me." His heavy breathing slowed. Though his charm was worthless in this environment, he would force a concession on some point by the sheer power of his will. "You're making a big mistake. You'll never get all of those properties free and clear without working through me. Some of those properties are held in trust. The city's action can't help you with that." He was bluffing, but it was the first thought that came to mind.

An unmistakable flicker of doubt crossed her face, and she dropped her eyes for an instant. Her gaze refocused, a sudden ferocity captured her expression, and when she spoke, she sounded like someone else.

"I tried to reach you at The Heritage Group. They've never heard of you. When I compared the number on your card with the one in the phone book, guess what? They're different." She had a way of letting the end of her sentences hang like a piano on a kite string. "I don't really know who you are, and I have a suspicion everything you've told me is a fabrication."

"I can explain." His chest constricted. "I brought you this deal because I knew the hospital would be the best end user for the land. I thought you appreciated my effort. You were going to get the property in the end. You said yourself the hospital didn't have any immediate plans for the property."

Katherine Cramer took another close look at him, then returned to the chair behind her desk. She pursed her lips. Her gaze carried beyond his shoulder. A weary expression replaced her hard countenance, and he knew she had won.

"As I said, I work for the hospital. If you were really on top of this acquisition, you would have made the property purchases and transferred the deeds into your name. You didn't. We checked. It's in the hospital's interest to get the land as quickly as possible and at the lowest possible cost."

She cut to the essence of every point. She was as stingy with verbiage as she was with cordiality. She gave him no openings to explore, no common ground to discuss. She was what? Early forties? And gorgeous for that age. With her caustic heart, how ugly would she be in a few short years? He felt hollow, helpless, and impotent.

"Now if you'll excuse me, I have to get back to work." She waited for him to turn. Desperately he wanted to say something, but he knew their conversation was over. He took a huge breath and stepped for the door.

"And Mr. Evans don't call, don't write. We have nothing further to discuss."

CHAPTER TWENTY-TWO

BRANDON FELT FAINT as he returned to his car. His mouth was dry, his heart numb. He had been double-crossed and hadn't seen it coming. He had to think things through and regroup.

For the umpteenth time in his young life Brandon wanted to see the one person who could soothe his soul and would let him tell how he'd been stabbed in the back. He drove straight to Cindy's apartment. Though she could do nothing for his dashed fortunes, she would comfort his ego and stroke his wounded pride.

Cindy answered the door with a shoe in one hand, her mobile phone in the other. She rolled her eyes when she saw him, ushered him in with a nod, and finished her call while standing in the doorway.

"Listen, I need to go," she said. "We can talk about this tomorrow. Bye."

"Who was that?"

"Marilyn. We work together. Can't you ever call? Just once, you know, out of courtesy."

"I thought you'd be glad to see me."

"I just got home. I'm tired. I've had a busy day. If you want to go dummying up more documents, we're going to have to do it some other time."

Brandon just stared. The defeat he'd suffered produced a dejected expression that said more than words could ever tell.

Cindy looked at him for a moment, and within seconds her eyes narrowed. "It's over, isn't it?" Contempt, not commiseration coated her words. "All that work... you barely got started. Did you even have a chance in hell of making it work? I doubt it. You, you big shot blabber mouth. Where's my money?" She threw the shoe at him and missed. She sucked in a huge breath and ran at him. He caught her shoulders, but her free hands beat on his chest.

"You dreamer, you liar. Why don't you leave me alone?" She yanked herself from his grasp. She glared at him, caught her breath, then marched to the dinette table, and ripped open a pack of cigarettes. She dropped in a chair and, when she looked back at him, Brandon knew she didn't have listening on her mind.

"They're talking about closing my store in the mall." Cindy drew a deep drag and blew out a cloud in front of her face. "Just like that, probably going from six stores down to three. I'll be out of a job for I don't know how long, and I'm still playing nursemaid to a twenty-four-year-old child who still hasn't even decided if he wants to be an astronaut or a fireman." She raised her hands, palms up, in utter exasperation.

"I'm sorry, Cindy. You've been super sweet to me, I know. I'll make it all up to you. I promise."

"Dammit, Brandon, there's only one thing I want you to do—just grow up, will you? I mean, how long have I known you? Years—and you're dealing with people like you did in the tenth grade."

"Maybe I better go."

"No, don't you dare go. You came over her for a reason. You wanted me to listen to how you were deceived and mistreated and all that. I know why you came. I've heard it all before. Well, I've got some things dragging me down now, so you can just stay." Cindy ground her cigarette out hard with her thumb. "Either that or don't ever come back."

"I'll stay," he uttered two of the most contritely spoken words he'd ever spoken.

But she wasn't through. Cindy stood, clasp her hands violently, then wrung them fiercely as she focused her tirade at him. "I'll get another job—one that pays real money. You won't see me chasing anymore daydreams. Good God, that crap's for children. Why did I ever listen to you?"

"You're just upset because of your job."

She dropped her hands to her side "Brandon, if I lose my job, it certainly won't help, but I'm talking about you. I'm so disappointed. You've got the smarts, you've got the looks. Why can't you just be straight with people? You have so much to work with, and all you do is cut corners."

"I thought I had a good idea."

"Whatever, Brandon. Careers aren't built on hitting the lottery. Only fools think that's going to happen. You have to work at something day-after-day to build it into something valuable, something worth bragging about."

He had no comeback to the truth in her rage. He was struck mute, and something like a conscience scraped inside his gut.

"What happened to all the money you were going to make in the stock market?"

He was unable to respond with a convincing answer and hung his head.

"Tell me, Brandon. Why have we been talking about real estate lately, and I haven't heard a word about the stock market?"

"I left that office."

Cindy's rage subsided, and she looked at him as something to be loathed as well as pitied. She sat back down in her chair beside her ashtray. "Aren't you going to do anything serious with your college degree?"

"I meant to."

Cindy took the jewelry off her wrists and lit another cigarette. "Well, I guess now would be a good time to make that move, 'cause I can't help you out anymore. Certainly not now, and I'd like to get my money back."

"I'll get it back to you."

"Yeah, until you get a real job, you probably shouldn't stop by anymore either. I think I've been making it too easy for you to be irresponsible, helping you chase cockeyed dreams at the end of the rainbow." Her voice cracked ever so slightly. "I can't chase anymore rainbows, Brandon."

He stood and began to walk her way. "I'm sorry. It's all my fault."

"No, don't," she said as she put up her hand to stop his approach. "Please, just go now."

He stood in place for a few moments longer.

"Please, just go."

CHAPTER TWENTY-THREE

THE MEETING AT McLINTY'S Restaurant had been productive, not to mention relaxing, all blended together over a leisurely meal. The rush of the lunch crowd had dispersed. They took a table in the back, quiet and secluded. Katherine Cramer's very presence made the hour enjoyable. A power broker in her own right, Katherine projected a sense of mystery all wrapped in a package of captivating elegance. Darrin Riley knew she eventually wanted to run the hospital and be appointed to the Western Heritage Museum's board of directors. Such promotions would satisfy her lofty aspirations for a year or two.

They had had an instant meeting of the minds. A condemnation proceeding for the purpose of exercising eminent domain provided the most expeditious path to secure the Kessler Park land for the hospital at a reasonable cost. It would score her significant credit. She was adamant about acquiring the land. She indicated she'd do whatever it took to insure the hospital gained control of the property.

Riley returned to city hall emboldened by their conversation. Accomplishing her interests wouldn't be easy, but he relished the challenge. Their leisurely lunch hammered down two points—the hospital wanted the Kessler Park land now that it was known to be for sale, and the hospital would pay whatever it took to get it.

Riley assured her a condemnation proceeding was the way to go. The city government would do the heavy lifting, and the neighborhood would be acquired all in one chunk, all at one time.

Two overriding principles guided Riley's professional existence. Would his efforts keep the city council members happy, and would his efforts put factions of the community in his debt? Political power was his motivation. A chance meeting with a future mayor had brought him the good fortune no amount of education or professional connections could have achieved. Now, at age thirty-three, he was already in the job he wanted for the rest of his life.

He would leave the front page pictures and sensational stories to the egomaniacs who paid dearly with their time and anxieties to coddle public adulation. Beyond that, Riley knew how to marginalize those who attached alphabets behind their names in the wretched hope their degrees would bring them the recognition they so desperately sought. He didn't need any of that. He already had his fingers on the pulse of the city. How insignificant is fleeting recognition when you already command the pistons of power?

The current city council had basically been together for three years; only Councilman Arlen Roberts from District Three was new, having come aboard the previous June. They were all old hands at the city governance game. They gave preference to influential contributors and paid homage to large employers. Pet projects came next, especially those that ranked high on the publicity scale. Such projects included the opening of a senior center or installing lights on a neighborhood ball field. The councilmen traded votes like baseball cards. Things got done, politicians got re-elected.

Riley would run Katherine's request by the mayor and get the city attorney to start the paperwork. The request would be placed on the council calendar. Three separate public notices, as required by law, would be placed in the newspaper, and a public hearing scheduled before the planning and zoning board. But Riley could start lining up votes now.

Zoning issues were a local matter. In actual practice, since the U.S. Supreme Court's 2005 ruling favoring municipalities over private property owners, the city could take any real estate in the city limits, for any reason and for any purpose, as long as they couched the acquisition in official language---for public benefit. With Saint Anthony's Hospital leading point on the legal process, Riley saw no obstacle in the path of the land acquisition that couldn't be successfully hurdled.

The main hospital campus was located in Councilman Decker's District One. Once he learned of the hospital's desire to obtain the land, he would support the measure wholeheartedly. In fact, Riley would exacerbate any difficulties to prepare Councilman Decker for votes on other matters down the line. All reality is perception. This, Riley knew better than anyone. Through continual exercises of procedural hocus-pocus were future political markers acquired.

Councilmen Fitzpatrick and Brunner might require additional coaxing. But the hospital had the balance sheet to make it work. If St. Anthony's truly wanted an expedited decision in acquiring the land, it might be the way to go. It wouldn't be the first time Riley accessed the Trevnor Trust---that wasn't a problem. Riley just didn't want his capricious councilmen getting overly greedy and fixating on the notion that hard assets were available on every vote.

When it came to the mayor, Franklin Patterson, his boss and power base, the road to an affirmative decision on the hospital's application would likely take a more circuitous route. The mayor would test the political wind before making any public statement on the subject. If grassroots opposition reared its head, he would no doubt issue a clarification. When the coast was clear, he would re-circle the wagons, reevaluate his stance, then make his position perfectly clear. In the end he would probably vote in accordance with Riley's gentle guidance. But the entire process, especially if the matter became a front page story, would tighten the vessels another millimeter in the old man's heart.

In the normal course of city politics, Riley knew he could get the votes needed to pass the condemnation of the Kessler Park property. But Katherine said she wanted the whole matter handled expeditiously. Riley would have to explore his bag of tricks and dangle some large, juicy carrots in front of the other four councilmen, especially the new guy, Roberts from District Three.

He knew these men wouldn't be against the hospital's land acquisition in principle; far from it. Across a sales counter or in the church vestibule, they would expound upon the hospital's expansion plans in glowing terms. In the days to come, they would make speeches and insist they be quoted, on the record, as supporting the foresight and advance planning of St. Anthony's to meet the demands of a growing city. But when they spoke with him, they would demand their pound of flesh. They were of a breed known as politicians. They hadn't fought to the top of Atherton politics to be relegated to 'yes' men. They would demand their cut, and they wouldn't vote their precious ballot until Riley delivered equivalent compensation.

The reality of the matter didn't bother Riley in the least. It was what he lived for, what made his professional juices flow, what ejected him from his bed at four-thirty every weekday morning. He still had weeks before the day to vote would arrive.

That day, after lunch with Katherine Cramer, when he returned from the restaurant and pushed on the revolving glass door at city hall, his insightful mind was firing full bore. He always found the political perks his city councilmen wanted most. He always had their votes locked up days before they cast them.

CHAPTER TWENTY-FOUR

TYPICAL MONDAY MEETINGS of the Atherton Planning and Zoning Board expanded the definition of routine and boring. But everything changed the evening Kessler Park residents descended upon city hall. At most meetings, the seven-member board easily outnumbered the audience. A city staffer and a petitioner would make brief remarks on a zoning application, little or no discussion would follow, and a quick vote would move the proceeding along. Within an hour, all requests dutifully heard and appropriate action taken, the session would adjourn. Board members would depart knowing they had done their part for democracy in general, and for the greater good of Atherton in particular.

The zoning board made use of the city council chamber and taped their temporary name plates over the permanent plaques of the city's elected officials. Members moseyed in as the appointed hour approached, casual summer dress the order of the day, 7-11 Big Gulps and 32 oz. water bottles in tow. A ring of bright light bathed the oval rostrum.

A dynamic mural of Atherton's economy painted in deep reds, rich earthen browns, and John Deere greens dominated the high curved wall behind them. The light remained dim in the rest of the chamber as few people ever sat in the amphitheater seats. But there was no doubt the auditorium was full, the swirl of movement in the shadows unmistakable. The planning commission members whispered to one another and peered into the darkened hall.

Rick arrived with Myron and Delores. Delores had insisted on coming. Pain or not, she wouldn't be denied her God-given right to participate in a matter of city government. Myron asked Rick to assist him getting her downtown. While he could get her in and out of their Towne Car, Myron appreciated all the help he could get. Myron wanted someone near Delores in case she had any difficulties as he was scheduled to be one of the speakers, and he took a seat down front.

Rick sat on the end of the back row next to Delores in her wheelchair. He was excited because everyone else was excited. Before they entered the building, he craned his neck, awed by the skyscrapers as he stood in their midst. The street sign at the corner of the giant, glass building of city hall read Trevnor Avenue and North Third. Seeing so many people he knew on the front steps of the fancy downtown building was proof enough something big was going to happen, something really big. Rick had dressed in a short-sleeved white shirt and a pair of clean blue jeans, and had exchanged his hiking boots for a pair of black loafers. They were the nicest clothes he had besides his pressed Sunday suit. He would have paid Mr. Holmes some of his own hard-earned money not to have to put on that thing in the hundred-degree heat.

Brandon attended by himself and sat quietly in the audience. He came to find out what he could. He knew full well any chance of making a buck from the transfer of the property was all but gone. Still, hope dwelt in his heart. If there was something he could do, some role he could play, some way he could get back into the picture he'd do it. He wouldn't give up until the hospital actually owned the land.

The auditorium seats were packed with white-haired ladies and wrinkled old men. A number of more able-bodied individuals stood in back, beside two sets of double doors. A few people sat in the aisles. The throng of attendees overwhelmed the air conditioning system. Every conceivable object readily available was converted into a personal fan. This public meeting might be the only opportunity residents of Kessler Park ever had to save their homes and property. The air was tense with anticipation. People fidgeted and engaged in rambling conversations which only heightened everyone's nervousness. The purpose of the hearing remained difficult to contemplate, and yet everyone possessed the uncanny feeling they had each walked willingly to their own execution.

As the board chairman peered from his perch and struck his gavel, a middle-aged gentleman in a white windbreaker unloaded several notebooks on the lectern in front of the stage and looked up at the commission. He glanced over his notes and began.

"Good evening, board members. I'm Greg Duncan with the city department of codes and zoning. Zoning change application #AZC- 2242 was received from Saint Anthony's Regional Hospital District on June 25th of this year. They're requesting the condemnation of the residential properties in the subdivision known as Kessler Park for the purpose of building an additional parking garage and a doctor's office building. The department has completed a full review of the request.

"The Kessler Park area is not a designated historic district, and there has never been an application presented to consider it. As board members may know, approximately fifty-four homes out on Montrose Avenue of similar architecture and date of construction were designated as historic homes in 1967, as were sixty homes in Richardson Terrace. Richardson Terrace and the properties in the request were once part of the same subdivision.

"The existing historical districts sufficiently preserve the city's architectural heritage. The request before you complies with all city ordinances, provisions of the city charter, and the requirement that the action be of public benefit. The department recommends that the board approve the request and place the measure on the calendar for consideration by the city council."

"Mr. Duncan." The lone woman on the panel spoke up. "We're entertaining a request to displace an entire subdivision for a parking garage?" Her incredulous tone was unmistakable.

"For now, commissioner, according to their application." Duncan perused his notes. "The remainder of the property would be held for future needs."

"For future needs?" The woman let a perplexed disdain roll off her tongue. "Mr. Duncan, the last time I drove through that area I remember some of those houses looked absolutely spectacular. The city is recommending demolition of well-maintained homes that have undergone major renovations, including considerable investments of time and money?"

"We audited every block as part of our review, commissioner. The condition of the properties spans a wide range. Some have been well maintained, that's true. But there are many others that probably wouldn't pass code inspection now, and should be designated uninhabitable. There's also a lot of mixed use in the neighborhood which is a violation of city housing regulations."

The lady raised her hand to cut him off. "I'm not asking you about code violations, Mr. Duncan. I'm asking you why we're considering this request when a number of people moved into that area not just because they thought it was a good investment, but because they wanted to preserve the heritage of this city."

"I'm sure that's true in some cases, ma'am, but if I may say, our physical review led to the conclusion that what you just described is the exception rather than the rule."

"Well, I've read the hospital's application on this request. I didn't see anything that leads me to believe they can justify condemning private property to build a parking garage." Her voice rose at the end, and she glared at Duncan over her reading glasses as she concluded. "Mr. Chairman, I think we have a lot to consider in this matter."

"Duly noted, Mrs. Swenson. We have four individuals who have signed up to speak. We certainly want to hear from them all," the chairman said without enthusiasm.

"Mr. Duncan, what kind of violations are you referring?" asked another board member.

"It's something we often see in older neighborhoods. In some ways it's more pervasive in Kessler Park because motorized traffic access is so restricted. You can't drive into the neighborhood from the north because there are no ramps off the freeway in that area, and rail lines block access from the east. A large number of the properties are now rentals where the estate homes have been turned into multi-family dwellings without proper permits. Some are used as places of business, again without proper permits or---"

"That's all I wanted to know," the board member interrupted.

A majority of the panel appeared relieved at the question and Duncan's illuminating response. The issue was refocused on the crux of the matter, back where it belonged. Kessler Park was a decaying residential island in the heart of Atherton. The hospital was providing a community service in its willingness to purchase the aged and underutilized area.

It wasn't that the men of the zoning board were intentionally callused. They were reasonable men with homes and families of their own. But their focus was on the city's modernization and growth. Rarely did they seriously consider questioning the recommendation of departmental staff on such matters. The city employees in Atherton's Planning and Zoning Department were the experts in municipal governance. If city staff recommended approval of a zoning application, then ninety-nine times out of a hundred the men of the board went along.

In addition, zoning commissioners were appointees. They received no pay for the service they performed. Job perks amounted to seeing one's name on city letterhead with an impressive bullet point on the personal resume.

They had nothing personal against the folks who lived in Kessler Park. Whatever that old secluded subdivision had stood for was all well and good. But these men lived in gated communities up north around the lake or along wide streets with basketball goals in the drive and swimming pools in the back yard. When it came to being educated about Atherton's early history, they weren't really interested. If the hospital said it could use the land that was good enough for them. If the city staff signed off on the proposal that sealed the deal.

When it came to the fate of Kessler Park, the majority on the zoning board just didn't care.

"Thank you, Mr. Duncan," said the chairman. "Our first speaker from the community will be a Mr. Gordon English."

A young man approached the podium. He was small in stature with a scrubbed face. He wore a brown suit with a bright white tie against a tan shirt, but his hesitant manner contradicted his sharp appearance. He squinted at the panel, cleared his throat, and took a noticeably deep breath.

"Good evening, commissioners. I'm an attorney with Dustin, Cushman, and Childs and represent the property owners of Kessler Park. We've conducted our own review of the hospital's application and find it to be punitive, over-reaching, and premature." He paused, took another deep breath, and flipped a page on the stand in front of him.

"We submit that nothing in the hospital's announced building plans for the next five years warrants this action, and that negotiating with each property owner over time is the more orderly and equitable way in which to proceed."

For their part, the panel sat back in their padded leather chairs, arms folded, patiently waiting, eyes beginning to glaze.

"I'd be happy to answer any questions." Mr. English concluded and closed his folder.

The chairman glanced to either side and, seeing no hands or even the slightest inclination to question the attorney, excused him and scanned his paper for the next name on his list. "Mr. Sherman Porter."

Sherman approached the podium with his shoulders back, his head high, a resolute expression chiseled into his face. His bearing and demeanor didn't reveal the slightest hint he was pushing ninety years of age, and he grabbed the podium with two hands, his eyes panned slowly across the stage making a final determination as how to begin, though he had rehearsed for days the comments he intended to make.

"Commissioners, my name is Sherman Porter. My wife and I have lived at 408 Lancer Street since 1945. I liked that old house when I bought it, and I like it even better now. You couldn't give me one of those cookie-cutter boxes they call houses now with their cheap pine studs and prefab trusses. My house was hand-built, every nail driven by hand with an eye for craftsmanship. So what if some of them are run-down more than others? You think your neighborhood won't experience the same thing over time?

"The hospital doesn't need our land, and you shouldn't let them have it. There are vacant lots all over the place, especially to the southeast. That old milk plant at 8th and Greenbrier has been vacant for years. If they need more land, why can't they start there?

"Kessler Park isn't empty and it isn't abandoned. A lot of good people live there, and it would be a hardship for many to move. Please listen to what our attorney said. If the hospital wants our property, let them negotiate individually with those who want to sell. Leave the rest of us alone."

Sherman took his seat without another word, and Louis Hilker stepped to the podium right behind him without being called.

By his very stance anyone could tell Louis was ready to deliver a scathing rebuke sprinkled with hell fire. To him, the political rubber-stampers seated before him were the unscrupulous underlings who did the bidding of the well-connected at the expense of the common man. His false teeth were in place, his sparse white hair combed back tightly above his ears. The bare skin on his head reflected the overhead lights like a polished glass ball. He wore a starched white, short-sleeved shirt that accented his hairy forearms, and his ever present contribution to male fashion, blue/green striped suspenders.

"I'm Louis Hilker, Mr. Chairman and board members. For this body to consider voting on this matter before a lot more study has been conducted is totally unacceptable. I know that we have been notified—the property owners—but does the rest of the public know what the hospital is trying to ram down our throats?

"The city's planning department may have approved the legality of this application, but what about justice and the rights of the people who live in our neighborhood? Do you want to be part of throwing old people out on the streets?" He locked his short arm at the elbow and pointed his stubby finger across the stage.

"There's a lot more to this matter tha---"

"Did you say it was Mr. Hilker?" another board member interrupted Louis. He looked to be in his mid-thirties with gleaming white teeth and what appeared to be a smirk forming on his lips.

"Yes, Louis Hilker."

"Mr. Hilker, you're overstating the matter before this board, and I think creating undo apprehension for many in the audience."

"I'm not creating undo anything. You people started this. Now let me finish."

"Mr. Hilker," the young board member raised his voice, "this body doesn't throw people out of their homes nor do we give special treatment to any person or group in this city. We do, however, endorse measures that improve the lives of everyone even if a few individuals have to make some adjustments."

"Please, Mr. Edwards," the chairman broke in. "That's not going to help us here. Please continue, Mr. Hilker."

Louis worked to relax his grip on the podium and unclench his jaw. He knew he'd been dressed down by a clueless political appointee, and he hadn't even finished his argument. He wished that for just ten minutes he could be forty years younger. Now he'd lost any inclination to appeal to them logically. He'd tell them exactly what he thought of their certified notice and official meeting.

"I'm telling you right now, if you don't refer this matter to another meeting, I'll make sure you have to change your home phone numbers and build a twenty-foot fence around your house to keep out the noise of the picketers. There's no overriding public need to legally steal the property in Kessler Park, and neither the city nor the hospital is going to get it without a fight." Louis glared across the stage and stormed back to his seat.

The audience murmured with audible whispers. A few scattered attempts at applause cracked through the crowd, but fizzled in a whirl of gossip. Several people jumped from their seats and hurried up the back steps. Someone turned on the lights, a cheer went up, the volume of the voices rose with the lights, the chairman called for order. But the genie was out, the people were free of any self-imposed decorum for official city meetings, and the conversations buzzed as though everyone was in attendance at an after-service Sunday social.

A curious surprise infected the expressions along the curved rostrum. Board members exchanged bewildered glances. Something new was happening in their solemn chamber. Commissioner Swenson smiled to herself as she scribbled on a legal pad. The board chairman glared wild-eyed at the swirl of unruly humanity before him and pounded his gavel. "Please, be seated. I ask for order during this proceeding." He checked his list of speakers and waited until the drone of voices and activity subsided into a manageable buzz. "Our final speaker is Mr. Myron Holmes. It's your turn to speak, Mr. Holmes."

Myron approached the podium with a stoop and a half-step shuffle borne of years of tightening hamstrings. His long fingers fidgeted with his notes. His milky eyes were restless and worried, but even with his nervousness the audience began to quiet.

Myron was a down-to-earth man and a serious thinker. He was neither given to exaggeration nor a person weakened by sentimentality. He would explain to the commission the error of this proposal and convince them of the vitality and value of Kessler Park.

Myron was actually a tall man, though the years had withered his stature, and he pulled himself up, sucked his rib cage high, and raised his chin to the mural on the wall.

"Commissioners, I must tell you, when I first got the notice from the city on this matter, it absolutely floored me. It occurred to me that something's not quite right when the hospital, an institution that claims to be so ready to help the community, has to pull an end run to create a legal house of mirrors and cry to elected officials to get their way. Why couldn't they have made an announcement they were interested in buying? I'll bet there would have been more takers than you can imagine."

Myron adjusted his feet and cleared his throat. "I think all of us here, myself included, would appreciate some straightforward dealing, the same thing all of you would expect and deserve. We need more time to fully present our arguments to the city. There are a myriad of reasons why this condemnation request is a bad idea, but we need some time to fully present our case. Why is everything moving so fast? What's the hurry?"

Myron looked across the stage, to his left, then to his right, and saw such disinterested faces he felt as though he was speaking a foreign language. A beefy fellow with thick glasses had fogged them with his mouth and was deeply involved in cleaning them with his handkerchief. Another man had his elbow on the desk, his chin resting heavily in his hand, his eyes wide open with such a bored expression one might assume he was in pain. "What is the hurry?" Myron repeated his overriding question with added emphasis, but his confidence waned.

They weren't listening. Louis's threats hadn't aroused them. Sherman's suggestion the hospital check on the availability of the abandoned milk plant had fallen on deaf ears. Their own hired attorney had stated little more than the obvious without any guts or conviction behind his legalese.

For the first time since he agreed to speak, Myron felt a panic in his stomach. This commission didn't care what anyone had to say. They were just being polite, part of the American democratic system, the non-confrontational brush-off. Unconsciously, and without preparation, he began to tell them the only thing he knew for sure.

"Commissioners, I walked through Kessler Park for the first time after I came back from the war in Europe. I could tell right then it was a special patch of land, one of those places on earth that people search a lifetime to find. In my case, I guess, I was just smart enough to know when I found it.

"A cute girl over in Clearview thought enough of me to wait until I got back to Texas. We moved to Atherton and got married. She's with me tonight, up there on the top landing. She's in a wheelchair now." Myron turned and gave a stiff wave in

Delores' direction. "I made the $300 down payment with money I got from the Army and a loan from my dad. The longer you're there, the more the neighborhood grows on you. I can't explain it, but it does."

As Myron's reminiscences went from the general to the personal an uncomfortable lump of self-pity crawled up his throat. He was thinking of things that made him sad; he was exposing his feelings which made him afraid.

"My wife and I never had any children. Sometimes life throws a couple a curveball like that. We spent our extra time helping the center for unwed mothers. Some even stayed with us in our upstairs bedrooms when the center ran short on beds. I guess, over the years, our house has become our baby." Myron sucked up a quick breath, and his voice began to break.

"I don't want to move. My wife doesn't want to move. It has nothing to do with finding another house. We don't want to move if you gave us a brand new house. Why should I have to move?" Myron's knees began to tremble.

From his top row vantage point next to Delores, Rick watched it all. He heard the crack in Myron's voice. He saw the old man begin to shake, the same quivering he'd witnessed the day the notice had arrived in the mail. Instantly, Rick sprang down the steps. When he reached the podium, Myron was barely able to stand. Rick grabbed him under the armpits so he wouldn't fall.

Myron babbled incoherently. Helpless fear and flabbergasted anger had boiled through him with such power he bit his lower lip, and a dribble of blood ran down his chin. Rick helped the old man to a seat, took out his handkerchief, patted Myron's bloody lip, and placed the cloth in his hand. Rick was about to kneel and stay with him until he regained his composure. But a statement from the committee chairman flashed in his mind, "Our final speaker is Mr. Myron Holmes," and an odd notion his friends might lose any chance to further address the people on stage, spurred Rick to turn, and he stood and faced the zoning board.

The auditorium grew silent. Everyone leaned forward. Rick raised his face to the panel of important city folk. He stared up at the giant mural of tractors plowing black Texas dirt, and beefy, white-faced cattle, and high rows of busted-open cotton. Rick spread his arms and took a deep breath, and any shyness that had ever inhabited his powerful body vaporized into the thirty-foot ceiling like a spirit ascending to heaven. Rick smiled, dressed in his white shirt and blue jeans, and looked individually at everyone on the stage and said, "Mr. Holmes couldn't finish everything he wanted to tell you, so I'll finish for him. If you'll be patient with me for a few minutes, I'll tell you what all these nice folks want you to know. Then I know you'll make the right decision."

Rick put down his arms and stood humbly before them as calm and relaxed as a minister beside a church's open door. His voice seemed to change. His words were distinct, rich, and mellow, and began to flow with a new-found authority. Even the most bored among the commissioners sat forward to hear this giant man with the deep, smooth voice. Rick resumed his speaking, not with any malice or anxiety in his words, just an easy, rhythmic tone like a father telling his children a bedtime story.

"I don't live in Kessler Park. I just work for the folks who live there, but I know them like neighbors just the same, or like family... yes, more like family. The whole neighborhood is like family.

"If you lived in Kessler Park, you'd never think of tearing it down," Rick said, his voice filled with forbearance they would even contemplate such action. "When you walk through Kessler Park when the sun is bright, the streets flicker as the light passes through the leaves, and the trees hold in the fragrance of the flowers. When you go down there, the trees welcome you—it's the birds, of course, but there's always music to be heard in Kessler Park, there really is.

"You can't put a price on beauty and peace, can you? Even if a giant oak tree stands beside a broken fence, it doesn't make the tree any less magnificent, does it? I'm sure you'd all agree there's not too much beauty in this world that you'd want to throw some of it away.

"And when I go in those houses, I'm amazed at how well they're built, and you would be, too. Those houses in Kessler Park are not the square boxes that get built today. Thought and care was given to every board that was cut and every nail driven. They were built to shelter, but also to inspire. Each house has its own personality because each house is different. So when Mr. Holmes calls his house his baby, there's a lot of truth in that. For the houses in Kessler Park are much more than real estate to be bought and sold. Each one is part of a family. Would you put a price on a family member? It doesn't matter that these houses are made of boards and stone. It's about love. Why would you ask these people to turn their backs on something so dear, especially when they're elderly?

"This meeting is about much more than a piece of land for the hospital. The hospital is asking for more than Atherton can afford to pay. You see, Kessler Park is alive—it's part of the town you're here to serve. If you kill Kessler Park, you'd be killing yourselves, too. You would be cutting off a piece of your body just as sure as if you took a knife to your own arm, because Kessler Park is about home. Where there's caring and commitment and security and love—we call that home. Home is the most important thing any of us has got."

The hall became sealed in an envelope of silence, of moist eyes, and tear-streaked cheeks as Rick turned and walked up the steps back to his seat beside Delores. The audience became lost in their memories, stirred to a happy nostalgia. It had taken the perceptive words of a simple man to evoke feelings in them of the most cherished things in life.

The board chairman appeared as if caught in a trance. Every face along the rostrum seemed tuned to the soft whisper of an angel at their ear. A gentle wave of reflection had passed over them. None on the board seemed anxious to challenge anything said or in any hurry to leave. Finally, they looked about. The chairman asked, "Anyone wish to make additional comments?" No one said a word.

Mrs. Swenson raised her hand. "I wish to make a motion to consider the condemnation application before the board."

"Do I hear a second?"

Quickly, the motion was seconded.

"All in favor?" he asked. A lone hand went up.

"Those opposed?" Six hands were raised.

"The motion is denied. This session is adjourned."

For one interminable second, as though a vacuum had sucked all breath from the crowd, the chamber fell silent. An instant later it exploded into cheers, applause, and hugs. People surrounded Rick, who sat wide eyed and bewildered, unaccustomed to such attention and confused by all the fuss.

"You did it, son," Louis Hilker proclaimed.

People patted him on his shoulders and reached for his hand.

"You're amazing, Rick," Cecil Nance declared. Rick caught a glimpse of Sherman and Grace Porter gazing at him in awe and admiration. Myron Holmes remained in his seat, silently weeping into his handkerchief.

CHAPTER TWENTY-FIVE

KESSLER PARK RESIDENTS were energized beyond repose. Octogenarians usually under their covers by eight had no interest whatsoever in going to bed. Porch lights lit the narrow streets like runways. Residents gathered on porches, rehashed the evening's events, and chuckled at how the members of the zoning board had broken under the persuasive power of their collective will. Phones lines hummed. Those who missed the meeting received a minute-by-minute account of the proceedings with sufficient pauses to heighten suspense. Late into the night, as the residents of Kessler Park talked about the momentous public meeting, they talked less about the zoning board's favorable vote, and more about Rick's incredible performance.

For his part, Rick headed straight home and went to bed. He was glad the vote went in favor of his friends, but he'd put in a full day and was tired.

He didn't fully understand the animated celebration that ensued. He expressed what he saw as the simple truth about the neighborhood, and the board made the only decision possible.

The next morning, a ringing phone awoke him. He rolled out of bed half asleep and grabbed the receiver from the night stand.

"Good morning, Rick. This is Sherman Porter."

"Good morning, Mr. Porter."

"You sure did a good job last night. Your talk to the commissioners was really good."

"I just wanted to help."

"You certainly did that, Rick. What you said made all the difference in their vote."

Rick scratched his head, his eyes closed as Sherman spoke. "I think it was everyone being there."

"You did a good job, Rick, you really did. I'm calling because I got a call from Mr. Dobson. He lives over on Ashford and he wants you to stop by and fix something on his house."

"I can do that. Where's he live?"

"At 1203 Ashford. His name is Everett Dobson. Go by as soon as you can. He's there all the time. He doesn't get out much. You should tell him about last night. I'm sure he'd be happy to hear the good news."

"Should I call him first?"

"You don't need to. I told him I'd have you stop by as soon as you could."

"Okay, thank you, Mr. Porter."

"Thank you, Rick."

By eight-thirty Rick was ready to go. He checked his calendar, saw he had nothing else scheduled until eleven, so he headed to the new appointment.

At the Dobson home, Rick admired the decorative inlay set between the arches along the porch that supported the second-story balcony. Foliate carved lintels crowned every window, each bracketed between functional shutters. Rick opened the wooden screen and knocked on the door.

Rick's never-ending fascination for the intricate construction of Kessler Park's Victorian homes pulled his gaze upward to marvel at the splendor of the old house. Above the front steps, a scroll-sawn spandrel with a saw-tooth border adorned the arched entry. It was a construction element that added nothing to the structural integrity of the house, yet everything to its aesthetics. Decorative scroll-sawn railings and cornice trim accented the structure's quaint charm. The wood needed sanding and paint, but a warm brown with white trim would be just the touch.

After a moment, the door opened a crack. "Yes?" answered a wispy voice.

"I'm Rick Stanton, the carpenter. You sent for me?"

The door opened wider. "Come in." A bent old man, his head a tangle of white hair, wrapped in a flannel robe, headed into the house before Rick was fully inside. "Please shut the door. This way."

Lamps with frosted glass bases of greens and reds offered the mainstay of the interior lighting. To one side of the entryway turned knobs crowned beaded posts, the entry to a four-foot wide staircase. Spiral balusters ascended into a cavernous second floor. On the opposite side of the entryway hung a full-length mirror adorned with an intricately carved gold-leaf border.

Once in the parlor, Mr. Dobson found himself a padded chair and laboriously settled into the seat. Dobson's face appeared as parchment stretched over facial bones. His lips were thin and translucent. Dot band-aids on his chin and forehead seemed to hold his skin together. A blotchy complexion only exaggerated his haggard appearance, but when he spoke he sounded absolutely serene.

"So you're Rick, the man who fixes anything?"

"Yes, sir."

"I've heard a lot about you."

"I do good work, the best I can, and if it isn't the way you want it, I'll do it again."

The old man nodded, and a lengthy pause passed between them. When he finally spoke again he said, "Winter's coming on, be here before you know it . . . that fireplace right there needs some work."

"The damper's broken, I think. I can't get it to close completely. Too much cold air comes down the chimney." Dobson seemed intent on explaining the scope of the repair, but the very mention of the fireplace arrested his thoughts, and he began to reminisce. "My Lizzy and I spent many a warm, peaceful evening sitting in front of that fireplace. Sitting by the fire when it was cold outside was our favorite way to spend time together."

Rick listened thoughtfully. He possessed an engaged manner of listening that never interrupted. When people talked to Rick they could unburden themselves in solitary dialogue, and all the while think they were carrying on a conversation.

Dobson stared into the cold, flameless hearth. "I was born in this house in 1924. I inherited it from my mother when she passed away. That was 1948. Lizzy and I hadn't been married a year. I decided to come back to the place and we moved in. I've always loved this house. Lizzy and I raised our two girls here. Wouldn't have had it any other way."

The old man turned Rick's way, but his thoughts remained in the dark, empty firebox, and he struggled to maintain the strength in his voice. "Lizzy and I went to the same grade school, you know, Lee Elementary, just eight blocks away. That's all gone now. The school district built a maintenance facility there. Our old playground is all concrete now." A long silence settled between the two men. "She's been gone five years next month."

Rick waited on the old man, lost in his memories. Finally, as the sight of Dobson's red, wet eyes pulled Rick's empathetic emotions to the fore, he said, "Mr. Dobson, I'm sure your wife was a wonderful lady."

Despair consumed the old man's expression. The lonely hurt in his eyes told his story.

"Mr. Dobson, do you have some pictures of your wife?"

Though his pitiful countenance remained, the suggestion motivated the man to move. He found a photo album in a bureau drawer and opened it on the dining table. For awhile he remained pensive as he prepared to turn the pages. Rick took a seat beside him.

"There." he pointed. "We were at Steamboat Springs. She loved it. The air was so cold and crisp, so clean in its iciness. It's a ski resort, you know, a beautiful place up in the Rocky Mountains."

Rick had never seen anything but flat Texas prairie but he sat quietly and nodded, and watched as the old man carefully turned the album pages, its plastic sleeves yellowed and cracked with age. For long stretches of time, Dobson just stared at the ancient photos without saying a word. He didn't acknowledge Rick or seem to know he was there. When he came to the end, he slowly closed the book.

Rick hardly said a word the entire half hour it took the old man to linger through his memories. He thought nothing of the time taken and wasn't perturbed with Dobson for his self-indulgent reminiscences.

He knew the old man needed fixing more than his fireplace ever did. The empathy in Rick's soul had him wishing he could do more than what he was doing already, so he placed his hand gently on the old man's shoulder and said what he knew was true. "Your wife sure was a pretty lady, Mr. Dobson. I know she was a real special person."

Finally, Dobson's thoughts returned to the present. He put the photo album back in the bureau and once again focused on the fireplace repair.

"If you would, see what needs to be done to fix that damper. You'll probably need to take the pieces with you so you can get exact replacement parts."

"Sure thing, Mr. Dobson." Rick removed his tool belt, grabbed his flashlight, and wiggled on his back into the firebox opening. After a minute he came out. "It's rusted through, sir. The hinge pins need replacing, too. I can have them out in a jiffy and be back tomorrow. I'll have it fixed in no time, and you'll be all ready for winter."

Dobson nodded slightly, his lips pressed tightly. His eyes, once again, assumed a distant gaze.

Rick maneuvered back inside the firebox and set to work. "You just let me know about any work you need done on your house," he said, his deep voice resonating up the chimney. "I specialize in restoring and maintaining houses like yours, Mr. Dobson. I take care to do all work just like it was done originally. Wood work, brick work, glass work, I know how . . ."

A crash came from the front of the house. Rick hit his head inside the firebox as he sat up. The disturbing sound dissipated as quickly as it had come. He heard nothing but his own groans as he held his head and struggled to his feet. What was that? The house fell eerily quiet. His eyes searched for the slightest movement. He listened for the faintest sound. He held his hammer high, cocked beside his head as he moved toward the front.

Broken glass littered the vestibule, easily seen as he approached the parlor door. Two more steps he saw it all. Illuminated by a single lamp, he saw

Dobson's broken body. A pile of rope lay on the corpse, one end looped around his neck. The other end had come loose from whatever it had been tied to above, but the fall had killed the old man as surely as any broken neck would have ever done.

Rick laid the hammer on a table. He was no longer concerned about the origin of the sound. No words of explanation were necessary to explain the sight before him. In that instant, a helpless, horrible loneliness overcame him. He wished he had said something or done something that would have prevented the man from committing the absolute act of despair. Hadn't he listened and tried to comfort him? What else could he have done?

He had never seen death before, but he knew there would be no more explosions. There was no more physical or emotional pain left for the old man to endure. Even in the carnage there existed a sense of peace.

He needed to notify others, but first he took a pillow and knelt beside the lifeless frame. The body was on its side, an arm grotesquely twisted behind his hips. Rick eased Dobson onto his back, brought the arm out, placed it by his side, and put the settee pillow under his head. As he did, Rick saw a folded white paper in the old man's robe pocket.

Rick took it and read it, and the hollow emptiness that had subdued him, a useless, reverent pity he mistook as compassion, was instantly replaced with boiling revulsion. Rick recognized the letter. It had sucked the last ounce of hope from Dobson. The paper had killed him as surely as if people from the city had come to his home and thrown him bodily from his second-floor landing.

Rick's whole being became incensed far beyond conducting more petition drives or making heart-felt speeches. The intensity of his disgust drove up his blood pressure. Tentacles of pressure crawled, once again, across his forehead.

He remembered Sherman's words, "He doesn't get out much. You should tell him about last night. I'm sure he'd be happy to hear the good news." A debilitating sorrow washed over Rick like a flood. He felt that in some way he should have known the old man's pain. He blamed himself and his forgetfulness and was unable to think beyond the anguish of regret that now consumed him. Unconsciously, his powerful hands began to shred the document into confetti, the letter with the legal language and the city's pompous seal, an official decree with the power to ruin lives---the hospital's condemnation notice to confiscate Kessler Park.

CHAPTER TWENTY-SIX

IN THE MIDST OF A SHOCKED, YET HAPPY throng of senior citizens, Brandon sat in disbelief. The Atherton Planning & Zoning Board had voted in favor of the Kessler Park homeowners. A cheerful effervescence filled the hall. People hugged anyone in sight. Their homes and sedentary pace of life had received a reprieve. The resulting relief was palpable. An old woman wrapped her arms around him and squeezed him like a long-lost son. For a moment, Brandon wasn't sure whether to be sad or delighted at the unexpected outcome. Apparently the hospital's land grab had been stopped. Would this turn of events put him back in the game?

Until now, Katherine Cramer's deceit had suffocated his motivation. The accompanying self-doubt and bitterness had wasted good energy. Katherine Cramer and her hospital cronies could second-guess themselves and deal with being blindsided by a reality check. Brandon sat in the city hall auditorium surrounded by an enthusiastic swirl of overjoyed senior citizens and relished the moment. His optimistic spirit bubbled back to the surface.

If indeed he'd been given a fresh opportunity, he would do things differently. Cindy's stark assessment of his manipulative behavior was correct. In the past, she let him run with a loose rein. She let him do things his way, always there to pick up the pieces when he invariably got into trouble. But the way she talked the other night, things had changed. No longer would she help clean-up his self-generated disasters.

He had to adopt a long-term approach. One way or the other, he would find the right investors, people with the financial muscle to hold onto the properties while the land appreciated in value. He would still make a fortune out of the dilapidated, ancient structures.

His mind grabbed the first twig of inspiration his thoughts could reach. He would contact his old acquaintance. Vic was the real estate professional. He should have called him sooner. Certainly Vic would see the value in the redevelopment of Kessler Park. Someone like Vic, with contacts in a large commercial real estate firm, could provide a competitive thorn in the hospital's flank if Katherine Cramer tried another ploy. Brandon thought about going to see him then, but decided instead to stop by Julio's Bar and Grill the following afternoon.

At happy hour, the bar was a sea of young professionals. He quickly located the table where his old friends stood, their beer bottles raised in another frat house salute. It was as though he could hear their individual voices above the din. Vic was there. Of all the times in his life when he enjoyed groups, indeed craved them, at this one moment Brandon wished he had found Vic alone. But Charles was there, the banker, and the computer programmer, Lance. Brandon headed toward the table, but then cut to the bar and ordered a beer. The bar was lush, fresh greenery placed strategically about, brightly lit, full of happy voices. None of it improved his outlook. He had a business matter to attend to and knew this would be a delicate discussion, at best. Brandon took a long, slow drink and headed to the table.

"Well, look who's here," Charles said. An inquisitive glint in his eyes quickly darkened and smugness coated his tone. "We thought you'd retired and moved to Palm Springs."

Brandon pursed his lips and exhaled an involuntary sigh. "No, not me. Atherton is my home. You'd have to haul me away in chains to get me out of Texas." Brandon wanted to smile, but he couldn't even force it. He knew he was on the spot. His understated reply was an attempt to inject levity, a refusal to concede all dignity. But no amount of glib talk could mask his internal agitation, and he felt disheveled in spite of his stylist clothes. "Just thought I'd stop by and check out the old stomping grounds."

"We're still stomping," Vic said as he crunched on a nacho. "Plowing the hard ground, so to speak." He eyed Brandon suspiciously.

Brandon looked directly at Vic. "Could I speak to you for a minute?"

"Hey, where have you been, man?" Lance blurted, "You used to be in here every day. I thought---" Charles put his hand on Lance's arm and gave him a little shake of his head.

"What do you want to do, take another boat ride?" Vic asked. The sarcasm in his voice was unmistakable.

"No—no boat rides. Just a moment of your time if I could."

Vic made eye contact with Charles and shrugged. "All right. One minute."

The two men stepped to an open space along the wall.

"I'm sorry about that day at the lake," Brandon said.

"You invite someone on your boat and an hour later you head back to shore? If all you wanted to do was pick my brain you didn't have to go through all that. I probably would have told you what you wanted to know over a couple of beers."

"I'm sorry. I apologize. I got so excited about what you were talking about I lost all interest in boating."

"Kind of what I thought."

An empty table opened up, and they sat down. Brandon drank the last of his beer and leaned across the table. "Listen, I found a prime piece of property. P R I M E." He let each letter roll off his tongue as though a distinct enunciation would imbue the word with magic.

Vic looked at him with disdain. "So?"

"You're the expert. I figured you'd know exactly how to handle it, and I'd just take a finder's fee on my first deal."

"What? Your first deal?" Vic raised his hands in exasperation and kneaded his temples for several seconds, then brought his hands together in front of his chest. "What do you expect me to do? I work for a major developer. I can't get involved in side deals. Besides, parcels for sale around this town are a dime a dozen."

"Not this parcel," Brandon said. Absolute belief exuded from his words. If he possessed anything, it was eternal optimism. With the least little opening he would sway Vic to his side. Brandon knew his assessment of the Kessler Park property was solid. He would find a way to spark an interest, fuel Vic's curiosity, ultimately sell him on the whole idea.

Vic wasn't persuaded. "Are you even licensed? You know, you can buy and sell for yourself all day long, but once you start involving third parties you have to have a Texas license. I can't pay you a fee of any kind if you don't have a license."

"I know, I know. That's why I really need you—your expertise—your company. I found something you don't come across every day. I know it. Let me show you. There's something in it for you. That's what you said you wanted, a chance to make a big score for yourself."

Vic hesitated. "Listen, pal, I drive nearly a thousand miles a week looking at property. I get sick of it. I'm busy enough as it is. If you've found some hot deal, go show it to any one of a hundred agents sitting in their offices now counting pencils."

"Yeah, but this land is going to go from residential to commercial. You'd know how to handle it. You'd know how to maximize the value," Brandon said.

Vic shook his head ever so slightly. "Sorry, minute's up. I'm not interested."

In the days that followed, Brandon got a job at a menswear store. A week's pay was about half what he'd made at the investment firm, but at least it was a job. He looked the part, tailored and stylish, and quickly learned all he needed to know about the brands.

He had his health, his looks, and his drive. Yet nothing ever developed as he envisioned. His life was a shamble of fast starts quickly spent. As much as he detested his father's legacy, he knew he was following the same path, destined to remain unfulfilled if not headed for jail. He didn't see himself as a bad person; he was outgoing and affable. Yet, his days around Todd brought home a truth he couldn't deny. Every time they were together, Brandon saw glimpses of himself in the other man. He had built nothing to brag about nor had he accomplished anything worthy of praise. He was just a well-dressed version of Todd.

Brandon spent more time walking the sidewalks of Kessler Park. His inner drive to possess the properties hadn't abated, but he throttled back his wishful thinking in an attempt to demand more of himself. Any prospect of buying the properties required he get to know the residents. He resolved to start at square one. The neighborhood wasn't getting any younger. It was the only plan of action with any hope of success, the proper way to conduct business.

Late one afternoon, as the sun fell behind the cooling, protective canopy of treetops, he saw a couple on their porch and decided to introduce himself. He waved as he approached. A slender, white-haired gentleman seated beside a woman in a wheelchair, waved back, their gazes patiently following him as he proceeded up the walk.

"Beautiful evening. My name is Brandon Evans. Your neighborhood sure has gotten a lot of attention lately. I wanted to come down and see for myself what all the talk was about. It certainly is peaceful along these streets."

"We like it," the old man said.

"With all the rundown buildings a few blocks away I never knew this place existed."

"Are you with the paper?"

"No, sir, I grew up in Atherton. Guess I just got curious when I read about your neighborhood."

"We're hopeful things get back to normal now that the city board put the hospital in their place," the woman said. "It's just home to us."

"*The Sentinel* sure played it up, all the history of this neighborhood and the legal fight you were going through."

"Yes, I read the paper. We got quite a scare. We just hope things get back to normal soon."

"May I ask, how long have you lived here?"

"Since 1947. The only place we've ever lived since we married. The only house we ever care to live in."

Brandon couldn't help but be impressed by what the old man said, not because of the span of time involved, but because of the emotion he put into every word. This was the half acre that identified their spot in the world. The old place obviously needed maintenance beginning with a fresh coat of paint, but to them it was home.

"May I sit down?" Brandon pointed to a stack of plastic chairs on the porch.

"If you intended to stay much longer I was beginning to wonder when you were going to ask."

"Thank you." Brandon sat where he faced them, but he could also see the yard and the street. "My, this is a tranquil view."

"We like it."

For several minutes Brandon watched the leaves, like flickering prisms, filter the evening sunlight into the colors of the rainbow. He listened to the rhythms of the yard, the pulsating hum of insects, and smelled the fragrance of the grass and flowers as a delicate aroma rose with the onset of dusk and drifted on the breeze.

"I suppose Atherton wasn't near the city it is today when you first moved here."

At first, neither acted as though they'd even heard his question, but the old man rubbed his finger on his chin and finally answered. "No, it wasn't. You got me thinking. Downtown's pretty much the same, 'course the names on most the stores are different. But the outskirts of town have exploded since those days. I didn't think much of that until I saw a city map awhile back. Yes, it's grown and changed a lot since we first moved here."

"I bet you had an interesting job."

"Who, me? Well, I don't know about that. I was an insurance adjuster." The old man's face rose to the sky as he thought. "Back then there was no such thing as claim centers or specialist. I handled everything, you name it." A twinkle in his eyes brightened his face. "House fires, wrecked cars--- one time a guy fell off an apartment balcony and broke his leg in three places. I had to make a personal visit to his hospital room to get all the details to process his claim. I traveled six counties. If it was something insurable, I handled a claim on it at one time or another."

"Sure sounds interesting to me."

"Well, I guess maybe it was. Certainly not routine, that's for sure. Something different every day."

"Did you work outside the home, ma'am?"

"Oh, yes, I most certainly did. I was a grade school principal for thirty years. I don't suppose you went to Eisenhower Elementary?"

"No, ma'am. Actually, I went to Lincoln."

"Yes, well, it's a wonderful profession. There was a shortage of teachers when I got my first job, and I decided to get into administration soon after that. It's a wonderful feeling knowing you had a part in the early lives of so many children. I loved every day of it."

Again, Brandon sat for awhile, enjoying the peaceful, secluded view.

"What do you think is going to happen to this neighborhood?" Brandon kept his gaze focused over the porch rail. He had no idea how they would respond. Beats of silence grew heavier as they lengthened, but Brandon said no more. It was up to either of these nice elderly people to reply, change the subject, or say nothing at all. But something in the question was more than the old man could contain, and after an indeterminable wait, he finally spoke.

"A month ago I wouldn't have had the foggiest idea what to say to a question like that or I would have told you to mind you own business. But now I know it's a legitimate question, one that requires some thinking on at any rate.

"It's just going to be sad to see this neighborhood go. I don't want to be around when it happens. My wife and I would like to live here until we're gone. After that, I guess, the city can do whatever they want with it."

"Sir, I know I have no right to ask you this," Brandon said, "but I've met folks who have never thought about who should get their property at their passing. It's really an important question to consider. Have you made that decision?"

"No, we haven't, and I'm not going to worry about that tonight."

"I'm sorry. I didn't mean to be rude."

"Are you a realtor?"

"No, sir, I'm not. What I am is a person who would like to see this location maintain its beauty and inspiration even as it changes. But there's no hurry. I'd like to help you pass on the value you've built here. I have no agenda more than that. I think this is a beautiful neighborhood, and I appreciate you letting me share your porch this evening."

"What's your name again?"

"I'm Brandon, Brandon Evans."

"And you are?" Brandon extended his hand.

"I'm Myron Holmes, and this is my wife Delores. Do you have a card?"

"No, I'm sorry, I don't. But would it be all right if I came back?"

Myron glanced at Delores, and unspoken communication passed between them. "Sure, young man, come back anytime you like."

CHAPTER TWENTY-SEVEN

A NEW AWAKENING took hold in Kessler Park. Residents stepped outdoors and looked about. Each had something new to be proud of. Revitalization took hold of the antiquated community, and a flurry of activity buzzed at every address. Sidewalks were cleared of litter, picket fences repaired and painted. Contractors hired, trees pruned, leaves raked, lawns mowed. Even those who usually stayed indoors hobbled in their front yards, stooped at the waist pulling at overgrown flower beds. Redmond's Hardware Store received so many orders a truck was dispatched, loaded with cans of paint, an assortment of brushes, leaf bags, hand tools, sections of fence, and trays of flowers in plastic starter pots—purple pansies, crimson clover, blue jasmine, and brilliant orange Texas Star.

The passing of Everett Dobson placed a respectful restraint on the barn-raising atmosphere. It was disheartening to consider the hopelessness that filled his final hours. Most everyone stopped by the funeral home and paid their final respects.

Rick worked from dawn to dusk. His uncomplicated mind appeared to protect him from the chaos he had endured at the Dobson home. He didn't seem to dwell upon the event. He focused on repairing, replacing, and fixing. As the neighborhood cleanup effort grew, Rick threw his energy into the endeavor. He completed carpentry projects up and down the streets. He dug holes and set fence post, single-handedly replaced rotted porch beams, lifted waning porch roofs with the power of brute strength. Between carpentry projects he poured and set concrete bases for the light poles at the garden park.

But all was not concealed in his vigorous activity. Rick accomplished the work of three men and hardly spoke. His strange silence was noticed by his elderly friends, and Sherman found Beatrice and Louis, and the three of them went together to speak with him. They got him to take a break, and they each took a seat on benches in the park.

"Rick," Sherman began, "I want you to know I'm sorry I sent you over to Mr. Dobson's house alone. You had never been there before. I should have gone with you and introduced you."

Even Rick caught the incongruity in the statement and his eyes widened. "I'm a big boy, Mr. Porter. I go to people's houses by myself all the time."

"Rick, we want you to know for sure, deep down, nothing that happened over there was your fault," Beatrice said. She sat beside him and put her arm around his broad back. "Do you understand me?"

Rick nodded hesitantly.

"The police could tell he had it all planned," Louis said. "There's a good possibility he just called someone over to his house so his final act would be discovered. We're sorry it was you. We're sorry he would do that to anyone. We just want you to know that no one is to blame."

Beatrice gazed at him. Wetness filled her eyes. "Do you believe us?"

"Yes," Rick said. His answer sounded like a question, but there was hope in the word.

"We want our cheerful Rick back. You have to tell yourself that there was nothing you could do. It wasn't your fault. You have nothing to feel bad about. Will you say that?"

Rick cleared his throat. "It wasn't my fault. I have nothing to feel bad about."

"Good," she said. "It's best to forget about it. It's all over now. Will you?"

He looked about and held each gaze, inhaled deeply, swallowed, and the pressure of the ordeal passed from him. His focus fell to his hands in his lap, and he whispered, "Thank you."

Lena got herself assigned to the Redmond hardware truck and she delivered orders to everyone's front door. When time allowed, she watched Rick work. She watched his defined shoulders and arms dig and lift, pry and carry. His body displayed raw power, but his work demonstrated the skill of a craftsman with a precise attention to detail. At the park, Lena screwed the fake cameras and rotating motors to the top of the poles, then stepped back while a group of men raised and held steady each twenty-foot pole section. Rick bolted them to their bases. Late in the afternoon, she left as she had to return the truck to the store.

In two short weeks the Atherton city council would officially vote to affirm the decision of the zoning board. The hospital's land grab would be relegated to the past. But the experience wouldn't be forgotten nor the awakening spark wasted.

Toward the end of another long day, as it approached eight, Rick hurried to the hardware store in hopes of getting there before it closed. The cool, orange glow of the setting summer sun now flickered through the canopy of leaves. A bolt of white light trimmed in gold pierced a billow of clouds. Reds and purples painted the western sky. In a matter of minutes the collage of color would fall into the horizon and pull a curtain of dusk over the city.

The bells attached to the front door clanged as Rick barged into the hardware store. A black woman fumbled for change at the counter. At the register, Lena turned and smiled as he came in.

"I'm glad you're still open," he said. "I need to get caulk and organic bug spray."

"Bug spray, aisle five." Lena was about to say she'd be right there when a crash of coins pulled her attention to the counter. "Oh, Mrs. Adams, don't worry about thirty-three cents, really. You've paid me enough."

The woman apparently didn't hear as she began to finger each coin, push them individually across the counter, and announce each denomination out loud.

Lena grimaced and began to clear the counter. "Here I have it—see? Thirty-three cents." She smiled. "Let me get you your receipt." She quickly gathered the remaining coins and dropped them into the lady's purse as the register spit out a foot of tape. "Here you are, Mrs. Adams. Thank you for shopping at Redmond's. You have a nice evening now." She rushed to aisle five.

"Find what you're after?"

Rick looked up with a start. "No—where's the ones with the big white labels?"
His concern had her kneeling beside him to aid in the search. "Do you know the brand name?"

"No," he said as though the question was irrelevant, "the bottles with the big white labels."

A sweet smile beamed from her oval face and lit her delicate features, but her reassuring tone didn't diminish his distress. White labels meant nothing by itself, but the store carried four brands of organic bug killer.

She took a chance and grabbed him by the shoulders. "Now look at me. I have what you want." She pulled two different bottles from the shelf and read the ingredients from each one. "See? They have the same stuff." She reached for another brand from a higher shelf and read the label to him word for word. "They're all the same, Rick. They won't hurt your gardens, and they'll kill the bugs." She held his gaze until the information registered.

"Okay," he said finally. "I'll take all those."

"Eight? My, you must have to kill all the bugs in the city."

The levity in her statement escaped him, and his response assumed the naïve, unfiltered truthfulness of a child. "I have a lot of gardens to care for with more flowers than I could ever count." He began to gather as many bottles as he could carry. "It's my job to take care of the gardens, and right now I've got a lot of bugs."

Lena listened intently and nodded. The weight of his words compared to the simplicity of his task bordered on the absurd, and part of her wanted to laugh. But the cherubic sincerity of his deep blue eyes made her want to pull him to her right there and then, and squeeze him, and press her cheek to his.

"It's okay. I'll tell you what. Let's put those bottles back on the shelves. I've got a better idea. I'll get you a four-gallon container with a hose and a pump from the back. It'll save money, and you'll have plenty of spray for all your flowers. How does that sound?"

"That sounds good, Miss Lena."

"Okay," she said. "You know where the caulk is. I'll meet you at the counter."

In all of his visits to the store, Lena always found herself instantly in good spirits when he walked through the door. It didn't matter that he wasn't an intellectual genius. She couldn't rightly say she'd ever met a guy who actually was. Telling spontaneous jokes or multiplying numbers in one's head were hardly traits she sought in a man. She knew he wasn't stupid just by the way he talked and the clarity by which he made his wishes known. She liked him, though she barely knew him. He was polite, and he smiled at her, and he looked into her eyes when he spoke. She knew he appreciated easy to understand suggestions about purchases he wanted to make, and she hoped someday he'd stop and take a more personal notice of the person making them.

As she handed him back his credit card she said, "It's closing time. Mr. Redmond will lock up the store. Would you—could you walk me to the bus stop?"

Rick blinked and thought for a moment. "Why, sure, Miss Lena. I can do that."

"Good night, Mr. Redmond," Lena called as the jangle of bells announced their exit. The street lights came to life as the warmth of the day ascended to the sky. The sweet coolness of the summer evening rolled over the streets. They appeared such a mismatched pair. Anyone noticing them would have said as much. His lumbering gait in hiking boots took one step for every two of hers. His dusty overalls contrasted strangely with her smart skirt and pressed blouse. He was twice her size; a bear escorting a lamb. For three blocks they walked side by side without a word. The clack of her footwear on the sidewalk lent a cadence to their stroll. Suddenly they both spoke at once.

"I was just going to ask, Miss Lena, how long you've been working at the hardware store."

"Four years. Please don't call me miss. I'm not that much older than you, Rick. You don't need to call me miss. It sounds so formal. It sounds like you think. . ."

"I'm sorry, I was just being polite."

"I know you were. I know you're a nice person. I've known since the first time you came in the store."

"You've always been a big help to me, like today," he said.

"I try." They walked to the end of the block. "Well, here's my stop."

Rick looked about seemingly deep in thought. "I can wait with you till the bus gets here if you want me to."

Her heart jumped with delight at his initiative. "I'd like that."

They took a seat under the awning of a dimly lit, newspaper-strewn wait station beside a row of tired, vacant-looking riders. Lena sat on the end of the bench, just enough room for an average-sized person beside her while Rick put down his can of insecticide and stood at the end of the row. The arrangement lasted all of twenty seconds.

"It's getting cooler," Lena announced. "You sit here." She forced some room for him to squeeze in along the bench, and Rick sat down without further coaxing.

No sooner had he seated himself than Lena took his arm with a faint possessive pressure and pulled herself against his side. Then she laid her head upon his shoulder.

"You should have worn a sweater," Rick said.

She scooted closer, felt the power in his arm, smelled the odor of his body, and smiled approvingly to herself. "I'm not cold."

They waited awhile and she said, "Do you like to go to the movies, Rick?"

"Sure, I like movies."

"I like them, too," she said. "If you wanted to spend time with someone, you could take them to the movies."

"And just watch the movie?" he asked.

"Well, after it was over you could go get something to eat and just spend some time with someone," she said. She waited. Rick said nothing. Finally she spoke again. "Rick, would you like to take me to a movie?"

"Oh, sure. That would be great."

"I get off work at six on Friday. Would you like to see a movie this Friday?"

"Friday would be just fine." He looked down at her, and she snuggled closer.

"So, would you pick me up at the store at six on Friday?"

"Sure thing. There's a movie house just up my street at 9th, I think."

"That's the one I was thinking of."

She quit talking, and they waited in silence. She didn't know how much time passed before the bus finally rolled to a stop. The other occupants at the station stirred and moved to the curb. She stood. A sleepy, dreamy expression set softly on her face.

"Thanks for walking me to the stop, Rick."

"Sure—oh, sure. Goodnight, Lena."

CHAPTER TWENTY-EIGHT

WHEN BRANDON RECEIVED HIS
PAYCHECK, he paid some personal bills, then
grabbed a blank check to write one more. He was
hardly rolling in money, but he wrote the check for
$200 and made it out to Cindy. He owed her, and
he would pay her what he could. After he addressed
the envelope, he pulled out a sheet of paper and the
words began to flow.

Dear Cindy,
I wanted to get this to you. I should be able to
send more by the 1st. I really appreciated your help.
If I ever said so, I know I didn't say it enough. I
hope you found a steady job you like. I got on with
Gibson Menswear. It's not too bad, and they carry
some good lines. I get 20% off if I want to buy
anything off the rack.
The city zoning board held a meeting last week
and turned down the hospital's application to

acquire that old neighborhood I've been looking at. I'm trying to get back in the picture, but I'm going about it differently. I've been getting around, introducing myself, talking to the owners about what they see happening to their property in the years to come. Most of them haven't given it much thought. I can see it's going to take some time, but I intend to keep at it.

I talked to a couple of sweet ladies yesterday. They're sisters and both taught school. They've been in their house since the thirties. They were raised there. Anyway, I met them before when I was doing the greeting card thing, and they were glad to see me. I even took them a box of cards. They really liked that. I think they're expecting me to personally bring them a box each month.

I asked them what was going to happen to their house in the future. They kind of came up with the idea that they intended to deed it over to their church. I asked if they would like to know how to go about making those arrangements now. The church would get the proceeds in the future, but without the trouble of selling the house. I explained how making a plan now would put extra money aside for unexpected bills they might encounter. They seemed pleased.

From the beginning, I knew bringing up the matter directly with those homeowners was the proper way to deal with them. I don't know why I get so short-sighted and go with what seems quick and easy. I know it wasn't the right thing to do, and it certainly wasn't productive. I admit I was wrong, but I still want to be a part of the redevelopment that will take place in that old neighborhood. Now though, I'm taking it slow, one step at a time.

I know you're upset with me. You have every right to be, but I hope you've seen some good things in me, too. I always thought we made a good pair on the town. I mean, if nothing else, you should let me take you back out on the lake. I was at the marina last weekend and fired up the engines on *Betty Sue,* but didn't take her out. There's no fun being on the water alone. You've always enjoyed the lake so much, I hate the idea of you missing it just because I've been a jerk.

I've called at all hours, but you never pick up. I don't want to leave messages. I hope you'll pick up. I admit I enjoy being with you. Since I've turned over a new leaf, you should give me a second chance. I thought maybe if we could just talk.

Brandon

The more time he spent in Kessler Park, the more often he ran into the neighborhood handyman, resident jack-of-all-trades---carpenter, painter, plumber, electrician, and gardener. Brandon now knew his name now, Rick Stanton, an able public speaker, too. The man was amazing, possessing not only exceptional skill in the building trades, but a down-home wisdom as well. Without knowing much, he seemed to know it all. His sensible take on life had to come from instilled values, for the big guy never wavered from an undercurrent of core principles.

Whenever asked his opinion, he was easy on the advice. Whenever questioned, he simply stated his position without apology or double-talk. Brandon envied the gentle giant and now sought him out, not for information, but for counsel. There was just something about listening to Rick talk about his day that soothed Brandon's anxious nerves. Something about Rick's uncomplicated insights gave Brandon a sense of peace.

One evening, just after he visited with a Mr. and Mrs. Hudson, he saw Rick on the sidewalk, using the last rays of daylight to finish work on a fence on the house next door.

Rick took a few nails from his mouth and looked up. "You again?"

"Yes, it's me. I was just talking to the Hudsons. You know them?"

Rick nodded. "Nice people."

"I sure like these evenings. Cools down quickly under all these trees."

"Uh-huh." Rick stood, surveyed his work, then looked directly at Brandon. "Are you the person who started all the trouble down here, where everyone could have lost their house?"

Brandon froze. The direct question caught him upside the head. For an instant, he was afraid to answer. Then he realized, if he could confess a lack of judgment to anyone, he could admit it to Rick. "Yes, I was involved. I didn't understand the special significance of Kessler Park." Brandon didn't mention he was still after the same result since the hospital and city had been cut out of the picture.

"That wasn't a nice thing to do. There's people I work for still aren't over the shock of it all. If I'd have known what you were up to, I would have run you off, for sure." Rick stuck the nails back between his lips, scooted on his knees along the fence, and kept nailing.

"I didn't want those notices to go out. That was the hospital's idea."

"But those letters wouldn't have gone out if you hadn't started it." Rick's tone indicated he neither wanted nor expected an answer. Somehow, he had pieced together the basics of what had been going on and simply made a statement.

"My dad was sent to prison recently. It's been a messed up couple of months. I think I was trying to do something to help him out, but I don't even believe that now. He's got time to serve, and nothing I do will shorten his sentence."

Rick said nothing. His head remained down as he worked on the fence. When he finished, he returned, sat on his toolbox, and wiped sweat from his face and neck. Dusk settled over the street. Brandon leaned against a tree trunk, and the two men continued their discussion in the dark.

"I guess you were saying your dad going to jail had something to do with you trying to push my neighbors out of their houses," Rick said. "I have a hard time figuring some things out, but that don't add up at all."

"Yeah, I know. What happened here is my fault. I just wished my parents, especially my dad, would have given me credit for a few things once in a while. With him put away though, it brought home that that wasn't going to happen."

Rick picked up his toolbox, stepped through the picket fence gate, and snapped it shut. "Perfect," he said. Then he stepped to the street, sat on the curb, and looked up at the rising moon. "I've known for years my parents were disappointed in how I turned out . . . but I never worried if they cared about me."

Rick's words resonated with such assurance Brandon fell under the spell of his voice. "How they feel about me is really about them. Their feelings for me have never had anything to do with what I became. They would always love me no matter what."

Rick's words were overwhelming in their simplicity, the way he could touch a thought with such child-like wisdom.

"Once we grow up," Rick continued, "it's time to move on. Be thankful for what we've been given. The future is up to us."

"I guess you're right," Brandon said. He couldn't have agreed more, but those were the only words he could force to his lips.

Rick stood and picked up his toolbox. "Good night then." Brandon watched him lumber up the sidewalk until he disappeared into the night.

The next evening, Brandon was back in Kessler Park talking to homeowners as they tended their flower beds or enjoyed the summer evening on their verandas. He began by asking about recent events. Everyone quickly condemned the hospital and their conniving ways, but they also told him stories about their wonderful years living at their particular address. Brandon listened, and the memories expressed began to form an idyllic picture, glossed over and embellished, he understood, but beautiful in their own little ways, and he enjoyed listening to their stories.

Some of the folks were infirm of body, others hard of hearing. Some were a little cantankerous if he came upon them when they were listening to the radio or busy in their garden. Still, he learned things he never knew, and he saw the caring eyes and heard the fragile fears of those near the finish line.

The more time he spent in Kessler Park, the more his opinions of the elderly changed, and for the better. He grew to like them all in one way or another as he acknowledged their individuality. A compassion for the elderly matured within him.

Near the south end of Cummings Street where it dead-ended into the litter-covered lot behind the pawn shop, he noticed city workers unloading concrete street barriers from a flat-bed truck. The workers moved the concrete barricades with the aid of chains attached to a front-end loader and set them across the end of streets. Brandon approached the obvious supervisor, an overweight guy in a hard hat who watched the proceedings from the curb.

"So what's all this?"

The heavy fellow gave Brandon a quick glance, then returned his attention to the front-end loader. "Work order."

"For what? You're not going to block up every street like that, are you?"

"Just the side streets for now."

"For now? Why are you blocking any of these streets?"

"Hey, pal, you'd have to ask my boss about that. I punch in and out every day, if you know what I mean."

"You don't have any idea why?"

The fat guy shook his head. "Like I said, you'd have to ask my department head."

"What department are you guys?"

"Streets and sanitation. Atherton's finest."

"I'm sure you are." With that Brandon walked away, his curiosity immediately bucked up ten notches. The city council meeting to officially consider St. Anthony's Hospital's condemnation request was just four days away. Brandon knew exactly where he'd be on Monday morning.

Saturday, Brandon went to work at the menswear store, their busiest day of the week. His cell phone rang, and he stepped out the back to take the call.

"This is Katherine Cramer, and I want you to know I'm aware of the games you're playing in Kessler Park."

"Games?"

"Listen, Mr. Evans." Her voice had lost the pleasant lilt of professional banter and had the edge of a taxi driver stuck in traffic. "St. Anthony's fully intends to pursue the acquisition of the Kessler Park acreage. This matter is not over by any means."

"Maybe you should take that up with the zoning board, Mrs. C. Last time I checked, they had a different take on the matter."

"You're an arrogant little nobody and quite clueless, I might add. If you know what's good for you, you'll butt out."

"What have you been smoking, lady? I don't know what you're talking about."

"You're down in that neighborhood, soliciting those homeowners to sell, arranging land contracts. That's what I'm talking about. I know good and well you don't have a Texas real estate license. That's misrepresentation and a felony for practicing without a license, mister. I'll have you brought up on charges if you don't quit that activity immediately."

Brandon swallowed, dumbstruck at the accusation. "Mrs. Cramer, you've got it all wrong. I'm not trying to put together any deals down there now at all."

"I don't believe you. You're trying to get the hospital to pay you for work you didn't really do. You just want to make it more difficult for the hospital to get the acreage at a reasonable price."

"Mrs. Cramer, please listen---"

"You heard me. If I get one more report of your busybody activities down there, you'll be sharing the same chow hall with that thieving father of yours." With that she hung up.

He could literally feel the heat radiating from his cheeks. If he weren't so bewildered, he'd probably have snapped the cell phone in his hands so great was his building anger. He had to wait ten minutes before he was able to go back inside the store.

    That evening, he picked up Jake and headed to the drag strip. Down a two-lane gravel road, a line of hot-rods, beat-up pick-ups, and family sedans waited to get into the parking area. During the week, the location was nothing but two parallel asphalt tracks in front of a rickety grandstand about fifty yards long. But on race day, the whole place erupted into a colorful tapestry of tents, vans, and trailers, and vehicles of every size and description.

    Jake watched everything with wide-eyed fascination. Brandon bought him a ball cap of a high-profile dragster. The hat was made of maroon corduroy with the driver's name etched in white script lettering. Jake handled the hat as though it were a bar of gold and creased it tenderly before putting it on his head. Brandon admitted the hat looked good, but who the driver was, he hadn't a clue.

    The smell of toxic exhaust and burned tire rubber quickly filled the air. The screaming roar of powerful engines encircled them like bolts of exploding thunder. Brandon bought some ears plugs, but they hardly helped. Jake cheered each race, screaming inaudibly against the deafening engine noise. He pumped his arm in the air when the cars took off from the start line and laughed in astonishment at the sheer power of the cars. Jake's tongue turned blue from the grape soda, his lips green from the cotton candy. He slapped Brandon on the back, bumped him in the shoulder, and jumped, and pointed as though Brandon may have missed something.

When the races were over, Brandon's ears rang all the way home. He was sure his brain had been tossed about in a hopper.

"Thanks, Brandon. Thanks so much. That was tons of fun," Jake said when he was dropped off in front of his house.

"Glad you liked it. Have a good week in school. I'll call you next week."

Whatever they agreed to do together in the future, Brandon swore he wouldn't return to the drag strip. He never wanted to lay eyes, or ears, on that place again. And yet, as he drove home, he knew he'd enjoyed every minute.

Atherton city council meetings began at ten on Monday mornings, if members of the council were in their seats, which was hardly ever the case. Once the meeting didn't get called to order until noon. A reliable factor in determining how close to the scheduled start time the session actually began was how well the Dallas Cowboys football team performed over the weekend. The better the team played, the sooner the meeting got started. Occasionally, if the team won and dominated their opponent, the meeting actually began on time.

Brandon arrived early, took a seat near the front in the half-full chamber, and observed others in attendance. He recognized three men from the neighborhood, Sherman Porter, Cecil Nance, and

Louis Hilker. Brandon moved to the row behind them and overheard their conversation. The city council's vote was a formality since the zoning board had rejected the hospital's application. They wanted to be there to watch the proceedings and witness the official end to the intrusion into their lives.

They watched Dan Beckerman across the auditorium conferring with someone none of them recognized. Gordon English, the attorney for Kessler Park, stopped to talk to the three men. He told them what they already knew. It had been over fifteen years since the council had overruled the planning board on any matter. There was no reason to think they would do it now. The vote in favor of Kessler Park's position was merely a procedural exercise.

At the Monday weekly council meeting, the city's elected officials publically declared their preferences, cast their votes, and faced the cacophony of the citizenry. It was a fair bet the citizens who made the trip downtown, scavenged for a parking spot, and hiked into city hall didn't do so to laud praise upon the council. It could be reliably assumed that most who signed up to speak at the weekly forum attended to beef about something.

Speakers were allowed to address one topic only, with a three-minute time limit. For the next hour, a parade of speakers stood behind the microphone for their allotted time crying about potholes and burnt-out streetlights. The abominable blight of graffiti was a prominent complaint as well as sluggish police response time.

New applications for council action were then read, discussed briefly, and tabled for any plausible reason that contained an air of even-handedness. City action delayed was government authority thoughtfully exercised. Decisions deferred generated fewer angry e-mails and nasty letters.

Finally, the time arrived for the council to consider old business. Votes would now be cast. Legal notices had been published with all relevant time frames adhered to strictly as required by law. Public hearings had been held. The condemnation application of Saint Anthony's Regional Hospital to acquire the area known as Kessler Park came up third on the docket, and the petition was read by the clerk in its entirety.

Sherman, Cecil, and Louis each held their breath. Their personal issue was now on stage. Though all seemed well-in-hand, the matter swelled in significance in the reading of the official application. It was as though they, together and personally, were being scrutinized, watched. Even as they sat, unmoving, their muscles tensed, their jaws clenched, every movement across the stage seemed to slow to an excruciating crawl. The clerk's voice dragged with an ominous tone as though she would never finish. The men strained to hear every word and leaned forward in their seats. When the clerk finished speaking, the accompanying silence held an uncomfortable pressure.

Finally, the mayor asked for a motion on the measure, and after receiving one, quickly received a second. "All in favor signal by raising your hand." Nine arms quickly filled the air. "Let it be noted that the measure passes unanimously."

It was as if an unholy vacuum had sucked all oxygen from the hall. After all they'd been through. When victory and the hope of returning to a peaceful life seemed once again within their reach the city fathers had snatched away their personal property and awarded it to the hospital.

Sherman's face visibly sank. Did the council know of the planning board's recommendation? Cecil gripped the arms of his seat until his knuckles turned white. Why wasn't there some discussion? Why no last minute questions or reservations by anyone on the council? It happened so quickly. When Louis looked around, their attorney, Gordon English, was nowhere to be seen. The men left the building drenched in utter disbelief. What would they tell their wives and friends? They were actually going to lose their homes. How much time would they be given to move out? Strange, debilitating feelings engulfed them. Sherman became so bewildered, his attention so blurred, on the way home he nearly sideswiped another car. On the trip back home, the three men traveled in a numbing cocoon of shock, and no one said a single word.

CHAPTER TWENTY-NINE

BRANDON SAT IN THE COUNCIL chamber as the session moved on to other topics and nodded. What had occurred, he had predicted. He wished someone had been taking bets. He'd have bet his last dime on the outcome he just witnessed. The fix was in, not just because the vote had been taken quickly, but because arrangements to expedite the outcome had been put into motion long before today.

He strolled through city hall, down its frosted-glass corridors to the information desk.

A matron at the desk peered at him through owlish glasses. "Yes, sir?"

"Do you have an organizational chart for the city?"

"Each department would have their own, sir."

"How about for the elected officials?"

"Yes, we do have something like that. It doesn't list names---just positions. Elected officials come and go, you know."

"Yes, ma'am, I understand. I'm sure I can fill in the blanks."

He walked three blocks to the main library, straight to the research department. Hopefully they kept the minutes of city council meetings. He wanted to learn about recent issues before the city and who benefited from actions taken by the council. How had each councilman voted in recent weeks, especially since the Kessler Park condemnation application first appeared on the calendar? He had a sudden passion for the study of local government.

He found a record of the council meeting minutes. Though detailed, they were too laden with governmental jargon to give him a sense of what had taken place. The actual applications on private sector requests proved more useful. There, a specific proposal was presented. Its origin, reason, and intended purpose could be tracked. He could determine who voted for each proposal and who benefited from the outcome.

He called Todd on his cell phone.

"What are you doing now?"

"Nothing. Sitting here looking at these walls."

"I've got a job for you. Get down here to the downtown library as fast as you can."

"Man, you know I don't have a car."

"Take the bus. You can get here in less than thirty minutes. Really, you aren't that far. You could walk here in that time. Just get here. I've got something in mind, and it'll be worth your time."

When Todd arrived, Brandon showed him documents of the city council's votes back to the first of the year. He had the folders on ordinance proposals, zoning request changes, and tax abatement applications. Brandon omitted capital expenditure votes because they dealt with normal and reoccurring city business.

"I want you to start with January 1st this year and track these initial requests all the way through to either being accepted or rejected. I want to know how each councilman voted on each measure."

A jaded boredom descended upon Todd's features as though he'd been asked to sharpen a box of pencils.

"I know you can handle this." Brandon infused his voice with all the enthusiasm he could muster. "I especially want to know who got the benefit from the proposals that passed."

"Got it," Todd said as he rolled his eyes.

"Here's twenty for lunch. I'll be back later. I have to go see someone."

Reluctantly, Brandon headed for Westchester Heights. It was an uncomfortable and anxious drive. He parked in the expansive driveway and ascended the white stones steps set into the hill. The curtains were pulled apart on the twenty-foot wide living room window. It was a good sign. He rang the bell.

He saw her through the door as soon as she turned into the entryway from the den, and he knew she saw him. But her pace didn't quicken. If anything, it slowed to a leisurely stroll. Brandon knew she would set her face to an expression appropriate for her mood, even clear her throat, and quickly consider the exact words she wanted to say. She opened the door.

"Good morning, mother."

"Brandon, you came to see me."

It was a good sign.

Brandon got his thick black hair from her. The rest of his good looks came from his father. She'd not be considered a beauty by most, her angular face too stark, a narrow chin with a slight overbite. But her eyes were absolutely holographic; emotion exuded from them in the form of light. Then again, he did take after his mother.

"May I come in?"

A hint of dejection crinkled her eyebrows. "Of course you can come in."

The house was light and cavernous. Brandon took a seat on a bar stool along an open counter between the kitchen and the den.

"Would you like some coffee? I can make some fresh." Victoria Evans leaned against the kitchen island, peering over her cup, her eyes aglow with amused suspicion. She was wearing a pink housecoat and slippers, but her hair was up in curlers. Maybe she had an appointment. Maybe she was going to get out of the house.

"I'm not much of a coffee drinker."

"How's your job doing?"

"Work's fine, mother. How have you been spending your time?"

"Oh, we play cards here on Thursday nights--- Texas hold'em. It's quite the rage. The girls love it."

"Mother, I need to borrow some money." He hated to say it, but being direct was the only way to deal with her. Beat around the bush and she'd suck you into her petty cycle of subtle recriminations.

"Are you in trouble?" For an instant she sounded genuinely concerned.

"No, mother. I'm not in any trouble—like you mean trouble." Brandon looked up and searched her eyes in the hope, just for a moment, he could have a conversation between two adults. If she would give him any money at all there would be conditions, but he had to ask. "Mother, I don't owe money, but I owe some time and effort to some people who need my help. I need the money to carry a project through. I'll pay you back however you want."

"How much?"

It was a good sign.

"Five thousand dollars."

"Good God, Brandon, I don't have that kind of money lying around."

Her reaction he expected. At least his request was now on the table. "Would you loan me the money if you had it?"

"Brandon, really, maybe, I guess. I'd have to know what you want it for."

"It's to help some people who really need it. Maybe I can stop something bad from happening that never should have started in the first place."

Brandon knew she was living on a nice cushion of bond payments and dividends allowing her to live a life of idleness and indulgence. It was all set up by his father for his own benefit, but since he was currently counting days in a four-by-eight cell in Huntsville, she benefited from the income. Her expression soured, and the mischievous glow receded from her eyes.

It was a bad sign.

"Why don't you move back here with me? This place is so empty. You could save some money that way for the Good Samaritan thing you're doing."

It was a very bad sign.

She was a manipulator, but then she had learned from the best. "Have you gone to see him?"

She turned her back and played with the coffee pot. "No. I've written, though. He wrote back, mainly to tell me how much I'm to blame for his predicament. I didn't know he was stealing from his company. He always wants someone else to blame for his problems."

"Any money left to pay his restitution?"

She nodded faintly. "The court recovered about half of it. I don't know where the other half will come from. The money I receive comes in monthly, and they haven't tied it to the money stolen from the company."

"What are you going to do when he gets out?"

"I don't know, Brandon. That's at least five years away. I'll worry about that when the time comes." She turned and faced him, and for a moment he saw the soft features of a caring mother. "I know he put so much pressure on you. He did to all of us. Why do you think your sisters live so far away? I just hope, in some way, with all the time he has to think, maybe he'll come out a little less critical, a little less bitter."

"Do you really think that will happen?"

"I just hope, Brandon. There's something in me that will always care about him. I just wish he'd ease up and find some joy in life."

"Mother, why did he just forget about us?"

Before she turned, he saw he'd hit a nerve. She walked across the room and played with a cigarette pack for what seemed like forever before she crumpled it in her fist and sat wearily onto a bar stool. "I don't know, Brandon. Maybe the pressure of his job got to him. Maybe he couldn't see past the notion he was supposed to be the provider, and everything else got lost along the way." She got up and went back to the coffee pot. Brandon waited. He could tell she wasn't through. When she refilled her cup, she walked back to where he sat.

"There comes a time, Brandon, when we have to do the sorting out for ourselves. Rehashing how we wished things would have been doesn't get you anywhere. Believe me, I know. We have to deal with things the way they are. It's time for that now, Brandon."

Brandon stood and took a deep breath. "I'm working on something that's right. If I have any success, it'll be worth the effort. I promise to come by more often, if that's what you want."

"Of course that's what I want."

That was a good sign.

"Can you give me something to get started?"

"Yes—yes, let me see." His presence seemed to take a weight from her heart, and she went to a desk drawer and took out a checkbook. When she looked up, her eyes were almost misty. "I can give you $2,000 now. Come by next Thursday, around six thirty, when the girls are here, and I'll see what else I can do."

"When the girls are here?"

"Yes, before we play cards. I want them to see how handsome you are. Here's my best number if you need to call. I got a new-fangled cell phone."

Brandon fought the urge to say something more. "Okay then, mother, thank you." He took the check and kissed her on the cheek.

When he returned to the library, Brandon found Todd overwhelmed with details, but jubilant on one point.

"This bunch don't disagree on nothing," Todd said, his long limbs and loose joints keeping rhythm with his enthusiasm. "I mean, they have a firm majority on every issue they vote on whether it's yea or nay, and most of them are unanimous."

"Shsssss," came from the next table over.

Brandon pulled Todd between the book racks. "Good job. Let's see what you got."

CHAPTER THIRTY

BRANDON TURNED HIS ATTENTION TO Atherton's fine mayor, Franklin Patterson. In his late sixties, Patterson had been a city hall fixture for close to thirty years, an unsuccessful bid for sheriff in the late seventies the only election he ever lost.

Brandon watched a town hall videotape in the library's media room and flipped through a book filled with the mayor's photos and public statements. He seemed an odd sort for the city's highest office. He spoke clearly, but in a monotone, evidenced no passion for any issue, and exhibited a mechanical way of sitting, eyes staring straight ahead as others spoke. He was photogenic, happy to accommodate group photos, and just as happy to move on. He rubbed elbows and glad-handed in an almost frenzied way.

An image began to emerge in Brandon's mind about the mayor. There was something about Patterson's demeanor that was too animated when he was onstage and too disinterested when he was off. His ruddy face and shiny head sported a rather cockeyed smile that was sufficient, if not endearing. A lawyer by profession, the political product of untold back-room compromises and last-minute deals, but something told Brandon that Patterson was more a marionette than a quarterback.

In his twenty-three years, Brandon had learned a thing or two about human nature. As he watched the videotape, a distinct impression formed concerning the mayor of Atherton, TX. The mayor was not the power behind the throne.

Maybe he was satisfied holding elected office. The title of mayor was no small feather in one's hat. Maybe he was just tired. After years of political battles, he may no longer care about the outcome of any of them. Then, too, it wouldn't be beyond the realm of possibility that he'd been a front man from the beginning of his mayoral tenure, either because of name recognition or because he proved a suitable compromise candidate among the power brokers of the city.

Brandon knew he would recognize what he sought if he came across it. If he could find even one shred of evidence of collusion regarding the Kessler Park vote, he would present his findings to the district attorney, the media, and anyone who would listen. He knew something shady had occurred. If there was any chance to save the old neighborhood, he would move heaven and earth to find it.

Mayor Patterson was scheduled to speak at a Rotary Club luncheon the following day, but once considered, Brandon found no reason to attend. The mayor's involvement in any vote fixing would be found in his past, not in his future. It was what he had recently supported and actually done that mattered.

Brandon returned to the library's main floor and slowly perused every document Todd had set aside. He ran across an innocuous petition for a zoning change for a two-story house to allow its use as a group home for developmentally challenged youngsters. A zoning change was approved in five weeks, an expeditious process from application to final approval for the normally lethargic and defensive Atherton council.

Brandon walked down the street to the county Hall of Records. Empowerment Charities, Inc. now owned the property. The previous owner was an Arlen Roberts. Brandon drew a quick breath. Was this the same man, the new city councilman from District 3? Elected June 6th, deed transferred on the house August 11th? Nothing trumps elected office to facilitate the sale of an unwanted piece of property.

The records didn't indicate the purchase price so Brandon drove to the property five miles northeast of downtown. He had to develop some leads and was willing to try anything to uncover useful information.

A middle-aged lady in a brown smock sat on the porch between two teenage girls. One girl rocked aggressively with great delight, while the other studied her fingers against the blue background of the sky.

"Can I go in or should I knock?"

"Go in," the lady said. "The office is on the left."

Just inside the door, he saw two teenage boys with video game controls in an adjacent room staring at an unseen screen. The rest of the main floor was empty. He rapped lightly on the office door and opened it. A heavy-set matron ceased her writing when he stepped in. Her expression seemed fixed, though cordial. Her eyes were gentle slits of light surrounded by grayish hair strained into a semblance of a wave and held in place with bobby pins.

"Good afternoon, my name is Brandon Evans. I was hoping to find out something about your facility."

"You have someone who needs special care?"

"Yes, my brother. I just wanted to inquire."

"Well, I'm sorry, Mr. Evans, but our referrals come from the state, and we have a lengthy waiting list."

"I see. I was hoping to learn a little about what you do and how someone would go about applying for services."

"Our residents are deemed to be able to live independently eventually, rather than in an institution. Those who reside here are on their road to independent living. We work to establish life skills and personal responsibility with all individuals placed with us."

"That's a commendable mission. The community needs many more facilities like this one if my experience is any indication. You haven't been at this location long, have you?"

"Moved here this summer. It's a perfect property for us, plenty of room. We have space for twelve residents."

"It's a lovely neighborhood—expensive, too. You could have gotten two houses in a more modest area, I would imagine, for what you paid for this one."

"Well, our governing board takes care of all of that," she said, "but I believe this property was a donation."

"Oh, that's different." Brandon was truly surprised.

"Mr. Roberts, the new city councilman from this district, gave it to us. He's a fine, upstanding gentleman and a credit to the city council, I would say. We desperately needed another facility and he stepped right in." The woman seemed especially pleased with herself having had the opportunity to make a personal endorsement.

"That's encouraging." Brandon found himself momentarily at a loss for words.

"I can give you a list of names and phone numbers to call for your brother's needs."

"Yes, that would be helpful. Thank you so much for your time."

Back in his car, Brandon suffocated in incredulity, a politician with a heart. He was too cynical for such nonsense. Life had taught him better. It wasn't that he had spent a life of depravation, far to the contrary. Yet, even an upbringing wrapped in the arms of abundance didn't blind him to the duplicity of human motivation. If anything, it illuminated it. He didn't believe the story the woman professed and was irked anyone would swallow such a line at face value. Councilman Roberts had gotten something of value in return for the house.

No one was going to convince him differently, especially when it came to a large, well kept property in an affluent neighborhood. But for now, there was nothing useful to learn here. Maybe improprieties by Roberts and other councilmen could be linked to this house. Presently, though, the trail led nowhere.

CHAPTER THIRTY-ONE

BRANDON RETURNED TO THE LIBRARY caught in traffic's evening crawl, exited the freeway as soon as he could, and wound through downtown streets. The ribbons of cars that lined the curbs during the workday were all but gone. The persistent haze of exhaust had lifted, brushed away by the breeze. Stragglers of work-a-day humanity claimed their vehicles from painted asphalt grids. Pigeons circled urban parks one last time, then took their roost. The western side of the city seemed ablaze, caught in the sharp angle of the sun. Brick and concrete took full possession of the streets, and urban towers of glass and steel began to meld as their folding shadows fell upon one another.

Of the hundreds of people he knew, no one quickly came to mind who could help him now. His old friends at the firm would shy away from checking on elected officials. The old gang from the frat house, plenty of whom lived in the Atherton area, ever willing to pull off a dangerous stunt like shooting tree squirrels with .22 rifles from dormitory windows across a populated campus, wouldn't have the nerve to probe into the lives of politicians. The extent of their bravery ended with feeding cat food and shoe polish to freshmen pledges. Their 'rally round the beer keg' bravado would be useless for what he had to do.

For that matter, he could think of no one who'd have a clue how to investigate people who worked within the mysterious shelter of a government entity. Even Cindy had turned her back on him. Never before had he seen her so abrupt and exasperated. They had been a fun pair. For a moment, he felt sorry for himself. He'd lost something he hadn't known he would miss. The only person readily available was Todd. If he could come up with anyone else, he would ask for their help. But Todd was all he had.

This time, at least, Brandon knew he'd be doing something for close to the right reasons. He had to find out how the vote to approve the Kessler Park condemnation had come off so smoothly. If his efforts thwarted the aspirations of Katherine Cramer, he would welcome that, too.

Brandon found Todd outside the library entrance smoking a cigarette.

"You find anything more?" Brandon asked.

Todd exhaled a long drag and gazed at his cigarette as though with each puff it were supposed to get longer. "Man, all that crap is boring."

"Well, it's research, but I'm paying you. Did you find anything?"

"Yes and no." Todd snuffed out his cigarette in a concrete ashtray that doubled as a trash receptacle.

"And?"

"I looked closer at some of the individual requests. You might find something in those."

"Like what?" Brandon was instantly attentive.

Todd lit another cigarette and repeated his protracted breathing cycle while his bloodstream rushed nicotine nourishment to his brain. "Well, if I was you, I'd look close at the businesses that made applications for the city to cut them some slack on their taxes. Seems to me, if an outfit had less tax to pay, there'd be extra money around to grease the process."

A glow came to Brandon's eyes. "Good point. You're pretty sharp."

Todd's response was another long pull on his smoke.

"Let's get all your paperwork, and I'll give you a ride home," Brandon said. "I've got a plan."

They drove a wide circuit out of the downtown area to get to one of the few underpasses below the freeway that ran south toward Todd's apartment.

"So why all this paper shuffling about the city government?" Todd asked. "You planning on running for mayor?" The comment instantly struck Todd as humorous, and he flashed his stubby teeth and dark gums.

"I screwed up---."

"Mr. big shot developer screwed up?" Todd interrupted.

Brandon cocked his eyebrows, but ignored the verbal jab. "Remember when you called me a

274

month ago and told me about that condemnation notice showing up at people's door? Well, the city voted on it today, made it official, the hospital gets all that land—unless I can stop them. Until today it looked like it might not go through, so I didn't say anything. But now the hospital definitely has city hall on their side."

"Damn," Todd sounded truly insulted. "All those signatures for nothing?"

"Yep." Brandon nodded and kept his eyes on the road.

"So what's going to happen to all those folks?"

"They'll have to move. The hospital will offer them a pittance. Some of them might file a protest, but the hospital will still pay them no more than they have to. The residents will have to move out even if the money part hasn't been settled."

"Damn, that's brutal." Todd was silent and slowly rocked his head in contemplation. "So how can you stop that?"

"My gut tells me some people at city hall have been accepting bribes, everything wrapped up quickly with an official bow. I intend to throw a monkey wrench in their plans."

Todd's brow crinkled as he studied Brandon across the car seat. "You're just pissed you lost out on the deal. You want the big shots to pay for horning in on your idea."

Brandon shrugged. "Think what you want. I think, I just wanted the recognition of putting together a big deal. Then, I kept at it when the zoning board voted the hospital out. But really, I've been fooling myself."

Todd wouldn't let the discussion die, and he jabbed contemptuously. "You still want those houses. You're just saying what you're saying now because you won't get them."

Silence settled in the car. There was nothing more Brandon could say that wouldn't sound like pleading. He changed the subject. "You and I are going to poke around and ask some questions."

"Me?"

"Yes—you. First thing I'm going to do is buy you some new clothes."

"But why? What's in it for you?"

"Exposing a crooked politician would make it worth my while. Maybe too, I could make it where those old folks won't have to move."

"Yeah but— " Todd attempted to wrap his thoughts around Brandon's magnanimous declaration, but the notion leaked away faster than his brain could compute as though his mind was little more than a sieve. "But what's in it for you?"

Brandon glanced Todd's way, a wry smile set firmly on his lips. "Nothing, but that's okay. It's something I need to do."

"Here's my place," Todd said. "Belmont Apartments."

"Here's thirty bucks for today. Help me out tomorrow, and we'll stir up a hornet's nest."

As soon as he stepped from the car Todd popped a cigarette in his mouth. "All right," he said after a brief yet intense personal deliberation. "I'll help."

"Be at the diner tomorrow morning. Eight sharp."

The next morning, both Brandon and Todd arrived at the diner before eight. Todd was quiet. The familiar shifty, nervous eyes had returned.

"What's up with you?" Brandon asked. "You want something to eat?"

"I changed my mind. I don't want to go messing with the local law."

"The law? I'm just talking about poking around some politicians. See what sticks to the wall. There's nothing illegal about asking questions."

"I don't want to do it." Todd was adamant. It didn't sound like money was an issue.

"What did you do, rob a bank?"

"No!"

Todd's stance was puzzling. Brandon hadn't seen the day Todd would turn down a buck. He cocked his head and remained quiet, his eyes asking for more information.

"I just changed my mind, that's all."

"You think quick on your feet," Brandon said. "I thought you'd love to mix it up with big shots who think they're better than everyone else."

"I can't do it. I just came here to let you know."

As Brandon stared across the table, the wave of irritation that rolled up inside him quickly dissipated. He hadn't relished the idea of working with Todd anyway. Still, he was surprised. Deep inside, he realized if anything was going to get done, it would be up to him alone. His overriding optimistic attitude stepped in and propped him up. It wasn't about being cheery or upbeat; it was about getting on with what he had to do. He tipped the last of his coffee to his lips and threw a couple bucks on the table. "Okay, suit yourself."

On his Trans Am passenger seat Brandon had his combat arsenal at hand. Everything he thought he could possibly need, he'd assembled over the last several days. The city of Atherton website carried photographs of all city councilmen and the mayor. He flipped through the portraits of smug, self-righteous dignitaries, each professionally lighted, meticulously air brushed. Brandon could now recognize each man on sight. Only the mayor held a full-time city position. The other men held regular jobs in addition to their official duties. Brandon knew where each of them worked and what they did for a living.

He flipped through the stack of papers of recent council votes on private business requests. Two kept grabbing his attention—the quick zoning change for the mentally-challenged halfway house he had already visited and a tax abatement request that passed in six short weeks for an agricultural equipment manufacturer called the Britton Cattle Equipment Company.

CHAPTER THIRTY-TWO

THE BRITTON CATTLE COMPANY WAS LOCATED in District Six, an amalgamation of human environs on the north side of town, retail, apartment buildings, tract homes, and warehouses. District Six extended to the city limits, butting against endless miles of scrub oak and mesquite trees, ravines, and pastureland that rolled on up to the Oklahoma line.

Councilman Don Martin held claim to the district, a three-term city official. A CPA by profession, he ran his own shop with the help of several secretaries, though he devoted a good deal of time to keeping tabs on the scuttlebutt downtown. Brandon called the office with a desperate plea for assistance due to a personal IRS letter and got an appointment for the next day.

Brandon read again the tax abatement application submitted by the Britton Cattle Company. The approval of the twenty-five acre tax abatement amounted to a sizeable loss of revenue to the city, and for an extended length of time. It was certainly possible Councilman Martin worked in some private capacity for the cattle equipment company. But if he uncovered shady dealing behind the tax break, Brandon figured it would involve cold cash under the table, not because of any professionally rendered services.

The following day, Brandon arrived right on time and was ushered into a formal conference room replete with a polished ebony table and black leather chairs. Martin entered with a yellow pad and a sporadic sniff. Enough strands of hair covered his head to give the illusion he wasn't completely bald. His shirt buttons fought a fierce battle to restrain his bulk. His eyes were focused, set deep in a fleshy face, his voice authoritative, yet friendly.

"How can I help you, Mr. Evans?"

Brandon proceeded with a fabricated story of unfiled returns, address changes, and failure to respond to previous IRS notices. Martin took notes, seemingly pleased, yet made enough empathetic utterances to not appear elated with Brandon's stated predicament. When Brandon finished, Martin immediately indicated he had just the answer. A thousand dollars would get the process rolling. Martin's office would respond to the IRS on Brandon's behalf, file all back tax returns, and once again, Brandon could return to his life, free of worry and stress.

"We'll find out exactly what the IRS has on you," Martin said with a vocal inflection that combined a nebulous threat with one of life's little ironies, and from the look on Martin's face, Brandon could tell he was supposed to be happy about the professional affiliation.

"I know I should have dealt with this sooner."

Martin sniffed in apparent agreement. "I need your approval here. Bring in all your receipts and W-2's."

"I was just wondering." Brandon made a subtle shift of topic. "I have my securities license, and I've sure noticed fewer people want a full-service broker since they can trade online for themselves. Has your business changed with all the tax preparation software that's available these days?"

"Oh, some, I suppose, but we keep books for people year 'round and prepare back taxes like we're going to do for you. I need your signature right here."

Brandon took the pen, looked at the paper, then raised his head as though a new thought had just crossed his mind. "Is there some sort of payment arrangement I could set up for this work?"

"What I quoted is based on what you told me and the scope of work required." Martin tried to come off as empathetic, but his voice carried a patronizing tone. "We typically get that up front. If there are additional charges, we'll bill you for those."

"What if I could bring you in more business to prepare back taxes?" Brandon's voice and body language projected a gung-ho confidence. Intensity spilled from his eyes, a dynamic determination that pulled women to him and made men pay attention. Everyone who knew him for any length of time had witnessed the performance before. Its sheer audacity contributed in large measure to its frequent success.

The idea caught Martin unprepared. "I suppose I could pay you a finder's fee."

"I bet addressing back tax problems would generate three times the income with half the work. Keeping books year 'round has got to be so time-consuming. Doing back taxes, on the other hand, you said yourself you can find out what the IRS already has on file, what penalties they've charged, what they're after. You can charge just about whatever you want to get someone off the hook. Am I right?"

"Mr. Evans, you paint an interesting picture." Martin let out a nervous chuckle. "But I'm not looking to add an employee. I just don't think---"

"Mr. Martin, I had a business professor once tell me if a person wanted a good job, he should create the job himself and prove the idea and the person were both valuable. Let me show you I can have them lining up at the door." Brandon exuded a tenacious expression and locked his gaze into the eyes of the astounded councilman. "Three times the revenue for half the work. Without a large volume of new business, you'll never know how profitable preparing delinquent taxes might be." Brandon paused for just an instant. "Pay me a set percentage based on the amount of business I bring in. You decide. I know you'll be fair."

"Good grief, young man. You do have an air about you."

"I wouldn't be an employee anyway. Strictly commission. That's what I'm used to, that's what I like. I'll start first thing in the morning." Brandon stuck out his hand, and the obese councilman shook it without so much as a gasp of protest.

That same day, the homeowners of Kessler Park received another official notice from the city. They had to be out by the first of the year. The final vote had taken place on September 20th. In real time, the city was giving occupants of the sub-division 100 days to move. The news gave Brandon a vague notion of hope, as well as nauseating sense of dread. He had time to uncover something that might change the course of events. He forced the fact that he'd been the cause of it all to the back of his mind. A definitive date was now known. It meant he had some time, but not much.

CHAPTER THIRTY-THREE

WHEN RICK BECAME INCENSED about the Kessler Park condemnation proceedings and undertook his petition drive, his mother became interested, too. Once the matter became front page news and Rick spoke at the zoning board meeting, she followed every development. Ann Stanton worked side-by-side the elderly residents when the neighborhood clean-up began after the favorable vote by the zoning board. She helped Ethel Barnes plant rows of pansies and daisies along her front porch flowerboxes. Ethel could do little more than shuffle about and display her radiant dentures in unmistakable appreciation. Ethel patted dirt around the new plants and thanked Ann for the colorful blessing for her porch.

When the city council voted against the zoning board's recommendation and in favor of the hospital's request, the neighborhood's reaction was abject despondency. Even the newly planted flowers seemed to droop in sadness. Everyone's bustling enthusiasm receded into cocoons of solitude and seclusion. Twice they had been hit; thinking of what lay ahead was almost too much to bear. Rick, too, was crushed. Content to live his life day by day, his world was thrown into uncertainty for he saw the very essence of life drain from his friends and neighbors.

The day after the city council vote, Ann received a call from Beth Dinkle at city hall. Beth's voice sounded anxious. It was more than a casual call. Ann sat back in her chair and focused on the voice at the end of the line.

"I just saw the official vote on that neighborhood you were interested in. I didn't know until today what had been decided on. I'm so sorry, Ann. From what I'd seen previously, I thought they were going to turn it down."

"We're all surprised. My son tells me it's a pretty gloomy state of affairs down there now."

"Ann, I know I shouldn't be telling you this, but I've always known you as a professional. It just struck me you have some sort of stake in that neighborhood and you ought to know."

"Know what?"

"I overheard two of the councilmen in the parking lot talking about how they could have gotten more money from the hospital if they'd just postponed the vote for a month or two. I was sitting right there, not two cars away, with my window rolled down. They didn't see me. They didn't even look around. One of them made it perfectly clear they blew a big opportunity. Nobody has deeper pockets than the hospital is what he said. Just like that."

"Are you sure he meant what you think?"

"Yes, I heard it all. They were both talking about how next time they would do things differently."

"Did they say how much?"

"No, I didn't get that—just a second."

"Who were they?"

"They're waving for me. I have to go. I'll get back to you."

The line went dead. Ann slumped in her chair. Her mind became a jumble of conflictions as the receiver slid down her cheek. Her first emotion was the elation of hope. Just as quickly, her mind soured. A course of action to right a horrible wrong was quickly dashed on rocks of realism. As promising as the revelation sounded, what did it really mean? Something told her it was practically common practice in city politics for under-the-table shenanigans to occur, but then, selling votes was illegal. Beth's information reeked of unmitigated corruption.

Ann wanted to be happy, glad Beth had the nerve to speak up. Rick's melancholy had already broken her heart. This news would beam a light of optimism into his outlook. Yet, what could she say? To tell him anything positive now, then for nothing to change, would put him through more anguish. She couldn't tell him what she'd heard. He wouldn't understand. Besides, even if Beth had proof, which was unlikely, what could happen now to change the past? She couldn't mention a word of this to anyone. As she sat staring at the dead receiver, part of her wished Beth had just kept her big mouth shut.

Brandon had an opening, a chance to increase Don Martin's cash flow, and with it an opportunity to get close to the man's daily activities. Brandon returned to his apartment and placed ads on free Internet sites using provocative fictitious testimonials. With the help of a web designer, he developed web pages targeted to young professionals with delinquent tax troubles. Within days, his cell phone rang with inquiries about his service.

He met with prospective clients wherever they wanted to meet. He got them to move forward, deal with their tax issues here and now, and steered them away from other preparers. He set appointments and, when possible, personally introduced them to Martin's office staff. Within two weeks, Brandon made regular stops at the office. Somewhere in that period, he took to sitting behind an empty desk. Brandon's charming smile soon became a welcome sight around the office, and he quit his job at Gibson Menswear.

Getting close to Councilman Martin had been the easy part; finding anything incriminating would be the challenge. It was possible Martin conducted his official responsibilities on the up-and-up, possible, but unlikely. The more time he spent around Martin, the more Brandon knew there were hidden political skeletons buried in his bottom desk drawer.

Martin's office door was usually open when he was in. Brandon listened intently to one-sided phone conversations where Martin laughed in off-color vulgarities about some local businessman or seethed about a worthless city employee. One day, Martin brought him into his office and shut the door. Brandon acted shocked to learn Martin was in fact an elected official on the Atherton city council. The awe that registered on Brandon's face was worth an acting award at the very least.

"I think you have what it takes to take on the world of politics," Martin said in his familiar ingratiating tone as though he were coaching a Little Leaguer.

Brandon shrugged. "Sir, I don't know anything about politics."

Martin vibrated in a heart-felt chuckle. "Oh, but you do. Politics is about people . . . getting to know them . . . learning what makes them tick. I already know you do that well. Everyone has their agenda, so you try to keep agendas on the same track as much as possible. When they differ, politics is all about getting more of your proposals through than the other guy." Martin became tickled and shuddered in his chair for fifteen seconds as another wave of mirth bubbled through him.

"That's kind of you to say."

"It's true, Brandon. You've got what it takes." Martin stopped for just a second and folded his hands slowly in a profound gesture. "I have a re-election campaign to run next spring, and I want you on my team. I'd like you to come with me to city hall and get a feel for the place, as well as meet some of the folks in the community who've supported me in the past.

"Certainly sounds interesting."

"And challenging," Martin interjected. "There's a lot to learn and hard work involved, but you've got the skill and the talent."

"I'd be honored, Mr. Martin. I love a challenge."

For weeks, the impending demise of Kessler Park received ample press. It made the evening news, the subject of front-page articles, a prominent topic of numerous editorials. Talk radio hammered away at the callousness of the hospital. Saint Anthony's Regional Medical Center had a public relations problem, but hardly a situation that would affect their bottom line or reduce their flow of patients. With the passage of time, the hospital would survive the scratch to its reputation and leave the faceless residents of Kessler Park to fend for themselves.

After awhile, some radio callers began to express support for the hospital's actions and their foresight in planning for Atherton's future need for modern, progressive medical facilities. Brandon knew the plight of Kessler Park would quickly fade as a news item. He had to find a crack in the council's vote-to-the-highest-bidder way of doing business. He had to find it soon.

The day after the final council vote, a group of twenty-five picketed the hospital's front entrance. The next day a group of close to forty showed up and marched for eight hours. Three weeks later, what picketers reported for duty were little more than weary stragglers with broken signs. The word "thieves" had been sprayed in reverse with red paint on the front glass by the hospital entrance so it could be read from the inside. It was quickly scraped off, the glass panel thoroughly washed.

Front-page stories with bold headlines that ran in the *The Sentinel* for eleven days straight, now appeared as summaries on page five. No longer did the newspaper express outrage of the historic neighborhood's demise. Instead, stories in the press began to speculate what the hospital intended to do with the newly acquired land.

CHAPTER THIRTY-FOUR

THE BAD NEWS REACHED RICK as a wisp of gossip drifting on the wind, an untidy rumor unmistakably apparent in downtrodden faces and bewildered gazes. No one told him directly about the council vote. No one needed to. He figured for himself all he needed to know. The important people in the fancy downtown building had crushed the vibrant life from Kessler Park. Even the fresh landscaping seemed to wither under the decisive proclamation. The air grew still in condolence; birds fell silent in empathy.

Though he could feel the sadness around him, Rick remained undeterred in his daily routine. He had appointments to keep, people to see. If his stops dispensed even a single smile he would maintain his schedule until the bulldozers came.

Today, he was scheduled to work at the sprawling two-story owned by Cecil and Clara

Nance. They had purchased the place several years earlier when Raymond retired after a thirty-year career as an industrial arts teacher. Cecil was sixty-eight, unusually spry for a man his age, with a motivation like Rick's to transform his house, and in time the whole neighborhood, back into the elegance that once graced the land.

Over the past month, the two men had erected scaffolding around the massive chimney. Today, Rick intended to help Cecil tuck-point the chimney and replace missing bricks in the impressive beveled crown.

"Good morning, Mr. Nance." Rick greeted everyone as though he were making their acquaintance for the first time. Rick wasn't fazed by the dejected look that greeted him. Sadness gripped him, too, but his outlook was too hopeful to countenance negatives. His attitude was sometimes seen as naïve, viewpoint mired in childlike immaturity. Rick's mind was unable to fathom great joy, but unable to succumb to lasting sorrow as well. Quite often, his simple perspective provided a healing balm most needed by people racked with despair.

Cecil sucked up a huge breath and blew it out in a slow, pitiful sigh. "Never in a million years would I have thought them sons-a-bitches downtown would have pulled the stunt they've done to this classic neighborhood. If I had only known. Them scum bastards. . ." His voice trailed off in profane mumbles.

"Keeping busy is the thing to do, Mr. Nance. It only gets worse when you sit and think about something bad. If you keep busy at least, you're not thinking about it."

The absolute simplicity of the suggestion was galling. Cecil stared back, about to take his frustrations out on Rick. One look at the young man's serene, sympathetic face stopped him from that. Still, Cecil was beyond depressed. He was about to suffer a serious economic loss. Everything he'd put into the house would never be recaptured. Even more to the root of his hostility was the blatant fact that his life-long dream to restore an historic structure had been yanked from his future, and for that he would forgive no one.

"There's no need to work on the house," Cecil said. "I should have called you. I forgot all about it."

"I come to work," Rick said. "The chimney needs fixing, and it seems wrong to leave it all broken up there when we got the platform built."

Cecil's eyes searched Rick's face anew. His expression struggled to exhibit some amusement at the idea, but it wasn't in him. Another tragic sigh shook his body. "It's not worth it. Let the whole damn thing rot where she sits. It makes me sick just to look at the house now."

"No! It's a beautiful house. It's almost perfect after all you've done. I hear other people talk, and they all wish their house looked like yours. It makes me so happy to see it 'cause I know I helped."

"It's going to be torn down." Cecil almost choked on the words.

Rick's face mirrored Cecil's grim reality, but his eyes exuded an optimistic light. He spoke with an unconditional conviction and the room seemed to brighten with his positive outlook. "But it's here now," Rick said.

Rick wanted Cecil up from his bench. He was ready to get to work. Moping about helped no one and got nothing done. "Everything's gone someday, Mr. Nance. But who wants to wait until things fall down or something dies? It's better to enjoy what you have today, don't you think?"

"What should we do?" Cecil asked. Rick's encouragement mentally knocked him from his apathy, though he was still immobilized by despair.

"Fix the chimney! I'll get the bricks and mortar up, and you make it complete and perfect." Rick beamed his radiant grin. "You make it the grandest chimney in the city."

Later that day, Brandon drove by the Nance house, and saw men working. Jake was with him. Brandon stopped the car, and he and Jake got out. As Cecil needed bricks, Rick sent them up four and five at a time in a box tied to a rope that Cecil hoisted to the chimney top through a pulley. Fresh mixed mortar went up the same way.

Brandon looked at the work in progress. He knew full well all the houses were slated for demolition, but said nothing about that. "Afternoon, Rick. Sure is an impressive chimney."

"Yes it is. I talked Mr. Nance into finishing the repair."

The three of them craned their necks and shielded their eyes against the sky as they watched for awhile.

"Don't I know you?" Rick addressed Jake.

Jake shook his head.

Rick's brow creased as his mind searched for a particular memory. "Bricks," hollered the voice from the top of the scaffolding as the wooden box descended. Rick filled the box, then turned to Jake.

"You came by the garden, didn't you?" The tone in Rick's voice indicated he was still trying to recall Jake's face. Brandon watched Jake stiffen.

"You came by the garden with your friends." Rick's voice grew more assured, but his body language didn't change. Nothing in his demeanor became accusatory. He was only trying to remember.

But Jake remembered, too, and the huge bulk of a handyman instilled him with panic. He remembered what had happened to Gary when he ripped the bluebonnets from the ground, and he remembered how they had pulled back the tree branch and smacked the big guy in the face.

"Look, mister. I don't know what you're getting at, but I don't think I've ever seen you before."

"I think it was you," Rick said as though he were about to recount an event, but that's all he said.

"Was what?" Brandon asked. He gaze darted between the other two. "What happened?" But Rick was again looking up at the chimney, and Jake had his hands stuffed in his pockets, his gaze now glued on his shoes.

"Jake?"

"What?"

"You know something, don't you?"

"No, sir. I don't know what he's talking about." The denial wasn't convincing. "Whatever it is, he has me mixed up with someone else."

Rick's attention remained high above. Brandon couldn't be sure he was even listening. Rick neither challenged the boy's statement nor asked another question. Brandon decided to let it go.

"We were headed to the mall," Brandon said to Rick to change the subject. "Is there anything you need from there? I could bring it to you tomorrow."

Rick shook his head. "I don't go to the mall much. Don't much know what's there anyway."

A shout of "mortar," came from overhead as the wooden box descended. Rick poured water on an already mixed batch of concrete, and he stirred it a bit more and dumped a shovel full in the box.

"All this is going to be torn down, you know," Rick said, as Cecil pulled the rope from above and fresh mortar headed up the scaffolding.

Brandon shook his head. "I heard," he admitted. He wondered why he would ever think that Rick wouldn't be aware of the latest neighborhood news.

"What you started is going to ruin the lives of all these nice people." A hard edge coated Rick's words, a bitterness Brandon had never heard from him before.

"Rick, everything that's going on is much bigger than me. The city and the hospital want this land. I'd stop it if I could, but it's way over my head."

"But all these homes are going to be torn down because you started it. You said so yourself. Why did you have to ever come around here?" Rick's tone expressed a deep hurt, as though Brandon had violated a sacred trust.

"What's going to be torn down?" Jake asked. His understanding hung outside the conversation, and his gaze darted between the older men. Neither Brandon nor Rick elaborated. For an indeterminable length of time a thick silence settled at the base of the chimney. "What are you talking about?" Jake insisted.

Finally, Brandon addressed the boy. "The hospital wants all this land for expansion."

"They're going to tear all these houses down?" Jake asked.

"That's the hospital's plan, along with help from the city."

"So that's what my mom and grandma's been talking about," Jake said to no one in particular. Then, he looked up and locked his gaze with Brandon's. "So, what's that got to do with you?"

Brandon glanced at Rick, but he was watching Cecil work high on the scaffolding. Having made his point, Rick seemed satisfied to let Brandon's conscience dish out whatever reprimand was due. Rick had said his peace. Further condemnation wasn't in him and would serve no useful purpose. It was enough he had let Brandon know he knew.

But Jake wasn't mollified. Brandon's silence ratcheted his curiosity up another notch, and his whole body began to fidget. "What's that got to do with you?"

Brandon gritted his teeth. Pressure built in his chest. Just moments before, the boy had refused to give a straight answer when Rick asked if they had met. Now, Jake was demanding that he divulge an indiscretion that already kept him awake at night. He wasn't about to be badgered by a pimple-faced kid who did nothing but take up his time.

"Don't worry about it. It doesn't pertain to you," Brandon said.

"Whaddya mean, it doesn't pertain to me? My grandma lives over on the next block."

"What?"

"Yeah. Mrs. Morgan---Mrs. Bea Morgan. Why do you think I live so close to here?"

"Beatrice Morgan is your grandmother?"

"Yes!" Jake looked at him like he was stupid. "Who do you think watched me and my sister all the time when my mom had to work?"

"You never told me."

"So? They've been saying for weeks grandma was going to have to move. She doesn't know where she can go, and she sure can't move in with us. We ain't got the room." Jake almost shook in his shoes. His stare filled with a mixture of bewilderment and fury. It was a look of having been betrayed. "What does all that have to do with you?" Jake asked for the third time.

Brandon couldn't think of what to say. Jake's face swelled with indignation, and the silence that permeated the atmosphere hung so heavy Brandon could hardly breathe.

He had to say something, but gagged on the thought. Jake was waiting. Rick was watching. The remorse Brandon readily declared to himself was nothing but a tiny slap on the wrist. Now he had to admit out loud a blunder of both judgment and decency. Like his father standing before the judge, Brandon stood convicted and exposed. His selfish deeds were about to see the light of day, and he wanted to crawl into a hole and sink into a coma.

"Back in May, I told some people at the hospital this area was for sale." Brandon exhaled, then sucked up a huge breath. "They grabbed onto the idea and took it to the city."

Jake's face contorted. The pained astonishment that etched his features was absolutely heartbreaking. "Why would you do that?"

There was no answer in the world that would suffice. An elaboration would only grind the pain in deeper. Brandon stood mute. The disappointment he saw on the boy's face hurt more than being whipped.

"You---" Jake's hands clenched and relaxed uncontrollably. "My grandma doesn't want to move from her house. She's never wanted to move."

Brandon prayed his sorrowful expression might convey the extent of his regret, but knew there was no apology sufficient for his actions. He'd never be able to look anyone in the face who lived in Kessler Park once they learned of his culpability in their troubles.

"So why did you start coming to see me? What do you expect to get from me?" If Jake's stare could kill, he'd be dead on the spot. And then, his words slow and deliberate, Jake screamed, "Don't you ever come around me again." Before Brandon could say a word, Jake dashed to the sidewalk and disappeared around the corner.

CHAPTER THIRTY-FIVE

BRANDON ASKED SUBTLE QUESTIONS
of everyone he met around city hall. Precious weeks
came and went, but no incriminating evidence
materialized. No loose tongues in the hallowed halls
of municipal government. No disgruntled city
employees who knew anything he needed to hear.

He met Don Martin's reelection committee, a
collection of middle-aged men short on fashion
sense, all cast from a similar die, with jowly faces
and belt buckles concealed behind aprons of flab.
The lot included a businessman whose vocation was
never made quite clear, an attorney who specialized
in traffic tickets, a carpet outlet owner, and a
druggist. Each man praised Martin's prowess as an
elected official. His successful candidacy held their
vicarious passports into the political arena, and for
such meager pickings they toiled in his campaigns.

Brandon was introduced to each in turn, and
when they met, they joked, and smoked, and drank
coffee by the pot. He fit right in. He made sure he

kept his references properly dated, sufficiently relevant, with an occasional hint of off-color humor that never failed to please. Brandon noticed how Martin watched him when he spoke. Brandon made the right comments, his approval rating rose. The man whose opinion mattered most appeared more than satisfied with his performance.

On his first visit to city hall Brandon was duly impressed. The coded security doors were opened wide. He was escorted inside by one of only nine elected officials of the fine city of Atherton, TX, Councilman Don Martin himself.

In the span of several hours, he brushed against the movers and shakers of a major city, an introduction that an entire semester of college political science lectures could only hint at. He met the mayor face-to-face, and his deputy, a man named Riley. He met the city manager and police chief, and toured Martin's city hall office. He received a councilman's view of the chamber where the public weekly sessions were held. Brandon's eyes rose in a brief, yet truly awed view of the amphitheater auditorium from Martin's official seat. The enormity of the chamber hit home, and his eyes didn't stop rising until they reached the ceiling.

Martin ended the session by poking his head in a half dozen rooms, painting the atmosphere with wisecracks and his raucous chuckle. They left the glass monolith of city hall and jaywalked to an Irish pub across the street named McLinty's. Martin led them through tables of lunch diners, past a bottle display of Irish ales and stouts, along a shiny brass rail to the back of the establishment. There, at a table for two, Martin ordered a plate of ribs, baked chicken breast, and red wine. Brandon selected a salad and a glass of water. The muffled din of pans and trays rattling in the kitchen came through the wall. Brandon noticed Martin look over his shoulder to insure the waiter was gone, and he leaned over the table with curious eyes and an expectant expression.

"So what did you think of that?"

"Impressive. I didn't realize so many people worked for the city."

"It's a big town," Martin said. "Regular folk take it all for granted, but running a city is a big operation."

"Yes, I see."

Martin leaned back. The lower half of his body settled into the seat. "Almost ten years I've been a councilman. Wouldn't trade it to be governor. Hands on the wheel of government, right in my own back yard."

"It's a lot of pressure, isn't it? I mean, there's no way you can please everyone."

"Sure, there's pressure." Martin's voice grew contemplative. "That's why everyone with good ideas or intentions doesn't make a good elected official. You got to be able to make a decision and not second guess yourself." Another thought obviously entered his head as Martin's expression instantly changed. "When you make the right people happy, it makes the residual pressure easy to bear." The comment tickled his fancy, and his merry chuckle bubbled up from his throat.

"I know you have the support of your district. I'll do whatever you need me to do to get you re-elected," Brandon said.

Martin's approving expression wrapped Brandon in a blanket of political affection. The food came, and Martin began his meal by downing a full glass of wine. He picked up a sparerib and began gnawing as he spoke.

"The pressure in this job doesn't come from the citizens. Hell no, I wish. It would be easy then. It's the other members of the council I have to watch out for. Such a bunch of crybabies, I swear. You've heard the saying, keep your friends close and your enemies closer? It's the damn truth. You cross some of these guys, they write it down in blood. Never forget nothing." Martin wiped his hands, switched to the chicken breast, and put his knife and fork to work.

"This new guy, Roberts, what an asshole. He went to UT in Austin. His uncle was mayor back in the eighties. Right out the chute he wants a special zoning exemption on one house up in the Heights. One house! Apparently he had a charity on the hook to pay top dollar for the place to use as a halfway house for trainable nitwits."

Martin's mind rolled with the recollection, and he recounted the story, speaking with his mouth full.

"Well, the Heights are in Joe Thompson's district, and there's no way anyone up there wants a halfway house in their neighborhood. You say halfway house and they think paroled perverts. That sounds dangerous and bad for property values, so the answer is no. Nobody bothers to find out that they only want the place for a bunch of docile retards." Martin got tickled and began to chuckle again. He spit chewed chicken in his napkin, wiped his teary eyes, drained a half glass of wine, filled it again, and resumed his meal and story. Brandon nibbled on his salad and listened.

"Thompson gets Brunner, Fitzpatrick, and Douglas to back him up 'cause they have high dollar neighborhoods in their districts, too. So before long, over this one little spat, we got an impasse on zoning changes. Brad Decker from District One is beside himself. St. Anthony's Hospital is in his district, and they want to acquire a good size parcel of land through a condemnation proceeding. But for several weeks, no one wanted to discuss it, and the mayor don't know who to side with. Believe me, it was a circus." Genuine laughter once again rolls out of Martin, and he tried to suppress his amusement with the back of his wrist.

"When was this?" Brandon could no longer restrain his astonishment.

"This past summer."

"So what happened?"

Martin was comfortable in his surroundings and with his dining companion. The meal was to his liking, and he poured himself another glass of wine. When he spoke again, he didn't even look over his shoulder.

"Mayor Patterson's right-hand man worked it all out. The man's a bona fide genius. He manages to keep everyone happy and city business gets done.

Without him, I think Patterson would have had a stroke by now."

Martin stopped and searched his plate of ribs for one last morsel. Brandon could hardly contain his curiosity. Martin was getting at something, but hadn't said it. Nervousness bubbled inside Brandon like a tiny geyser preparing to blow. Now may be the only time he would ever hear this story, but if he asked too many questions Martin might seal up like a vault.

"So those two councilmen aren't still at each other's throat?" Brandon asked. It was the most innocuous question he could think of.

"Oh no." Martin took something from his mouth with two fingers and stuck it under his plate. "Everything's back to what we call normal." He smiled, meat stuck in his teeth. "In this instance, the hospital was adamant about getting their petition through. They didn't want any delays—said they couldn't wait. They were willing to grease the wheels of efficient government." Brandon cocked his head. Martin's smile became a grin, and his familiar chuckle rattled at the back of mouth.

Martin's voice became a whisper. "Thompson got $20,000 supposedly for his campaign fund. That got him off of his soapbox about halfway houses in upscale neighborhoods. Brunner, Fitzpatrick, and Douglas all got compensated for their votes too. The hospital was more than willing. The hospital got their application approved, and Roberts got the zoning change on the house he wanted to sell."

Martin pushed his plate forward, poured himself the last of the wine, and set his elbows on the table. "I didn't take anything from the hospital, but I've traded in favors before, and they're worth money. I tell you this just so you know politics involves doing what it takes to get good things accomplished. I can honestly say that every vote I've cast has benefited this city and the people who live here."

"I understand. You do what you have to do to get things done."

"You catch on quick. You're a natural for this game."

Far from understanding anything clearly, Martin's ramblings raised a hundred new questions. But one question, in particular, pressed on his mind. Brandon struggled to keep his voice calm. "So how did the hospital know they could get their application approved?"

Martin finished his wine and looked longingly at his empty glass. "Like I said, Patterson's assistant. You met him today. He looks like your typical civil servant, but the guy has an encyclopedic mind. He made all the connections. He keeps tabs on everything."

"You better let me drive back to the office," Brandon said.

"That's a good idea."

It all was so simple, yet so complex. Brandon envied this guy who worked for the mayor, though he didn't remember meeting him or understand what he actually did. The man had the city council in one hand and the business community in the other. The very thought was exhilarating; the golden keys of power. He remembered how he used to lie awake for endless hours imagining such influence.

What he really wanted now was proof of what he'd just been told. Martin's smug, condescending, self-serving words had dissipated into thin air, and his sweaty mug made Brandon nauseous. The idea that people who held public positions with power over others could run roughshod over the trust handed them was something he couldn't abide. Somehow he would expose their deceit and corruption. Brandon was now more determined than ever. One way or another, he would bring them down.

CHAPTER THIRTY-SIX

FOR DAYS, BRANDON TRIED without success to reach Cindy by phone. Late one afternoon, after three earlier attempts, she answered.

"Thanks for answering."

"I've been busy. I've got a minute."

"So you've decided you don't hate me?"

"Please—don't start. I don't need any of that now. I said I've been busy."

"Have you found a job?"

"Part-time, still looking for something permanent."

"What is it?"

"I don't want to get into it, Brandon. I don't want you getting one of your sudden urges and going over there when I'm working."

"Just curious."

"I got your letter. Please tell me you're calling to say you've got more of my money?"

"I have some money."

"That's not what I asked."

"I've got money. I know I owe you. I can pay you $500 now, if it would help?"

"If it would help? Yes, it would help." A pause overtook the line when Brandon didn't answer. The silence grew. "You being up front with me, Brandon? I mean, this isn't just another game to waste my time?"

"I have the money. I just want to see you. How 'bout I take you out tonight to a nice dinner?"

"Jeez, that's sweet, but I have other plans."

"What plans?"

"Brandon---if you could just hear how you sound."

"It's been a while. I miss you."

Another long pause held the line. When Cindy spoke again her tone was more conciliatory. "I'm going over to Marilyn's. I promised to help her. Maybe you could take me out tomorrow."

"Sure, that'll work. I'll see you tomorrow."

"Wait! What time? You know, you could be nice and ask me for a date and tell me what time you'll pick me up. I'd like that a lot better than you just dropping by."

"You're right. Would you like to go out to dinner tomorrow?"

"Sure, I'd like that."

"I'll pick you up at seven then, okay?"

"That sounds nice. I'll be ready."

Brandon stared at his cell phone as though the device held some sort of magic. Just keep asking, never give up. Anything was possible. Her acceptance of such a simple request was just what his tattered ego needed. Progress at anything, however slight, tended to brighten his outlook for the moment. When the success pertained to Cindy, his improved attitude easily lasted for days.

Brandon returned to Kessler Park and drove the narrow streets. He gazed at the towering houses as he rolled by, the sprawling homes, steep roof lines, vast porches. A strange sense of wonder infused him. The smaller houses appeared as quaint gingerbread cottages, elegant in design and adornment, warmth and safety built into every board and beam. He perceived the neighborhood anew and wondered why it took so long to see the inherent beauty in the old structures.

He pulled along the curb and parked near several benches he could see on the crest of a vacant lot. The air floated on the breath of autumn. Birds fluttered in the branches. Brandon became aware of singing. No longer did he hear harsh cackling and shrill whistles. Now the oaks and elms held a choir of golden melodious thrums. The air hummed with tongue-trilling chirrs, contented coos, and honey-nugget warbles of harmonic smoothness and sweet clarity. Brandon listened intently, alone in his thoughts.

Somewhere near his heart a new and different feeling began to demand a measure of attention. His mind slowly awakened to a different perspective into his own being. He climbed a set of concrete steps imbedded in the earth up to an upper level where the park benches sat, and there, unseen before, he saw Rick on his knees working in a patch of flowers.

Brandon walked over. "Still working on the neighborhood, aren't you?" Brandon would have expected nothing less. The big guy was so steady, so consumed by everything he worked on, so precise in everything he did.

Rick looked up and shaded his eyes from the sun. When he recognized Brandon, he put his head down and continued working.

"So this is the garden." Brandon took a seat on a nearby bench. "Is all this your doings?"

"Everyone helps. This is a neighborhood garden."

From the street to the alley the lot was awash in a rainbow of blooms. A wide walking path crisscrossed the flowers. Low shrubs bordered clusters of benches. Gentle waving rows of blossoms painted the lot in the center of the old subdivision in a swath of natural color.

"Anything I can do to help?"

"And get your pants dirty?"

Brandon leaned over, put his elbows on his knees, and his chin on folded hands. The scene brought an ache to his chest. There was nothing he could possibly do in restitution for his selfish actions. Councilman Martin hadn't elaborated on what he'd said the other day at lunch. He had no hard evidence that bribery had occurred and, without it, he was powerless. The tiny knot in his throat grew with the realization he was out of options.

Brandon watched Rick pick at the tiniest of weeds between the flower stems. The meticulous gardening seemed absurd. Within weeks this entire area, blocks of it, would be leveled, piles of dried lumber and broken fence, twisted tree roots and busted stones.

"Why are you weeding those flowers?" Brandon couldn't control the emotion that churned within him. "You know they're as good as dead. They'll be bulldozed before the next good rain." Brandon stood, turned about, and pulled at his hair. "Everything is going to be destroyed."

Rick glanced at him from his knees. He set aside his hand spade, got to his feet, and wiped his dirty hands on his overalls. Brandon finally put down his arms and quit looking in every direction.

"But the flowers are here today," Rick said, and he looked at Brandon with a calm yet profound understanding of what this one day was all about. "I came to enjoy them today."

Rick took a seat on a bench across the walkway and waited for Brandon to sit back down. Rick closed his eyes and turned his face up to the sun and spread his arms across the back of the bench. "I often get confused. Sometimes I get scared. Sometimes I get lonely," he said slowly, and he paused, seeming to check his memory. "No matter if I'm tending the flowers or just sitting--- being in this garden makes me feel better. It's a special place in the middle of this big town. Sometimes I come here in the middle of the night when the moon is out, and sometimes I just sit here in the sun in the middle of the day. I know it's 'cause the flowers are pretty. But I like them, too, 'cause the flowers are perfect. Every one of them—they come up perfect—they look perfect—they smell perfect. They all have something special about them. Look at all the different colors." Rick smiled a proud, powerful grin. "And look at all those pretty shapes, big ones and tiny ones. Just look."

Brandon felt the pressure inside his body relax. Rick looked directly at him with an easy, non-judgmental expression. It was a trusting look Brandon had never seen before from anyone he could remember, certainly not from his father, who always scowled at him as though he were incapable and unreliable.

Brandon wanted to know what this plain, yet skilled man would do once all of this was gone. But he wasn't going to ask. It didn't matter anyway. Rick had just said so. He was concerned only with today. That idea alone instilled an ounce of calm in Brandon's heart. Just concern yourself with today.

"Where you from, Rick?"

"Oh, I'm from here."

"You grew up in Atherton?"

"Uh-huh."

"Do you live around here?"

"I have an apartment over on Eighth Avenue."

"There sure has been a lot of commotion going on around here lately," Brandon said. "Do you know what all these people are going to do?"

Rick's face fell slightly. Brandon had brought up a subject Rick had satisfactorily filed away and was now forced to reconsider.

Brandon saw the uneasiness. "I mean, I feel bad myself, and I don't even live here."

"I've been helping people pack and move boxes for days. I've been getting everyone's new address so I can send them a card once in awhile. I'll probably never see any of them again, but I just wanted to write, in the future, if I wanted to."

Rick looked straight at him and Brandon could see the ordeal was taking its toll on Rick as well. "This is the first time I've had to myself for quite awhile. See? There's a van right over there. I don't know where everyone is going. I just know they're all leaving their hearts here." Rick clenched his jaw.

"Maybe I could change clothes and help you put these flowers in new pots. You could give everyone some flowers for their new homes. Flowers from here."

Rick stared straight ahead, lost in thoughts of his own. "No---where these people are going isn't home. There're just going to a place to live. They don't need these flowers or want them either. They belong right here 'til they die. Then I'm going fishing. I haven't been fishing in a long time. I'll just sit out by the lake and see what I can catch."

"You mean Johnson Lake?"

"The big lake out that way." Rick pointed.

"That's Johnson Lake. Nice, isn't it?"

Rick nodded vigorously. "It's got some nice fish."

"Where do you fish?"

"At the lake up that way, like I said."

"No, I mean, where on the lake?" Brandon smiled. He wanted now, more than ever, to talk about something other than what had brought him to the neighborhood today. Though he couldn't care less about fishing, at the moment he found the topic absolutely fascinating.

"Not far from the dam are quiet coves where the lake widens out. That's where I fish."

"I bet you're good at it."

Rick took the compliment in his usual subdued, reflective way. "I enjoy it. I guess I do good. The sunfish are fun to catch 'cause they're so beautiful, and the catfish put up a real fight. There's bass, too, but I can only catch the small ones from shore."

"Well, you know," Brandon said, "I've got a boat. Maybe you'd like to come out on my boat sometime and fish in the middle of the lake?"

"You have a boat?" A sense of wonder infused Rick's words.

"I sure do, a thirty-four footer." Brandon watched Rick's eyes brighten as he processed the idea. "Have you ever been on a boat?"

"No," Rick said, awe evident in his breathless answer. "Never have."

"Would you like to?"

"I sure would." Rick spoke as though he would soon be standing on the moon so complete was his joy.

Never before had Brandon seen Rick so excited. Even though it was just a boat ride to him, it obviously meant a lot to Rick. The big fellow stared at him intently, apparently waiting for him to confirm his offer, this Brandon could sense. He felt better, just knowing he would do it. He would take this guy out on the water, because now, he would do just about anything to relieve some of the guilt in his soul. Even if the water was choppy, or the sun too hot, or anything else that could possibly make him want to change his mind, he'd do it just because it would make this simple handyman happy.

"We can go tomorrow if you want to," Brandon said.

"I'll have to check my calendar."

"Well, let's see. How about Sunday? You don't work on Sunday. That's just three days away. We can go whenever the fish are biting best, early morning or toward the evening. You tell me. You're the fisherman." Brandon smiled.

Rick gasped a breath of total enchantment. "Morning is best. Can I bring my friend?"

"Sure, what's his name?"

"It's a lady."

"Oh, do you think she'll want to go?"

"I don't know, she might."

Brandon wasn't sure how many women would want to go boating at the crack of dawn just to throw a few fishing lines in the water, but he didn't question the notion. "She's your friend, you say?"

"Uh-huh. She's my friend."

"Well then, you should ask her for sure. I know she'd like you to ask her. What's her name?"

"Lena. She's real nice."

"Well, good, Rick. I'd like to meet her, too. Sunday morning then. Guess I'll have to get up early." Brandon got up from his park bench. "I can pick you up. What's your address?"

"I'm apartment fourteen. That's the first floor at Belmont Apartments on 8th Avenue."

"I'll find it," Brandon said. "You'll enjoy being on the lake. Don't think I've been on the water at dawn, but it sounds like a great idea to me." Brandon paused, and his easy smile faded. "Listen, Rick, I'm going now, but I'd like to come back tomorrow and help you, whatever you're doing. Would that be okay?"

"Sure. I'll be loading a truck. I forget where, but I'll be around here somewhere."

"I know there's a lot of work to be done." He liked Rick, and not because of anything or anybody he knew. Whenever he was around Todd, he was aware of the seamy deceit that lived in his heart, but when he spoke with Rick, he knew that goodness dwelt there also.

Things were obviously not playing out the way Rick would have liked, yet, he seemed to harbor no ill will. Dwelling on negativity wasn't part of his nature. There was something about the big guy that embodied the spirit of this historic enclave, and Brandon wanted to do whatever he could to help him. He didn't know exactly why or how, but he knew he'd do whatever he could to see this likeable fellow reestablished after the neighborhood was gone. "I'll see you tomorrow, and we'll make definite plans for Sunday morning."

Brandon gave a thumbs-up sign, turned, and walked to the street, leaving Rick standing wide-eyed and speechless in the midst of the garden.

At his apartment that evening, Rick called his mother to tell her the exciting news. He was going fishing on a boat. They talked for nearly an hour. Rick told her every detail of his preparations for the excursion. He recited a list of fishing tackle he needed to get at the store. He told her of the fish in the lake he was never before able to reach, what bait he would use, and how deep in the water he needed to troll. Ann Stanton sat back on her couch, muted the TV, and listened to every word.

The following morning at eleven, Beatrice Morgan called Rick's apartment, attempting to locate him. He had agreed to be at her home by nine to help load her belongings. Getting no answer, she called Sherman Porter, who in turn called Cecil Nance. By one o'clock Ann Stanton was knocking on her son's apartment door. No response was forthcoming. She got the building manager, and he opened the door.

Rick was still in bed lying on his side, still in his nightwear of a T-shirt and briefs. One leg was under his cover, the other on top. His pillow had fallen on the floor. His breathing was shallow, his skin cool and sweaty. Ann approached his bed without apprehension or fear. She had prepared herself for this day long ago.

She touched his cheek and said his name. Rick didn't respond. She knelt beside the bed and brushed back the hair stuck to his temple. Tiny slits in his half-closed eyelids revealed the whites of his eyes and seemed to flutter as she repeated his name. "Momma's here. Talk to me, Ricky."

She took his limp wrist and squeezed his cold, meaty fingers. "Help me roll him on his back if you will," she said to the manager with absolute calm, though her eyes had crested with tears. When they spilled down her cheeks she neither acknowledged them nor wiped them away. They pulled the blanket back, straightened his legs, and adjusted his head and shoulders. "Do you want me to call EMS?" the manager asked with an anxious voice. Ann nodded, and the manager dashed from the room as she tucked the blanket around Rick's shoulders.

She put her hand through his hair and kissed his cheek. "You're such a good son, Ricky. I'm so proud of you." Then she put her arm across his chest, and settled her cheek on his shoulder, her face kissing his neck. She whispered his name over and over as she waited for the ambulance to arrive.

At the hospital Rick was given oxygen and an IV to administer fluids. Ann and Michael stayed at the hospital around the clock. His sisters drove into town from Houston and Abilene. Residents of Kessler Park came by, one by one, hour after hour. They brought so many flowers they overflowed his room and the waiting area and began to fill the chapel.

It was an aneurysm. There was no way to predict or prevent it. With Rick's previous head injury, there was a possibility that subsequent cranial problems could occur, but nothing was certain. Considering his coma, his complete lack of response to any form of stimulus, his prognosis was extremely poor. But again, it was all wait and see.

On the second day, while visitors gathered in the waiting room, a lone woman stopped at Rick's hospital room and stared at the name in the slot outside his door. She pushed open the heavy door with great hesitancy. She approached in silent trepidation, her breathing deep and labored by the time she stood beside the bed. All the joy in her life flushed away in one big sigh as she looked upon the white, comatose face of the nice man she had come to know. The news she'd been forcing upon herself as a lie was undeniably revealed as the truth. He looked so sick, so helpless, so gone.

Lena lowered the side rail and stepped on a foot stool to stand above Rick's prostrate body. She touched his cool cheek with the back of her hand and leaned over the bed.

"I found another movie, Rick, you might like to see," she whispered, hopeful he could sense her voice. "We can go whenever. . . you know. . . any day is fine with me." Pent-up anguish erupted into a tremor of convulsive sobs, and Lena clung to the bedrail until her heart became exhausted, her body washed of its sorrow.

Four days later, Rick's body gave up the fight. The funeral was attended by hundreds. Almost everyone who lived in Kessler Park came. Many who had already moved made the trip from wherever they were to pay their last respects to the kind carpenter who was always available to help with a practical solution and a friendly smile. The preacher delivered a gentle sermon. A classmate who had known him in junior high said a few words. Four men from the neighborhood spoke about how truly blessed they were by Rick's presence in their lives.

The last speaker was Brandon. He approached the lectern without prepared remarks, placed his hands on the sides of the lectern, and surveyed the gathering. Although personally unknown to them, Brandon had made a special request to Michael and Ann Stanton to be allowed to speak at the service.

"Good afternoon, everyone, my name is Brandon Evans. I wanted to say a few words, for the very reason that I didn't grow up on the same block or attend school with Rick. I never knew him as a boy or watched him struggle after his accident. I wasn't around when he learned his trade, though I've seen countless examples of his handiwork.

"Actually, I knew Rick for all of three and a half months. In that short time, I learned a few things. Things, I must admit, I'd been searching for quite some time to understand. And Rick taught me much of that, just by being Rick.

"The first day I met Rick, he graciously answered some questions I had, and the last time I saw him he was just as helpful. He was always busy, but never so rushed that he couldn't lend a hand or an ear. The most important thing Rick taught me was to slow down. Let your mind be unhurried and let your senses linger---long enough to smell the flowers.

"Early on, Rick understood that personal influence and individual prestige can be held for just an instant. All fame is fleeting. More money than you need to meet basic needs can bring more sorrow than happiness. Our true intentions are more transparent than we realize, and too often when we try to impress others we only fool ourselves. Rick knew that only friends have lasting value. He lived his life that way, and the overflowing number of people in attendance here today is ample proof of that. It's your friends that make you rich. Rick was truly a friend. He was certainly my friend."

And at the end of his struggle, four months shy of his twenty-ninth birthday, Rick was buried in east Atherton just a few miles from his boyhood home.

CHAPTER THIRTY-SEVEN

AN OVERWHELMING SENSE OF LOSS consumed Brandon in the days after Rick's death. The simple fellow had been a towering presence. Brandon's sadness stemmed from an admiration that went far beyond the man's quaint unpretentiousness. He had embodied a tenacious work ethic and a fathomless optimism that surpassed his own. He'd had so much less to work with and still had proved himself a leader. The whole community mourned his passing. Not a single person thought less than the world of Rick.

Brandon tried to dig deeper into the corruption at city hall, but met dead ends at every turn. Councilman Thompson worked in the finance department at a downtown oil and gas firm. He didn't meet with the public in the course of his day job, and he was impossible to get near. Brandon managed to get Councilman Roberts on the phone. He tried to get him into a conversation about the wonderful halfway house he made possible, but the man was shifty, vague, and non-committal. Roberts refused any credit for the project. He cut short the conversation. Brandon's attempt to arrange a face-to-face interview never got off the ground.

The sky turned winter gray as Thanksgiving rolled into December. Christmas was on the wind. Lights, bells, store displays, and music brightened the city. But no mistletoe hung in Kessler Park, no decorated trees, no door wreaths. Eggnog and hot chocolate wasn't served as families came together. In Kessler Park kinfolk gathered only to box up old memories and haul them away. Brandon spent much of his time in the increasingly deserted neighborhood. Wherever he saw people moving furniture and loading boxes he went to help.

One of the last to leave was Myron and Delores. Brandon stood at the gate as young men about his age hauled out a threadbare recliner, a grandfather clock, and a solid wood dining table. A debilitating winter cold accentuated the dreary day. No wind, no snow, only the depressing gloom of an overcast sky. The falling temperature bit exposed flesh and discouraged the spirit. The high apex of the house's roof line peered down upon him as he moved up the walk, somehow knowing the end was near.

Brandon went inside to help. The house was all but empty. Myron sat near the window in a straight-backed chair. Delores was beside him in her wheelchair. Their faces were blank slates, no sadness, no apprehension. They almost looked serene. Their eyes followed him as he approached.

Brandon knelt in front of them. "Can I get you anything?"

"No, thank you," Myron said, but a slight change in his expression indicated he appreciated being asked.

"Where are you all going, if I may ask?"

"Just a few miles from here," Delores said. "It's a nice little place, two bedrooms."

"Brick," Myron interjected.

"I beg your pardon?"

"It's covered with brick."

"That sounds nice."

Myron nodded vacantly.

"It's got a nice little yard," Delores said, "but there's no room for my garden." The blank expression left Delores' face in a heartbeat, and her chin began to quiver as her eyes brimmed red and wet.

Brandon took her tight-skinned hand of knuckles and bruises. "I'll stop by after you've had some time to settle in. What's your new address?"

"I don't remember," Myron said. "I think the driver has it."

Brandon stood. He wanted desperately to say something of comfort. The Holmes gazed about for the last time at their home of sixty years, and Brandon knew it was foolhardy to try. No one could possibly know what they were remembering in these last few hours. It would take a person wiser than Solomon to say something appropriate or soothing at this moment. So, he didn't say a word.

He backed slowly away from the window and silently walked from the house.

Brandon returned to his car and drove down deserted Atoka Avenue. Demolition was to begin the day after tomorrow. He set his jaw and shook his head. The city could schedule destruction for any day they wanted. It didn't mean they'd get to keep their timetable. He wasn't finished. Not finished at all. An expanding idea took shape in his mind. He'd throw a monkey wrench in the bureaucratic arrogance of the hospital brass and generate a snippet of news to embarrass city officials.

He spun around a corner and headed to Pioneer Boulevard and car dealership row. A four-mile stretch on both sides of the road, home to spectacular displays of balloons and pennants, and an endless floating wall of gorillas, dinosaurs, and ducks greeted every passerby. If that didn't attract enough attention, the new car dealerships competed to see which could get an American flag the size of a football field atop the highest pole.

Brandon dipped into Williams New & Used Cars, Trucks and Vans. The Williams brothers weren't keen on letting the merchandise sit, especially the used vehicles, and for a fifty-dollar bill a person could rent about anything for a couple days. Just top off the tank before bringing'er back. Full means seeing fuel in the neck of the tank. Full means having the dial pegged hard right on the gauge. Don't return the damn vehicle with the needle quivering below the full mark. Returning the vehicle full means every drop the tank will hold.

He rented a Ford Econoline with a sliding side door and headed for the Salvation Army clothing store. He bought every blanket and quilt in the place, thirty-three in total, and stowed them in the van. He grabbed a burger and fries and called Cindy. No answer. Dusk settled on the city, the winter cold drilled quickly to the bone on such sun-shortened days, and by six o'clock it was dark. He pushed the van heater to high and began driving the city's side streets looking for the homeless, anyone still out in the weather.

First, he saw the flames. A 55-gallon barrel belched fire near a retaining wall under the freeway. He drove closer and saw the huddle of humanity. Brandon drove over the curb onto an endless apron of concrete under the bridge and parked. The moment he stepped from the van and buttoned his coat he realized he should have changed clothes. His pressed slacks and L.L. Bean winter garb overstated his humble mission. Already the four people around the fire had turned to check out the van. They could easily mug him for his wallet. Brandon approached the fire. It was too late to change plans. When it came right down to it, he figured the people standing around the barrel would be more interested in his proposal than his money.

A low octave rumble rolled overhead, spiked with sharp clicks as traffic crossed the expansion joints on the overpass. Brandon stopped well short of the barrel and raised his voice above the din.

"You all want to stay warm tonight? No bed checks, no rules—just someplace warm."

Four sets of wide eyes, illuminated by the fire, peered back at him. The lone woman took a step his way, her matted white hair sticking out from under a child's pink knit bonnet. She wore layers of tattered clothing, her outer layer a greasy, army fatigue jacket frayed at the hem.

"It's a little on the cold side tonight," she said.

"You gotta place we can get inside?" asked a gaunt black man, his words ground through his lips as though he had gravel in his throat.

"Yes, I can get you all inside tonight, and a blanket for each of you."

The mass around the barrel began to move from the fire. No urgency, no enthusiasm, nothing more than one step in front of the other. Even the sight of a warm van didn't quicken their pace. They moved as though what they had heard may well be a dream, a hallucination brought on by hunger and cold. To hurry was to hope. Brandon saw only too well reluctance on the part of any of the four to rush into anything. Why run to disappointment?

Brandon opened the side door and beckoned them inside. "I don't have any coffee or anything to eat, but I'll stop later."

A short white man, surely much younger than his appearance suggested, thanked Brandon as he climbed aboard. He had a face covered in soot and no hat. The fourth man was wasted thin like the black fellow with bony hands and protruding cheekbones. They all went for the blankets and squeezed together on the one bench seat at the back of the van.

"Where's some others we can get inside tonight?" Brandon asked, knowing full well they'd know where to look.

"The next underpass down that way," the black man said and several arms pointed the direction.

The van stopped at the next underpass. Brandon and the black man got out and hollered up at the shadows under the bridge. Figures on a high ledge began to move. Once they'd heard the offer, five people came off their cardboard mattresses and shimmied down the embankment. One man had on a brown tweed suit jacket as his outer coat and a few T-shirts on under that. Brandon gave them the quick rundown of his purpose. They loaded up without any questions, no concern for where they were going or how long they'd be gone. It wasn't here, and anything else beat that.

In thirty minutes the van was packed. Brandon drove to Kessler Park, over the Baker's tired picket fence and across their yard to bypass the street barricades, and stopped a few doors down. He threw open the sliding door and gave them his speech.

"These houses are empty and available. The city wants you to use them until this cold weather is over and maybe longer than that. The doors are unlocked." He motioned to the three nearest him. "You guys got on together. You take this house. Now, there's no heat in them so you'll have to build a fire. Just make sure the chimney flues are open. Scrounge what you can for wood. Here's some matches. One blanket per person." When they were out he stirred another group and sent them to the house across the street.

The van's cargo light illuminated the grimy faces as the people exited, and one man paused, just for an instant, and looked at Brandon as he neared the open door. Brandon didn't recognize the clothes nor even the face, but one glance into the man's eyes and Brandon remembered the library. It was the same guy he'd sent on his way with a sharp, uncaring rebuff the day he went to look at city maps. Now he was lending the guy a hand along with dozens like him. The ironic justice was neither uplifting nor disheartening, just strangely sobering, and Brandon dropped his gaze until the man exited the van.

At the end of the block Brandon turned to find the first four he'd picked up still squeezed together on the bench seat at the back. "This is your house." He pointed at the Queen Anne cottage and knew immediately it was old man Warrren's place, the first house he and Todd had gone into together, the guy Todd had conned for his signature by telling the old man he was entitled to a magazine subscription refund. Brandon shook off the memory and threw open the side door. "Come on, people, this is the end of the line."

Then he softened his tone. "Okay, hold it a second." The evening was bitter and raw, but the van was warm. The heater droned, and he stopped them before they exited.

Brandon addressed the two white men. "Will you guys go inside and start a fire?" The small fellow with no hat nodded. Brandon gave the tall, lean man a book of matches. "You two come with me, and we'll get some sandwiches and coffee." The woman and the black man headed back to the rear of the van. "You can sit up here for now." Brandon helped the bundled woman into the passenger seat, and the black fellow sat on the van floor behind them.

"What's your names?" Brandon asked once they began rolling.

"Mary," was all she said as she rubbed her hands together under the heater vent.

"My name's Carl."

"How long have you been under that bridge?"

"I've been there going on three months," Carl said. "It was okay 'till the weather turned bad. There's a chicken shack up the street that'll give you their surplus if you don't go by too often." His baritone was distinct, but grating, too, like he was gargling rocks. "I've only seen her around this past week."

"You know where we can find more people who need shelter tonight?"

"Won't be difficult, mister. The downtown shelter is full, no doubt, and they don't have enough room for half who needs it."

"Good," Brandon said. He stopped and picked up coffee and cellophane wrapped, cold cut sandwiches for Carl and Mary, and drove back into the darkness and filled the van again. On the way back to Kessler Park he stopped and bought five cases of bottled water and fifty loaves of French bread. There was no way he could buy hot coffee and sandwiches for everyone tonight. Maybe tomorrow he could come up with something better.

He delivered fifteen more people to the empty houses in Kessler Park and dropped Mary off as well. "Do you think we can fill'ur up again, Carl?"

"Oh, yes, sir."

"And Carl, everyone who needs a roof doesn't have to be brought here by me. Pass the word around. Anyone who needs a place to bed down can come around and stake out a space."

Brandon and Carl kept working until ten o'clock. When they were through, seventy-one people got some extra warmth by being indoors for the night. All available blankets were quickly taken; all the bread instantly disappeared. A few people got an extra bottle of water, but that, too, was quickly gone. Brandon felt physically exhausted as he drove to his apartment, but not mentally tired in the least. In fact, his mind was invigorated. It was possibly the most rewarding day of his entire life, and all he had to show for it was dirty slacks and a dented wallet. The best part of it all was tomorrow was another day, and he planned to do the same thing all over again.

CHAPTER THIRTY-EIGHT

DURING THE FITFUL NIGHT, a to-do list flickered through his mind with items added and others falling away before his skittish dreams could peg anything down. Brandon intended to get as many homeless people into those empty houses as possible and let the city sort through the mess. Let the homeless have a change of scenery, and some excitement injected into the humdrum monotony of their usual existence. Let them witness first-hand elegant old dwellings. They wouldn't be hurt at any rate and may damn well enjoy the whole affair.

The next morning, Brandon popped awake before six. He dressed in scuffed work boots, tattered blue jeans, a pullover wool sweater and a pile-filled nylon coat, realization of the long, cold day he faced. He headed straight to Kessler Park and drove the empty streets. Smoke billowed from dozens of chimneys and curled against the frosty air. Everyone, it seemed, had gotten through the night. No one passed out in a yard or asleep on a porch. A fear that some unforeseen incident would arouse city officials before the homeless benefited from the empty houses now abated, he parked in front of Mr. Warren's house.

Quietly, he stepped through the front door and walked into the parlor. Carl and Mary and the other two men slept in a semi-circle around sputtering embers. As a whole, the house held a foreboding chill, the dank odor of frosty dust. Near the fire, the pervading smell was the sweaty stench of toasted clothes, but as he observed for a moment, Brandon knew they had slept well. A stack of broken posts filled the corner. Obviously they had torn into the stairway banister to build their fire.

"Let's stoke that fire," Brandon said with as much good humor as the cold morning and early hour would allow. "Up and at 'um."

Mary's puffy face, pasted with disdain, gave him a quick once over before her head turned and fell back into the bend of her elbow. Along with Carl, the small fellow began to move, and together they rose with uniform sluggishness until finally they stood erect.

"If you guys will help me, we'll go 'round up some grub." Brandon said the magic words. They picked up their blankets and bags and followed him to the van.

The men headed for the New Hope Mission near the railroad right-of-way parallel to Station Road.

"Everyone has to be up and out of the mission at a certain hour, right?" Brandon asked.

"Yeah, usually seven-thirty, but when it's this cold probably not until nine," Carl said.

"Good, we have time. We'll grab some breakfast. Then I want to drop you guys off. Tell everyone you see down there about the vacant houses."

They stopped at Maria's Restaurante, a sixteen-hour-a-day Mexican establishment that fed the early morning crowd of every working stripe a hot blend of breakfast burritos and black coffee. Brandon ordered through the drive-through window, and the three men ate in the van.

"I'll be right back." Brandon rushed in the side door and immediately found himself in the kitchen. Grills sizzled with green peppers and jalapenos, sausage and eggs. Voices fought for attention at the order window. A wide-set woman caught him with her bright, brown eyes the moment he entered.

"May I help you?"

"Are you Maria?"

"No," She smiled and wiped her hands in her apron as she took a break from chopping peppers. "But I am the manager."

"Great. I need to give you a really big order. I don't need it for an hour or so. I can come back. Will you help me?"

"Well, sure, if I can. We're here to sell food. What can I get for you?"

"I want a hundred of your breakfast burritos, a hundred Styrofoam cups, and two urns full of coffee." The woman's eyes widened, quickly gleaming. "I'll need the urns, too. I'll rent them for a couple hours. Your breakfast rush will be over by then. Can you have it ready by nine?"

"I can have it ready in twenty minutes." She smiled again. "But why do you need my urns?"

"I figured I needed at least ten gallons of coffee. How else could I move it?" He shrugged.

"Oh, that's no problem. I have large thermos containers you can use, and I'll have you twelve gallons. How's that?"

"Great."

"We'll have it ready. I need a hundred dollars now and the rest later," she said, the friendly light still beaming from the brown eyes in her chubby face.

"Thanks so much. I'll be back as close to nine as I can."

Brandon dropped the two men off at New Hope Mission. Then he headed to a familiar, yet infrequently visited apartment complex. It had been nearly a month since he'd seen Cindy. With Rick's death, everyone's move from Kessler Park, and his ongoing preoccupation with snooping into activities of city council members, time had slipped away.

Their dinner date had been a disaster. The whole evening had come off so formally, so sterile, like two absolute strangers just sharing a table to consume a meal. She hardly talked. He tried to get her to open up. Was she having problems at work? Was there some difficulty in her immediate family? She refused to elaborate on any subject, insisting that everything in her life was proceeding on an even keel.

337

Yet, when she looked him in the eye he could see a disappointment that sustained her expression. It was a face of loss, with an air of pity, as though there was nothing she could do to change the facts as she interpreted them, and her presence at the restaurant table was just an act of courtesy, void of any hope for the future.

She had given up on him. He realized that now. He had been so busy before he hadn't thought it through. As he pulled into the apartment parking lot, a debilitating, empty nervousness grabbed him. He liked her. He enjoyed being around her. Partying with Cindy made the expense and hangovers after a night on the town worth all it cost.

He sat in the van listening to the heater hum. He knew there was more to her change of attitude than just being fed up with his impetuous ways. She wanted more, but he wasn't sure what he had to give. Part of him still had the need for immediate gratification, the fun of flirtatious freedom.

His better judgment told him to leave. He could get a few hobos to help him distribute the grub and get back to work filling the houses. Here it was, eight-fifteen on a freezing Saturday morning. Even with the possibility she didn't have to work, it was obvious he was harboring fanciful daydreams. Maybe she had the day off, but why would she go with him to hand out burritos to street-grimy strangers? Why would she even open the door? Why had he come this way?

He decided to leave and pulled from the parking space, drove to the entrance of the complex, but made a quick u-turn and came right back.

Leaving without trying to see her wasn't an option. He would take no for an answer, but he had to hear it. He wasn't going to talk himself out of what he came for. Even though he liked to call it optimism he knew sometimes he was just downright stubborn. If stubbornness was what he needed at this moment, he was glad he had it to back up his intention. He was certain what he was about to do didn't come from an abundance of good sense.

He knocked on her door. After a minute she answered, wrapped snuggly in a pink robe, her face smeared with night cream. Her expression exploded with incredulity, but she let him in to check the outside arctic blast.

"I thought we had an understanding about showing up unannounced?"

"You look absolutely gorgeous this morning."

"Why are you here, Brandon? What time is it anyway?"

"About eight-thirty. I'm helping homeless people get in from the cold. Worked at it all last night, too. I rented a van. In less than an hour I'm picking up breakfast and coffee to distribute to the homeless. I thought you'd like to go and help."

He could see his early appearance and verbal onslaught caught her off guard. She studied his face through sleepy eyes and yawned. "I thought maybe I'd get to sleep in for one day—my one day off this week. Would you make some coffee?"

Her request made him beam. The satisfied glow that lit in his chest warmed his entire body, and he pulled off his stocking cap and set about work in the kitchen. Cindy sat at the dinette table and lit a cigarette.

"So let me get this straight," she said, "you're getting the homeless indoors?"

"That's right."

"And you rented a van?"

"Yep."

She exhaled a relaxing plume of smoke. "I don't get it. Is this a part time job?"

"No, actually it's called community service. I realize other people have problems and needs. I came on a way to get some street people out of the cold, and I'm doing it."

"That's good of you, Brandon." She crushed out the cigarette. "Is this something you plan to make a habit or is this a one-time thing?"

He brought in two cups of coffee and sat at the table. "Look, I'm doing what I can, when I can. I'll never claim to be a saint. I found an opportunity to be helpful, and I admit I feel good about it. It's not about me." He paused and sipped the coffee. "I'm glad you're off work today. I think you'd like to be in on this. I need more help, and I'd like it to be you."

"You wake me up from a sound sleep and now you want to drag me out in the cold." She stirred her coffee and took a sip. He could see wheels turning in her waking mind. He answered her rhetorical question with a question of his own.

"Do you think I'd be doing something like this just to kick up some fun?"

She peered over the rim of her cup. "No, I don't guess I'd accuse you of that."

"Come on." He beamed his warm, engaging, brilliant smile. "You don't want to stay cooped up all day. It's really worthwhile, and I'll buy you breakfast, sausage and egg burritos and more coffee."

"Oh, well then, if you're going to splurge on breakfast." She tried to smile.

"Throw on anything. We're working with the homeless."

"You wouldn't mind if I washed my face?"

"No, babe. Dress warm."

Maria's had the coffee in four-gallon push-button thermoses, and the burritos in foil lined picnic baskets covered with gingham cloth. Brandon drove to Kessler Park and knocked on doors while Cindy manned the mobile food distribution center. Everyone who was up and hadn't left the area on their daily scavenging excursions got something to eat. The hot coffee brought toothy grins to grimy faces. Rough, dry hands extended in gratitude. Even the crusty and indifferent said thanks.

At a soup kitchen few would have thought much of the meager meal. Yet out on a cold, empty street the food and humble gathering acquired a feeling of community, a brief moment in time for sure, but different and worth savoring. People invited each other into their houses and showed them off like they owned them. Brandon escorted Cindy around, and they saw where people had unpacked their gear and set up spaces they could call their own.

After an hour, Brandon and Cindy drove to The New Hope Mission. Carl and Jerome had rounded up folks who were ready for the ride back. People hopped in the van. The buzz about the empty houses had hit the streets, something new, anything but the cramped, double bunked, smelly quarters of the mission with all its rules and restrictions. By two in the afternoon, sixty more people had been moved into the empty homes of Kessler Park.

With the van finally empty, and now alone with Cindy, Brandon drove to Norma's diner for a hot meal. A waitress came along with a pot of coffee and took their orders.

"I told you it would be a full day," Brandon said as he rubbed his hands around the mug. "I think everyone appreciates those houses, cleaner and more secure. None of the utilities are on, but they're warmer than being outside. Those fireplaces can really hold a flame."

Cindy stirred her coffee and listened. Her perceptive, hazel eyes rested on his face. Her thick black hair was now hidden, all stuffed under a knit cap pulled over her ears. The winter air's cold bite had turned her nose into a red, wet bulb. Pink flared in her cheeks, a hint of blue lined her lips, and moisture sat in the corners of her eyes. But as he gazed upon her winter-bitten face, Brandon beheld a breathtaking countenance, utterly fresh and alive as though never before witnessed, and he fell silent at the sight of her natural beauty.

She appeared serene, content to be a part of the proceedings, happy to lend a hand. Still, a hesitation shadowed her expression as though she knew not all had been revealed. Around Brandon, having the other shoe drop when a person thought everything was copacetic was more troubling than just remaining apprehensive until it did.

"So what prompted all of this?" she asked, her gaze now focused across the top of her coffee cup as though it were a gun sight.

Her words pulled him from his thoughts. "I knew those houses were available. It's the neighborhood I was working on, you know. I got attached to the area even though the hospital is going to get the land."

"So that's the neighborhood. It looks so desolate. I hadn't thought much about it," she said. Their food came, and they were silent for awhile as they ate. "So why are they all empty?"

"Move out orders were issued weeks ago. The city council approved the hospital's formal request to acquire the land. Since the houses are going to be torn down anyway, I thought the homeless ought to use them until then."

"When is that?"

"Next week sometime. Tomorrow actually, I think."

Cindy's expression cracked with something akin to relief. The information sounded about right. Her brow pinched, and she sucked up a huge breath. "You've gone to all this trouble to get people off the streets for a couple of nights?"

"Yeah, I guess. I figured anything was better than being out in the cold."

Her focus narrowed at him like a laser. "Did it ever cross your mind those people might have thought they were going to get more than a one-night stand of warmth out of those houses?"

"It's not going to be cold forever."

"I wonder if you care about those people at all. What are you up to this time, Brandon?"

He hesitated and avoided her stare. "It's not how you make it sound. Ask them, any one of them. I'll bet they're happy to be out from under their bridges or wherever no matter how long."

The waitress returned and refilled their cups with a glare at each of them as their voices were rising. She left without a word, but the tension grew thicker, and a recriminating pall settled over the booth.

"But that's not why you're doing it, is it, Brandon?"

"Well, maybe not." He had to think for a moment, but he wasn't ashamed of his reasoning. "You haven't a clue how many decent, kind folks lived in those houses and what the city has done to their lives. I want to throw off the city's plans. I want to put them behind schedule." He'd about reached his limit with her quick accusations. So what if he wasn't perfect. He didn't see her out there saving the world.

"And it's perfectly all right to toy with a bunch of destitute people so you can make a point? Is that it or am I missing something?"

Brandon stared across the table. "What's got into you? I've been down there for three months trying to help those old folks save their homes. Don't I get any credit for that? I admitted I was wrong the way I went in there at first. I made a

344

mistake. But now---you get on my case because I'm doing anything at all." He grabbed the sugar dispenser and squeezed it around and around in his hands, then set it tenderly back beside the salt and pepper shakers lest he yield to the urge to smash it against the wall.

"I do things, Cindy. That's me. Do you prefer resignation over initiative? I mean, really, what's your point?" He paused, both puzzled and disappointed in her criticism. "I don't quit just because things aren't perfect. Are you lowering your expectations so you can control everything in your life? Are you preparing yourself to be satisfied with whatever comes your way, Cindy? Is that it?"

She blinked and set her cup on the table as his words pushed her back in her seat. "No, I was just asking."

He took a deep breath and tried to relax. "I'm sorry. I'm stressed out. This whole thing has me in knots." He stopped and worked to collect himself. After a moment, he caught her gaze and captured her complete attention. "I listened to you when I knew you were right. But now I'm right. I'm doing something, and I'll be damned if I'll sit idly by while the city and the hospital get a free rein completing their legalized extortion."

"I didn't know you were so committed," she said.

"Well, I am, and I'm positive illegal activity took place to get this deal through. I'm going to find out what happened one way or the other. What's so frustrating is that I'm afraid the old neighborhood will be torn down before I find anything." He dropped his gaze and shook his head. "It's going to happen, and there's nothing I can do. I did this to slow it down. I probably should have saved my money."

"Oh, no, Brandon, you did good." She reached for his hand across the table. "You're helping a lot of needy people get in out of the cold, and you bought them food, too. That's worth a lot. That's worth an awful lot. I'm sorry I jumped on you about it. I didn't understand."

At that moment, all of his effort since he rented the van seemed worth it. He could have gloated in a psychological victory of sorts, but he was more pleased not by having won, but by having pled a heartfelt case. He had swayed her because he told the truth. He convinced her because he talked about others over himself. She wanted to believe in him. He could see it in her eyes. He longed for her acceptance; now he had more. Affectionate warmth emanated from her gaze, declaring she wanted to trust him.

In those few ticks of the clock, on a cold, overcast day, dressed in frumpy clothes, nursing a cup of bitter coffee, he learned something about himself and how to lead a life---he learned more than a lifetime of living had taught him until then.

CHAPTER THIRTY-NINE

TRAFFIC ON SIXTH AVENUE moved at a subdued pace as rush hour ended and dusk approached. Cars rolled by in clouds of frosty exhaust. Occasional pedestrians scampered along, hunched over, shoulders against the cold, the corner bus stop kiosk now vacant. The looming skyscrapers of downtown Atherton appeared as a backdrop of gray icicles to the leafless canopy of branches that identified Kessler Park.

A gleaming, sleek black Cadillac Escalade rolled from the hospital's underground parking garage. Katherine Cramer sat in the back as two property managers and a secretary escorted her on a tour of the property. She could think of nothing but the new land acquisition and needed to assure herself all was proceeding according to plan. She couldn't go home until she had one last look at the old houses. Tomorrow the demolition work would begin. Beginning tomorrow she would be near the site around the clock. At dawn, no technicality or unseen stumbling block would continue to frazzle her sensibilities or potentiality thwart her triumph.

The bleak drabness of the evening seemed to cheer her. The frigid air and empty streets infused her with a sense of dominion, and she told the driver to hurry as though he were her personal chauffeur. They entered the neighborhood by cutting across a curb behind street barriers and driving across a yard. At first glance all seemed quiet and empty. They proceeded no more than a block when Katherine told the driver to stop, and the four occupants of the SUV watched two scruffy men in tattered clothes wrestle a length of picket fence up the front steps of a residence and into the house.

"What the hell was that?" said the driver.

"I don't know," Katherine said. Confusion filled her thoughts before anxiety found a base from which to grow.

"Look at that chimney," said the female secretary in the front passenger seat, her eyes craned to the top of the door window.

"What do you see?"

"Smoke from that one----and there. Oh my God!"

Katherine yanked open the door and stepped out. "Where?" Immediately, she saw two belching chimneys and, though the sight was curiously disturbing, it didn't account for the young woman's cry of distress.

Everyone else jumped from the SUV, and the young woman pointed. Everyone looked, and now everyone saw. Between two houses, over on the next block, rolling smoke bubbled from a roof, a flicker of flame from behind a window.

"Get around there," Katherine commanded.

No sooner had they rounded the block and stopped when smoke poured from under the eaves. Flames danced frantically behind second-story windows in one of the largest houses in Kessler Park. The house was a massive structure with a curved balcony over the front porch, a turret above a bay window, and sprawling, steep rooflines butted up against a line of trees.

The driver called the fire department on his cell phone.

Curtains vaporized like crepe paper. Everyone watched the growling blaze eat at the ground floor interior. Glass panes popped and exploded. The fire sucked in fresh breath, and with it, a roar of destruction groaned from within the house. The fire pulled the homeless from their dwellings, and they wrapped their meager garments around themselves and watched the show.

Tongues of fire reached through broken windows. Clouds of black smog bubbled like boiling molasses through a roof that finally succumbed to the searing heat. Flames claimed the roofline, and in less than a minute turned the cedar shakes into a torch. Beams and planks split, staggered, and snapped in a tortured symphony of rips and groans. A row of elm trees began to smolder. Flames licked their way to the back of the house. The heat became so intense it actually warmed the yard, and people moved closer on the frigid night in spite of the crackling inferno of the firestorm.

Katherine was beside herself. Disgust was her reaction at the sight of the grimy street people. She cared nothing of their troubles. Their plight didn't even enter her mind, but she felt vulnerable for her own person as she stood in their midst and was incensed they stood so near.

But the fire captured most of her attention. The house was slated for demolition, but this wasn't good. Every fiber of doubt in her body tingled with anxiety, and she wanted a stiff drink. This was going to cause delays, of that she was sure. The rock of composure she could summon when in her office crumbled within her, and she felt the need for someone to tell her what she should do. This was a terrifying dilemma for which she had no reference for handling, but nonetheless felt responsible. Darkness fell and flames reached high and lit the night sky, and Katherine was unable to form a definitive thought or utter an instructive sound.

Fire department sirens could be heard blocks away. Street barricades hampered access to the fire, and when the first trucks arrived, embers were landing on the roof next door. The firemen threw off their hoses, carried one several houses down, and connected it to a hydrant. No water, no pressure. More trucks arrived. An emergency call went out for a pump truck while the firemen unloaded their gear and pushed back the crowd.

The captain-in-charge, a tall, barrel-chested man clothed head-to-toe in a yellow slicker, stood by his truck shouting into his two-way. Katherine summoned her entourage, approached the captain, and pulled on his arm. He stopped talking long enough to peer down at her.

"I'm with St. Anthony's, and all these houses are scheduled for demolition."

He studied her as if he'd missed something or if she had more to say. "Yes?"

"It's okay if they burn. They're going to be torn down anyway."

"What?" He blinked disbelievingly at what he'd just heard and was even more nonplused by the silly expression that nodded back at him. "Are you out of your mind, lady? You can't just let a building burn."

His response knocked Katherine mute, and she slunk back.

"Get her out of here," the captain shouted to a fireman and went back to his radio.

The grass was now on fire and lapped at the foundation of the neighboring house. Glowing embers rained on dormant trees and the roof next door. Chunks of burning shingles, blown skyward by blistering updrafts, fell like sparkler showers, found rest on balconies and in roof valleys, and within minutes two more houses were on fire. Until the water trucks arrived the firemen watched the structures burn along with the ever growing throng of spectators. When the first pump truck finally arrived the firemen sprang to their stations.

Hoses crisscrossed yards in an instant spider web of canvas tubing. A third alarm went out. The first house was totally engulfed in tumultuous tornado of roaring flame. Firemen attacked the two new fires, containment their priority. A two-hour battle ensued, man against nature, water against fire. One house collapsed on itself in showers of orange embers and crashing lumber. Others, partially ablaze, sizzled against the spray of water hoses, spitting defiantly, flames subsided, only to rise again. Finally, the steady battle of the firefighters gained the upper hand. The brilliant light of the inferno was extinguished. Darkness reclaimed the sky. The bone-numbing chill of the winter night returned. A smell of soot and charred lumber drifted on the breeze. A square block of ground was soaked. The homeless milled about, excited far beyond any thought of sleep. Firefighters worked into the morning to gather their gear and secure the houses for inspections that would begin the next day.

Brandon and Cindy watched it all along with the others. Brandon had a good idea how the fire began, innocently enough in all likelihood, but with devastating consequences. Three perfectly good homes completely destroyed. He hoped none of the elderly owners would find out about the fire before the whole area was razed. Something told him having one's house burn was emotionally worse than having it leveled. In any case, he hoped none of them would come around, especially Myron and

Delores in whose house the fire had begun---the one house burnt completely to the ground.

The fires merited a front page photo in *The Sentinel*, and repeated segments on television news. Until the investigation was complete, the fire marshal took control of the neighborhood. It was quickly determined the cause was a fire built too big for the hearth. With the ongoing investigation and related commotion, the homeless got extra days of free accommodations. Even when the city realized they had a squatters' convention going on in a neighborhood scheduled for demolition they conducted evictions at a leisurely pace. The chore fell to a couple of constables who searched the houses, padlocked the doors, and posted signs. Anyone found in a residence was sent on their way, but no one was charged or hauled in. The city had to reschedule the demolition anyway as other projects now had to be completed first. In all, Kessler Park lived another nineteen days before the fateful morning arrived.

CHAPTER FORTY

THE WORKERS CAME AT DAWN. Track-driven backhoes and long-necked scoop shovels rolled down steel ramps off forty-foot trailers. The air filled with belching exhaust and the defiant grumbles. A deafening clatter accompanied the firing of powerful diesel engines. Fifteen-ton behemoths were ready to gouge the soil and strip the land. But they needn't bow their backs. They wouldn't even break a sweat. Their job of knocking over a hundred or so dried-out houses wouldn't take long at all.

Birds flitted from tree to tree oblivious to the reality that many of their roosts would soon be gone. Rabbits and opossums, field mice, stray cats, and a few dogs sniffed and meandered through their morning routines, unaware all hell was about to be visited upon their territory. Residents and curious onlookers watched from vantage points around the perimeter. Some, it seemed, wanted confirmation it wasn't a bad dream. Others waited in rapt anticipation to see what it looked like when those gigantic wooden things broke apart.

From where he stood looking down Atoka Avenue, Brandon saw the houses he had looked at almost every day for months. In the morning haze, they almost looked as before. But there were no chairs on the porches, no cars in the street, no furniture of any value left inside. Some of the stain glass windows had been removed, though not all. No matter how they looked outside. They weren't the same. The houses had been condemned long ago. Now vacant, they stood hauntingly silent, standing on death row.

Not a soul remained in a single one. A wave of self-contempt consumed him. All his efforts to find a solution, to right his wrong, to mitigate his careless, stupid, selfish actions had resulted in nothing. As a massive, earth-moving trencher approached the first house, Brandon stood silently, alone and hollow.

The massive machine crawled to the side of the nearest house, raised its long arm, then with a clanging shudder dropped its huge bucket into the roof, and that section of the house imploded in a cloud of dust. The bucket rose again, the machine crawled closer, and swung the boom at the chimney. The bucket's tooth caught a brick and the tall, majestic ribbed chimney buckled like a bird shot from the sky and crashed into the roof with the sound of cannon fire. Across the street, another belching machine charged the side of a tired, old house.

Sherman stood at the main entrance on Ashford Street with Louis and Cecil. They staked-out the weathered-brick entry to the subdivision. They wanted to save the tarnished brass plaques recessed high and set into the stone façade. Two plaques, one on either side of the street that simply read:

KESSLER
PARK

The men had no particular use for the plaques. They just wanted to save them. As their final community act they would retrieve the signatures to their neighborhood before they got crushed and lost in the rubble.

Sherman approached an operator as he was about to climb into his machine. He pointed and yelled his request above the rising racket, and the man nodded. As soon as the machine lurched to life, the operator knocked down the entryway columns and scraped the debris from the street. The elderly men retrieved the plaques, knocked away bricks and mortar, and put the two plaques in the trunk of Sherman's car.

When the bulldozers had scattered their devastation upon the lawns, they moved to the next address. The air filled with drifting dirt and ripping, tearing sounds of cracking, splitting, grinding. Dust clouds as thick as smoke choked the site. Previously nurtured gardens and flower beds were ground into oblivion, machine trampled without notice or concern. The land looked like a war zone. Front-end loaders chewed at foundations. Torn, scarred, splintered, and busted, sections of walls and floors, beams and studs, large and small were snatched in iron teeth, smashed into groaning trucks and hauled away.

Each proud old home stood in defiance as a dozer approached, each death so magnificent, poignant, and sad. Vaulted rooflines and spectacular chimneys, curved balconies, and giant windows held their faces high to the sun, ready to meet their doom. And then, so quickly the air of stately honor gone, vaporized in demolition dust, a mass of rotten splinters and shards of glass, grotesque piles of worthless boards.

Onlookers came and went, but few stayed long. There wasn't much to see; nothing exciting to watch for any length of time. Only the residents of Kessler Park shed any tears. By the evening of the second day everything was gone. Only the tallest, healthiest and straightest of the oak and hackberry, juniper and cottonwood remained, saved by bright red ribbons wrapped prominently around their trunks. The streets were now covered in dirt and tire tracks. Nothing but the few trees remained and scattered unrecognizable debris. When the workers loaded the last of their machines and drove away, the rising moon peered down upon the patch of churned earth, now gouged and scarred, desolate and barren.

CHAPTER FORTY-ONE

THAT EVENING BRANDON drove to a bowling alley near the tracks, sat at the bar, and got drunk on cheap vodka as gutter balls and crashing pins decimated the formation of any intelligent thought. He had a good job. He had the confidence of a city councilman. He was earning good money. Everything was going great except his life. He drove home in a stupor and slept till noon.

He awoke with a headache, but was over his self-loathing. Everything had been lost, and still people remained in official positions who had misused their authority. He dismissed any inclination to forget it and pursue his lucrative relationship with Councilman Martin for his own self-enrichment. His father's ruin proved short cuts only lead to dead ends. Even Cindy's drastic change, her refusal to any longer coddle his shallow schemes, focused a beacon of reality in his face. He knew what he had to do no matter how long it took.

He knew he was close if he just kept digging, asking questions, snooping around, paying attention. He showered, dressed in a tailored gray suit with a white tie, and headed to the office.

Maddy flashed her coquettish glance when he entered. Pamela waddled to the copier, her face in constant torment with a nasal twitch. The women were polite, married, and overweight. They were efficient in their work, but set in their ways. Weeks earlier when he had spoken with each of them, he had quickly determined they were unable to do anything beyond what they had been trained to do, and whatever daring to chart unknown waters they may have once possessed had long ago sunk to the ocean floor.

"Afternoon, ladies," Brandon said without looking at either of them. He pulled a printout from his briefcase of recent inquiries to his "delinquent tax" website and sat down to call them all to bring in more business. He called the first number and spoke at length with a back-of-the-truck contractor. The man agreed the time had come to file his returns. He was resigned to paying his taxes, because he now had too many customers and was making too much money to escape paying his tab to Uncle Sam.

The afternoon rolled by. Brandon set the receiver down, checked off another prospect, and looked up to see Maddy approaching his desk. Her big, round eyes sparkled when he made eye contact.

"Could you set the alarm system when you leave?" she said with melodic sweetness.

Brandon blinked and looked about. "What time is it?"

"Five-thirty. I've never seen anyone work so hard." The candy-coated voice obviously intended to enhance the compliment.

"I have four appointments coming in tomorrow. I may get some more."

"That's excellent."

Maddy was nice enough, but he wasn't going to encourage her. "What's the code?"

"9753 then push alarm. Lock the door and exit within sixty seconds."

"Will do. Where's Don?"

"Oh, he's been downtown all afternoon. He left in a hurry just before you came in. Are you coming in tomorrow?"

"I'll be here part of the day for sure."

"Goodnight then."

As the front door closed behind her, Brandon sat up and stretched his back for the first time all afternoon. Without the familiar ambience of clipping heels, chattering printers, and grating file drawers, a strange silence rolled over the office. He heard a single horn blast from the parking lot as someone secured their car. He glanced over the list of prospects he'd called, then set the list aside. A new thought came to him, and he leaned back and let it mature in his mind.

Brandon swiveled in his chair and looked at the back office. The door was closed as he knew it would be. It would also be locked. But why? One instruction to the secretaries that the room was off-limits would settle the matter. He'd never seen them so much as knock on the door.

He leaned back and closed his eyes against the fluorescent light. A thought passed though his mind, found heat, and began to ferment. Curiosity arose within his contemplation. Even so, if there was anything to find, it was too late. There was nothing left to save; no one to help. Brandon leaned over his desk and put his head in his hands.

Effervescent bubbles of possibilities began to swell inside his skull, and he knew, once again, he couldn't absolve himself until he uncovered the truth. No matter the risk, no matter the cost, he could never end his search until he uncovered the evidence he knew existed. If any of it lay back in that office, he had to know. It was no longer about what could be accomplished once it was found, but the knowledge that he couldn't live with himself until it was.

He hadn't asked to remain in the office. No suspicion would fall upon him because of his presence. He went to the window and closed the vertical blinds halfway. Light slipped through, but no one could see in directly. He turned off the front bank of lights. He tried Martin's office door. It was locked, as he expected. He bent open a large paperclip and jimmied the lock. The paperclip caught, then broke free. He bent a tiny hook in the end. Again, it seemed to be ready to move, then slipped again. He bent the clip, this time at a ninety-degree angle about two inches from the tip. He rotated it in the key slot like a crank. Something caught; he heard a faint snap. Quickly he gripped the knob with his other hand, and it turned.

Martin's cluttered desk faced the door. Computer monitors sat along the back wall with blank screens. The blinds were closed. Brandon cracked them to get enough westerly light to see. He turned off the remaining office lights and locked the front door.

Back inside Martin's office, he opened the top drawer of the first file cabinet. Everything appeared to be copies of normal tax returns for individual clients. He scanned more file drawers, perusing them randomly, and found more of the same. He noticed the two computer hard drives; on one a steady green light glowed. He sat at the station and moved the mouse. The computer screen burst to life. Maybe Martin always left his computer on in the middle of his work. Doubtful, but it was on now.

The screen held a tax return being processed. He recognized the name and knew it was one of the delinquent tax cases he'd brought in. He made a mental note of the page number, saved the information, closed the file, then clicked the documents folder.

Most names on the list were individuals. When he came to a business, he stopped and looked up the paper copy in the file drawer. Grier Pharmacy. From what he could see, it looked legit. He flipped through files for Reynolds Packing, Simpson Motors, and Koppel Road Satellite Entertainment. His eyes felt strained. There was nothing obviously out of order. Martin apparently had a boringly humdrum profession of pushing numbers. No wonder he looked to politics for a kick.

When he was about to give up and put the computer page back where he'd found it, he came to the T's and a file simply labeled TT. He opened it and read the heading---Trevnor Trust. Such a title hardly indicated a business, but aroused no suspicion either. It was a ledger file, not a tax return. At first glance it seemed as nothing more than what it appeared, an income and expense log for a club possibly, or a non-profit.

But the use of initials was puzzling. Not a single word spelled out for any entry. Brandon ran his finger down the column. The deposits were significant, $40,000, $15,000, $20,000, $50,000, $150,000, all in round numbers, large round numbers. The payouts were for smaller amounts, but round numbers, too. This wasn't the account for the Northridge Businessmen's youth basketball program or Sterling Acres beautification fund.

For a moment, Brandon studied the initials on the payouts. There was no way to know what they meant. He scrolled to the bottom of the document and back to the top. Then he saw the tiny gray boxes at the far outside of each line, the same color as the background on the page and easy to overlook. He placed the cursor on a gray box next to a deposit labeled BC, and it changed to a glove. He clicked. The facsimile of a check appeared, and all he could do was stare.

A check in the amount of $30,000 written by Britton Cattle Equipment Company covered the screen, reproduced in a computer ledger in Councilman Don Martin's private office. Brandon jumped to the file cabinet "B's" and searched the tabs. There was no file for the cattle equipment company. And yet, Martin had handled a $30,000 check from the company, now entered in a nebulous account labeled a trust. Brandon clicked on the next gray square and a deposit for $50,000 from Rhodes Development Corp appeared.

A creepy tingle of anticipation crawled along his arms. The light from the screen hurt his eyes. His breaths came quick and shallow. Brandon moved the computer cursor across the screen and clicked an entry marked JD. A check flashed on the screen in the amount of $10,000 made out to Joe Douglas. Was this the same Joseph Douglas as the Atherton city councilman from District Eight?

Brandon clicked on MT, and a check for the same amount written two weeks ago to Mike Thompson flashed on the screen.

The purpose of the account became clear. The fictitious trust was one big slush pool. Its purpose could only be to corrupt Atherton city councilmen and sway their votes. He found the copy of another check, this one made out to Don Martin himself for $10,000, dated less than a month ago. The name printed on the check read simply Trevnor Trust with no address or other information and was signed by Martin using his full name.

Brandon was ecstatic. Both outrage and elation pumped through him. Now he had uncovered proof. Martin had consistently lied to him, no doubt of it now. What was the man trying to do? Give him an early lesson on the sleazy side of politics? Martin was awash in the corruption. Somehow it made perverse sense. Martin was the obvious man for the job. He had the accounting background and the unmitigated gall to handle the money. It must have given him an ungodly rush to boast at the restaurant and without the slightest hint of concern. The man must be completely stupid to think he wouldn't one day be found out. Either that or his balls were covered in cowhide.

Brandon opened all the deposit entries. Just a few mouse clicks later, air rushed into his lungs as though he had sucked up the room. There it was--- dated in mid-August, five months ago, a check from St. Anthony's Regional Medical Center to Trevnor

Trust in the amount of $150,000. An anxious fear gripped him. Queasiness invaded his chest as he searched the desk drawers for a blank flash drive. He wanted the entire file, but at least a copy of that check. He hit the print button on the computer while he searched. He couldn't find a flash drive anywhere, and he turned to rise when a voice came from the door.

"What are you doing in here?" It wasn't a question. Before Brandon could move, the skin on his back rolled as though touched with a hot poker. An oily sweat seemed to ooze from his pores. The hair on his arms stood erect. Brandon turned and saw Martin's huge bulk in the doorframe.

The shock in Martin's eyes dissolved into a threatening sneer. He came at Brandon with the power of an NFL fullback plowing through a huddle of children, threw a chair into the wall on his way across the room, and drove his desk backward, pinning Brandon against the computers.

"Stop! I'm not doing anything."

The cry gave Brandon the three seconds that probably saved his life. By the time Martin glanced at the computer screen, and saw for himself exactly what had been uncovered, Brandon forced a space to clear his legs, jumped on the desk, and seized the table lamp. Martin grabbed for his ankle. A tortured roar bellowed from Martin's throat. Brandon had the lamp firmly in his grasp, the shade crushed between his forearms. Martin's fingers crawled at his leg to pull him down. Brandon swung the lamp with two hands and all his might. The heavy base struck Martin's head and he crumpled to the floor trailing a slobbering groan.

Brandon jumped to the floor and pulled back the desk. Martin tried to rise. Brandon took aim and kicked him squarely in the groin. Martin moaned in agony as he rolled about in a fetal ball. His scalp appeared as if it had sprung a leak, but the blood flow was small. Brandon tore the lamp cord from the base, tied his hands behind him, pulled loose Martin's belt, and tied his feet.

Brandon resumed his search for a useable storage device. He found one in Maddy's desk drawer. He took the copy of the $150,000 check from the hospital out of the printer and proceeded to download the entire ledger file onto the portable drive.

"Don't take anything," Martin pleaded. "I'll pay you whatever you want."

Brandon listened to Martin's plea. The words pressed upon the decision-making lobe of his brain. He means it now, but would he ever pay if I let him go? "How much?"

"Fifty thousand dollars," Martin blurted without hesitation. "No questions, no trail. You have to let me explain how all this fits together. . ." Martin's face flushed beet red from the strain, and he sucked up a breath. ". . . with more to come. I'll show you how it all works."

Elected crooks---they'd offer tens of thousands to keep their little secret. Talk about launching a political career. He could have the power elite of the city licking his boots. Brandon looked at the computer monitor. The program was still loading.

"Whatever you want, Brandon. You name it. No one, absolutely no one, is going to benefit if you let that stuff out," Martin begged. "I can make you rich."

Brandon wished the human body had an anatomical way to shut out sound the way it could shut out light. Brandon wanted to close his ears. He wanted Martin to shut up. The possibilities rolled through his brain. Was this the break he'd dreamed of for years? After all, the reason he pursued this information was gone, torn down, bulldozed, and hauled away. Why shouldn't he change his mind? What would be so wrong to take advantage of beating people at their own game? They were doing it. On the floor in front of him lay one of the highest officials in the city—nothing but a thief. Everything in his background cried for him to use this moment and milk it for personal power and financial gain.

The flash drive was ready. Brandon yanked it from the computer, then reloaded it to check that indeed the file had been recorded. Everything was there.

Brandon ripped away another lamp cord and tied Martin's feet to a knob high on the windowsill, then loosened his tie and pulled it from his neck.

"You're a fat ass, Don. You need to lose some weight."

When he began to gag the councilman, Martin pleaded once again. "I trusted you, Brandon. Don't do this." Brandon took his handkerchief, forced it in Martin's mouth, and secured it with the man's own tie.

"Yeah, Don? Well, the people trusted you."

Martin was on his back, his hands tied under him, his feet awkwardly strapped in the air. He could kick the wall, but that was about all. It would be a miracle if he could roll over from that position. Brandon went to the door and pushed in the lock on the knob. "I know that won't hold you forever, but it may hold you long enough." Brandon set his jaw and focused his mind. He took one last look at the wrecked office and the wide-eyed councilman bound on the floor. He stepped back, shut the door, and it snapped shut, Martin with the only key. Brandon hurried from the office, grabbed a phone book on his way out, and locked the office door.

There was no time to lose. It was seven-forty. The sun had disappeared, trailed by a dying orange glow in the west. Brandon looked up Gordon English's phone number and called him from the car.

"Mr. English?"

369

"Yes."

"My name is Brandon Evans. I'm calling about the Kessler Park project."

"Pardon me, Mr. Evans, but I don't take business calls at home. Besides, you're aware that matter has been settled, aren't you?"

"No, sir. That matter is far from settled. I just got hold of evidence that may shake this city apart, and Kessler Park is smack in the middle of it. I need you to help me get this in front a judge."

"What are you talking about?"

"Bribery on a massive scale, and I have the proof."

"Well, I don't know---"

"Mr. English, those people lost their homes. They paid you and your firm good money. Now I know you did your best, but this is new. The city council vote was fixed. You owe it to them for this evidence to see the light. Your firm doesn't represent the city, does it?"

"No."

"Okay then, what I have will give a huge boost to your firm's reputation. Think what it might do for your career?"

"Mr. Evans---"

"Just get me in front of one of your managing partners. Nine o'clock tomorrow morning. You won't be sorry." What that Brandon hung up.

His shin throbbed, his knuckles were skinned. He was running on a dwindling supply of adrenaline. Think, Brandon, think. He had only so much time. By this time tomorrow the Atherton media wouldn't be complaining about a shortage of newsworthy copy. He intended to rock the downtown glass tower called city hall to its very foundation. Lies were going to see the light of day; let the chips fall where they may. Some good-ole-boys were going to have their cozy lives turned upside-down. Heads would roll. Lawsuits would be filed. People would be fired, impeached, and shamed. His dad may hear of this in his four by ten foot cell in Huntsville and be proud of him in some perverse way. The knowledge of all of the upcoming turmoil settled in his thoughts nicely, and Brandon smiled. He was going to make his mark after all.

He drove straight home, made a dozen copies of the flash drive, left one in plain sight beside his computer, packed two changes of clothes, and checked into a hotel for the night. Martin may have already freed himself. He didn't want to be anywhere he could be found until he'd left the evidence all over town. At the very latest, Martin would be discovered in the morning shortly after Maddy and Pamela opened the office. Then, too, it wasn't beyond possibility Martin could have a heart attack and die right where he lay. He shook such thinking from his head. No matter what, he couldn't look back. He had made his final, irreversible decision when he gagged Martin and silenced his pleas. He had to see things through no matter what lay ahead.

Brandon thought of Vic and his real estate company. He wanted badly to call him, but knew he needed to talk to the attorneys first.

He wanted to get in touch with the Stantons. Rick had told him something he needed to confirm. Brandon remembered them from the funeral. Stoic and proud, Rick's parents sat impassively through the service and never shed a tear. His sisters cried, but not them. They sat quietly, hand-in-hand, resilient and humble. They had made Rick's damaged life productive, and he had given special meaning to theirs.

He called Cindy, but no answer. He called Todd and hung up after one ring. He took a hot shower, then fell onto the hotel bed. Finally, he drifted into an elusive shadow of sleep and tossed in fits the entire night.

CHAPTER FORTY-TWO

BRANDON WAS UP AS SOON AS morning light touched the hotel curtains. He drove downtown to the Watson Building and took the elevator to the top. The law firm of Dustin, Cushman, and Childs occupied the entire floor. Their vault of legal profundity was guarded by two massive ten-foot doors. The reception area was a tribute to ostentatious opulence. Brandon hardly noticed and cared even less.

He approached the receptionist determined, solemn, and serious. For the first time in his life the use of cute remarks and twinkling eyes didn't enter his thinking as a way to get what he wanted. Everything he would do or say would be accurate, to the point, unwavering.

"Good morning, I'm Brandon Evans. I'm here to see Mr. English."

"Certainly. If you'll have a seat, I'll see if he's available."

Dustin, Cushman, and Childs specialized in real estate law and handled everything from property foreclosures for financial institutions to commercial contracts and mineral leases. But they also had a litigation team. They weren't averse to suing someone criminally or defending them either if the price was right. An occasional trip into the courtroom kept the mind sharp, generated renewed vigor when legalese pumped through the veins while cross-examining a witness.

Within minutes, Gordon English came to greet him and escorted him into the interior sanctum. English was sharply dressed, but appeared nervous, a condition he could not hide despite his steady voice. He had arranged an audience with managing partner R.W. Cushman.

Cushman was a tall man, angular of face and trim of build. His white hair had a steel tinge, and he rose from behind his desk as the two men entered. He shook Brandon's hand as English introduced them, offered them each a chair, and returned to his seat behind the desk.

"Gordon tells me you have some information that implicates some of our city officials in unethical practices."

"Yes, sir, that's correct. But I wouldn't characterize this evidence as muddying the waters about unethical behavior," Brandon said, his eyes locked fiercely with Cushman's. "I have undisputable evidence that the city council has been systematically squeezing businesses for favorable council votes, enriching themselves under the table, and making a mockery of fair and unbiased-decision making." Brandon paused a second for his words to soak in.

"Recently, these crooks stole the Kessler Park subdivision from a bunch of old folks. I know for a fact these people got paid a pittance for their property. The appraisals were depressed because the neighborhood was old, in disrepair, and zoned residential. It's already been torn down, but I want these people to get the money they deserve. No— what I really want is for them to get their property back so they can make their own choices about it. The property will go commercial. Whatever is built there eventually will make the land worth ten times what the hospital paid for it."

Cushman paid attention. Brandon was clear, direct, and laid his position on the line. He wasn't like the mealy-mouthed, equivocating "professionals" who so often wasted his time by spilling out a lot of double-talk forcing him to translate everything they said. "So what have you got?" Cushman asked.

"The whole thing. It was all kept in one account, the slush money paid in by businesses and individuals wanting special treatment and the corresponding payoffs to elected officials."

"I'd like to see it."

"I have it with me. I want you to see it. And I want you to help me. If what I've just told you is just as I've explained, will you help me?"

"I have to know what we're dealing with," Cushman said frankly, but with obvious interest.

"You need to know. I've already made a dozen of copies of this file. The word is going to get out one way or the other. Does this firm currently represent the city or any of the councilmen?"

"No, we do not."

"The hospital paid at least $150,000 to grease their agenda through city hall, and the city council divvied it up to insure a favorable vote. It makes me madder than hell to think they thought they could get away with it."

"I agree. I'm deeply concerned if it's a bad as you say."

Brandon stared fiercely at Cushman. He'd walk right out and take his chances elsewhere if he got even a hint the man might sell him out. "How bad does it have to be?"

"If they did it once, they'll do it again," Cushman acknowledged. "We'll help you if you have the evidence." Brandon studied the man for five seconds more, then handed over the flash drive. Cushman stuck it in his computer and within a minute his face fell, heavy in contemplation. "Take a look at this, Gordon."

Brandon added something he just remembered. "The widow of one of your former law partners lived in Kessler Park. That little lady was devastated when she was forced to move."

"Who was that?"

"Her name is Ethel Barnes."

A slight grimace settled on Cushman's face, and he nodded ever so slightly. "That would be Marvin's wife. I knew him well, a good man. He was my mentor. Actually, he helped everyone here, but I especially appreciated everything he did for me." Cushman turned back to the computer. "You see all of that?"

"I see it, sir," Gordon said.

Cushman turned toward Brandon, his eyes laced with concern, thoughts obviously racing through his brain. "We'll do it! Gordon, I want you to prepare an Appeal of the Kessler Park Condemnation Order and get it over to Judge Appleton's courtroom. He's the best person for this, and he'll look at it today."

To Brandon he said, "You have our full cooperation. I'm sure we can get a court order for the bank records. We'll concentrate on the Kessler

Park issue first. That will uncover other buried secrets. Eventually, I'll have to turn this over to the D.A."

"Fine—one more thing," Brandon said. "You might call the police department. I had to leave Councilman Martin tied up in his office. He came in right when I found the computer file."

Cushman couldn't conceal his astonishment. "It's a gutsy thing you're doing, Evans. Did one of your relatives live there?"

"No."

"So why are you pursuing this, if I may ask?"

Brandon stood and took a deep breath. "I'm not completely sure."

During the night, Don Martin broke the cord that held his ankles to the window ledge. He rolled onto his stomach, but with his hands tied behind him, was unable to get to his knees. When the secretaries came in at eight-thirty, he made enough commotion for them to track down the custodian who opened his office door.

The police were called. Martin was bloodied, sweaty, grimy, and stressed. He couldn't speak without gutter-slime, four-letter words spilling from his lips. He yelled so many instructions he became faint and had to sit down. He called his lawyer. He demanded to hear from the mayor. When the police arrived they inspected Martin's office and took a statement, but quickly departed when he began his harangue. The police department had already received some pertinent information on the matter from a prestigious downtown law firm.

"You've got a bad bump there, Mr. Martin. I'd have that looked at if I were you," said the lieutenant in charge as he walked out the door.

Brandon sped from the attorney's office to the Stanton residence. He parked at the curb and knocked on the door. Ann answered.

"Brandon Evans, ma'am, I hope I'm not interrupting anything, but I sure could use a moment of your time."

She opened the door, and they took a seat in the living room. Brandon could still see sorrow in her eyes. It had been just over a month since Rick's passing. His appearance on her doorstep probably had a lot to do with her mournful expression, since she only knew him in connection with her son, but he had come to further Rick's efforts. Once she understood, hopefully it would brighten her day.

"Mrs. Stanton, Rick told me he collected the new addresses of everyone in Kessler Park so he could write them. Do you happen to have a list like that?"

"Well, let me think. I remember him mentioning that, too. It's surely in his belongings, probably in his notebook. I haven't thrown anything out."

"Would you mind checking?"

Ann hesitated. "Those people have moved. They're gone. Rick's gone. Are you going to bother them now?"

Brandon could feel a brittle tension engulf the room. There was a hint of accusation in her tone. He needed her help, but he didn't want to get her upset. He measured each word he was about to say, and said a silent prayer they would come out right.

"Mrs. Stanton, I just discovered that the entire governmental procedure to get that land for the hospital was a scam. I knew something shady was going on, and I've been working for months to come up with the proof. I finally found hard evidence. I just didn't find it before they tore the neighborhood down. I want the new addresses so we can let the people know they might get more money or even get their property rights back."

Ann Stanton's eyes grew wide. A debilitating gloom seemed to invade her body. Brandon thought she'd be pleased to hear the news, but such was not the case.

"It was Rick who helped me see something had to be done to help those people," Brandon said.

As soon as he finished, he watched the woman fall prostrate across her couch. A wail of untold heartache screamed from her throat, and her entire body convulsed with sobs. One mention of her son and a flood of emotion poured forth. Brandon was dismayed, then concerned. What had he done to bring on such an outburst? Ann buried her head in the cushion. Her breaths came in stuttered gasps. For more than a minute, Brandon could only watch in a state of confused apprehension. But soon, he realized her anguish was not because of him. It was a sorrow that had to be expelled. From wherever it came, it could no longer be contained. Eventually, the emotional purging began to taper, and he waited patiently for the episode to pass. When Ann finally looked up, her eyes were red, her nose runny, her hands soaked with tears.

"Oh, excuse me." A cathartic sigh finished it, and she went to the bureau for a box of tissues. She dabbed her eyes and blew her nose. "I'm so sorry." She sat on the couch, still struggling to rein in her composure.

"There's nothing to be sorry for."

"Yes, in a way there is. You see, I'd heard something about under-the-table deals myself from someone at city hall, and I just wanted to forget about it. I didn't think it would make any difference. After Rick died, I tortured myself for a week thinking that if an appeal had been made, if he thought nothing had been decided for sure, maybe he wouldn't have slipped away."

Brandon remained silent and listened.

"I know that's not true, though. He called me that very night. He was so happy you were going to take him fishing. That meant so much to him. You're a wonderful person, Brandon. The world could use a lot more people like you." Ann walked over and gave him a big hug. "I loved my son dearly, but I wish he could have grown up to have been just like you."

"I don't know what to say." Her heartfelt compliment stirred unfamiliar emotions, joy even in sadness. He felt a sense of something accomplished in spite of the loss.

"Sit back down. I'll be right back," she said. "I'm sure I can find those addresses."

CHAPTER FORTY-THREE

BRANDON HEADED FOR Trinity Plaza, a
maze of offices and bistros, spas and boutiques. He
had one last call to make, one more presentation,
and at least one more person to persuade.
Henderson Commercial Properties resided on the
fifth floor of the plaza tower, and he took the
elevator up.

Brandon took a deep breath at the door and
approached the receptionist with a confident,
serious demeanor.
"Good afternoon, my name is Brandon Evans.
Is Vic in?"

"Well, no. Just about everyone is out. Did you
have an appointment?"

"No, I had other business in the plaza. I
certainly need to speak with someone. I came across
an opportunity, and I knew Vic would be the person

to talk to. Is your broker in?" Brandon worked to heighten the urgency of his call.

"Maybe I could help you with an appointment?"

"No, this can't wait. Is there another agent in the office who has two minutes?"

"Maybe I can help you."

Brandon turned. A burly man stepped from an office across from the reception area. Immediately Brandon could tell the guy was in charge of something. A clump of white hair burst from his open collar and rolled up sleeves exposed thick, hairy arms with huge hands. He had a heavy brow and a solid jaw. A curiosity sparkled in his eyes indicating he was neither averse to talking with drop-in callers nor afraid to get rid of them. He gestured with his hand, and Brandon stepped into his office.

"Have a chair."

"Brandon Evans, sir. Two minutes." Brandon extended his hand before he sat.

The man shook it. "Dwight Henderson. I'm the owner here," he said without any added inflection or self-serving pomp. He set his elbows on his desk as he took his seat, pressed his lips with an index finger, and studied Brandon. "Which Vic were you looking for? We have two Vics here."

Brandon didn't miss a beat. "Well, sir, I don't know his last name. We're just casual acquaintances." The thought rolled around in the back of his skull, this honesty thing was actually relaxing. No scrambles for past answers or attempts to concoct an interesting tale. Just shoot straight, tell it like it is. Brandon saw the answer he gave was sufficient. If he'd tried to dredge up a convoluted back story, he'd have wasted time and possibly be ushered out the door.

"So you have an opportunity that can't wait to be told. Is that what I heard you say?" Henderson leaned back to listen.

"That's correct, sir. You may be aware the neighborhood between St. Anthony's and the freeway has just been demolished and cleared. I've uncovered proof the decision to approve that condemnation was greased with bribes. A legal team is working to get the decision vacated.

"Most of those property owners were elderly with medical problems living on fixed incomes. I want them to get fair value for their property, and I'm looking for a buyer who wants prime commercial property in the heart of the city."

Henderson leaned forward, and a furrow crinkled his brow. "Most of the property we acquire is for a specific purpose. We have end-users who need certain locations or specific amounts of land, and we buy and develop those properties. We're not in the business of acquiring property and waiting for someone to come to us."

"Then I suggest you go take a look at the tract and see if you can use it," Brandon replied.

Henderson's eyes flashed. He studied Brandon as though there might be something he'd missed. An added interest lit his features. "You're pretty confident this land has potential?"

"The hospital wants it. Sell it back to them. They're trying to steal it. I want those old homeowners to get a fair dollar."

"You been peddling this idea all over town?"

"No, sir. I brought it here because Vic says you're a good company. He said it more than once. I figured you have the ability to buy it and the expertise to move it. I don't want anything. I'm not licensed anyway, and that's not why I'm here. It's just that I know almost everyone who owned property there, and I know I can get it put together for you quickly. Their homes are gone. They'll sell. I just want them to get what they deserve."

Henderson became silent in contemplation. "You know how big a tract it is?"

"Close to forty acres, I think. I don't know exactly."

"That's not huge, but not bad for property close to downtown. Not bad at all. Okay," Henderson said, "we'll go look at it. We'll come up with some figures. All I can do now is check it out."

"Fair enough. I think you'll see the potential. Like I said, I'm not looking for any compensation, but I will ask for one small favor if you decide to purchase."

"What's that?"

"It's not for me. If you decide to move ahead, I'd prefer to tell you then. Thank you for your time, Mr. Henderson. I appreciate you listening to my proposal."

"Certainly, young man. You're welcome."

A *Sentinel* reporter who spent his days loitering in the courthouse corridors got the first whiff of the story. A legal secretary mentioned Judge Appleton was in hubbub about something at city hall. "He's more excited than ever. Been on the phone with the district attorney for an hour. Told me to call his wife because he'd be home late."

The next day, TV and newspaper reporters roamed in packs about city hall. City employees barricaded themselves behind security-coded doors. The mayor's office closed up like a clam. It issued a one-paragraph statement in answer to the barrage of questions. City councilmen were conspicuously difficult to reach. It was rumored that some of them had retained counsel, but as yet, no accusations had been made.

On the third day, a Friday, Gordon English filed his appeal on behalf of the former residents of Kessler Park. The district attorney's office was duly notified as their office would represent the city in the proceeding. Judge Appleton scheduled the hearing for the following Tuesday. He was the senior jurist on the three-panel state appeals court for North Texas. His associates on the bench, Judges Herron and Williams, were each well-qualified in their own right with equal power concerning decisions of the court. But Judge Appleton was known for his sober judgment and decorated for his four decades of service to the bench. His colleagues frequently deferred to him when it came to setting the priority of the docket.

Over the weekend a buzz and bitch about the conduct of city officials dwelt on every tongue. No tidbit of speculation was too outlandish for the radio call-in shows. Little was actually known because little had been revealed. But those close to the action knew something was up, and conjecture ran wild. Reporters desperate for a scoop would take one kernel of possibility and spin it into a three-minute TV segment or a half-page of newspaper copy.

Mayor Patterson took the brunt of it all, mainly because he was well known. The city manager wasn't on safe ground either. No one knew exactly what the city fathers were supposed to have done, but the idea of political corruption was easy to sell. If someone had potholes on their street, it was easy to make the connection that the money for the repair had lined the pockets of someone at city hall. When the truth finally came out, all the unsubstantiated guessing was chalked up to sound judgment.

At ten the following Tuesday morning, the courtroom was packed when the three-member appeals court took their seats. Gordon English made his motion short and sweet.

"We ask the court to vacate the condemnation order of the Atherton City Council on the tract of land known as Kessler Park. We submit that uncovered evidence reveals illegal and unethical influence brought to bear on the decision."

Having seen the full contents of the ledger, the district attorney replied with four unenthusiastic words, "No objection, your honor."

The panel conferred with one another all of twenty seconds. Judge Appleton was as demonstrative with his words as the district attorney had been brief. "The decision of the City of Atherton versus the subdivision known as Kessler Park is hereby vacated by the order of this court." The sharp crack of the gavel punctuated his words.

Appleton and his colleagues quickly whisked the district attorney to chambers. They had further matters to discuss concerning the contents of the ledger.

CHAPTER FORTY-FOUR

ADDITIONAL INFORMATION QUICKLY came to light. Citizens of Atherton experienced outrage, then shock, and finally the bleary emptiness of despair. It was worse than they had ever dreamed. The facts underscored a wholesale breach of trust. A violation of this magnitude would require a total change of direction to correct and a long time to heal. All the councilmen implicated by the ledger resigned, and lawsuits were filed against them. The Texas State Attorney General became thoroughly involved in the matter. It was determined that Mayor Patterson hadn't taken a dime nor had Councilmen Garrett nor Decker, but they were forced to resign as well. No one believed they hadn't known of the payoffs.

For ten weeks, new candidates ran for council seats, as city-wide, special elections were scheduled for every district. The city manager operated the city and maintained basic services. No new business was considered; no new plans were made. The city languished in a leadership vacuum. It would take years for Atherton to regain its prestige among regional cities. It would take even longer for city officials to win back the respect of the electorate.

Katherine Cramer was summarily fired. As the head of the hospital's real estate department and the point person on the Kessler Park acquisition project she was the most likely one to take the fall. And she did, without a severance package or a heartfelt goodbye. Though others were certainly involved, the hospital hierarchy circled the wagons and shifted to damage control.

Darrin Riley slipped through the cracks and was never charged and only routinely questioned. He hadn't signed any checks; he hadn't taken a penny. Since Patterson had to resign, Riley was out of a job for the time being. But he still knew the movers and shakers about town, and the department heads within city staff. The mastermind of all the underhanded dealings slipped under the radar, and took a well-deserved vacation to Europe. Once he got back in town he could put out feelers and see who among the newly elected could use some political expertise. Riley was sure at least one of them would be interested in how to get things done around Atherton City Hall.

Two weeks after the court decision, Dwight Henderson gave Brandon a call. "I'd like you to come in so we can talk about Kessler Park."

"When?"

"This afternoon would be fine."

The receptionist escorted Brandon into the conference room where three men were scanning papers. Two of the men he knew.

The man closest to the door stood and shook his hand. "Hi, Vic," Brandon said, "good to see you."

"Same here. Was this the parcel of land you were trying to tell me about?"

Brandon nodded.

"It is unique. I'm sorry I didn't take you more seriously."

Brandon didn't dwell on the apology. "I'm glad you've seen it now."

"Brandon, this is James Livingston," Henderson said, "our in-house counsel. Jim, this is Brandon Evans." The men shook hands across the table.

"Brandon." Henderson brought his bare arms out from under the table, his sleeves rolled past his elbows, and folded his hands on top of the papers. "This Kessler Park parcel poses some challenges.

It's probably going to go to high-rise office buildings eventually, but right now the office market is saturated. But it's also a one-of-a-kind property. There'll never be another parcel this big, close to the heart of the city."

Henderson reached for a sheet of paper and began reading. "We got the figures the hospital was paying out for each lot. On the small lots of $1/4^{th}$ of an acre the hospital paid $15,000. We can give those homeowners $60,000 and still make money. On the half-acre lots the hospital paid out $30,000. We can offer $120,000. Of course, these amounts don't include the actual homes. We would pay extra based on the square footage of each house."

Brandon couldn't even swallow. His face flushed warm.

"Yes, they were trying to steal the land. And just so you know, if anyone has already been paid, all they have to do is send a certified check back to the hospital, and the property is theirs once again," Henderson said. "Our attorneys will get the property deeds back in their names."

"So you're going to buy it?"

"We're going to buy it," Henderson said with a grin. Vic patted Brandon on the back.

"That's great. All the trouble I went through to uncover that scheme wouldn't have meant much if I couldn't get those folks a better deal."

"Well, you did, and I wouldn't be surprised if someday you don't get a commendation from the police department or the city or both."

"I'm more interested in telling you what I'd like to see happen since I brought this deal your way."

"Sure. I remember you mentioning it." Henderson leaned back in his seat. "I'd expect you to ask for something."

"Well. . . " Brandon glanced at each of the men as he collected his thoughts. "I'd like you to set aside a couple acres in the middle of that plot of land and dedicate it as a little park in remembrance of that neighborhood. It should have some picnic tables and benches and a walking path and shrubs. Most of all, I'd like to see it covered in flowers. I want Henderson Properties to build the park so it's done right, and I want to have it deeded as a park so no one can ever change the use of that little plot of land."

When he finished, Brandon gazed into three serene faces as if his voice had been lake waters gently washing on shore. He spoke with such confidence and conviction a person could almost see the park there now.

"The people who eventually work in those office buildings will appreciate it," he said, "and it'll help me get all the paperwork back for you from the individual owners. I don't think there'll be any problems, but I do believe it would be a nice gesture from Henderson Properties considering the way they lost their homes."

Henderson brushed his lips with his finger and nodded. "I think we can work your park into our figures," he said. "I'm assigning Vic to help you with the paperwork that needs to be done."

"Thank you, sir, but it's not my park. There was a handyman down there all the people really loved. He cared for a number of gardens, and it got me to thinking about a park. His name was Rick Stanton, and he passed away several months ago."

Henderson nodded. "I doubt if many of those people will know how much you've done for them."

Brandon mentally shrunk from the endorsement. He'd done his best to atone for his greed. But he knew, given a choice, most of the residents of Kessler Park would turn down the money and choose to be back in their ancient, run-down homes.

"There's one more thing, Mr. Henderson. It's not about the property or the company doing any additional work. It's just that I'm interested in the real estate business, and I want to go to work for you."

Henderson appeared pleased.

"I can start studying for my license even while I'm helping Vic get the properties signed over. I know this is what I want to do. I believe I can be an asset to your company."

"I think you would be, too," Henderson said without hesitation. "You brought in an excellent property. The key to this business is working with people. You need a conviction in your proposal and the resolve to see it through. You've already shown me that. We'd be happy to put you through our training program."

CHAPTER FORTY-FIVE

AROUND-THE-CLOCK ACTIVITIES filled the weeks that followed. Word of the court order needed to be communicated to displaced Kessler Park homeowners. Negotiations to repurchase their property rights had to take place with each one individually. Only Dan Beckerman, resident slum lord of Kessler Park, expressed displeasure over the eminent domain procedure being annulled; that was, until he learned of the substantial new offer being made by Henderson Commercial Properties. Then, he tried to hold out for even more. Brandon explained it was a take it or leave it deal. Leave it and Beckerman could see how well his finances held up waiting any number of years with nothing to show for his lost rentals other than several hundred square feet of fresh dirt.

Henderson Properties selected a site and work began on the new park. The land was graded and a sprinkler system installed. A figure-eight sidewalk was poured as a walking path and four-foot high evergreens planted around the perimeter. Four covered pavilions housed two picnic tables each with more set in the open around the park. The tables were made of hard weatherproof plastic, colored in earth tones of green, light blue, soft yellow, and tan. Curved metal benches were set in concrete along the walking path with bushes planted throughout. Then, the open ground was prepared with mulch, sand, and clay. Potted blossoms were brought in by the truckload and planted across the park in a broad spectrum of color. It was an inspiring sight to stand in the middle of the park and turn full about. Rick would have been at home and happy.

Brandon divided his time between real estate training classes, meeting with Kessler Park homeowners, and enduring grueling depositions at the hands of defense attorneys, one for every ex-city councilman charged with bribery and public corruption.

As winter turned to spring, he had talked to Cindy just a handful of times since their cold Saturday, feeding the homeless. The previous week he caught her on a lunch break and bought her a sandwich. She seemed pleased to see him, but appeared tired and rushed. She had gotten on at another jewelry store working full-time. She had enrolled in night school, taking classes in elementary education. She wanted to get her degree and loved the prospect of working with children. She wasn't going to build a career standing eight hours a day behind a retail counter.

He could tell she had boxed up her daydreams and locked away her thoughts of shining knights and floating castles. She wouldn't run away with him for a weekend even if he offered to pay for it all. She wouldn't entertain more outlandish plans. Something had been lost in that, but then he, too, had changed.

Brandon remembered how fun and carefree she had been, how she had laughed at his every story and welcomed his outrageous ideas, pumped up his enthusiasm with her rapt attention for his schemes that were dumber than fairy tales. It had been fun. Like children, they had carried on as though tomorrow was meant for only them. Lately, the adult side of life had taken prominence, and Brandon knew this was where he should be, and now must live.

Cindy knew about the public corruption indictments and Brandon's efforts to get elderly homeowners just compensation for their property. Brandon brought the conversation around to the upcoming park dedication.

"We're going to dedicate the new park a week from Sunday. It's at one, so church services will be over, and the seniors will have plenty of time to get there. Would you like to come?"

Her face fell slightly as though he'd asked her to a boxing match. "Marilyn and I have been going to estate sales on Sundays."

"Estate sales? When did you start that?"

"Oh, I don't remember, awhile back."

"Do you buy much?"

"No, not really. I can't afford it. But it's interesting."

"Can I tag along? I'll be your driver. I might learn something, too."

She smiled. "If you want."

"Listen, if it's a nice day, we can take the boat out. It's up to you. You never can tell. It might be a perfect day to get on the lake."

"Maybe, but Marilyn's going, too."

"Absolutely. A week from Sunday."

"Sure, I'll go now that I think about it." She paused and gazed straight into his eyes. "Brandon, I want you to know, I'm proud of what you did for those people, especially after the way things started. You could have silently slipped away and no one would have known of your involvement. But you didn't. If you want me to attend this park dedication, I'll be happy to go."

"Great! You want me to pick you up at, say, ten-thirty? We'll have brunch before we go to the park dedication."

"That sounds perfect," she said. "and thanks for lunch."

Brandon learned Todd had been caught shoplifting and thrown in jail. Due to his inability to pay the fine, Todd's restitution for his secular sin came in the form of a thirty-day donation of his life to the county lock-up. Brandon went to the jail and paid the fine.

"He'll be released around three this afternoon if you want to come back."

Brandon didn't want to come back. He hadn't wanted to go to the jail in the first place. But he had. Though he couldn't express it in words, he knew why. With an investment of time, compassionate counseling, and choice words, others had opened a window for him on a new beginning. They hadn't had to fork over $700 to pay a fine, but it was only through the grace of God. How close had he come to falling off the deep end?

Things were getting better. He felt good about what he was doing in Kessler Park. He'd done his best to right a bad situation. Everything wouldn't always go as planned, but he intended to always do what he knew in his heart was right. He knew much of how he had dealt with people stemmed from

401

what he'd taken from his father. That was hardly an excuse. It was like Rick had said, there comes a time to move on, and accept responsibility for your future.

At 3:10, Todd walked out of the jailhouse in familiar wrinkled attire. Brandon honked the horn as he stood beside his car. "I thought I'd get you out," Brandon said. "I imagine your wife and baby could use you."

Todd looked at him curiously. "I was kind of getting used to it in there. Three meals a day. It's a little noisy, but least there ain't no squalling babies."

"I don't think you mean it. You're too smart to settle for that."

"Yeah, well, what am I supposed to do now? You got any work lined up?"

"No, I don't. I don't know what your next move will be, but I think you can do a lot better than conning a bunch of old folks into buying a bunch of stuff they don't need."

"Yeah, well, you did it, too. You don't need to be preaching to me, college boy. I know all about giving it a shot."

"I'm just saying, I think you've got it in you to do well. You've got to make some tough choices, but there are no choices back there." Brandon glanced back at the jailhouse as they pulled from the parking lot. "In there they do all the deciding for you. That's why I paid to get you out. I figured I owed someone a second chance. Guess I thought it ought to be you."

For a moment, Todd appeared baffled, but then he nodded. "I do appreciate that, man." The two men rode in silence. Brandon pulled into the apartment parking lot and stopped.

"This is goodbye, Todd. I don't have any money. The jail got it all." Brandon reached across the seat and extended his hand. "Good luck."

Todd took it, shook it, and got out of the car. Before he shut the door he leaned back in and repeated, "I really do appreciate it, man."

Sunday morning broke sunny and clear. The Texas breeze blew soft as a whisper. It was a perfect day to inhale the fragrance of spring and behold the color of a park in bloom. Lawn chairs were unfolded on the walkway and in the grass.

Grandchildren and great-grandchildren scooted together along picnic tables. The permanent metal benches were reserved for the elderly. The pageantry of the blossoms was breathtaking. Pinks and red petals washed into yellows and golds. Purples and shades of blue spilled into the white stars and orange trumpets, and in the rising warmth of the day, tiny swirls of insects danced across them all. The gathering of chairs formed a circle around a

403

plaque in the center of the garden. It was anchored in the ground on a pipe and shielded by a small gabled roof. The plaque displayed a meticulously carved bronze etching of Rick. Reproduced from a photograph, it depicted Rick dressed in his everyday overalls, an infectious grin on his face, the sun catching the twinkle of his eyes, a ladder behind his shoulder. The inscription under the etching read:

The splendor in this park exists in memory of

Rick Stanton, a man who saw potential

and beauty in everything and everyone.

Residents of Kessler Park had paid for Rick's memorial, and for the installation of the old bronze KESSLER PARK plaques now set in concrete in the sidewalks at either end of the park. Sherman Porter had rid them of tarnish and grime. The bronze plaques had survived over one hundred thirty years set in the brick wall at the entrance to Kessler Park. They would survive another one hundred thirty years where they now lay.

Someone tapped him on the shoulder. Brandon turned to see the engaging smile of Beatrice Morgan. "You've done a wonderful job here, Mr. Evans," she said as she extended her hand and he shook it lightly. "With all the houses gone, this park

404

looks spectacular in the midst of the remaining trees. It's a breath of life."

"Well, thank you." Brandon was truly humbled. "I thought it was the least we could do."

"I have someone with me who'd like to speak to you," she said.

Brandon had already noticed the boy, but now he turned his way. "How are you, Jake?"

"Fine." For a moment they just looked at each other. "My grandma tells me how you've done the best you could down here. I think it looks pretty neat myself. I'm sorry I blamed you for everything."

"Apology accepted. I've learned from my mistake, and now it's time to move on." Brandon stuck out his hand, and Jake took it. The boy was dressed in a blue sports shirt and press slacks. He'd let his hair grow out on the sides and gotten the top trimmed. "You're looking pretty sharp, Jake."

"Thanks. One other thing. I just want you to know, that handyman guy did recognize me. I was there when one of my friend tore up his garden. I wasn't real proud of that then, and I just wanted you to know."

Brandon pursed his lips and nodded. "I know. Rick filled me in. He told me later he knew you were with the other boys." Brandon turned and opened his arm to the majesty of the garden. It's because of him that all of this is here now. That's him there on the plaque."

"I saw it," Jake said. "It's good."

"I'm glad you're man enough to tell me about it, Jake. I'm really glad. I'm sure your grandma is proud of you, too." Brandon glanced up at Beatrice, then back to Jake. "Maybe something soon, you'd like to go back to the drag races?"

"Oh, yeah," Jake said immediately, his voice full of anticipation.

"I'll give you a call real soon," Brandon said as he ruffled Jake's hair.

At one o'clock, Brandon moved to the center of the gathering, raised his hand, and looked about. He saw Michael and Ann Stanton. They knew everything done to leave a heartfelt memorial to Rick had been his doing. He smiled at Cindy and Marilyn seated in lawn chairs to his side. He saw Wallace and Lydia Baker. Ethel Barnes was unable to attend. She now lived in Little Rock with her daughter, but she sent in twenty-five dollars toward Rick's plaque.

Brandon noticed Judith Hilker and beside her Louis, dressed in short-sleeved shirt and black pants with bright red suspenders, something new for the special occasion. He nodded at Cecil and Clara Nance and Sherman and Grace Porter as he turned full circle. Myron Holmes sat on a park bench with Delores in a wheelchair by his side. Her often misplaced ruby red pendant glittered in the noonday sun as it hung around her neck. Brandon couldn't help but notice they all seemed pleased if not completely happy. If today was to be the final mention of their beloved neighborhood, they would go away with a measure of contentment.

"Good afternoon. We certainly have a fantastic turnout, and it's fitting that we do. We're here today to dedicate this park as a memorial to the vibrant neighborhood that was originally laid out in the 1870's, and through the years became home to many, many wonderful families. This city was enriched by all who called this neighborhood home. This garden park will continue to enrich all who come to enjoy its location and behold its beauty.

"We want to thank Henderson Properties for making this park possible, and we want to pay a special tribute to our dearly departed friend, Rick Stanton, who did so much for this neighborhood. Everyone, be sure and take a look at the memorial erected in the center of the park in Rick's honor.

"The name of the original community was Kessler Park, and this park will retain the name. Bronze plaques once set at the entrance to the subdivision are now embedded in the concrete walk at either end of the park. An endowment to maintain this public garden has already been established. People will be enjoying this Kessler Park for many years to come. Please signal your enthusiasm as we officially dedicate the new Kessler Park."

Applause erupted from the gathering along with a chorus of cheers. Heartfelt hugs were passed around. More than a few tissues got put to use. Multi-colored balloons were released from nets stationed around the park, and everyone watched the colors race into the sky. When the celebration began to taper, Brandon raised his hand again.

"Everyone, please be seated. I have one more thing to say." He waited a moment while everyone settled down. "I figured since we were all gathered in this beautiful garden on such a lovely day, I should take advantage of this inspiring setting."

Then he paused. The crowd waited patiently for him to continue. Brandon turned and looked to his side. There, his eyes found Cindy, and even the rumble of nearby traffic couldn't invade the deafening silence that seized everyone gathered. Brandon approached Cindy's chair and knelt at her side.

"As God is my witness, I don't know why it took me so long to see what a beautiful person you are." He took her hand. "You've always been my best friend and my most steadfast supporter. When I'm away from you, I can't get to sleep. When I'm with you, I think anything is possible. I want you to know I love you---probably always have. Until recently, I never slowed down long enough to know." He stopped and swallowed. "I'm not usually at a loss for words." Cindy's fingers touched his temple and gently brushed back a lock of hair that had fallen in his eyes. Her wide-eyed initial shock softened even as her eyes brimmed with tears.

"I know it took me a long time to get things straight, but I'm doing my best to do what's right. I did everything---for you---and because of you. I promise I always will."

He took a black box from his pocket and opened it to reveal a twinkling diamond ring. "Cynthia Bradshaw, will you marry me?"

She blinked and tried to smile, and through the tears Brandon saw unequivocal love captured in her expression. "Oh yes, Brandon, I'll marry you. Yes, yes, yes."

About the author

Clifford Morris was born and raised in Dodge City, Kansas where he learned a lot about the history of the Wild West, mainly that most of what you saw in the movies never happened. He's an Army veteran and widely traveled, courtesy of the United States military. He spent an illustrious career in sales promoting items too new to be appreciated or too old to be useful to people who had already purchased from the competition or who didn't have two nickels to rub together. A lifetime sports enthusiast, Mr. Morris spends much of his time reading good fiction, and the rest of it trying to write some. He currently resides in North Texas.